Sons of the Oak

Tor Books by David Farland

The Runelords
Brotherhood of the Wolf
Wizardborn
The Lair of Bones
Sons of the Oak

SONS OF THE OAK

❧ DAVID FARLAND ❧

A TOM DOHERTY ASSOCIATES BOOK
NEW YORK

This is a work of fiction. All the characters and events portrayed in this novel are either fictitious or are used fictitiously.

SONS OF THE OAK

A Tor Book
Published by Tom Doherty Associates, LLC
175 Fifth Avenue
New York, NY 10010

www.tor.com

Tor® is a registered trademark of Tom Doherty Associates, LLC.

Library of Congress Cataloging-in-Publication Data

Farland, David.
    Sons of the oak / David Farland.—1st ed.
        p.   cm.
    "A Tom Doherty Associates book."
    ISBN-13: 978-0-765-30177-2
    ISBN-10: 0-765-30177-6 (acid-free paper)
   1. Supernatural—Fiction. I. Title.
    PS3556.A71558S66 2006
    813'.54—dc22

                                                   2006005729

First Edition: November 2006

Printed in the United States of America

0 9 8 7 6 5 4 3 2 1

To Rick and Amy White, with gratitude for their friendship
and support through a difficult time

SONS OF THE OAK

Asgaroth sent his consciousness across the stars, past nebulae of flaming gases, past black holes that sucked in all matter, beyond galaxies dying and gone cold, until he stood upon the broken remnants of the One True World before his master, Shadoath.

She appeared to him as a goddess of shadow, a petite woman, sleek and elegant, her supple limbs the very definition of grace, raven hair cascading down bare shoulders, her smooth skin as flawless as perfect virtue, her lips so red that blood would envy it.

A shadow slanted across her face, hiding her features, but her eyes sparkled like black diamonds.

She sat upon a marble dais in a garden, with trees twisting up like thick serpents, their dark leaves hissing in a hint of wind, while among them sweet doves sang their night songs.

In the hollows among the trees stood her guardians, those who worshipped her, those whose love enslaved them. Once, in a previous life, Asgaroth had grown a cancer on his shoulder. For weeks a fevered hump had amassed, swelling so quickly that he could almost watch it. He knew that it would kill him in time, and had watched it with morbid dispassion, until finally one day the skin above it had grown so taut that it could no longer hold, and a rip appeared. From out of it he saw the cancer: a grotesque fleshy head with a mouthful of crooked teeth, a single milky eye, and some ragged hair.

He had looked upon it with dispassion, laughing. "It is my true self revealed at last!" he'd whispered.

But those who guarded Shadoath were more twisted still, mere humps of flesh with crooked backs that surely could not attain higher thought. They seemed to sprout heads and arms almost at random. He saw one that had three full hands budding from a single arm, yet it held a silver scimitar in one of those hands with expertness, its swollen fingers like red claws wrapped painfully about the hilt.

Shadoath watched him approach with dispassion. They had spoken countless times before, over the millions of millions of years.

"Mistress," Asgaroth whispered. "The torch-bearer has chosen a new form."

Asgaroth showed her a vision of Queen Iome Sylvarresta, her womb swelling with new life, a spirit shining like a fallen star beneath the flesh.

Shadoath showed no emotion. It had been ages since this torch-bearer had last shown himself. He had been in hiding, for centuries, purifying himself, firming his resolve.

"What does he desire?" Shadoath asked.

Asgaroth showed her a vision of the world of the Runelords, a world healing after the fierce battles between the reavers and the Earth King, a world healing more than any world should, a world remaking itself in the shape of the One True World. "He has found it: a world that holds the memory of the master rune. The restoration is at hand!"

This caused Shadoath to rise. Once, so long ago that even the memory of the events had faded, so that now it was only a legend, the Dark Master had sought to seize control of all creation, had sought to bind all that existed to her. But her efforts had failed, the master rune itself was broken, and at that time, the One True World had shattered, splintering into a thousand thousand shadow worlds, each but a dim reflection of the perfect world that had been.

With its destruction, the knowledge of the master rune was lost. Long had Asgaroth believed that reality was like a shattered crystal, each shadow world a shard of what had been. And one of those shards would still know the shape of the master rune.

Now, they had found that shard. And with the knowledge, the master rune could be rebuilt. The shadow worlds could be bound in one, all worlds colliding to make a perfect whole.

"He will seek to bind the worlds," Shadoath said.

Both Shadoath and Asgaroth had amassed a wealth of knowledge about magic. But neither knew the key to binding the worlds, to bringing forth the restoration.

"Then we must make sure that he is under our sway," Asgaroth said. "After his birth, it will take time before he fully awakens to his power. The torch-bearer will be vulnerable."

"Then we should plant the seeds of his destruction now," Shadoath said. "You know what to do. Open a gate to his world, and I will bring my armies and join you."

Asgaroth smiled. Shadoath's resources were unbounded, her cunning unsurpassed, her cruelty inspired. Compared to her, the monster Scathain who had lost against the Earth King was but a worm. She had defeated the torch-bearer countless times before. She would defeat him one last time, in this the most desperate of contests. For this time it was not a single world that hung in the balance, it was all creation.

"An open gate awaits you," Asgaroth said, and he showed her a vision of a tiny village, burned to slag there among the woods. Chimneys of blackened stone were all that was left of the houses. On a patch of ashes, among ash-covered bones, green flames glowed, creeping along the ground.

At that moment, the Earth King Gaborn Val Orden was taking a late meal. He set down his wine goblet and felt vaguely disturbed. He tilted his head as if listening. He felt something. . . . A keen sense of danger that prickled the hair on his scalp. But it was distant, in the future. And it was not targeted at a certain person. It was diffuse, and vast. It was an evil large enough to lay waste to an entire world.

❧ 1 ❧

PERFECTING THE DARKNESS

No one can truly be called a man so long as he basks in the light of his father and mother. For until we are forced to stand alone, we never know the measure of strength that abides within us. And once a boy's father dies, he cannot be called a child any longer.

—*The Wizard Binnesman*

This was the face of the Earth King: Skin the shade of dark green oak leaves, fading in the fall. Old man's hair of silver webs. A sorrowful face as full of furrows as the rind of a rotting apple. And green-black eyes that were wild, hunted, like the eyes of a stag in the forest.

That is how Fallion, at the age of nine, remembered his father. A father he had not seen now for three years.

Strange then, that on an autumn evening as Fallion rode on a mountain track outside Castle Coorm with his younger brother Jaz and Hearthmaster Waggit beside him, and a small contingent of guards bristling front and back, the image of his father should intrude so heavily on Fallion's mind.

"Time to turn back," the point guard, a woman named Daymorra, said in a thick accent. "I smell evil."

She nodded to her right, up a hill where fences of stacked gray stones parceled out some cowherd's lands and formed a dam that held back the leaning pine forests of the mountains above. There, at the edge of the forest rose a pair of barrows, houses for the dead. In the swiftly falling darkness, the shadows under the trees were black. And above the mountain hovered a haze, purple and green like a bruise in the sky. Strange lights flashed among the gauzy clouds, as if from distant lightning.

Fallion's personal guard, Sir Borenson, laughed and said, "You don't smell *evil*. It's a *storm* you smell."

Daymorra glanced back, troubled. She was a rugged woman from beyond Inkarra, with strange skin as gray as a tree trunk, black hair as fine as flax, and black eyes that glinted like lightning. She wore a simple outfit of ebony cotton covered by a supple leather vest, with an ornate steel buckler that covered her belly, and a slave's collar of silver around her neck. Neither Fallion nor anyone that he knew had ever seen anyone like Daymorra until she had shown up at the castle six months earlier, sent by Fallion's father to join the guard.

"Humans may not smell evil," Daymorra said. "But I've garnered endowments of scent from a burr. They know the smell of evil. Something is there, in trees. Evil spirits, I think."

Fallion knew of men who had taken endowments of scent from dogs, but he had never even heard of a burr. Daymorra claimed to have taken endowments of hearing from bats, grace from hunting cats, and brawn from a wild boar. The skill to draw attributes from animals other than dogs was unheard of in Fallion's land. If her story was true, hers was an exotic amalgam of powers.

Fallion rose up in his saddle, drew a deep breath, and tasted the air. It was so heavy with water, he could smell tomorrow's morning dew, and the air was just cool enough that he could feel the first thrill of winter in it.

I do smell something, he thought. It was like an itch, an electric tingle, across the bridge of his cheek.

Daymorra eyed the barrows distrustfully and shivered. "One should give dead to fire or water, not leave evil spirits in the ground. We should turn back now."

"Not yet," Waggit argued. "We don't have far to go. There is a thing that the boys must see.

Daymorra's nostrils flared; she reined in her horse, as if thinking, then urged it ahead.

Fallion's younger brother Jaz had been watching the side of the road for small animals. Fallion's first vivid memory had been of discovering a frog— like a bit of gray-green clay with a dark mask. It had hopped over his head and landed on a lilac leaf when he was only two. He'd thought it was a "squishy grasshopper," and felt the most amazing sense of wonder. After that, Fallion and his brother had become obsessed with hunting for animals—whether they be hedgehogs in the fields above the castle, or bats in the guard towers, or eels and crayfish in the moat. Jaz spoke up, "What is a burr?"

Daymorra frowned, then made big eyes and spoke as she rode. "A fawn, I think you call it. It is a forest fawn?"

Jaz shrugged and looked to Fallion for help. Though Fallion was only a few months older than his brother, Jaz always looked to him for help. Fallion was both much larger than Jaz and more mature. But even Fallion had never heard of a "forest fawn."

Waggit answered, "Among the islands where Daymorra's people come from, the burr is a small antelope—not much taller than a cat—that lives in the jungle. It is a timid creature. It is said that the burr can taste the thoughts of those that hunt them. The fact that Daymorra was able not only to catch one, but to take an endowment from it is . . . remarkable."

They rode around a bend in silence, plunged below a thin cloud, and climbed again, only the thud of iron-shod hooves and the slithering sound of ring mail announcing them. To the left, the dull sun floated on the horizon like a molten bubble in a vat of ore. For the moment there were clouds above him and below, and Fallion pretended that he was riding through the clouds. The road ahead was barren, riddled with rocks and roots.

Fallion caught a movement out of the corner of his eye, glanced to his right, under the shadowed pines. A chill crept up his spine, and his senses came alive.

Something was under the shadows. Perhaps it had just been a raven flitting under the trees, black against black. But Fallion saw Borenson reach down with his right hand and grasp his long-handled warhammer, whose metal head had a bird on it, with spikes sticking out like wings.

Fallion was young enough to hope that a bear hid in the woods, or a huge stag. Something better than the ground squirrels and cottontail rabbits he'd been spotting along the road.

They crested a small hill, overlooking a vale.

"Look there, my young princes," Waggit said soberly to both Fallion and Jaz. "Tell me what you see."

A cottage squatted below, a tidy home with a freshly thatched roof, surrounded by ruby-colored roses and butterfly bushes. Birds flitted everywhere—yellow-headed bee eaters hovering and diving around the bushes.

A woman was out late, handsome, in a burgundy work dress, her hair tied back with a lavender rag, raking hazelnuts onto a ground cloth while her red hens clucked and raced about pecking at bugs and worms in the freshly turned leaves.

The woman glanced uphill at the riders, no doubt alerted by the thud of hooves on hard clay, the jangle of weapons. Worry showed in her eyes, but when she saw Borenson, she flashed a smile, gave a nod, and went back to work.

Hearthmaster Waggit whispered to the boys, "What do you know of that woman?"

Fallion tried to let his mind clear in the way that Waggit had taught him, to focus. He was supposed to gaze not just upon her face or figure, but upon the totality of her—her clothing, her movements, the house and possessions that she surrounded herself with.

Waggit was teaching the boys to "read." Not to read characters or runes upon a parchment, but to read gestures and body language—to "read" people. Waggit, who had mastered several disciplines in the House of Understanding, insisted that "Of all the things I teach you, reading the human animal, as is taught in the Room of Eyes, is the skill that you will invoke most in life. Reading a person well can mean the difference between life and death."

"She's not married," Jaz offered. "You can tell because she doesn't have any clothes but hers drying on the line." Jaz always tried to speak first, making the easy observations. That only made Fallion's job harder.

Fallion was being tested; he struggled to find something more insightful to say. "I don't think she wants to get married . . . ever."

Behind him, Sir Borenson gave a sharp snort of a laugh and demanded, "Why would you say that?"

Borenson knew this land, this woman. His snort sounded almost derisive, as if Fallion had guessed wrong. So Fallion checked himself, and answered. "You and Waggit are her age. If she wanted a husband, she'd smile and look for a reason to talk. But she's afraid of you. She keeps her shoulders turned away, like she's saying, 'Come near me, and I'll run.'"

Borenson laughed again.

Waggit asked, "Is he correct?"

"He's got the widow Huddard right," Borenson said. "Cool as midwinter.

Many a man has wanted to warm her bed, but she'll have nothing to do with any of them."

"Why not?" Waggit asked. But he didn't ask Borenson or Jaz. Instead he looked at Fallion, probing, testing.

What he saw was a handsome boy with black hair, tanned features, nearly flawless. His face still swelled with the fat of a child, but his eyes held the wisdom of an old man.

Waggit studied the boy and thought, He's so young—too young to plumb the depths of the human soul. He is, after all, only a child, without even a single endowment of wit to his name.

But Waggit also knew that Fallion was of a special breed. The children born in the past few years—after the Great War—were different from children born in the past. Stronger. Wiser. Some thought that it had to do with the Earth King. As if the rise of the first Earth King in two millennia had bestowed a blessing upon their seed. It was said that children in the rising generation were more perfect than their forefathers, more like the Bright Ones of the netherworld than normal children.

And if this was true of the get of common swineherds, it was doubly true of the Earth King's firstborn, Fallion.

Fallion's brother Jaz was nothing like Fallion. He was a kind boy, small for his age, and already distracted by a salamander pawing through the dead leaves by the roadside. He would be a thoughtful prince someday, Waggit imagined, but nothing special.

But Fallion had a greater destiny. Even now he gazed down upon the widow, trying to discover why she would never marry.

Her little cottage at the edge of the wilds was so . . . lush. The garden behind the house was lavish for a lone woman, and it was kept behind a tall fence so that her milk goat, which stood in the crook of a low apple tree, could not get the vegetables.

Bushes and trees had been planted around the house to break the wind and offer shelter to birds—bee eaters and sparrows that, like the chickens, cleared the garden of worms and beetles.

Wicker flower baskets hung from the eaves of the cottage, drawing honeybees, and Fallion did not doubt that the widow Huddard knew where the hives lay.

This woman lived in harmony with nature. Her home was a little island paradise surrounded by rocky hills.

Fallion said, "She works hard. Nobody around her works as hard. We've seen a hundred cottages along the road, but none like hers. She doesn't want to raise some man like he was a baby."

Sir Borenson laughed again.

Waggit agreed, "I suspect that you're right. The other shacks that we've passed were poor indeed. Their owners merely *survive*. They look at the hard clay, the rocky ground, and don't have the heart to work it. So they let their sheep and cattle crop the grass short and live off what scraps of meat they can get. But this woman, she *thrives* on ground that breaks the hearts of lesser men. One widow with the heart of a warlord, forever battling the rocks and clay and cold up on this hillside. . . ." Waggit spoke with a note of finality. The lesson was done.

Fallion asked Waggit, "Did you bring us all of the way up here, just to see one old lady?"

"I didn't bring you up here," Waggit said. "Your father did."

Jaz's head snapped up. "You saw my da?" he asked eagerly. "When?"

"I didn't *see* him," Waggit said. "I heard the command last night, in my heart. A warning. He told me to bring you boys here."

A warning? Fallion wondered. Somehow it surprised him that his father had spared him a thought. As far as Fallion knew, his father had forgotten that he even had a pair of sons. Fallion sometimes felt as fatherless as the by-blows that littered the inns down on Candler's Street.

Fallion wondered if there was more that his father had wanted him to see. Fallion's father could use his Earth Powers to peer into the hearts of men and see their pasts, their desires. No man alive could know another person or judge their worth like Fallion's father.

Fallion's horse ambled forward, nosed a clump of grass by the roadside. Fallion drew reins, but the beast fought him. "Get back," Fallion growled, pulling hard.

Borenson warned the stallion, "Careful, friend, or the stable-master will have your walnuts."

All right, Fallion thought, I've seen what my father wanted me to see. But why does he want me to see it now?

Then Fallion had it. "With a lot of work, you can thrive in a hard place."

With rising certainty he said, "That is what my father wants me to know. He is sending us to a hard place."

Borenson and Waggit caught each other's eyes. A thrill passed between them.

"Damn," Borenson said, "that boy is perceptive."

Movement up on the hill drew Fallion's eye—a shadow flitted like a raven between the trees.

Fallion could not see what had drawn his attention. The wet trunks of the pines were as black as ruin. The forest looked as wild and rugged as Fallion's father.

He focused on the tree line. A few great oaks sprawled silently along a ridge, offering shade to a pair of brown cattle, while smaller oaks crowded the folds. But still there was no sign of what had drawn his eye, and again Fallion felt uneasy.

Something is there, Fallion realized. Something in the shadows of the trees, watching us—a wight perhaps. The ghost of a shepherd or a woodsman.

The loud bleat of a sheep rode down from the woods above, echoing among the hills in the crisp evening air.

"Time to go," Borenson said, turning his horse; the others fell in line.

But the image of the cottage lingered, and Fallion asked, "The widow Huddard, she . . . makes a lot of her own things. She sells milk and vegetables, honey and whatnot?"

"And your question is?" Waggit asked.

"She lives well from her own labors. But I was born a lord. What can I make?"

Fallion thought of the craftsmen at the castle—the armorers, the alewives, the master of the hounds, the dyers of wool. Each jealously guarded the secrets of his trade, and though Fallion suspected that he could master any of those trades, he had no one to teach him.

Waggit smiled with satisfaction. "The common folk manipulate *things*," he said. "Blacksmiths work metal, farmers till the land. That is how they earn their living. But a lord's art is a greater art: he manipulates *people*."

"Then we are no better than leeches," Fallion said. "We just live off of others."

Sir Borenson sounded so angry that his voice came out a near roar.

"A good lord earns his keep. He doesn't just *use* others, he empowers them. He encourages them. He makes them more than what they could become by themselves."

Maybe, Fallion thought, but only because they know that he'll kill them if they don't do what he says.

With a sly grin, Waggit added, "A lord's craft can indeed be marvelous. He *molds* men. Take Sir Borenson here. Left to his own devices, he is but the basest of clay. He has the natural instincts of a . . . cutthroat—"

"Nay," Daymorra threw in with a hearty laugh. "A lecher. Left to his own ways, he'd be a lout in an alehouse, peddling the flesh of young women."

Borenson blushed, the red rising naturally to his face, and laughed. "Why not both? Sounds like a good life to me."

"But your father turned Borenson into a lawman," Waggit said. "And there are few better. Captain of the Guard, at one time."

Fallion gave Borenson a long look. Fallion had heard that Borenson had been powerful indeed—until his Dedicates had been killed. Now the guardsman had no endowments of brawn or of speed or of anything else, and though he had the respect of the other guards, he was the weakest of them all. Why he had not taken new attributes was a mystery that Fallion had not been able to unravel.

Fallion knew that there were dangers in taking endowments of course. Take the brawn from a man, and you become strong, but he becomes so weak that perhaps his heart will fail. Take the grace from a woman, and suddenly you are limber, but maybe her lungs won't unclench. Take the wit from a man, and you have use of his memory, but you leave an idiot in your wake.

It was a horrible thing to do, taking an attribute from another human being. Fallion's mother and father had abhorred the deed, and he felt their reluctance. But why had Borenson turned away from it?

Borenson wasn't a real guard in Fallion's mind. He acted more like a father than a guard.

Waggit said softly, "The shaping of men is a—"

There was an odd series of percussive booms, as if in the distance up the mountain, lightning struck a dozen times in rapid succession. The sound was not so much heard as felt, a jarring in the marrow.

Waggit fell silent. He'd been about to offer more praise for the Earth King. But he often worried about praising Fallion's father in front of the boys.

Gaborn Val Orden was the first Earth King in two thousand years, and most likely the last that mankind would see for another two thousand. He cast a shadow that covered the whole world, and despite Fallion's virtues, Waggit knew that the boy could never come close to filling his father's boots.

Waggit had an odd sensation, glanced up the hill. Almost, he expected to see the Earth King there, Gaborn Val Orden, stepping out from among the shadow of the trees, like a nervous bear into the night. He could nearly taste Gaborn's scent, as rich as freshly turned soil. Nearby, a cricket began to sing its nightly song of decay.

Borenson drew a deep breath, and raised his nose like a hound that has caught a familiar scent. "I don't know about evil, but I smell *death*. There are corpses in the forest."

He turned his horse, and with a leap it was over the hedge and rushing up toward the pines. Waggit and Daymorra looked at each other, as if wondering whether they should follow, and Fallion made up their minds for them. He spurred his horse above the hedge and gave chase.

In moments, they thundered over the green grass up the hill, leapt another stone fence, and found themselves under a dark canopy. The pine needles lay thick on the ground, wet and full of mold, muffling the footfalls of the horses. Still, with each step, twigs would break, like the sound of small bones snapping in a bird.

It seemed unnaturally bleak under the trees to Sir Borenson. He'd been in many forests. The clouds above and the setting sun had both muted the light, but the black pine boughs seemed to hurry the coming of the night.

In the solemn forest, mist rose from the ground, creating a haze, like an empty songhouse once the candles have been snuffed out, after the last aria of the evening.

They rode through deep woods for nearly half a mile before Borenson found the bodies. They were riding up a steep draw, through trees so thick that even ferns could not grow beneath them, when they came upon five girls lying in the crooks of a mossy old oak—pale flesh, white and bloodless, fingers and toes turned blue.

Each body was at a different height. But all of them were well above the reach of wolves. All of the girls were young, perhaps five to thirteen years old, and most were naked. Their bellies looked swollen, as if they were pregnant.

But most horrifying were their expressions. They stared up with eyes gone white, and their mouths gaped wide, as if they had died in inexpressible fear or agony.

Both, Borenson suspected. His heart sank. His own daughter Talon, the oldest of his brood, was eight. At that moment he felt that she was the most precious thing in his life. He glanced back, afraid that Fallion and Jaz would see the bodies, but it was too late. The princes were staring in shock.

Fallion peered up, horrified by what he saw. As yet, he had not learned the mysteries of how children were formed. He had never even seen a girl with her clothes off, and he knew that what he saw now was evil and unnatural.

Up the hill, there was a cracking sound in the woods, as if a horse had stepped on a branch. Everyone stopped and glanced uphill apprehensively for a moment, then Borenson turned back to the princes.

"Get them away from here," Borenson told Waggit and Daymorra.

Borenson rode his horse near, placing himself between the princes and the girls in order to obscure their view. And for a moment he just stared at two of the girls, wedged in the crook of the same branch, whose bodies lay almost even with his eyes.

Both girls had rips and cuts on their flesh, bruises from rough handling. Both had obviously been violated by a big man, for there was bleeding and tearing in their most sacred places.

Borenson glanced at the ground and saw huge tracks—as if an impossibly large bear had been circling the tree.

Waggit rode up and whispered, "The girls taken from Hayfold? All the way up here?"

Borenson nodded. Three girls had been kidnapped a couple of nights before from the village of Hayfold. Such crimes were almost unheard of since the coming of the Earth King. Yet more than three bodies were here now. Borenson wondered where the other two had come from.

"I'll cover the corpses," Borenson said. "We can bring a wagon up tonight to retrieve them."

He reached up, feeling more fatigued than his labors of the day could account for, and unpinned his green woolen cape. The lowest two girls were laid out side by side, and he imagined that his cape would cover both of them.

But just as he pulled the cape up, one girl moved.

He grunted in surprise and quicker than thought his boot-knife leapt from scabbard to hand. He stared at the girl for a moment, and saw movement again—a shifting in her belly.

"Is . . . is there something in there?" Waggit asked, his voice shaken.

And now that Borenson thought about it, he realized that the girls were too bloated for such cold weather. They shouldn't have swelled so much in a pair of nights.

He saw it again, as if a child kicked inside the dead girl's womb.

"There are babies in there," Fallion said, his face a study in horror and amazement.

Leaning forward, Borenson plunged in his knife, penetrating the skin, so that the smaller girl's belly flayed open. Out spilled its contents.

Borenson saw several creatures—wet, slimy, squirming. Like black malformed pups feeding at their mother's teats.

One spilled out onto a limb, rolling to its back. Its eyes were lidless, like a snake's, and vast and soulless in a wolflike face. Its tiny paws looked powerful, with claws as sharp as fishhooks. Its body looked too long for those legs, almost otterlike, with folds of skin that ran from leg to leg, like a flying lizard. But the creature had black hair, and its mouth held far too many teeth.

"What in the world?" Waggit intoned with revulsion.

The girl's innards were mostly gone. Tripe, guts, liver. The monsters had been feeding on them.

"Eating their way out," Waggit said. He asked the others, "You ever heard of anything like this?"

"You're the scholar," Borenson shot back.

Both men looked to Daymorra for an answer. She was the one who had traveled most widely in the world. She just sat astride her horse, nocking an arrow to her great bow, and shook her head.

Suddenly, from the highest branch above them, there was movement. A pale face turned to them, and a small and frightened voice whispered, "Get away from here. Before *they* come back!"

A young woman with hair as red as cinnamon was staring down at them—fierce eyes as blue as summer skies, the eyes of a savage. With her pale complexion, Borenson had just thought her to be another one of the dead. She looked to be twelve or thirteen, her small breasts just beginning to form. Her clothes were sodden rags, and her windblown hair had bits of leaves, lichens, and bark caught in it.

He stared in surprise. The girl's teeth were chattering. Strange, Borenson thought; I did not hear it before. She still clung to a scrap of cloth, a dark green coat. Her thighs were bruised and bloody, but her stomach was not yet bloated. Her rape must have been very recent.

Borenson glanced back at the others, to see their reaction, but the young woman begged, "Please, don't leave me!"

"We won't," young Fallion said, spurring his horse. In an instant, he was under the limb, reaching up.

The girl leaned forward, grabbing him around the neck. She felt shaky and frail as she half slid, half fell into the saddle behind him.

Fallion worried for her, hoping that there might be time to save her still. He wondered if it was safe to touch her—if the creatures inside might eat their way out.

Borenson threw his cape around her shoulders. Fallion felt her tremble all over as she hugged his chest. She clung to him as if she'd die before she let go.

"Do you have a name, child?" Borenson asked.

"Rhianna," the girl said. Her accent was one common to folk in the far northwest of Mystarria.

"A last name?" he asked. She made no answer. Fallion turned to see her. Her blue eyes were filled with more terror than he had ever seen in a human face.

Fallion wondered what horrors she had seen.

For her part, Rhianna stared at the men, and she was too afraid to speak. She could feel something hurting her inside. Was it fear that gnawed at her belly, or something worse? Why were these men still here? Everyone else was dead. She could tell them later what had happened—about the dark stranger, the summoner. She forced some words past lips that would not let her speak. "Please, let's go. Get me out of here!"

In the woods above them there was a distant crack, like a wet limb snapping under heavy weight.

"I smell evil," Daymorra whispered. "It's coming."

Suddenly a voice inside Fallion warned, "Flee!" It was his father's voice, the warning of the Earth King.

All the others must have heard the same warning, for Waggit instantly grabbed Jaz's reins and went thundering downhill through the woods.

Borenson fumbled with his boot-knife for an instant, thinking to put it away, but then stabbed the damned creature that lay on the limb through the belly, and it wriggled on the end of his blade. He marveled at its strength, until it let out a shrill bell-like bark.

And in the woods, uphill, an enormous roar sounded, shaking the air, a mother crying out to her young.

There was the sound of limbs snapping and trees breaking, and Borenson looked back. Fallion was trying to turn his mount, mouth wide in horror. Borenson slapped its rump, and the horse lunged away uncertainly.

Rhianna wrapped her arms around Fallion. He locked his own small hand over her fist and thought, We were all wrong. My father didn't send me here to see some old woman. He sent me to see *this!*

He glanced back into the woods, trying to discern what gave chase, as Borenson sheathed his knife.

Fallion's heart was pounding like a sledgehammer upon an anvil. His father seldom sent warnings, and only did so when a man was in mortal danger.

There was a sound like the churning of wind, or the rising of a storm up the hill, as if something were rushing through the trees. Fallion peered up through the woods, and it seemed that he saw movement—dark forms leaping and gliding through the trees. But it was as if light retreated from them, and the harder he squinted, the less certain he could be of what it was that he saw.

"Ride!" Daymorra shouted as she drew back her arrow. "I will hold them off!"

Waggit and Jaz were already gone, leaving Daymorra to her fate. Borenson spurred his own horse and kept just off Fallion's flank. Soon the horses were galloping at full speed.

Fallion's training took over and he clung to the saddle and crouched, offering less wind resistance as an aid to his swift force horse and making a smaller target of his back. Rhianna clung to him, warming his back. With his ear pressed against the horse's neck, he could feel the heat of its body on his cheek as well as between his legs, could feel every thud of its hooves against the soft humus, and could hear the blood rushing through its veins and the wind wheezing through the caverns of its lungs.

He was suddenly reminded of an incident from his childhood: on a foggy morning, not five years ago, he and Jaz had gone out on the parapet. The streets had been all but empty so early in the morning, and Fallion had heard a strange sound, a panting, as if someone were running, followed by a call: "Wooo—OOOO. Wooo-oooo."

Both boys thought that something was coming for them, scrabbling up the castle walls, and they tried to imagine what it might be. So they ran into the room and barred their doors in fright.

They tried to imagine what kind of animal might make such a noise, and Fallion had ventured that since it sounded like a horn, it must be an animal with a long neck.

In their room, the boys had a menagerie of animals all carved from wood and painted in their natural colors. Jaz suggested that it might be a camel that was chasing them, though neither boy had ever seen one. And in his mind, the sound immediately became a camel—black and huge, like the war camels that were ridden by the Obbattas in the desert. He imagined that the camel had sharp teeth dripping with foam and bloodshot eyes.

Four-year-old Fallion and Jaz had rushed out into the Great Hall of the castle, stumbling in fear and shouting to the guards, "Help! Help! The camels are coming!"

Sir Borenson, who was taking breakfast at the time, had laughed so hard that he fell off of his stool. He took the boys outside in the fog and drew his sword very dramatically, cursing all camels and commanding them to do no harm.

Then he led them toward the sound of the eerie calls. There, in the courtyard, they found a puppy chained to a stake—a young mastiff that alternately howled and panted as it tried to pull free.

"There's your camel," Borenson had said, laughing. "The Master of the Hounds bought him last night, and was afraid he'd try to run home if we took him off his chain. So he'll stay here for the day, until he figures out that he's family." Then the boys had laughed at their own fear and had petted the puppy.

Now as Fallion rode, he heard trees snapping, saw the fear on Borenson's face.

We're not children anymore, he thought.

He looked to his brother Jaz, so small and frail, riding in his haste. Fallion felt a pang of longing, a stirring desire to protect his brother, something that he'd often felt before.

Fallion suddenly heard a strange call, like deep horns ringing one after another, all underwater, then a sudden screeching and the sounds of trees crashing, as if some enormous creatures tangled in battle.

Fallion imagined Daymorra fighting there against the creatures, and whispered the only prayer he knew, "May the Bright Ones protect you, and the Glories guard your back!"

Fallion opened his eyes to slits. Darkness was coming fast even as his horse lunged out of the woods and leapt down a sloping field. The garnet air seemed wan and diffuse, as if filtered through fire-lit skies. Fat grasshoppers leapt from the stubble as the horses pounded past, and there in the grass, white flowers yawned wide, morning glories with petals that unfolded like pale mouths, getting ready to scream.

There were more cries in the woods as the party reached the road. Somehow they had circled behind the widow's place. Her black dog raced out from under her porch, giving chase, but could not keep up with the force horses. Soon it dropped away, wagging its tail sheepishly as if its defeat were a victory.

Something stirred inside Fallion, and he heard his father shout, "Run!" Fallion spurred his horse harder. "Run! The ends of the Earth are not far enough!"

Again his father's image intruded in his mind, a dimly recalled green figure, a shadow, and Fallion felt his presence so strongly that it was as if the man's breath warmed Fallion's face.

"Father?" Fallion called out.

Fallion looked behind him, wondering what could be giving chase, when he felt something pierce his stomach.

He glanced down to see if an arrow was protruding from his ribs, or to see if one of the black creatures that inhabited Rhianna was there. His wine-colored leather vest was undamaged. Yet he could feel something vital being pulled from him, as if he were a trout and a giant hand had pierced him and now was yanking out his guts.

He heard a whisper, his father's rambling voice. "Run, Fallion," he said.

"They will come for you." And then there was a long silence, and the voice came softer. "Learn to love the greedy as well as the generous . . . the poor as much as the rich . . . the evil. . . . Return a blessing for every blow. . . ."

Suddenly the voice went still, and there was a yawning emptiness in Fallion. His eyes welled up. Fallion saw sheep running headlong down from the hills, and everywhere, everywhere, from all of the guards, grunts and cries of pain issued. Fallion could feel keenly a wrongness descending upon the world.

"Sweet mercy!" Waggit shouted.

Borenson growled, "The Earth King is dead!" and somewhere in the distance, from Castle Coorm, whose towers rose above its gray weathered walls, a bell began to toll.

Fallion had never known a world without an Earth King. All of his young life, he had felt secure. If danger arose, whether from assassins or illness or accident, he had known that his father's voice would whisper in warning, and he would know how to save himself.

Suddenly he was naked and bereft.

The horses galloped hard along the dirt track. Borenson cast a fearful glance uphill.

"Above us!" Borenson shouted. Darkness thickened all around, as if the last of the sun had dipped below the horizon, sucking all light with it.

Tears of pain filled Fallion's eyes, and he looked up the mountain. Daymorra came riding hard from under the trees. It seemed that a wind swept toward her, rattling the pines along the mountainside, causing whole trees to pitch and sway and crack and fall. But it was no wind. Instead Fallion saw creatures—like scraps of blackest night, floating about in a mad dance, landing in the trees and shaking them. Their growls rose, deep and ominous, like distant thunder, but they held to the woods, and did not dare race into the open fields. Instead, they leapt from tree to tree, following through the woods, while the trees hissed and bent under heavy weight.

And then all of the horses were speeding away, down the long winding road, while the enemy fell behind. Borenson brought out a warhorn and sounded it, in hopes that the far-seers at Castle Coorm would hear and know that they were under attack. The far-seers with their many endowments of sight might spot them from the castle. But Fallion knew that at such a great distance, he would look as tiny as an ant.

The night suddenly descended, falling instantly and unnaturally to smother the world.

It was the end of a golden age of peace. Fallion knew it. Everyone knew it. Even the sheep felt it.

Fallion squinted in the unnatural darkness as the horses thundered. Rhianna clung to him, gibbering with pain or terror, and he felt hot tears splash down from her eyes to his back.

Are there monsters in her? Fallion wondered. Are they eating their way out? What are we running from?

And instantly he knew: for years the old folks had said that the world was becoming more like the netherworld. They said that fresh springwater tasted better than old wine. The hay in the fields smelled sweet enough to eat, and often folk spoke in awe at how vivid the stars now burned at night. And the weather: the lazy summers let fruit grow fat on the trees, while the winters came with a sharper bite. Some said that the world was becoming more "perfect," bringing perfect weather, perfect children, perfect peace. But there was a dark side, too. New terrors were said to be hiding in the mountains, creatures more vile than anything the world had known.

And now, Fallion thought, perfect evil has been unleashed upon the world.

THE CUT THAT CURES

Not all pain is evil. Sometimes we must pass through greater pain in order to be healed.

—The Wizard Binnesman

As night fell, Queen Iome Sylvarresta clutched the ramparts of Castle Coorm beside her far-seers and watched breathlessly as Sir Borenson fled down the mountains, blowing his warhorn again and again.

Iome had as many endowments of sight and hearing as any far-seer. Each time her children rode over a hilltop, she could see their frightened faces, pale and round in the failing light.

But she could not discern what enemy chased them. Her tears at the loss of her husband kept welling up, and though she wiped them away savagely with the sleeve of her cloak, new ones kept filling their place.

"There's something in the woods above them, keeping pace," one far-seer said. Indeed, whole pine trees shook and swayed on the ridge above, and black shades floated among the branches. Iome could hear distant bell-like barks, animal calls. But no amount of squinting would reveal the enemy.

"The boys look well," the far-seer said, trying to comfort Iome.

The words had little effect. Iome felt numb with grief at the loss of her husband. She'd always known that this day would come, but it felt far worse than she had expected.

I should not mourn him so, she thought. I lost him years ago when he became the Earth King, and his duties stripped him from me. I should not mourn him so.

But there was an ache deep inside her, an emptiness that she knew could never be filled. She almost felt as if she would collapse.

She mentally tried to shove the pain back.

The sun was falling, retreating to the far side of the world. Already the vale around the castle was shrouded in darkness, and all too soon the last rays of sunlight would fade from the hilltops in the east, and the world would plunge into blackest night.

Iome bit her lip. A dozen force knights were already galloping into the hills to the children's aid.

I've done all that I can, Iome thought bitterly.

And it did not seem enough. Worry fogged her mind. Gaborn had not been dead for two minutes before the boys fell under attack.

It reeked of a plot, of enemies lying in wait. Iome looked back into the shadows behind her, where her Days stood quietly studying the scene. The Days was a rail of a woman, with long trestles of hair braided in cornrows, a doe's brown eyes, and the sullen robes of a scholar.

If there was a plot, the Days would probably know of it. Every king and queen had her own Days whose sole purpose in life was to chronicle their lives. And each Days had given an endowment of Wit to another of his order, thus sharing a single mind, so that in some distant monastery, this woman's other half scribed Iome's life, while others scribed the lives of other lords. If any king or queen in the land had a hand in her husband's death, the woman would know.

But she would not tell, not willingly. The Days were sworn to strict noninterference. The woman would not warn Iome if her life was in danger, wouldn't give her a drink if she was dying of a fever.

Yet there were sometimes ways to gather information from them.

Iome glanced at the far-seer, pretended to rivet her attention upon him, and said, "Gaborn was not dead five minutes when the boys were attacked. Could it be a plot?"

Iome glanced back to her Days, to see her reaction. She showed none. Inwardly, Iome grinned. When the Days had first come to her, she had been young and immature. Iome had been able to read her as easily as if she had been a child. But she could not do that anymore.

Iome felt old and weak, full of pain.

Suddenly the boys topped a hill three miles off, and there met the knights that Iome had sent to their aid.

For the moment they are safe, Iome thought. Now I must take measures to ensure that they remain that way.

By the time that Rhianna reached Castle Coorm, she was sick with grief and fear, and felt certain that something was gnawing at her belly. A few dozen commoners had begun to gather outside the castle walls to pay their respects to the fallen Earth King.

They had lit torches, which now reflected from the waters of the moat, and guttered in the evening breeze, filling the vale with sweet-smelling pine smoke.

As their mount descended from the hills toward the castle, she could hear hundreds of peasants singing:

> "Lost is my hope.
> Lost is my light,
> Though my heart keeps beating still.
> Oh, remember me when
> we meet again,
> my king beneath the hill."

Borenson shouted for people to clear the road, and Rhianna heard cries of "Make way for the prince!" followed by gasps of astonishment as people looked up at the boy who rode in the saddle before her.

Only then did she realize that she rode behind Fallion Orden, the Crown Prince of Mystarria.

Rhianna was weeping bitterly for each precious lost second spent behind the armored knights that guarded the way and the townsfolk that gawked at the prince.

Fallion squeezed her hand, which was wrapped around him from behind so that she was clutching his chest, and whispered, "Don't be afraid. We have good healers at the castle. They'll take care of you."

He seemed to be a kind boy, quick to give comfort, and she remembered how he had been the first to offer her a ride.

He's quick to help, as well, she decided.

And what seemed to be long wasted moments later, the horses finally thundered over the bridge into the castle.

Fallion shouted "Make way, make way!" and the horses cantered through the streets up to the keep. In minutes Rhianna dismounted and was whisked inside, where she gaped at the splendor of the Great Hall.

Servants had begun preparing a feast. Maidens had begun bringing bowls of fruit—local wood-pears and shining red apples, along with more exotic fare all the way from Indhopal—star fruits and tangerines to set upon the tables. Children were strewing pennyroyal flowers upon the stone floor, raising a sweet scent. Huge fires blazed in the hearth, where young boys turned the crank on a spit, cooking whole piglets that dripped fat and juice to sizzle in the flames. A pair of racing hounds barked at all of the excitement.

No sooner had the party entered than a knot of maids surrounded Fallion and Jaz, offering sympathy for the death of their father. Fallion tried to look stoic while wiping away the tears that came to his eyes, but Jaz seemed to be more sentimental, sobbing openly.

At the far end of the hall, Rhianna saw the queen herself hurry forward, an ancient woman with watery eyes and hair as white as ice, prematurely aged from having taken numerous endowments of metabolism. She stood tall and straight like a warrior, and moved with the grace of a dancer, but even Rhianna could see that her time was near. Even the most powerful Runelords died eventually.

Amid the bustle, Sir Borenson grabbed Rhianna and picked her up, hugging her to his chest as he shouted, "Call the surgeon, hoy!"

For his part, Borenson planned to leave the boys in the care of the cooks and maids and their mother. The boys were well liked by the help. As toddlers, Iome had sent them to the kitchens to work, as if they were the get of common scullions. She did it, as she said, "To teach the boys humility and respect for authority, and to let them know that their every request was purchased at the price of another's sweat." And so they had toiled—scrubbing pots and stirring stews, plucking geese and sweeping floors, fetching herbs from the garden and serving tables—duties common to children. In the process of learning to work, they had gained the love and respect of the common folk.

So the maids cooed at the boys, offering sympathy at the death of their father, a blow that one heavyset old matron thought could somehow only be softened by pastries.

Borenson told Waggit, "I need to get this girl to a surgeon, and learn what I can from her. Her Highness will be eager for news. Give her a full accounting."

Then he carried Rhianna through a maze of corridors and steps, and soon was panting and sweating from exertion. As he carried her, he asked, "Where can I find your mother or father?"

Rhianna was almost numb with fear. She didn't know how much she could trust this man, and she dared not tell him the truth. Her stomach hurt terribly. "I don't have a da." And what could she say about her mother? Those who knew her at all thought that she was daft, a madwoman. At the very best she was a secretive vagabond who traveled from fair to fair to sell trinkets, staying only a day or a few hours at each before she crept off into the night. "And my mother . . . I think she's dead."

Wherever Mum is, Rhianna thought, even if she's alive, she'll want people to think that she's dead.

"Brothers? Sisters? Grandparents?" he asked as they bustled up some stairs, brushing past a maid who was hurrying down with a bundle of dirty bedding.

Rhianna just shook her head.

Borenson stopped for a second, peered deep into her eyes, as if thinking. "Well, when this is all over, maybe you can come live with me."

If I live, she thought. Rhianna could feel the mail beneath his robe, hard and cold. The epaulets on his shoulders dug into her chin. She wondered if he was a hard man, like his armor.

"I think you'd like it at our house," he continued. "There's plenty of room. I have a daughter a little younger than you. Of course, you'd have to put up with some little brothers and sisters."

Rhianna bit her lip, said nothing. He seemed to take her nonanswer as an acceptance of the offer.

They reached a tower chamber, a simple room with a soft cot. The room was dark but surprisingly warm, since one wall was formed by the chimney from a hearth. Borenson laid her on a cot, then ducked into the hallway with a candle to borrow light from another flame. In a moment he was back. The ceiling was low, and bundles of dried flowers and roots hung from the rafters. A single small window had heavy iron bars upon it to keep out the night. Rhianna found her eyes riveted to it.

"The creatures were following hot after us, weren't they?" she asked. She'd heard the bell-like calls all down the mountain, had seen dark shapes, larger than horses, gliding among the pines.

"They followed us," Borenson said. "But they didn't dare come into the open. They stayed in the woods."

"It's the shadows they love," Rhianna said. "I think they were mad that I left. They want their babies back."

She tried to sound tough, but her courage was failing. Dark fluid had begun to dribble out from between her legs.

They're eating me, she realized.

She looked up at Sir Borenson. "I think I would have liked to have lived with you."

Borenson paced across the room peering at the bundles of herbs, as if wondering if one of them might be of some help. He went to a small drawer and opened it, pulled out a tiny gold tin. It held some dark ointment.

He took a pinch and rolled it into a ball.

"Are you in pain?" he asked.

"A bit," she said, trembling. But to be honest, she wasn't sure of the source. Her stomach was cramped part in fear, part in hunger. She hadn't eaten in two days. She felt weak from hunger and constant terror. She hadn't slept much, and now she felt as if she were in a dream and dared not hope for a happy ending.

"Take this," he said, offering her the dark ball. "It's opium, to get rid of the pain." He took a small pipe from the drawer—a pretty thing shaped like a silver frog upon a stick. The bowl was in the frog's mouth, while the stick served as a stem. Borenson lit it with the candle.

She took the end in her mouth and inhaled. The smoke tasted bitter. She took several puffs, then Borenson uncorked a wine bottle that was sitting on a stand by the bed and offered her a drink. The wine tasted sweet and potent, and in a moment the bitter taste faded.

There was a soft tap at the door, and Fallion entered. The boy looked very frightened, but when he saw that she was awake, he smiled just a bit.

"Can I stay?" he asked. He did not ask Borenson. He asked her.

Rhianna nodded, and he came and sat beside her, taking Borenson's spot.

Rhianna leaned back upon the bed, and Fallion just sat beside her, holding her hand. He was trying to offer comfort, but kept looking to the door, and Rhianna knew that he was worried that the healer would not come in time.

At last, Borenson asked the question that she knew that he must. "The creatures in the wood . . . where were you when they took you?"

Rhianna didn't quite know what to answer. Once again, he was prying, and she knew that, as the old saying went, A man's own tongue will betray him more often than will an enemy's. "We were camping near the margin of the old King's Road, near Hayworth. My mum had gone to Cow's Cross to sell goods at Hostenfest. We were shanking it home when a man caught us, a powerful man. He had soldiers. They knocked Mum in the head. It was a terrible sound, like an ax handle hitting a plank. I saw her fall by the fire, practically in the fire, and bleeding she was. She didn't move. And then *he* took me, and wrestled a bag over my head. After, he went to town and nabbed other girls, and he hauled us far away, up into the hills—" The words were all coming out in a rush.

Borenson put his finger to her lips. "Shhh . . . the man with soldiers—do you know his name?"

Rhianna considered how to answer, shook her head no. "The others called him 'milord.'"

"He was probably a wolf lord, an outlaw," Fallion said. "I heard that a few of them are still hiding in the hills. Did you get a good look at him?"

Rhianna nodded. "He was tall and handsome in the way that powerful lords are when they've taken too much glamour. You looked into his eyes, and you wanted to love him. Even if he was strangling you, you wanted to love him, and even as he killed me, I felt that he had the right. His eyes sparkled, like moonlight on snow . . . and when he put the bag over my head, he had a ring! Like the ones that lords wear, to put their stamp on wax."

"A signet ring?" Fallion asked. "What did it look like?"

There was a bustle at the door as a pair of healers entered. One was a tall haggard man with dark circles under his eyes. The other was an Inkarran, a woman with impossibly white skin, eyes as pale green as agates, and hair the color of spun silver.

"Iron," Rhianna said. "The ring was of black iron, with the head of a crow."

Borenson stood up and stared hard at her, almost as if he did not believe her. Fallion squeezed Rhianna's hand, just held it tight. "A king's ring?"

"He wasn't a king, I'm thinking," Rhianna objected. "He seemed to be taking orders from someone named Shadoath. He was telling the men, 'Shadoath demands that we do our part.'"

"Did you see this man, Shadoath?"

"No. He wasn't near. They just spoke of him. They said that he's coming, and they were worried that everything be 'put in order' before he gets here."

Borenson frowned at this news. "Shadoath? That's not a name that I've heard before. So your captor, once he had you, where did he take you?"

"I don't know," she said. "When they took off my hood, it was dark again. There was a town, a burned-out village in the woods. I saw black chimneys rising up like the bones of houses. But the fire there had been so hot, even the stones had melted. And we were sitting in the dark, on the ground, while around us there were ghost flames, green ghost flames."

The opium was working quickly. Rhianna could no longer feel the clenching in her stomach. In fact, her whole body felt as if it were floating just a little, as if it would rise up off of the cot and just float like a leaf on a pond.

"Ghost flames?" Borenson asked.

"They burned, but there was nothing for them to burn," Rhianna explained. "They just floated above the ground, like, as cold as fog.

"The soldiers set us there, and invited the darkness. Then the shadows came. We screamed, but the men didn't care. They just . . . they just fed us, gave us . . . to them."

Fear was rising in Rhianna's throat, threatening to strangle her again.

"Twynhaven," Borenson said. "You were at the village of Twynhaven. I know the place. Raj Ahten's flameweavers burned it down, years back. What more can you tell me about the beasts that attacked you?"

Rhianna closed her eyes and shook her head. The creatures had carried her so tenderly in their mouths, as if she were a kitten.

"They licked me," she said. "But I never even got a good look at them. But they washed me with their tongues, before . . . And I heard the leader talking. He called them *strengi-saats*."

"'Strong seeds,'" Borenson said, translating the word from its ancient Alnycian roots.

Rhianna looked up at him, worried. "Do you know what they are?"

"No," Borenson said. "I've never heard of them. But I'll soon find out all that I can."

By now, the healers were examining Rhianna; the man set some herbs on the table, along with a small cloth with some surgeon's tools—three sharp knives, a bone cleaver, and some curved needles and black thread for sewing.

Fallion must have seen her looking at the knives, for he whispered, "Don't worry. We have the best healers here."

The male healer began to ask questions. He prodded her stomach and asked if it hurt, but Rhianna's mind was so muzzy that she could hardly understand him. It seemed like minutes had passed before she managed to shake her head no.

Fallion began to tell her of the huge feast that they would be having downstairs in a couple of hours. Eels baked in butter; roast swans with orange sauce; pies filled with sausage, mushrooms, and cheese. He offered to let her sit by him, but Rhianna knew that he was just trying to distract her.

Sir Borenson had pulled the Inkarran woman into a corner and now he whispered fervently. Rhianna blocked out Fallion's droning voice, and listened to Borenson. The woman kept shaking her head, but Borenson insisted fiercely, "You have to cut it out—now! It's the only way to save her. If you don't, I'll do it myself."

"You not healer," the woman insisted in her thick accent. "You not know how. Even I never do thing like this."

"I've sewed up my share of wounds," Borenson argued. "They say that you cut children out of wombs in Inkarra."

"Sometimes, yes," the woman said. "But only after woman dead, and only to save child. I not know how do this. Maybe this kill her. Maybe ruin her, so she no have babies."

Rhianna looked at the big guard, and for some reason that she could not understand, she trusted him. His inner toughness reminded her of her mother.

Rhianna reached over to the table beside her cot and grabbed a knife. Not the big one, a smaller one, for making small cuts. Fallion grabbed at her wrist, as if he were afraid that she'd stab herself.

"Sir," Rhianna said, her vision darkening in a drug-induced haze. "Cut me, please."

Borenson turned and stared at her, mouth open.

"I'm not a healer," he apologized. "I'm not a surgeon."

"You know how to make a cut that kills," Rhianna said. Her thoughts came muzzy. "You know how to hit a kidney or a heart. This time, make one that heals."

He strode to her and took the knife. Rhianna touched its blade, tracing a simple rune called harm-me-not.

The Inkarran woman came up beside him, and whispered, "I show where to cut." Just then, the healer who had been preparing the tools put one large hand over her eyes, so that Rhianna would not be able to see what was done to her.

Rhianna surrendered.

ಖಿ 3 ಅ

OF RINGS AND THRONES

*Every man rightfully seeks to be lord of his own domain, just as every spar-
row wishes to be a lord of the sky.*

—*Emir Owatt of Tuulistan*

Night descended upon Castle Coorm. The clouds above were worn rags,
sealing out the light. The air in the surrounding meadows grew heavy and
wet, and in the hills, bell-like barks rang out, eerie and unsettling.

The peasants who had come to mourn the passing of the Earth King
issued through the gates like nervous sheep, and the atmosphere soon
changed from one of mourning to uncertainty and anticipation. The
inhabitants of Castle Coorm bore themselves as if in a siege.

It was more than an hour after Fallion had made his way home, and now
his mother waited, pacing in her quarters, often going out onto the
veranda to gaze at the hills, where every cottage was as empty and lifeless as
a pile of stones. She ignored the local dignitaries that arrived, hoping for
news of Gaborn's death. How had he died? Where? She had no answers for
them yet, none for herself.

Iome hoped that messengers would come. But she could not know for
certain that anyone would bring news. She might never learn the truth.

In the past few years, Gaborn had taken to wandering afar. With his
dozens of endowments of metabolism, he had become something of a loner.

How many folk in far lands had met her husband, a stranger in green
robes whose quick movements baffled the eye and left the visitant wondering if he'd really seen the Earth King or was only having a waking dream?
Often Gaborn merely appeared to a peasant who was walking the highway
or working in the fields, looked into his eyes for a moment, pierced his soul,
and whispered the words, "I Choose you. I Choose you for the Earth. May

the Earth hide you. May the Earth heal you. May the Earth make you its own." Then Gaborn would depart in a blur as soundlessly as a leaf falling in the forest.

He lived at dozens of times the speed of a normal man, and had aged accordingly. For him, a winter's night would feel like more than two months of solid darkness. For him, there was no such thing as a casual conversation. He had lost the patience for such things years ago. Even a few words spoken from his mouth were a thing to be treasured.

Iome had not seen him in three years. Ten months ago, Daymorra had met him on an island far to the south and east of Inkarra. Iome felt sure that he was working his way across the world.

But why? She suspected that it had to do with Fallion.

It was while Iome fretted that Sir Borenson stalked into her private quarters bearing a bowl, with Fallion in tow. The servants closed the door, and even her Days would not enter the sanctum of her private quarters, leaving them to talk in secret.

In the bowl were half a dozen eggs, black and leathery, floating in a thin soup of blood. Iome could see through the membranes of the eggs—eyes and teeth and claws. One egg had hatched, and a tiny creature thrashed about in the blood, clawing and kicking. It was as black as sin, with vicious teeth. Even as Iome watched, a second creature breached its egg, a gush of black fluid issuing forth.

"It looks almost like a squirrel," Iome mused, "a flying squirrel."

"It doesn't have any ears," Fallion said.

It was not like a squirrel at all, Iome knew. It was more like the egg of a fly, planted into the womb of its victim, then left to eat its way out and dine on the girl's dead remains. Apparently the egg didn't need the blood supply of a mature woman to hatch—perhaps only warmth and wet and darkness.

Sir Borenson cleared his throat. "We got all of the creatures out. Only one had hatched, and it only moments before."

Iome had already heard some of the news of their adventure. Fallion and Jaz had given a wild account, nearly witless with terror. Daymorra and Hearthmaster Waggit had been more cogent.

And in the midst of the questioning, Fallion had gone to give the girl comfort as others cut her open. He'd seen the eggs torn from her stomach, and now he looked very wise and sad for a nine-year-old. Iome felt proud of him.

"Do you even have any idea what these creatures are?" Iome asked.

Borenson shook his head. "Rhianna told me that they were summoned from the netherworld. The summoner called them strengi-saats. But I've never heard of them."

He went over to the hearth, hurled the bowl and its contents into the flames. The young monsters made mewling noises as they died, like kittens.

Rhianna, Iome thought. So the girl has a name. And so do the monsters that she held within her.

"I wish that Binnesman were here," Fallion said. The Earth Warden Binnesman had made detailed studies of flora and fauna in the hills and mountains of Rofehavan, in the caverns of the Underworld, and had even collected lore from the netherworld. He would know what these creatures were, if anyone would. But he had gone back to Heredon, home to his gardens at the edge of the Dunnwood.

"Will the girl survive?" Iome asked.

"I think so," Borenson said. "We found her womb easily enough, and I got all of the . . . eggs out." Iome didn't imagine that anyone had ever said the word *eggs* with more loathing. "The healers sewed her back up . . . but there was a lot of blood. And I worry about rot."

"I'll see that she's well tended," Iome said.

Borenson said. "I was hoping that you could spare a forcible. . . ."

"An endowment of stamina?" Iome asked. "What do we know of her? Is she of royal blood?"

There was a time in her life when Iome would have allowed such a boon out of pity alone. But the blood-metal mines were barren. Without blood metal, her people could not make forcibles, and without forcibles they could not transfer attributes. So the forcibles had to be saved for warriors who could put them to good use.

"She has no parents," Borenson said. "I'd like to take her as my daughter."

Iome smiled sadly. "You were ever the one for picking up strays."

"There's something about her," Borenson said. "She knows some rune casting. At least, she put a blessing on the knife before she would let it touch her. Not many children her age would know how to do that. And she didn't do it out of hope. She did it with confidence."

"Indeed," Iome said. "Too few even of our surgeons know such lore. Did she say where she learned it?"

Borenson shook his head. "Fell asleep too soon."

"We'll have the healers watch her," Iome said in a tone of finality.

Borenson bit his lip as if he wanted to argue, but seemed to think better of it.

Fallion cut in. "Mother? Won't you give her one forcible?"

Iome softened. "If her situation begins to worsen, I will permit her a forcible." She turned to Borenson. "Until then, perhaps you should ask your wife to wash the child. Myrrima has a healing touch."

Borenson nodded in acquiescence.

Iome changed the subject. "Daymorra told me of bodies in the hills," Iome said. "I've sent her to lead twenty men to burn the corpses. We can't let these monsters continue to breed."

"I agree," Borenson said. "But there is something else. Rhianna did not see the face of the man who summoned the creatures. She only saw his ring: black iron, with a crow."

Iome stared hard at Sir Borenson, unsure whether she should believe it. She looked at Fallion, hesitant to continue speaking in front of her son.

Fallion must have sensed something amiss, for he said, "An iron ring, with a crow. For Crowthen?"

"King Anders, you think?" Iome asked. "Back from the dead?" That drew Fallion's attention. Fallion peered up at her with eyes gone wide, riveted.

"It couldn't be. I saw his body myself," Borenson said. "He was cold when they took him from the battlefield at Carris. No matter how much of a wizard he was, I doubt that he could have come back."

Yet Iome gave him a hard look.

Fallion asked, "How can a man come back from the dead?"

"Anders was mad," Iome answered, "wind-driven. He gave himself to the Powers of the Air. As such, he could let his breath leave him, feign death."

Fallion looked to Borenson. "Can he really do that?"

"I've seen it," Borenson said. "Such men are hard to kill."

Iome dared not reveal more of what she suspected about Anders. Borenson put in, "Whoever he is, he isn't working alone. He mentioned a superior: someone named Shadoath. Have you heard the name?"

Iome shook her head no. "It sounds . . . Inkarran?" she mused. It didn't sound like any name that she had ever heard. "If Anders is back, that could explain much," Iome said. She turned to Fallion. "You were attacked only moments after your father . . . passed. I doubt that anyone could have known that he was going to die—unless they had a hand in it."

Fallion shook his head and objected, "No one could have killed him! His Earth Powers would have warned him."

That was the kind of thing that the cooks and guards would have told Fallion. Gaborn was invincible. Iome half believed it herself. But she also knew that Anders was both more powerful and more evil than her son could know.

"I'm with the boy," Borenson said. "It seems more likely that his enemies just waited for him to die. His endowments were aging him prematurely. He was old, even for a wizard."

Fallion had to wonder. His father should have known that he was going to die. His Earth Powers would have warned him weeks, perhaps months, in advance. And thus if he had foreseen his own death, why had he not avoided it?

Perhaps he could not avoid it, Fallion thought. But at least, he could have come home to say good-bye.

He said good-bye in his own way, Fallion realized. But it seemed a small thing.

And for that matter, why had Gaborn sent Fallion into the mountains toward danger as his last act? Had his father meant for him to find Rhianna, to help save her?

That didn't make any sense. Rhianna wasn't one of the Chosen. His father couldn't have known of her distress. The Earth King's powers were limited. He didn't know everything.

Fallion was in a muddle.

"Why would anyone want to kill me?" Fallion wondered aloud. He saw his mother stiffen, exchange a look with Borenson.

She knelt, bit her lower lip, and seemed to search for the right words. "There are many men who might want you dead. I haven't wanted to alarm you, but you need to know: your father traveled through many realms, seeking out the good people of the world. He Chose those that he liked best, and with his blessing, he helped them to prosper, and protected them from harm."

She held her breath a moment, letting this sink in. "Now those people venerate him. They love your father like no king before him. And you are his heir. There will be many who will want to serve you more than their own kings. Who would want to serve an old warlord in Internook, for example, when he could have the son of the Earth King as his lord?"

"No one," Fallion said.

"Exactly," Iome said. "Which is why, when the last Earth King died over two thousand years ago, other lords banded together and slew his offspring, in order to protect their thrones."

"But I don't want anyone's throne," Fallion objected.

"You don't now," Borenson said with a note of hope in his voice, "but if you were to stake such a claim . . ."

"Wars would rage across the land," Iome said, and Fallion imagined millions of people, rising up at once, to subjugate their lords.

"But I wouldn't do that," Fallion said.

Iome looked to Borenson, unsure what to say next, and Borenson whispered, "Not now," he said. "Maybe you'll never want that. But the time may come. . . ."

Fallion looked at his mother, saw her blanch. Borenson had just suggested the unthinkable.

Iome had to deter the child from that line of thinking. "What is the duty of a Runelord?" Iome asked Fallion. She had made him memorize the words as an infant.

"The Runelord is the servant of all," Fallion said. "It is his duty to render justice to the aggrieved, to foster prosperity among the needy, and to establish peace whenever peril looms."

"That was your father's creed," Iome said, "and the ancient creed of House Orden. But it is not the creed of every king."

"Certainly it is not the creed of Anders," Borenson said. "Or of those who followed him. He fears you, fears the kind of king that you could become."

"But I've done nothing to him," Fallion said.

Iome knelt, looking into his eyes. "It's not what you have done, it is what you *could* do. When you were born, your father looked into your heart, and saw that you had an ancient spirit, that you had been born many times. He said that you came to the Earth with a purpose. Do you know that purpose?"

Fallion felt inside himself. He didn't feel special at all. He was just frightened. And he wasn't aware of any powerful desires, except that his bladder was full and would soon need to be emptied. "No," Fallion said.

Iome peered into his face, and her features softened as she smiled. Fallion could see wetness in her dark eyes. "Your father said, 'He comes to finish what I could not.'"

Fallion wondered at that. His father had been the most revered king in two thousand years. He had led an army against the reaver hordes and won. People said that there was nothing that he couldn't accomplish. "What does that mean?" Fallion asked. "What am I supposed to do?"

Iome shook her head. "I don't know. But in time it will become clear to you. And when it does, Anders will indeed find that he has a worthy foe."

Fallion wondered what to do. He couldn't fight. But suddenly he knew the answer. Fallion turned a step, peered out through the open doors, to the veranda, where a sudden breeze gusted, blowing the curtains inward toward him. "When he was dying, Da told me to run. He said that they would come for me, and I was to keep running. He said that the ends of the Earth are not far enough."

Iome made a choking noise, and when Fallion turned, he saw her dark eyes glistening with tears. She looked to Sir Borenson, as if to confirm what Fallion had said. Borenson peered at the floor as if he were a wizard staring into some dark orb, and he nodded. "Those are the words he gave me," Borenson said. "He told me to take the boys and run, and said, 'The ends of the Earth are not far enough.'"

From the window, there came a sound, a distant rumble, the growl of one of the strengi-saats from the woods. Iome strode to the veranda, and considered closing the doors.

She stood listening for a moment. Across the fields, the cottages were all dark. Not a single lamp shone in a window. And now a ghost mist was rising from the warm River Gyell, spreading through the downs. A bell-like call sounded to the north of the castle, and Iome thought it odd. The creatures had come from the south.

She waited a moment, heard an answering call from the south, and two from the west.

They're circling the castle, she realized. Perhaps they're after more women. Or after my son.

She dared not ignore Gaborn's warning or even to hesitate to act. "I think that you're right," Iome said. "It would be best to leave quietly, and soon. Fallion, go and find Jaz. Tell him that you are to go to your rooms and pack three changes of clothing, your long knives, and perhaps a few trinkets, but no more than each of you can easily carry. Then go straight to bed and get some rest."

"Yes, Mother," Fallion said.

Iome watched as he hurried from the room, his feet rustling across the stone floor. She stood for a moment, thinking, then sighed deeply. She turned to Borenson. "You think well of Fallion. You could not hide the hope in your voice when you spoke of him challenging Anders."

"I watched his father grow," Borenson said. "He was a good lad, and I knew that he'd make a great king. But Fallion will be better."

Iome smiled. No one could do more for his people than what Gaborn Val Orden had done. "All parents hope that their children will be better than they are." She thought a moment. "But don't speak of those hopes to Fallion. He's just a child."

"With enemies that are more than man-sized."

"We'll leave before dawn," Iome said.

"Do you plan to come?" Borenson asked. "It's a far journey."

"I'll come," Iome said. "You know where to go?"

"I have an idea, milady," Borenson said. "When I received the command, I had an . . . impression."

"Speak of our destination to no one," Iome said. "Not me, not the children. The fewer people who know the way, the fewer who can reveal it."

"I understand," Borenson said.

"We must consider which guards to take with us. I'll want Daymorra and Hadissa, I think."

"The fewer the better," Borenson argued. "If we're to travel discreetly, exotic guards will attract attention."

"Of course." There was so much to plan, Iome's mind was spinning. If the boys did not have guards, then perhaps they'd need to protect themselves. "Do you think the boys are ready for their first endowments?"

Borenson gave her a hard look. Iome and Gaborn had both been loath to let their sons taste the first kiss of the forcible, to let them feel the ecstasy of having another's attributes flow into them, lest they yearn to repeat the experience over and over, and thus become corrupted.

Worse, Iome knew firsthand the toll paid by those who gave endowments.

She'd seen her own father become a drooling idiot after he gave his Wit to the wolf lord Raj Ahten. Iome had given her glamour to Raj, and had watched her own beauty turn to corruption.

"It's a heady thing for a child," Borenson said. "Jaz isn't ready yet. He acts like any other child his age, but Fallion's a good boy, very mature for his age. He could bear it . . . if you are ready to lay that burden on him."

Iome bit her lip. She knew what he meant by "burden." Iome had laid endowments upon her own husband, had given him endless strength and stamina with which to fight the reavers. And as a result, she had lost him.

In the very same way, she would be sacrificing her sons if she gave them endowments now. Their childhood would end the instant the forcibles touched their flesh. She might give them greater strength, speed, wit, and stamina with which to fight their battles, but in doing so she would lay upon them an onus, a burden of responsibility that no child should have to bear. The very attributes that saved them would warp them, suck the joy from their lives.

It was a quandary. Do I ruin a boy's life in order to save it?

"A thought, if I may?" Borenson said. "Your sons are going into hiding. But how long can they remain hidden if they bear the scars of the forcible?"

He had a point. If her boys had the strength of three men, the grace of two, the wit of four, the speed of three—how long could they hide such powers? Even if they managed to hide them, the runes that the forcibles branded into their skin would mark them for what they were.

And it would leave them only half alive, as she'd left Gaborn only half alive when she sacrificed him for the good of her people.

"Very well," Iome said, letting out a sigh. "If my children cannot protect themselves, then we will have to protect them." She gave Borenson a long, appraising look. "Sir Borenson, you were once the greatest warrior of our generation. With a few endowments, you could be again."

Borenson went to the window and looked away, uncertain what to say, considering the offer. He had thought about this many times, and had turned it down just as many.

He had taken endowments when he was young, and in doing so, had turned strong men into weaklings, wise men into fools, hale men into sicklings—all so that their attributes would be bound into him.

But for what?

When a lord took endowments, those who gave them, his Dedicates, lost their attributes and stood in need of protection, protection that never seemed quite ample.

For once Borenson took endowments, every lord and brigand would know that the easiest way to take him down would be to kill his Dedicates, stripping Borenson of the attributes that they magically channeled to him.

Thus, in the past, those who had served Borenson the best had all paid with their lives.

Worse than that, Borenson himself had been forced to play the assassin, slaughtering the Dedicates of Raj Ahten, killing more than two thousand in a single night. Many of those had been men and women that were numbered among his friends. Others were just children.

Nine years past, Borenson had put away his weapons and sworn to become a man of peace.

But now, he wondered, dare I take this charge without also taking endowments?

I made that choice long ago, he decided. When I became a father.

"My daughter Erin is still in diapers," Borenson said. "If I were to take three or four endowments of metabolism, she'd be ten when I died of old age."

"So you dare not make my mistake?" Iome said.

Borenson had not meant to offer this painful reminder, but Iome had to understand what he was faced with.

"I want to grow old with my children. I want to watch them marry and have my grandbabies, and be there to give them advice when they need. I don't want to take endowments of metabolism. And without those, the rest would be almost meaningless."

It was true. A man might take great endowments of grace and brawn and stamina, but that would not make him a great warrior—not if an opponent charged into battle with three or four endowments of metabolism. Borenson would die in a blur to a weaker man before he could ever land a blow.

"Very well," Iome said. "I not only respect your position, I wish that I had been as wise in my youth. But if you will not take the endowments necessary to ensure my son's safety, then I will be forced to ensure his safety. At least, I'll come with you as far as I can."

Borenson felt astonished. He had not expected her to abandon her kingdom. At the most, he'd thought that she might only accompany him to the border. He gave her an appraising look. "As far as you can, milady?" Then he asked tenderly, "How far will that be?"

Iome knew what he meant. She hid the signs of aging from others, but she could not hide them from herself. Though she had been on the earth for less than twenty-five years, her endowments of metabolism had aged her more than a hundred. She moved like a panther, but she could feel the end coming. Her feet had begun to swell; she had lost sensation in her legs. Iome felt fragile, ready to break.

"You and my son had the same warning," she said. "'Hide.' But my husband's last words to me were, 'I go to ride the Great Hunt. I await you.'"

Iome continued. "I suspect that I have only a few weeks left, at best. And it is my greatest wish to spend that time in the company of my sons."

As she spoke, Iome felt a thrill. She had never considered abdicating her throne. It was a burden that she had carried all of her life. Now that the choice was made, she found herself eager to be rid of it, to relinquish it to Duke Paldane. No more meetings with the chancellors. No more court intrigues. No more bearing the weight of the world upon her back.

"I see," Borenson said softly. "I will miss you, milady."

Iome gave him a hard little smile. "I'm not dead yet."

Borenson did something that she would never have expected: he wrapped his huge arms around her and hugged her tightly. "No," he said. "Far from it."

She escorted him to the door, let Sir Borenson out. Outside, her Days stood beside the door, waiting as patiently as a chair.

Iome smiled at the woman, feeling a strange sense of loss to be losing this piece of furniture. "Your services will no longer be required," Iome said. "I hereby abdicate my throne in favor of Duke Paldane."

The rules were clear on this. Once Iome abdicated and named her successor, the Days was to leave.

The young woman nodded, seemed to think for a moment as she listened to the counsel of distant voices. "Will Fallion be needing my services?"

Iome smiled patiently. The Days performed no "services." They merely watched their lords, studied them. Perhaps at times there were lords whose endowments of glamour and Voice could sway a Days, but Iome had not known of one. Iome had had a Days haunting her for as long as she could remember. She would be glad to be rid of the woman, finally. "No, he won't be needing you."

The Days took this in. She had to know that Iome was taking her sons into hiding. An ancient law forbade a Days from following a lord into exile, for to do so would be to alert the very people that the lord was forced to hide from.

"Then I shall hurry on my way," the Days said. Iome wondered at the use of the word *hurry*. Was it a subtle warning? The Days turned toward the tower door, looked over her shoulder, and said, "It has been a pleasure knowing you, milady. Your life has been richly lived, and the chronicles will bear witness to your kindness and courage. I wish you well on the roads ahead. May the Glories guard your way and the Bright Ones watch your back."

∞ 4 ∞

THE STRONG SEED

No man is as strong as a mother's love for her child.

—Iome Orden

Fallion worked breathlessly to finish packing in his bedchamber while Jaz did the same. It wasn't that Fallion had much to pack; it was that he felt excited. He only recalled ever having one real adventure in his life: when he was four, his mother had taken the boys to Heredon. He remembered almost nothing of the trip, but recalled how one morning they had ridden along a lake whose waters were so calm and clear that you could see the fat brook trout swimming far out from shore. The lake seemed to be brimful of mist, and with the way that it escaped in whorls and eddies, Fallion almost imagined that the lake was exhaling. The vapors stole up along the shore and had hung in the air among some stately beech and oaks, their tender leaves a new-budded green.

Their expert driver kept the carriage going slowly and steadily so that Fallion and Jaz could sleep. As the horses plodded silently on a road made quiet by recent rains, Fallion suddenly found himself gaping out the window through the morning mist at a huge boar—a legendary "great boar" of the Dunwood. The creature was enormous; the hump on its shoulders rose almost level with the top of the carriage, and the long dark hair at its chest swept to the ground. It grunted and plowed the fields with its enormous tusks, eating worms and soil and last season's acorns.

The driver slowed, hoping to pass the creature quietly, for a startled great boar was as likely to charge as to flee. Fallion heard the driver mutter a curse, and suddenly Fallion looked off out the other window and saw more of the beasts coming out of the fog and realized that they had inadvertently driven right into a sounder of the monsters.

The driver pulled the carriage to a halt. For long tense minutes the boars rooted and grunted nearby, until at last one beast came so close that it brushed against a wheel. Its casual touch devastated the carriage; suddenly the axle cracked and the vehicle tilted.

Fallion's mother had been sitting quietly, but now she acted. The royal carriage had a warhorn in it, for giving calls of distress. The bull's horn, lacquered in black and gilt with silver, hung on the wall behind Fallion's head.

Quietly, his mother took the horn down, and cracked the door just a bit. She blew loudly, five short blasts, a sound that hunters made when chasing game.

Suddenly the great boars squealed and thundered away, each lunging in a different direction.

But one huge boar charged straight out of the fog, its snout lowered, and slammed into the carriage. Fallion flew against the far door, which sprung open on impact, and hit the soggy ground. Bits of paneling rained around him, and for a long minute he feared for his life.

He sprawled on the ground, heart pumping, fear choking him.

But in moments all that he could hear was the sound of the great boars thundering over the hard ground, and his heart thumping, and he realized despite his fear that he had never been in real danger: his father had not used his Earth Powers to whisper a warning. If Fallion had been in real danger, his father would have told him.

Now, outside his window, Fallion heard a strange howl. It started like distant thunder, turned into a long catlike yowl, and ended like some bizarre animal cry.

Jaz looked up to the window, worried.

Now, Fallion knew that he was going into real danger, and he had much to prepare. He put his clothes into a bag: a pair of green tunics heavy enough for traveling, a warm woolen robe the color of dark wet wood, boots of supple leather, a cape with a half hood to keep off rain. And that was it.

But as he worked, he had to put up with Humfrey, his pet ferrin. Humfrey was only six months old, and not much larger than a rat. His back was the color of pine needles on the forest floor, his tummy a lighter tan. He had a snout with dark black eyes set forward, like a civet cat's.

As Fallion and Jaz worked, Humfrey hopped around them, "helping."

The small creature understood that they were going somewhere, so he made a game of packing, too.

Peeping and whistling, he shoved the mummified corpse of a dead mouse into Fallion's pack, along with a couple of chestnuts that he trilled were "beautiful." He added a shiny thimble, a silver coin, and a pair of cocoons that Fallion had been saving over the winter in hopes that he might get a butterfly in the spring.

Fallion reminded Jaz, "Don't forget Mother's birthday present," and pulled out a small box of his own, checked to make sure that Humfrey hadn't gotten into it. Inside was an oval cut from ivory, with his mother's picture painted in it, from when she was young and gorgeous, filled with endowments of glamour from beautiful young maidens. Fallion had been working for months, carving a tiny, elegant frame out of rosewood to put the picture in. He was nearly finished. He made sure that his cutting tools were still inside the box. Humfrey liked to run off with them.

When he was sure that he had everything, Fallion pushed the box into his bag.

Humfrey hopped up onto the bed and whistled, "Food? Food?"

Fallion didn't know if the creature wanted food, or if was asking to pack food.

"No food," Fallion whistled back.

The little ferrin seemed stricken by the statement. It began to tremble, its tiny paws, like dark little hands, clutching and unclutching—ferrin talk for "worry."

Humfrey made a snarling sound. "Weapons?"

Fallion nodded, and Humfrey leapt under the bed where he kept his hoard of treasures—silk rags and dried apples, old bones to chew on and shiny bits of glass. Fallion rarely dared to look under his bed.

But Humfrey emerged triumphantly with his "weapon"—a steel knitting needle that he had filed to a point—probably using his teeth. He'd decorated it like a lance, tying a bit of bright red horsehair near the tip.

He jumped up on the bed, hissing, "Weapon. Weapon!" Then he leapt about as if he were stabbing imaginary rats.

Fallion reached down, scratched Humfrey on the chin until he calmed, and then went to the blades mounted on the wall above his bed to select a knife. There were many princely weapons there, but he chose a simple one, a long knife that his father had given him, one with a thick blade of steel and a solid handle wrapped with leather.

As he took it from the wall, he marveled at how right it felt in his hand. The blade was perfectly weighted and balanced. For a nine-year-old, it was almost as long as a sword. At the time that his father had given him the blade, a belated gift for his sixth birthday, Fallion had thought it a trivial thing.

It was a custom in many lands for lords to give young princes weapons with which to protect themselves, and Fallion had been gifted with many knives that had greater luster than this one. Even now some were mounted above the bed—fine curved daggers from Kuram with ornate golden scroll-work along the blades and gem-encrusted handles; long warrior's dirks from Inkarra carved from reaver bone that glimmered like flame-colored ice; and a genuine assassin's "scorpion" dagger, one whose handle was a scorpion's body and the tail its blade—complete with a hidden button that would release poison onto the blade.

But for right now, his father's simple knife felt right, and Fallion suspected that his father had given it to him for just this time in his life.

Did my father's prescience extend this far? Fallion wondered. His mother had told him that his father sometimes sensed danger toward a person weeks or months in advance. But it only happened when his father looked long at that person, and then he would cock his head to the side, as if he were listening for something that no one else could hear.

Yes, Fallion decided, his father had recognized danger. And so Fallion claimed his knife now, believing that his father had known how right it would feel in his hand, perhaps even knowing that Fallion's life might depend upon this blade.

Even as he drew the weapon from the wall, a strange compulsion overtook him, and Fallion found himself strapping the blade to his side.

Just to be safe, he told himself.

Indeed, everyone in the castle was trying extra hard to be safe tonight. Jaz had lit a dozen candles in the bedchamber, and the scent of precious oils filled the room along with the light. Every lamp had been lit in every hallway. It seemed that everyone was wary of what might be lurking in the shadows.

As Fallion considered whether he should hone his blade now or wait until morning, Jaz went to the window and opened it, looking out.

"Fallion," Jaz said in wonder, "the hills are on fire!"

Fallion strode to the window, peered out. Humfrey scurried up Fallion's pant leg and then leapt onto the windowsill. The window was too small to let a man climb through, and too small for both boys and a ferrin to all peer out of at once.

Fallion's nostrils flared at the taste of fresh air.

There in the distance, high up in the hills above the fog-covered bottoms, an angry red star seemed to have fallen to the earth.

"They've set the forest on fire," Fallion said. "Mother sent Daymorra to find the bodies of those girls—the ones that had the babies in them. But the strengi-saats must have carried them away first. So Daymorra probably set fire to the hills, to burn them out."

"I'll bet that the monsters carried them in their mouths," Jaz said, "the way a mother cat will move her kittens once you've found them."

"Maybe," Fallion said.

One of the monsters snarled in the distance, across the river to the north of the castle. Jaz turned to Fallion, worried.

"Fallion, I think we're surrounded. Do you think that Mum will have us fly out?"

In Mystarria, each castle had a few graaks, giant flying reptiles with leathery wings, to carry messages in times of distress. The graaks could not carry much weight for any distance, and so the graak riders were almost always children—orphans who had no one to mourn them if they were to take a fall. But if a castle went under siege, as a last resort the royal children would sometimes escape on the back of a graak.

Fallion felt an unexpected thrill at the thought. He had never flown before and would soon be past the age where he could ride a graak.

Why not? he wondered. But he knew that his mother would never allow it. Graak riders were given endowments of brawn and stamina, so that they could hang on tightly and endure the cold and lonely trips. His mother wouldn't let him ride a graak without endowments.

"She won't let us fly," Fallion said. "She'll send us with an escort."

"*Let* us fly?" Jaz asked. "Let us fly? I wouldn't get on a graak for anything."

"You would," Fallion said, "to save your life."

Humfrey darted under the bed and came back up with a wilted carrot. He threw it up on Fallion's pack, and snarled, "Weapon. Weapon, Jaz."

Fallion smiled at the ferrin's sense of humor.

Jaz picked up the limp carrot and swished it in the air like a sword, and the ferrin cried in glee and thrust with his spear, engaging the human in mock combat.

Fallion glanced back at the fire and wondered about the strengi-saats. He didn't always think quickly, but he thought long about things, and deeply.

When Borenson had cut Rhianna open, all that Fallion had seen were eggs—ghastly eggs with thin membranes of yellow skin, cast off from a hideous monster.

But what would the monster have seen? Her babes. Her love. And a strengi-saat would want to protect her young.

How far would she go to do it?

Fallion remembered a heroic tabby cat that he'd seen last spring, fighting off a pair of vicious dogs in an alley while she tried to carry her kitten to safety.

With a dawning sense of apprehension, Fallion got up and ran out into the hallway. Humfrey squeaked and followed. As Fallion raced out the tower door, along a wall-walk, he grabbed a torch from a sconce.

Sir Borenson and Fallion had left Rhianna in her room, to sleep off the effects of the drugs she'd taken. The healers had said that she needed rest.

Perhaps she'll need more than that, Fallion thought. Perhaps she'll need protection.

As he ran, Fallion tried to recall their retreat from the hills. The strengi-saats had given chase, but had not attacked. Like mothers protecting their young, he thought, just trying to drive us off.

And now he realized that once they had driven off the men, they'd gone back to their children. In fact, Fallion realized now that as they had run, he had heard bell-like calls in the woods far behind them. At least one of the strengi-saats had remained to guard the young.

With rising apprehension Fallion redoubled his pace.

But when we first went up there, he wondered, why hadn't the strengi-saats stayed at the tree to guard their young? Most animals would have stayed to protect their offspring.

Then he recalled the cracking sound in the woods when he'd first found the bodies. It had been loud. Too loud for a creature that moved as silently as a strengi-saat.

The monsters had been trying to draw us away from their young, Fallion realized, the way that a peeweet will fly up and give her call to draw you from her nest.

Breathlessly, he raced to the lower levels of the keep, burst down the short hallway, and threw open the door to Rhianna's room.

He found her lying quietly in bed, her face unnaturally pale, almost white, drained of blood by the healers' opium. Someone had brushed the twigs and leaves from her hair, and washed her face, and Fallion felt astonished that he hadn't noticed before that she was pretty, with flawless skin and a thin, dainty mouth.

The room was dark. There should have been a candle or two burning by the bed, but either the candles had gone out, or the healers had blown them out so that Rhianna could sleep more easily.

Yet as Fallion held his torch aloft, it seemed that its light grew wan, unable to penetrate the gloom. He felt a faint breeze tickle his right cheek, and glanced toward the window. Shards of glass showed where it had been broken, and other shards lay on the floor. Something had hit the window from the outside.

Humfrey came creeping into the room, hissed a warning. "Dead. Smell dead."

Fallion inhaled deeply, caught a whiff of putrefaction. He could not see beyond the bars of the windows. It seemed that the gloom grew deeper there, so deep that even the torchlight could not penetrate it.

Humfrey hissed in terror and bolted out the door.

Fallion's heart raced, and he held the torch aloft. He drew his dagger and held it before him. "I know you're there," he said weakly.

There came an answering growl, so soft, like the whisper of distant thunder rolling down from the hills. The torch sputtered and began to die.

Fallion saw the flames suddenly diminishing in size, fighting to stay lit. There was no wind to blow them out.

The strengi-saat is doing it, Fallion realized, sucking away light, the way that it had in the forest.

Fallion's heart pounded, and he suddenly wished for light, wished for all of the light in the world. He leapt toward the window, hoping that like a bear or a wolf the monster would fear his fire. He thrust the torch through the bars, and suddenly it blazed, impossibly bright, like the flames in an ironmonger's hearth.

The fire almost seemed to wrap around his arm.

And then he saw the strengi-saat—its enormous head and black eye right outside the window, so much larger than he'd expected.

Many creatures do not look like their young. Fallion had expected from the young that the monster would have soft black fur like a sable or a cat. But the thing that he saw was practically hairless. Its skin was dark and scabby, and though it had no ears, a large tympanum—black skin as tight as a drum—covered much of the head, right behind its eye. The eye itself was completely black, and Fallion saw no hint of a pupil in it. Instead, it looked dull and lifeless and reflected no light, not even the fire of his flaming torch.

If evil could come to life, Fallion thought, this is what it would look like.

"Yaaah!" Fallion shouted as he shoved the torch into the monster's face.

The torch blazed as if it had just been dipped in oil, and the strengi-saat gave out a harsh cry—not the bell-like tolling that it had given on the hunt, but a shriek of terror. It opened its mouth wide as it did so, revealing long sharp teeth like yellowed ivory, and Fallion let go of the torch, sent it plunging into the monster's jaws.

The torch blazed brighter and brighter, as if the beast's breath had caught fire, and giddily Fallion realized that this creature feared fire for good reason: it seemed to catch fire almost at the very smell of smoke.

The strengi-saat leapt from the wall and Fallion saw it now in full as it dropped toward the road. The light shining through the membrane in its wings revealed ghastly veins.

Outside, a guardsman upon the walls gave a shout of alarm. Fallion saw the gleam of burnished armor as the man rushed along the wall, drawing a great bow to the full.

The monster glided from the window and hit the road, perhaps thirty yards out, and crouched for a moment, like a panther looking for a place to spring. It shook its mouth and the torch flew out, went rolling across the ground, growing dim as an ember.

To Fallion's surprise, it seemed that the torch was almost gone, burnt to a stub, though a moment ago it had been as long as his arm.

Fallion feared that the beast would escape in the darkness.

But at that moment an arrow flashed past the torch and Fallion heard a resounding *thwock* as it struck the beast's ribs. The wounded strengi-saat appeared only as a shadow now, a blackness against the night, as it leapt into the air. But Fallion heard the twang of arrows from three or four directions, and some shafts shattered against stone walls while others hit the beast.

He drew his head back from the window, wary of stray arrows, and heard triumphant shouts. "We got it!" "Damn it's big!"

Fallion peered out. The ground was only two stories below and the monster had not gotten more than two hundred feet from him. The guards rushed to it with torches in hand. These were force soldiers, rich with endowments, and they ran with superhuman speed, converging on the beast as soon as it hit the ground, plunging swords into it.

It lay on the cobblestones, a looming shadow, and gave one final cry, a sound that began as a snarl as loud as thunder, and ended with a wail. The noise made Fallion's heart quaver, and hairs rose on the back of his neck.

Then it succumbed, dropping as if its life had fled in that horrible cry.

Fallion peered out the window and drew a breath of astonishment. He had only seen the strengi-saats from a distance, shadows against the trees, and had thought them to be a little longer than his horse. But now he saw that the beast was four times the length of a tall man, and that it dwarfed him.

The guards were talking, babbling almost giddily, like young hunters after their first kill. Fallion couldn't make out all of their words.

"How did it get over the walls?" someone asked, and another added, "Without being seen?"

There were mumbled responses. No one seemed to know, but one guard, the one who had first raised the cry, said distinctly, "It came from there," nodding toward the keep. "It's all shadows there. I would not have seen it if someone hadn't launched a torch at it."

The guards stared up at the window: at Fallion. Even though the room was not lit, Fallion had no doubt that they saw him, for these were force soldiers, gifted with endowments of sight.

They peered at him in breathless silence, and someone said softly, "Fallion."

He saw fear in the men's faces. They were imagining the punishment they'd get for letting such a monster near the royal heir.

"I'm all right," he said weakly, reassuring them.

But from the far-seer's tower came the long plaintive bellow of a warhorn, and suddenly the warriors were bounding off, running up to defend the castle walls.

Fallion's heart raced as he imagined strengi-saats attacking in force.

ಬ 5 ೧೩

ASGAROTH

Every lord at some time must resort to intimidation to govern his people. I find it best to be consistently swift and brutal, lest my enemies confuse my kindness with a lack of resolve.

—Shadoath

But it was not strengi-saats that came against Castle Coorm.

Iome stood upon the walls above the gate and looked down upon a small contingent of warriors, perhaps fifty in all, mounted upon their horses out in the darkness, out beyond the moat. Three of them bore torches, and Iome could see the party well. They were a mixed bag—knights from Crowthen in their black mail upon black horses; minor nobles from Beldinook in their heavy steel plate, their tall white war lances raised to the sky; burly axmen from Internook dressed in gray.

Behind them came a train of long wagons, the kind used for transporting horsemen's lances.

Taken altogether, they looked as scruffy as poachers, as cruel as a band of brigands.

Their leader though, he was something altogether different: he was a tall man, and lean, and sat aback a reddish destrier, a blood mount from Inkarra, bred to travel dark roads.

The leader wore no armor or device to tell where he came from. Instead he wore robes all of gray, with a deep hood that hid his face. His cape pin was made of bright silver—an owl with flaming yellow eyes—and his only weapons seemed to be a boot dagger and a war bow of black ash that was very tall, strapped in a pack on the back of his horse.

There was a darkness about the man, as if shadows bled from his pores and drifted about him like a haze.

He is not of this world, Iome thought, her heart pounding in fear. King Anders of South Crowthen had given himself to a locus, a creature of the netherworld, a being of pure evil, and if anything was left of Anders, Iome could not see it. The creature before her had been transformed into something altogether different.

Iome studied the warriors around the dark rider, looking for anyone that might be his accomplice, the man she had heard called Shadoath.

One ruffian spoke up, a fat strapping warlord of Internook, "We come to parley." Iome recognized him.

"Draw near, Olmarg," Iome said, "and speak."

Olmarg glanced at the shadow man, as if seeking his permission, then spurred his own potbellied war pony to the edge of the drawbridge.

Olmarg looked up at Iome, the old cutthroat's face a mass of white scars. He wore gray sealskins, and his silver hair was braided in ringlets and dyed in blood. "We've come for your sons," Olmarg said.

Iome smiled. "Never one to mince words, were you," Iome said. "I appreciate that. What happened to your face since the last time I saw you? Was it eaten by wolves?"

Olmarg grinned. In his own lands, friends often exchanged insults as a form of jest, and Iome was relieved to see that he took her cut in the proper spirit. Olmarg shot back, "Harsh words—from a hag. To think, I once dreamed of bedding you."

"Eunuchs can have such dreams?" Iome asked.

Olmarg chortled, and Iome felt that she had won. She got to the point. "So, you want my sons?"

"Give them to us and we'll raise them like our own: good food, ale in their bellies, women in their beds. And a promise: your boy Fallion, he can have the run of Heredon when he's fifteen."

Iome grinned, a smile that was half wince, amused that Olmarg would think that she'd want women in her son's bed. "Royal hostages?" Iome asked. "And if I say no?"

"Then we'll take them," Olmarg said, "dead, if need be."

Fifty men didn't represent much of a threat. But these weren't commoners. They were Runelords, and would put up a fierce battle. More than that, they represented half a dozen nations, and might well have powerful allies back home.

And then there was the shadow man. Iome couldn't even guess what powers he might bring to bear.

"I see," Iome said. "You want to make it easier for the assassin's knife to find them?"

"We're coming as friends," Olmarg said. "We want Fallion to know us as friends, and allies. That's all." He smiled as persuasively as possible, the scars on his face rearranging into a mockery of friendliness, and his voice became sweet. "Come now, think on it. You're wasting away. You'll be dead in no time, and who will raise the boys then?"

Iome gave Olmarg a dark look. Olmarg was a pig, she knew. A murderer and worse. She could dismiss his request without a thought. But she gazed down upon the shadow man. "And what of you? Do you wish to raise my sons as your own?"

The shadow man rode forward, stopped next to Olmarg. He did not look up, and Iome could not see his face. Thus he kept his identity hidden, causing Iome some lingering doubt.

It's not Anders after all. If it were, he'd show me his face.

"You have my word," the shadow man said, his voice as resonant as a lute. "I will raise the boys as my own."

His tone drove a spike of fear into Iome's heart. There was something wrong with it, something dangerous, as if he had taken hundreds of endowments of Voice. Iome could not tell if it was Anders who spoke or some other being. He sounded too pure and lofty to ride with these men.

And Iome knew that he would be handsome, that he had taken endowments of glamour. If so, the luster of his appearance and the persuasiveness of voice would combine to seduce the boys, bend them to his will. He'd have them eating from his hand in no time.

In Rofehavan it was said, "When you look upon the face of pure evil, it will be beautiful." Suddenly Iome wished that the shadow creature would pull back his hood, reveal his beauty.

"I know you," Iome said, and she spoke the name of the locus that had crossed from the netherworld, "Asgaroth."

The stranger did not deny it. "If you know me," he said, "then you know that you must submit."

He glanced back at his men, gave them a nod.

Half a dozen men dismounted and rushed to the lance wagons, then removed their wooden lids. What they pulled out were not lances.

Instead, they pulled out three large stakes, like thickened spears with dull points, and even in the shadows Iome could see that each was elegantly carved and painted, like some gift that a foreign dignitary might offer a neighboring lord.

Yet impaled upon each of these stakes was a human form. The bodies were not just thrust through. Instead, the victim's hands and legs had been tied, and the stakes had been driven up through their nether regions with great care and threaded upward until the lances' points broke through their mouths, like trout upon a skewer.

The soldiers rushed forward and shoved the stakes into the ground so that the bodies were raised up high. Then they stood beneath, waving their torches so that Iome could see the identities of their victims.

What she saw shook her to the core of her soul. Among the impaled were Jaz's personal guard Daymorra. Next came Iome's childhood friend, Chemoise. And last of all was Gaborn's uncle, Duke Paldane, the man that she had planned to place in charge of her kingdom as regent.

Iome gaped in amazement. Of all the dark deeds she had ever witnessed, none struck her with as much force. It wasn't that she couldn't imagine such evil having been done. It was that she couldn't imagine *how* it had been done so quickly.

All three of these people had been under Gaborn's protection, and he had been dead for only a few hours. Chemoise had been in Heredon, hundreds of miles away, in the Dedicates' Keep. Paldane had been in his own castle. For both of them to have been abducted and put to torture—it could only mean that Asgaroth had known for weeks that Gaborn would die this day.

How can I fight such foreknowledge? Iome wondered.

"So," Iome said, looking at the grotesque forms on their splendid skewers and trying to remain calm. "I see that you have made an art of murder."

"Oh, not just of murder—" Asgaroth said, "of *viciousness*."

There was a soft moan from Daymorra. Paldane moved an elbow. Iome realized to her dismay that both had survived the impalement. The stakes had been threaded past vital organs—heart, lungs, liver—in the most ghastly manner.

Through the haze of shock, Iome registered a movement at her side. She glanced down, becoming aware that her sons had come up to the parapet despite the fact that she had ordered them to stay in her rooms. Iome felt angry and alarmed, but she understood how hard it was for the boys to restrain themselves. Now the boys leaned over the merlons to get a better look.

Fallion seemed to stare calmly at the impaled, as if he would refuse to be intimidated, while Jaz gaped in shock, his face leeched of blood.

Iome feared how such a sight might scar the boys.

The shadow man shifted his gaze slightly, stared hard at Fallion, and Iome suddenly realized that this demonstration had not been for her benefit as much as it had been for Fallion's.

For his part, Fallion could almost feel Asgaroth's eyes boring into him. It was as if Asgaroth looked into Fallion's chest, into his soul, and everything was stripped bare to see, all of his childhood fears, all of his weaknesses. Fallion felt that he had been weighed and found wanting, and now Asgaroth scorned him.

Fallion's knees trembled no matter how hard he tried to stand still.

That's what he wants, Fallion realized. My fear. That's why he did this. That's why he brought the strengi-saats.

And with the realization, Fallion suddenly felt a sullen rage blossom, one that left him in a numbing trance.

There is an end to pain, he realized. There is only so much that he could do to me.

Fallion said steadily, and not too loudly, "I'm not afraid of you."

The shadow man made no move. But as if at some hidden signal, Asgaroth's soldiers went to the impaled victims and clubbed their shins with the torches so that Fallion heard the snapping of bones, and then held the torches to the victims' feet. Both Daymorra and Paldane cringed and writhed, and Fallion could hear them choking back sobs, but neither gave in. Neither of them cried out.

Fallion saw Asgaroth's game. He would try to enlarge his realm through intimidation.

Fallion reached down to his sheath and pulled his own dagger, then held it up for Asgaroth to see.

"Is that the worst that you can do?" Fallion asked. He stabbed himself in the hand, drew the dagger across his palm, opening a shallow wound. He raised his palm in the air so that the blood flowed freely. "I don't fear pain," he said, then added calmly, "Is that why you *fear* me?"

Asgaroth trembled with rage. He sat upon his destrier, clenching the reins, and Fallion looked over to his mother's soldiers on the wall, many of whom were staring at him in open amazement. Fallion curled his bleeding hand into a fist, and drew it down quickly, as if striking a blow, and against all of the rules of parlay, he shouted, "Fire."

Fallion had never ordered a soldier to kill. But in an instant, every archer upon the wall let fly an arrow, and the marksmen fired their ballistae. It was as if they had been aching for permission.

Arrows swept down in a dark hail. A dozen cruel Runelords were slaughtered in an instant, and many others took wounds. Horses screamed and fell, bloody rents in their flesh. Fallion saw dozens of men, arrows lodged in them, turn their horses and beat a hasty retreat.

But Asgaroth went unharmed. Before the command to fire had even left Fallion's mouth, the shadow man reached over with his left hand and grabbed the fat old Olmarg, lifting him easily from the saddle, and threw him upon his pommel, using the warlord as a human shield.

It happened so swiftly, Fallion barely saw the movement, attesting that Asgaroth had many endowments of both metabolism and brawn.

Then, as Olmarg filled up with so many arrows that he looked like a practice target, Asgaroth raised his left hand and a powerful wind screamed from it. In seconds every arrow that flew toward him veered from its path.

Fallion could hear the twang of bows, could see the dark missiles blurring in their speed, but Asgaroth tossed Olmarg to the ground and then sat calmly upon his horse, taking no hurt.

Many an arrow landed nearby, and soon Asgaroth's victims, impaled upon their stakes, had each been struck a dozen times, putting an end to their torment.

And though the archers kept firing, Asgaroth gazed hard at Fallion and shouted, "If viciousness be art, then of you I shall make a masterpiece."

Asgaroth calmly turned his blood mount and let it prance away, its hooves rising and falling rhythmically as if in dance, until it rode off into the darkness. The shadows seemed to coalesce around the rider, and in moments he became one with the night.

He's coming back, Fallion thought. In fact, his men are probably sur-rounding the castle now as they wait for reinforcements.

Fallion looked up at his mother. Her jaw was clenched in rage, and she looked at the blood dripping from his palm. He thought that she would scold him, but she merely put a hand on his shoulder and whispered, pride catching in her voice, "Well done. Well done."

Iome strode from the castle wall, hurrying down the steps. At her back, she heard an old veteran soldier telling Fallion, "You ever need to go into battle, milord, I'd be proud to ride at your side."

It was a sentiment that Iome suspected more than one man shared at this moment.

A healer in a dark blue robe, smelling of dried herbs, brushed past Iome on his way to bandage Fallion.

Sir Borenson met Iome in the courtyard, rushing up as if to ask orders.

Iome said swiftly, "How soon can we leave?"

"I need only to get the children," he said.

Iome had not packed a bag, but it was not a hundred miles to the Courts of Tide, and the heavy cloak and boots that she wore would suffice until then. She carried a sword beneath her robe, and a pair of dueling daggers strapped to her boots, so she would not lack for weapons.

"Get your family then," Iome said, "and I will meet you in the tunnels."

Borenson turned, racing toward his quarters, a small home beside the barracks, and Iome hesitated.

After what she had just seen, she felt certain that Fallion was almost ready to receive endowments.

It isn't age that qualifies a man to lead, she thought. It's an amalgam of traits—honor, decency, courage, wisdom, decisiveness, resolve. And Fal-lion has shown me all of those tonight.

But dare I take his childhood from him?

Not yet, she told herself. But soon. Too soon, it must come.

Which meant that she needed to take only one thing on this trip: Fal-lion's legacy.

She raced up to her treasury above the throne room, where she kept hundreds of forcibles under lock and key.

6

THE FLIGHT

No man ever truly leaves home. The places we have lived, the people that we know, all become a part of us. And like a hermit crab, in spirit at least, we take our homes with us.

—*The Wizard Binnesman*

Sir Borenson was loath to tell Myrrima that they would have to leave Castle Coorm. It is no small feat to uproot a family and take your children to a far land. Even under the best of circumstances it can be hard, and to do it under this pall of danger . . . what would she say?

Borenson's mother had been a shrewish woman, one who drove her husband half mad. Privately, Borenson held the belief that nagging was more than a privilege for a woman, it was her right and her duty. She was, after all, the one who ruled the house when the man was out.

Sheepishly, he had to admit that his wife ruled the house even when he was home.

Myrrima had become entrenched at Coorm. She was a favorite among the ladies and spent hours a day among her friends—knitting, washing, cooking, and gossiping. Her friendships were many and deep, and it would be easier for Borenson to cut off his own arm than to cut her off from her friends.

So when he went to their little house outside the main keep, he was surprised to find the children already packing.

"We're leaving, Dad!" little five-year-old Draken shouted when he came in. The boy displayed a pillowcase full of clothing as proof. The other children were bustling in their room.

Borenson went upstairs and found his wife, standing there, peering out the window. He came up behind and put his arm around her.

"How did you know?" he asked.

"Gaborn told me. It's time that we take care of his boys. It was his final wish. . . ."

Myrrima peered out the window. Down in the streets, a group of peasants had gathered outside the Dedicates' Keep. The facilitators were gathering those who would grant endowments to Mystarria's warriors—attributes of brawn, grace, metabolism, and stamina.

The peasants were excited. To give an endowment was dangerous. Many a man who gave brawn suddenly found that his heart was too weak to keep beating. Those who gave stamina could take sick and die.

Yet this was their chance to be heroes, to give something of themselves for the good of the kingdom. To give an endowment made them instant heroes in the eyes of family and friends, and it seemed that the darker times became, the more willing folks were to give of themselves.

Myrrima felt inside herself. She had not taken an endowment in nine years. In that time, several of the Dedicates who had granted her attributes had died, and with their passing, Myrrima had lost the blessing of their attributes. Her stamina was lower than it should be, as was her brawn and grace. She still had her endowments of scent, hearing, sight, and metabolism. But in many ways she was diminished.

In the parlance of the day, she was becoming a "warrior of unfortunate proportion," one who no longer had the right balance of brawn and grace, stamina and metabolism, to be called a true "force warrior."

Against a more-balanced opponent, she was at an extreme disadvantage.

She caught sight of a light in the uppermost tower of the Dedicates' Keep. A facilitator was up there singing, his voice piping in birdlike incantations. He waved a forcible in the air, and it left a glowing trail. He peered at the white light, which hung like a luminous worm in the air, and judged its heft and depth.

Suddenly there was a scream as the attribute was sucked from a Dedicate, and the worm of light flashed away into the bosom of some force warrior.

Myrrima felt a twinge of guilt. It was more than the act of voyeurism. She'd always been on the receiving end of the ceremony. They said that there is no pain on earth that compared with giving an endowment. Even childbirth paled beside it. But it was equally true that there was no greater ecstasy than receiving one. It wasn't just the rush of strength or vigor or intelligence. There was something primal and satisfying about it.

Borenson was watching, too, of course. "Are you tempted?" he asked. "We're going into danger, and we'll have the king's sons in our care. Iome would feel more confident if you were to take further endowments. . . ."

But Myrrima and Borenson had talked about this. He'd sworn off endowments nine years ago, when his Dedicates were slain at Carris. He'd had enough of gore. Dedicates were always targets for the merciless. It was far easier to kill a Dedicate who lent power to a lord than to kill a lord himself. And once a lord's Dedicates were slain, and he was cut off from the source of his power, killing him was almost as easy as harvesting a cabbage.

So a lord's Dedicates became a prime target for assassins.

No longer was Borenson willing to risk the lives of others by taking their endowments.

He had children to care for, and he couldn't count on Myrrima. She was aging faster than he.

Myrrima's endowments of glamour hid it, and her wizardly powers would probably extend her life, but the truth was, Myrrima suspected that even without taking more endowments, she would pass away years before him.

And like her husband, Myrrima wanted to be a commoner.

It should be our chance to grow old together, she told herself. It should be our time to fade. . . .

She didn't want either of them to take endowments. But there were the children to worry about.

"Are you sure we can protect them, even without endowments?" Myrrima asked.

"No," Borenson said candidly. "I'm not sure that we can protect them even if we take endowments. I only know . . . that I'm done. Many a peasant raises his family with nothing but his own strength. So will I."

Myrrima nodded. She still had some endowments, and she had a few wizardly powers to lean on, small as they were. They would have to be enough.

In her room, Rhianna drifted through dreams of pain, a recurring dream in which a strengi-saat carried her in its teeth as it leapt through the woods, landing with a jostle, then leaping again, landing and leaping. Each time that she closed her eyes, the dream recurred, startling her awake, and she would lie abed and try to reassure herself, until her eyes succumbed to sleep once again.

So it was that the strengi-saat bounded, twigs snapping between its feet, the darkness of the woods all around, a soft growl in its throat like thunder, and for an instant, as happened each time that it landed with a jar, Rhianna feared that its sharp teeth would puncture her for certain this time.

She came awake with a cry and found Sir Borenson trying to quietly lift her.

"What are you doing?" Rhianna asked.

"I'm leaving," he whispered. "I'm going to a far land. Do you still want to come with me?"

He let go of her, laying her back in bed. Rhianna opened her eyes, and in her drug-induced haze, reality felt oily, as if it would slip from her grasp, and she had to look around the room and focus for a moment, reassure herself that this room was the reality, and that the strengi-saat had only been a dream.

She realized that Borenson had decided to let her make up her own mind. She wasn't used to having the freedom to choose.

She felt terrified at the thought of leaving the security of the castle.

"Is it through the woods we'll be going?"

"Only for a little way," Borenson said. "But you'll have me to guard you."

She didn't want to tell him, but she didn't believe that he could do much to protect her. Still, he must have seen the doubt in her eyes.

"I don't look like much," Borenson said. "My middle is all going to fat. But I used to be the Earth King's personal guard, and now I serve his son. I've killed men, too many men, and too many reavers. I'll protect you, as if you were a princess, as if you were my own daughter."

Rhianna wondered if that could possibly be true. Sir Borenson was going bald on top, and he didn't look like some great warrior. Could he really protect her?

More important, what would he think once he got to know her? Rhianna knew that she was no one special. She wasn't worth taking chances for. In time he would see that, and he would hate her.

It was still the dead of night, and Rhianna looked up, saw a woman in the door. The woman had dark hair, long and elegant, flowing over her shoulders, and eyes so black that they gleamed like the waters roiling deep in a well. Her face was kindly, loving. Several children huddled beside and behind her, clutching at her midnight blue dress, peeking shyly into the room.

Almost, it seemed a dream.

"I'm not fit to ride," Rhianna said, all business.

"We'll not be going by horse," the woman said. She drew near, smiled down at Rhianna for a long moment, and took her hand. Rhianna's heart was still thumping in fear, troubled from her nightmares. The opium had diminished her pain, and it had left the world seeming fuzzy, disturbing. But the woman's warm smile seemed to wash away Rhianna's fears.

"This is my wife, Myrrima," Borenson said. "And my children—" He nodded toward a tough-looking girl with dark red hair who held a babe in her arms. "Talon, Draken, Sage, and the little one, Erin."

"Hello," was all that Rhianna managed to say. She couldn't think straight. Did this man really want her, or was he just trying to be kind? And what of Myrrima, what would she be thinking? Would she want another child clinging to her dress?

Rhianna couldn't imagine it.

But as she looked into Myrrima's eyes she could see depths of peace and calmness that defied all understanding. Rhianna's own mother had been a terrified creature, tough but fearful, living on the edge of madness. Rhianna had never imagined that a woman could feel the kind of peace that emanated from Myrrima.

"Come," Myrrima whispered seductively, as if inviting Rhianna to join her in a game. "Come with us."

"Where to?" Rhianna asked.

"To a place where children don't have anything to fear," Myrrima promised. "To a place where the skies are blue and daisies cover the hill, and all you have to do all day long is roll in the grass and play."

Rhianna's mind balked at such notions. She didn't trust strangers. The opium haze held her, and she tried to imagine a place where the skies were blue, and daisies bobbed in a summer breeze, and it almost felt as if no such place had ever existed.

Rhianna smiled, and Myrrima peered at that innocent smile, relieved to see it, happy to see Rhianna grinning the way that a child should.

"All right," Rhianna agreed.

"Fine," Myrrima said. "I'm glad that you're coming."

Could it be true? Rhianna wondered. Could she really be glad? What did Rhianna know of these people?

I know that others trust them, she realized. Kings and lords trust them with their own lives, even with the lives of their children. Maybe I can trust them, too.

"Okay," Rhianna said, surrendering completely.

And then Sir Borenson checked her wound, peering under the bandage. "It's healing some," he said, but looked worried. Very tenderly he lifted her, and bore her as if she were as light as a maple leaf, floating down the hallways of the castle, past nooks where bright lamps glowed like small stars, to a worn cellar door beneath the buttery where an old crone in dark robes waited with Jaz and Fallion, who had a bloody rag wrapped around his hand.

Rhianna was borne into a dank tunnel, where men with lanterns waded ahead of them, splashing through shallows as black as oil, in a tunnel where the walls of rounded stone were covered with green algae, and water and slime molds dripped from every crevice.

Rhianna peered up at Sir Borenson and admired his fine beard, which was red at the chin but going to silver on the side. In her opium haze she felt that every hair looked abnormally strong, as if each was spun from steel, while the sweat rolling down Borenson's cheek was like wax melting off a candle. She imagined that he too would melt away.

She closed her weary eyes for a bit, and her heart seemed to soar.

Do I want to go with them? she wondered. What would Mother say?

But Rhianna didn't even know if her mother was still alive, or if she was alive, how Rhianna would ever find her.

And she knew one other thing: her mother would want her to leave this place, run far away to hide.

She woke to find that Sir Borenson had stopped and that he was setting her in the back of a boat.

They were in a cave now, and above them she could see muddy gray stalactites dripping mineral water. Dark water churned and swirled all around the boat; they were in an underground river.

The smell of minerals and ripe cheese filled her nostrils. Rhianna peered up to a tunnel overhead.

Of course, she realized, the water keeps the tunnels cold and moist, perfect for aging cheese. That's probably how they discovered the river, cheese-makers tunneling through the rock, widening the caves.

The boat was long and wide of beam, like the ones that traders sometimes used to cart freight up and down the River Gyell. At the prow, the carved head of a heron rose up, its long beak pointing downriver; the gunwales were wide and carved to look like feathers, but there was no other adornment. Instead the boat had been painted a plain brown, and was loaded with crates. A crevasse between the boxes made up the sleeping quarters, and a dingy canvas stretched over the top served as a small tent.

Myrrima knelt at the edge of the water, drawing runes upon its surface with her finger, whispering as if to the river. Rhianna saw her draw a rune of fog, a rune of protection from Air, and runes of blessing for battles ahead. She dipped her arrows in the water one by one.

For a moment Rhianna had a vision of her uncle in the morning sun under the Great Tree, teaching her to scry runes as he traced them for her in the dust, then erased them with his hand, and had her repeat each one. Those had been happy times.

The old crone was at the front of the boat, loading the boys in, her voice tender and comforting, and Rhianna thought that this woman must be their grandmother.

"Where are we?" Rhianna suddenly asked, worried.

"We're on the Sandborne," the crone whispered, "above where it flows up out of the ground."

Rhianna tried to focus. The Sandborne was a small river that came out of the hills three miles from Castle Coorm, then joined the River Gyell. She puzzled for a moment, trying to imagine just where they might be.

Borenson laid her under the tarp, upon a bed of straw. His daughter Talon came and sat beside her, giggling, as if this was some great game, all the while balancing baby Erin, who was still just a crawler, asleep in the crook of her arm. Then Borenson handed them a basket full of fresh beer bread, a shank of ham, a few pear-apples, and candied dates stuffed with pistachios.

Rhianna felt frightened and tried to rise up, but Borenson saw her fear. He spoke to one of the guards that bore a torch, "Your dirk."

The man tossed it to Borenson, and he passed it to Rhianna, let her hold it close, as if it were a doll. "Quiet now," Borenson said. "Make no noise."

Then the other children piled into the tiny space as Rhianna traced a rune upon her blade: death-to-my-enemies.

Rhianna glanced up. The old crone was staring at her severely, but to Rhianna it was not a look of anger—more of a question.

Rhianna suddenly realized that this was no grandmother at all. This was the queen. But without her courtiers and finery, Rhianna had not recognized her.

Iome studied the injured Rhianna and thought, She is a rune-caster. What a special child. I should have let her have a forcible when I could.

The Lady Myrrima finished drawing her own runes, and then looked up at Iome, as if seeking her approval, and assured her, "There will be heavy fog on the river tonight."

Iome nodded, grateful to have Myrrima beside her. Once, years ago, they had been young maidens. Iome's own endowments of metabolism had aged her, and though Myrrima had taken such endowments, too, she still looked young, perhaps in her early forties, still beautiful and voluptuous. Myrrima's powers in wizardry kept her young. Any man who saw her on the street would ache for her.

Iome felt like a wraith in her presence.

Don't flatter yourself, Iome told herself, there isn't even a ghost of beauty left in you.

And it was true. Iome had aged gracefully in some ways, but her skin and flesh were going. After having given up her own endowment of glamour to Raj Ahten, she'd never been able to force herself to seek glamour from another woman. Draining a woman of both her physical beauty and her self-confidence was too cruel. Iome would never subject another person to such torment.

And so I am a wraith, she thought, and I will leave my children in Myrrima's care. In time they will grow to love her more than they could ever have loved me.

Myrrima walked around the boat, and with her wet finger, she anointed the eyes of each person. "This will help you see through the fog," she whispered.

Iome took her own place, standing at the rudder, feeling both sad and comforted by her vision of the future. She threw her cowl over her face and shrugged her shoulders, adopting the part of some anonymous old trader, while the children lay down in hiding, and Borenson and Iome's own guard, Hadissa, sat just under the lip of their shelter.

Fallion's pet ferrin whistled and lunged out of the cubbyhole, then hopped around the boat, giving soft little barks of alarm at the idea of being surrounded by water.

Fallion whistled, "Hush," in Ferrin, a command that was soft and not too judgmental, a command that might be spoken by a ferrin mother to her child. Not for the first time Iome marveled at how swiftly the boy had learned the creature's tongue.

Like his father, she thought.

Rhianna backed away from the creature and asked, "What's that?"

"That's Humfrey," Jaz said. "Our ferrin."

"Oh," Rhianna said. But there was a hesitancy in Rhianna's tone that made Iome suspect that the girl had never seen a ferrin before.

"Did you know that ferrins lay eggs?" Jaz asked. "They're not like other mammals that way. They lay eggs. We saw the cobbler and the baker digging out a ferrins' lair last spring, and there were eggs in it. Humfrey hatched out of one of the eggs."

A young page set a small chest at Iome's feet, and it tinkled softly with the sound of metal clinking against metal.

Borenson looked up at the page and said needlessly, "Careful!" but the damage had already been done.

In the box was a fortune in forcibles, hundreds of them, like little branding irons, each painstakingly crafted with runes on the end that would allow her sons to draw attributes from their vassals. Surely a few of the forcibles had been damaged—nicked or dented.

"They can be repaired," Iome said.

As the guards shoved the boat from the dock, out into the oily waters, Iome took comfort.

Things can be repaired, she thought: Fallion's hand, the forcibles, our kingdom.

And as she steered out into the current, which would carry them inexorably through the tunnel, past columns of twisted limestone, Iome whispered to herself, "Hurry the day. Hurry the day."

ಕಾ 7 ಚ

SWORN TO DEFEND

A man who has not sworn himself to the service of the greater good is no man at all.

—Gaborn Val Orden

The longboat cast off, water lapping at its sides, and thudded against the cavern wall. Fallion's wounded hand still hurt, and he had to wonder at his own bravado.

He peered around at the other children hidden among the crates. Their eyes were still bright in the torchlight, and their faces frightened.

In the mornings and evenings, when the guards traded shifts at the castle, they would hail each other, raise their blades to their foreheads, and salute one another.

Fallion now drew his own blade, turned first to Rhianna, then to Talon, then to Jaz, and softly spoke the oath, "Sworn to defend."

It was more than mere words to Fallion, more than idle comfort that he offered. It was a bond that he knew would have to define him for as long as he lived.

Rhianna studied him. She had seen her mother's trinkets stolen, along with her most beloved possession, her horse. Her mother had taken counterfeit coins in trade. She'd been lied to and hurt and used by men who professed love. Finally, she had been hunted down and killed by the man who professed to love her most.

Never trust anyone. It was a promise that Rhianna had made to herself long ago. But sometimes, she found, you had to trust people a little.

Could Fallion be one of these people? she wondered. We'll see. . . .

Rhianna saluted him with her own dirk, and Jaz likewise, while Talon merely gave him a determined look and clutched baby Erin to her chest as each of them said in turn, "Sworn to defend." Even the little ferrin Humfrey, excited to see so many drawn blades, leapt up with his sharp knitting needle and chirped a single word, "Kill!"

And it was done. The guard Hadissa turned back, looked at Fallion and the other children, smiling, and at first Fallion imagined that the dangerous little man was laughing at them, as if it were child's play, but then he saw a gleam of approval in the assassin's dark eyes. Hadissa smiled because he understood. They were children no more, for the four of them were sworn as one.

The longboat caught the current and slid from the docks into the darkness so that suddenly they were in shadow. Fallion could not see the faces of the other children at all.

He peered forward as the boat glided past pillars of dripping limestone into the oily darkness. Everyone fell silent. Water dribbled from the ceiling, so that silver notes plinked magically all around. There was nothing to hear but the sounds of the boat and the small sounds of children breathing, and there was little to smell.

In the utter darkness, Fallion felt that he was sliding away from his old life, into a new one, and there was little that he could take with him. He caught himself falling asleep and, raising his head, decided to practice an old trick that Waggit had taught him.

"Remember this day," Waggit had said. "Hold it in your mind for half an hour before you go to sleep, and the lessons that you have learned will remain with you for a lifetime."

So Fallion tried to hold the day in his mind, recall all of his lessons. At the widow Huddard's cottage, he had learned that a Runelord's art was to learn to see the value hidden in others, and to then mold men and use them as tools. So he swore that he would seek to understand others, to recognize their hidden assets and help them become the best that they could be.

He had also learned that he was to flee to a hard land, and that he could thrive there if he worked. He swore to himself to work hard.

Then he had met Rhianna, and Fallion wondered if his father had sent him to save her.

She could be important to my future somehow, he thought.

And from Borenson and his mother, Fallion learned that he had had powerful enemies even before he was born, and that he had come to this world with a purpose, one that he still did not understand.

Sir Borenson secretly hoped that Fallion would lay hold on the world, claim the throne of every evil lord and usurper, but his mother was afraid for him to even think that way.

And then Fallion had faced Asgaroth, who also hoped to lay hold on every throne, and he would do so using terror as his weapon.

It seemed a great deal to hold in one small mind. Fallion thought about these things and realized that yesterday he had been a child, hunting for shiny stones beside the streambeds and lifting up logs by the mill to look for mice.

Now, he had fallen into affairs far beyond his ability to understand.

Jaz crouched beside Fallion, his breath coming ragged, and whispered, "I wish that they would have let us fly."

Fallion smiled. So now Jaz wanted to fly?

Fallion felt trapped here on the boat, too.

"Did you see the snails on the bottom of the boat?" Fallion asked, wanting to comfort Jaz. Jaz loved just about any animal, and Fallion knew that talking about such things would distract Jaz from his fears.

"Snails?" Jaz asked.

"Big ones," Fallion whispered, "big pale ones." Fallion had seen one under the hull, the yellowish brown of ground mustard. He'd tried to reach down to catch it, but the water was so cold that it bit, and so clear that the snail was farther away than it looked.

"I saw a fish, I think," Jaz said, "a shadow in the water. Did you know these caves were here?"

"No," Fallion whispered.

Hadissa turned, hissed through his teeth, a sign for them to be quiet.

Hadissa came with us, Fallion thought, and he took some comfort in that. Hadissa had been an assassin, the grand master of the Muyyatin, and thus it was rumored that between his training and endowments he was the most dangerous man in the world.

So it was that the boat jostled down its dark course, until at last there was a thin light ahead, and the boat neared a curtain of ivy. Jaz suddenly threw his arms around Fallion and squeezed, trembling with fear.

I'll take care of you, Fallion promised silently, hugging his brother.

Because Iome had taken endowments of metabolism, she bore her two sons only four months apart. Though he was only four months older than

Jaz, Fallion was the larger and the smarter. It was Fallion's self-appointed duty to watch over Jaz.

Rhianna reached out and clutched Fallion's leg, and he patted her hand.

The dry vines hissed over the canvas roof as they passed beneath the mouth of the cave and rode out under the stars.

Fallion peered up through the flaps of the tarp.

This was the most dangerous moment, for they came out in a narrow gorge with steep canyon walls, into cold night air that smelled thickly of hoary woods and bitter pine bark—the kind of woods that the strengi-saats seemed to like.

The stars burned brightly through a thin haze that lumbered over the water. A reedy breeze wound down the canyon, lightly stirring the air, which was so heavy with water that Fallion could nearly drink from the air alone.

Fallion's heart hammered, and he peered about, watching for shadows flitting by.

Humfrey came and snuggled against Fallion's chest, his paws wet from the deck, and Fallion reached down and scratched the ferrin's chin.

They rode quietly for several moments, and he remembered a boating trip that he had taken with his mother on the River Wye when he was five.

The sky had been pristine blue and the day warm, with dragonflies darting above the water and perch leaping after them. Mallards had flown up from the cattail rushes, quacking loudly to draw attention away from their nests, and Fallion had watched a mother muskrat paddle past the boat with fresh grass in her mouth for her young, and had watched a water shrew bob up from the surface and crouch on a rock to eat a crayfish.

It was one of his best and brightest memories, and as he lay back down in the boat now, he tried to pretend that this trip was like that one.

There are turtles that live on this river, Fallion reassured himself, imagining how they would sit sunning on logs, like muddy rocks, until you got too close.

And in the springtime the frogs probably sing so loud that you couldn't sleep if you wanted to. And I'll bet that there are river otters here that slide down muddy trails into the water, just for fun.

Fallion was just beginning to think that they had come through safely when he heard a sound up in the trees like rolling thunder: the snarl of a strengi-saat.

❧ 8 ☙
THE SIEGE

Peace comes not from an absence of conflict, but from an absence of despair.

—Duke Paldane

In the watchtower at Castle Coorm, Chancellor Waggit—who only an hour before had only carried the title of Hearthmaster—paced beside the far-seers, expecting a siege. By all of the signs, it appeared that he had one.

He had often come to the watchtowers at night, looking to the far-seers for news. The far-seers had many endowments of sight, hearing, and smell. Little happened near the castle that escaped their detection.

On most nights they kept their silent watch, amusing themselves and the chancellor with the antics of the townsfolk. The cobbler's wife had several lovers, and could often be seen tiptoeing to some tryst while her husband slept off his nightly drunk, blissfully unaware that there was only a slim chance that he had fathered even one of his nine children. Other nights, the far-seers would relay the words to screaming fights that took place outside the alehouses, or just watch the stags and bears sneak into apple orchards on the hillsides to eat the fallen fruit.

But tonight, there was danger afoot. A wind picked up just after midnight, less than an hour after Prince Fallion had ordered the slaughter of Asgaroth's troops, and it blew this way and that, signaling a storm. The air was thick and fetid, as if it had blown out the Westlands from the swamps at Fenraven.

It sat heavy in the lungs, and made breathing tiresome. Worse, the air carried clouds of gnats that seemed to want to lodge in Waggit's throat when he breathed, and mosquitoes that acted as if his was the only blood to be found for twenty leagues.

Heavy clouds began to lumber over the horizon, blotting out the stars, and grumbling could be heard, the voice of distant lightning.

Sometimes a bolt would sizzle through the clouds, creating a burst in the heavens. By that light, the far-seers reported strengi-saats at the edge of the woods in the southern hills, dark shadows flitting between trees. Earlier in the day, Waggit had thought that there were perhaps a dozen of the beasts, but with each hour the count grew. Strengi-saats were filling the country-side, and Waggit realized that he and Sir Borenson had only stumbled upon their advance guard. There were not just a dozen of them. The far-seers reported several dozen, perhaps even hundreds.

And over the hill to the north, even Waggit's poor eyes could see that campfires glowed, limning the hills and trees with light. An army was gathering. From time to time, the far-seers reported that troops rode in haste over a distant hill to the north, lances like a forest against the sky, or they would spot small groups of warriors scrounging around cottages, poking through barns.

Warning of the siege had come too late, and most of the livestock was still out there, waiting to fill the bellies of enemy troops.

No sooner had Asgaroth made his retreat than Waggit sent out three graak riders to nearby castles, calling for troops. He hoped that reinforcements would arrive soon.

But the heavens filled with black clouds, and the air grew heavy with the smell of rain. His messengers would not be able to fly in this storm, not with lightning bolts sizzling past their heads.

An hour before dawn, Waggit stood marveling at his own meteoric rise to power. Nine years ago he had been working as a miner and his only title, if he'd had one, might have been "village idiot." But when the reavers attacked Carris, by virtue of his strength and stupidity Waggit found himself in the front lines, swinging his pickax for all that he was worth. The minstrels claim that he killed nine reavers that day. He doubted it. He could only remember killing a couple. But for Waggit's valor the Earth King gave him the title of Baron, along with nine forcibles. Five of them he had used to take endowments of Wit, so that now he recalled all that he saw and heard. The other forcibles he had used to give himself strength and stamina, so that he might study long into the nights.

Thus he had raised himself to the status of Hearthmaster, a teacher in the House of Understanding.

And only moments before she left, the queen had named him Chancellor and bestowed upon him the task of caring for Castle Coorm and the lands roundabout.

It would have been a pleasant task in fairer times. Coorm was called the Queen's Castle, for over the centuries many a queen had made it their summer resort when the air got too muggy at the Courts of Tide. It was a pretty castle, one might even say dainty, with its tall spires and pleasant views.

But now it seemed a death trap.

Waggit was determined to defend it to the best of his ability, and he had good captains under him who knew how to wage a war. But he couldn't help but worry. His own wife and daughter, both of whom were named Farion, were trapped within the walls.

So it was that just before dawn a large force of soldiers came sweeping toward the castle on foot, racing down over the hill from the north. The men sprinted through the damp fields with unnatural quiet, it seemed, or perhaps it was the contrary winds that blew away the sound of their approach. There were thousands of men—archers with longbows, force soldiers with spears and axes.

Asgaroth rode before them, upon his red blood mare.

One of the castle guards winded a horn, his plaintive notes warning almost no one, for the walls were already well manned.

The signal was mostly for the benefit of the queen, to let her know that the battle had begun, if any of her folk were still within hearing range of the horns.

But the signal served another purpose, one closer to Waggit's heart: from the graakerie, eight graaks suddenly took flight at the sound. Upon the back of each sat a young boy or girl, cowled and anonymous.

One rider was Waggit's own daughter, seven-year-old Farion.

The graaks split off in groups. Four of them went northeast toward Courts of Tide. Three winged northwest toward Heredon.

And one flew straight up toward the far-seer's tower, thundering above it, the wash from its vast leather wings stirring the air.

From atop it, Waggit heard a small voice call, "Good-bye, Daddy."

Waggit's heart skipped a beat. Farion sounded so tiny and frightened to be riding such a great beast.

The graak let out a plaintive croak, then suddenly turned and followed the three that headed for Heredon.

Waggit smiled sadly, relieved to see that his daughter had made it through the takeoff, worried about how far she had to go.

It will be storming soon, he thought. The rain and thunder will drive the graaks to ground. But hopefully it will be many hours from now, and the great reptiles will be far away.

Waggit stood, leaning upon a staff, watching the children fly off into the night.

Let Asgaroth puzzle that one out, he thought. If it is the princes he wants, he'll have to send men to follow the decoys.

But suddenly there arose grunting sounds from the north, the sound that graaks make when they take flight, and Waggit watched in horror as dozens of the creatures rose up from the woods.

They had no riders upon their backs, no saddles even, and when they saw the riders, they let out frightful cries and climbed like hawks.

With rising horror, Waggit watched the cloud of winged beasts, and realization came to him.

There were stories, ancient stories, of such graaks—trained not as mounts, but as winged assassins.

None had been used in nearly two hundred years.

The lords of the Earth had a tacit agreement: children, even messengers, were never to be targeted in war, and since assassin graaks would of necessity kill children, their use among civilized folk had long since been abandoned.

Apparently, Asgaroth was not civilized folk.

"Farion!" Waggit shouted in warning. "Come back!" But she was too far away to hear.

Amid cries of dismay, the young riders hugged the necks of their mounts as the killer graaks swept toward them. Some children turned their mounts, tried to veer away from the killers, but such a race was bound to end badly, for there were two or three killer graaks to each mount, and they would not be hindered by riders.

Waggit winded his own horn, calling retreat, and watched in terror to see if the children would give heed.

Six of the children heard.

Two others, two that had been heading toward Heredon, seemed to freeze with fear. Waggit watched in dismay as killer graaks swept up and deftly plucked the children from their mounts, then dove and brought the children to earth kicking and screaming, to make of them a meal.

Not my Farion, Waggit told himself. Not my daughter.

He had lost track of where Farion might be. He knew that she was upon a graak, and he also knew that she was the least adept of the riders. Had she been able to turn in time?

The others raced back toward the castle, their mounts veering and swerving as killer graaks gave chase. As the graaks neared the castle walls, archers let fly a hail of arrows, trying to deter the attackers, but it was little use. The assassin graaks kept coming.

One child took an arrow in the shoulder. He cried out and fell from his graak, hundreds of feet, to land with a crunch just outside the castle wall.

Another dove toward the graakerie and hit the landing pad, and as he tried to leap to safety, a killer graak dove like a giant gull and took him in its teeth.

The rest of the children veered between towers, screaming for help as enemy fliers gave chase. Waggit watched them fly by, the wingtips of their graaks nearly clipping the towers, the stark fear showing in every line of their faces.

Two passed him, a third.

Then the last of the children came, racing toward his tower, and Waggit heard Farion's voice, so full of terror that it broke his heart, crying, "Daddy!"

A killer graak was racing up behind her.

Arrows whipped up toward the killer, and Waggit wondered if he could leap onto its back, use his own weight to bear it to earth.

But it stooped above him, screaming down in a dive, and the worst that he could do was to throw his warhorn.

The warhorn bounced off its chest. The graak didn't even seem to notice.

Farion dove straight toward the gate, hugging the leathery neck of her graak, screaming in terror.

Arrows blurred up, hitting the killer graak as it raced down to snatch her. Waggit heard the snick of arrows, saw them bounce off its breast, and then one struck home, blurring into the monster's breast, and the killer graak made a croaking sound, veered left, and began to fall rapidly.

Waggit saw Farion's own graak hit the ground fast, and Farion was thrown onto the cobblestone streets on impact.

She rolled down near the wall of an inn, and a force soldier hastened to her side, grabbed her.

For a brief moment, the girl was silent, and Waggit held his breath, afraid that she'd taken injury in the fall. But within moments she began to scream in terror and fight the guard, breaking free, and then she scrambled into the door of the inn.

In the end, only five children made it back safely.

When it was done, the assassin graaks flapped heavily out toward the woods, and Chancellor Waggit gazed down into the fields to the north.

Asgaroth sat straight in his saddle, gave a nod of satisfaction.

Now the siege begins in earnest, Waggit thought. For certainly Asgaroth believed that if any of the princes were alive, they had just been driven to ground at the castle.

But Asgaroth waved his men forward. Dozens of them swept over the fields, into the woods east of the castle, and Waggit was left to marvel.

Asgaroth had suspected that it was a ruse. Perhaps he had even *known* that it was a ruse.

Yet he had let his graaks murder innocent children anyway.

What kind of man would do that? Waggit wondered.

Waggit had studied much in the House of Understanding. He had read histories of ancient lords, befouled and evil, and in time had begun to understand a little of how they thought, how they gained power.

But no one could ever really understand them. No sane man would want to.

Now that he had finished terrorizing the castle, Asgaroth left a contingent of warriors to beat back any attempt that Waggit's troops might make to sally forth while he went to search for the princes in earnest.

෨ 9 ෬

TRUST

The art of raising a child comes in knowing when to hold his hand, and when to let it go. Once he learns to trust you, he is ready to learn to trust himself.

—Jaz Laren Sylvarresta

At the snarl of the strengi-saat, Rhianna rose up on her elbow, edged to the open flap, and peered out over Hadissa's shoulder: the stars shone down through a thin haze that clung to the river. Starlight gleamed on the water, upon the slick round stones along the bank, and upon the glossy leaves of grass and vines along the shore.

Rhianna wished fiercely that there was more of a fog. Myrrima had promised them one, but Rhianna could see plainly through the thin haze.

Enormous pine trees crowded the banks along the steep sides of a hill; beneath them, all was shadows.

The strengi-saats will be on us before we ever see them, Rhianna thought.

And then there was a hiss in the trees, pine boughs brushing against one another, as something huge leapt from a large branch, and Rhianna clearly saw a shadow glide across the water ahead, only twenty feet in the air, and land among the rounded boulders at the edge of the river.

Rhianna dared not cry out, for fear that she would attract the monster's attention. Besides, she was sure that Borenson and the others could see it.

The strengi-saat dropped silently to the ground and merely crouched in the shadows on the riverbank. It sniffed the air and peered about, searching for prey, and then cocked its head to the side, listening.

It can't hear us, Rhianna thought, even though her heart beat so loudly that it thundered in her ears. It can't see us, either.

But she knew from her time among the strengi-saats that they had powerful eyes, and seemed to travel well even in total darkness.

So why doesn't it see us now?

The fog, Rhianna realized.

Myrrima had anointed Rhianna's eyes, promising that she would be able to see through the mist. Could it be that the strengi-saat really was blinded by the haze that crept along the river?

If that was true, then Myrrima was a wizardess, and suddenly Rhianna knew that it was true and some white-hot part of her soul burned with a desire to be like the stately woman.

Rhianna glistened with sweat. It was as if her body was trying to reject the opium that the healer had given her, so that it purged the drug from every pore. She licked her upper lip and found that it tasted bitter from opium and from the acids in her body.

She felt that surely the strengi-saat would hear them or smell them. But the beast just held still as the boat glided swiftly downriver toward it, and for their part, as the boat drifted slowly and began to spin, the adults on the boat remained still, like frightened rabbits that hold and hold right until the time when you reach down into the tall grass and snatch them up.

Water lapped softly at the sides of the boat, but the river here was swift; it burbled among the rocks and hissed through the canyon. Perhaps the small sounds of their passage were masked by the larger waves lapping the shore.

Rhianna's gut ached from her wound. As they neared the strengi-saat, the terror that she felt of the monster, the fear that it would violate her again and try to fill her with its children, was overwhelming. She bit down, clenching her jaw, afraid that if she did not, the beast would hear her teeth chatter, or that she would let out a scream, and she realized that her hand was clenching her dirk so hard that it ached.

And suddenly, there was a movement from the boat. Hadissa, the dark-skinned little man from Indhopal, silently rose to his feet, cocked an arm, and let something fly. A dagger flashed end over end, and lodged into the head of the monster, striking deep into its tympanum with a solid *thunk*.

The strengi-saat gave a startled cry, almost a whine, and leapt forward, lunging into water up to its chest. There its head sank beneath the waves, and it thrashed about, kicking with its back legs.

Without warning, a second shadow dropped from the woods, arced toward the spot, and landed without a sound on the riverbank.

It cocked its head, then lunged out over the water, not a dozen feet in the air.

As it neared the boat, Hadissa made a fantastic leap, launching himself at the monster. He had numerous endowments of brawn and grace, and he seemed almost to fly up into the air to meet the beast.

His scimitar sang from its sheath, and the strengi-saat gave a bark of astonishment.

At the last instant, it must have seen its foe. It raised a claw.

With a vicious swipe of the sword, Hadissa struck. There was a crack of metal as his sword shattered against the strengi-saat's bony claw.

The strengi-saat dropped, crashing onto the boat, which rocked wildly. The children cried out in terror, fearing that they would capsize. The beast raised its head and snarled, a deep roar, as Myrrima spun and swung a pole, cracking it over the monster's head.

Rhianna heard a thump and a splash as Hadissa hit first the side of the boat, then water.

There were thuds on the boat planks as Borenson rushed to attack, but in that instant, the strengi-saat's nostrils flared and it lunged toward the opening in the boxes, its mouth wide, as if to take Rhianna in its teeth.

But Rhianna had a secret of her own. When she was a child of five, her father's men had been sent to hunt her. In an effort to disguise her, Rhianna's mother had given her a single endowment of metabolism, taken from a whippet.

Thus, over the years, Rhianna had aged at double speed. Though she had only been born nine years ago, she looked like a girl of thirteen—and she could move with blinding speed.

In stark terror, Rhianna twisted away from the strengi-saat, and the pain of the stitches in her belly flared as she swung her dirk, burying it up to the finger guard into the monster's tympanum.

Rhianna's mother had once told her that if you ever needed to stab something, that you should never settle for one blow, but to keep striking again and again.

So her hand blurred as she buried the dagger into the monster again, again, again. And suddenly she realized that Fallion had lunged forward and was plunging his own long knife into the tympanum on the strengi-saat's other side. The strengi-saat was lunging toward her, trying to take her in its mouth, and distantly she became aware of Fallion shouting, "Get away from her! Get away!"

Fallion edged his body between Rhianna and the monster. He was simultaneously trying to drive it off and to defend her, as he'd sworn.

So few people had ever kept their word to Rhianna that she stopped to stare at Fallion, her mouth falling open with a little startled "Oh!"

The creature cried out, appearing astonished at Fallion's ferocious assault, wrenched back, and then Borenson was on it, burying his warhammer into its back.

The beast sprung into the air, flung itself backward over the boat, and then lay splashing in the water.

Rhianna crouched, hot blood dripping onto her hand, her heart pounding so hard that she was afraid that she would die. She gaped at Fallion, who grinned wickedly and wiped his blade clean on his tunic.

Mist came to Rhianna's eyes as she peered at him.

Here is someone I can trust, she told herself.

Hadissa suddenly pulled himself over the gunwales, and plopped in a sopping heap in the bottom of the boat. The boat rocked just a little. Then he stood, crouching like a dancer, waiting to see if more of the monsters would come.

Myrrima took an oar and righted the boat. There was a roar of rapids ahead, and she aimed the boat toward a dark V of water. No one spoke. Everyone listened. Only the wind hissed through the branches of the pines.

Rhianna reached down, felt her stomach to make sure that she hadn't ripped her stitches open. When she found a warm dot of blood, she pushed herself to the back of the shelter and tried to hold still.

Don't sleep, she told herself. Don't let yourself sleep. Sleeping is stupid. People die when they let themselves get caught asleep.

But she dared to close her eyes.

Fallion is watching for me, she told herself.

❧ 10 ☙

THE CHARGE

Every man is born and every man dies. The important thing is to celebrate all of the moments in between.

—Hearthmaster Waggit

Asgaroth had hardly escaped into the woods when Chancellor Waggit brought his mounted troops onto the commons, just inside Castle Coorm. He knew that he would have to break the siege and send men into the woods to hunt Asgaroth's troops. But he dared not have his men charge into the darkness, and so he waited for dawn, a dawn that refused to come.

Instead, thick clouds drew across the heavens, like a slab of gray slate, blotting out the light. Sodden curtains of rain began to fall, adding to the gloom.

When dawn came, it seemed almost as dark as midnight, and the field was too muddy for the horses to make a safe charge.

But Waggit had no choice. He had to act soon. So he left three hundred men to guard the castle walls, and let the drawbridge fall amid the rattle of chains and the groaning of hinges.

Then a thousand lancers rode out in an ordered line, the horses walking slowly, followed by two thousand archers with their steel bows.

The air was thick with water. It caught in the lungs and ran down the back of one's throat.

Sounds became elusive. The creaking of leather, the plod of horses' hooves, muffled coughs, the soft clanking of oiled armor beneath surcoats— all such sounds seemed to become elusive, like rabbits leaping through the brush from the beagles, their white tails flashing as they dodged through tufts of gorse.

And so the lancers took to the gray field, and the archers marched out behind them.

Off in the distance, up the gentle rolling hills of the village, warhorns blew, and through a curtain of rain Waggit could make out the shadows of men flitting away from stone cottages, racing behind high hedges toward the woods.

Waggit chuckled. Asgaroth's men had no stomach for a fight, he could see. They would make a hunt of it, their men fading into the trees and sniping with arrows from thickets where the horses could not charge.

There would be no easy way to get to them. The sodden weather wouldn't allow him to put fire to the woods.

So, he told himself, we'll hunt them, man to man.

Waggit suspected that his men outnumbered Asgaroth's, but he couldn't be certain.

He'd see their number soon enough.

He raised his horn to his lips. It was an ancient thing; the ebony mouthpiece smelled of lacquer, sour ale, and the previous owner's rotting teeth. He blew with his might, a long wailing burst that made the horn tremble beneath his palm.

His troops began advancing slowly, and suddenly the rain pelted, becoming a gray veil that blocked out the hills ahead.

Riding forward, Waggit turned his mount, sent the charge south, and hurried his pace, racing blind, his horse's hooves churning up mud.

He was alone with his thoughts, and fear rose to his throat. He would be glad when this day was done, glad to ride home to his wife and sit beside a roaring fire with his daughter on his knee. He conjured a scene where Farion giggled as he sang to her and fried hazelnuts in butter and sea salt over the open hearth, while their yellow kitten crept about, trying to see what they were up to.

That is the way it will be, he thought.

He could not face any other alternative.

And all too soon, they came out of the rain. Ahead lay a stone fence, with a high hedge that blocked his way to the right and left; barring the road ahead was an old sheep gate made of wooden poles. Beyond, a lonely-looking road stretched through sodden woods.

Asgaroth's soldiers guarded the road. Waggit could see warriors of Internook hunching down behind the gate in their sealskin coats, horned helms making them look laughably like cattle, their huge battle-axes at the ready.

Others hid behind the stone fence to the right and left of the gate, their bows drawn.

"Clear them out!" Waggit shouted to his men. "Clear them out!"

Holding a shield in his left hand, and a black lance in the crook of his right arm, he nodded sharply so that the visor of his helm dropped. He spurred his mount.

Arrows began flying past as he raced toward the gate. One blurred toward his chest, and only luck let him angle his shield to catch it on the edge, sending it ricocheting into the sky. Another glanced off of his epaulet, and a third struck his mount near the throat, shattering in the barding, and the broken shaft went flying into his leg.

Waggit heard horses scream and men grunt in surprise behind him as arrows took them.

Then his own archers began firing back, sending a hail that blackened the skies.

Ahead, some of the axmen roared in anger as arrows plunged into them. Waggit saw one huge axman, his golden hair flowing down his shoulders in braids, pull an arrow from his gut, shake it in the air, then lick the blood from it, as if to mock the attacker's petty efforts. At the last, he bit the arrow in two and spat it out, then shouldered his ax, eyes blazing as he held his post.

That man is mine, Waggit thought.

His horse was charging directly toward the fearsome warrior.

He'll cut my mount's belly open when it tries to leap the fence, Waggit thought. That's what he's after.

But Waggit had a lance in his hand, a cold wet lance that was growing slippery in the rain. He gripped it tightly, tried to steady his aim as he squatted low.

Suddenly Waggit became aware of a dozen riders thundering at his side and behind him. The riders on the left held their shields in the left hands, while those to the right shielded the right. Thus they rode in a shield wall to meet their destiny.

And suddenly Waggit's horse was leaping in the air to clear the gate, and his own lance was aimed at the warlord's head.

The warlord grinned, bloody teeth flashing, and tried to duck and swing his ax all in one swift motion, aiming to disembowel Waggit's leaping mount.

But Waggit quickly dropped the point of the lance, taking the warlord in the face.

As the metal point of his lance bit into flesh, snicked through bone, and clove through the warlord's skull, Waggit shouted, "Chew on this!"

Then the weight of the carcass dragged the lance from Waggit's hand and he was over the wall. His horse hit the muddy road and went down, sliding.

Arrows whipped overhead and one snapped into Waggit's helm.

The other horsemen were coming, and Waggit realized that their mounts would trample him to death if he didn't get out of the way.

Waggit tried to leap from his own saddle and pull out his saber as the horse skidded.

He hit the ground and went down, skidding as he fell, realizing too late that the enemy troops had trampled this part of the road and peed on it, turning it into a muddy brew, all in an effort to slow just such a charge.

He heard other horses falling behind him, and he had the good sense to try to get out of their way.

Keeping his shield high, Waggit tried to leap up, but found himself scrambling and crawling through the mud toward the safety of a beech tree. Another horse fell behind Waggit, clipped his leg, and sent him sprawling backward.

A swordsman of Ahshoven, in battle armor as gray as the rain, raced up toward Waggit, intent on dealing a death blow, his breath fogging the air around his black beard, and all that Waggit could do was to raise his sword and parry feebly.

But suddenly a horseman came thundering down the road, and a lance struck the swordsman in the gut, lifting him from his feet.

So powerful was the grip of the lancer that the man was borne away, his face a mask of shock and regret, until the lancer deigned to hurl him and his lance aside.

Waggit whirled and searched for more attackers.

But Waggit was a scholar more than a warrior, and better fighters with grand endowments of brawn and metabolism were already ahead of him, masters of the slaughter. Asgaroth's troops were no match.

Waggit saw that there had only been a hundred men or so at the gates, hardly enough to slow his troops, much less stop them. And now they were running along the hedgerow, heading toward the wooded hills, hoping to escape.

Waggit suddenly became aware of a sharp pain in his leg, a pinching sensation.

Reaching down near his crotch, Waggit felt the broken shaft of the arrow that had pierced his thigh. In the heat of battle, he'd forgotten about it.

He pulled, felt a sharp pain as the bodkin came clear. The arrowhead was not a broad tip, thankfully. Such a blade would have been likely to sever an artery. Instead it was long and sharp, like a nail, meant to pierce armor.

He peered down at his wound. Blood wasn't pumping out. The shaft had missed the artery. He licked the tip of the arrowhead, in mockery of the enemy warriors that were dying on the battlefield, and tasted the salt of his own hot blood. He hurled the broken arrow to his feet, where he crushed it in the mud.

Then he pulled out his kerchief and tied it around his leg. The best thing that he could do now was to apply some steady pressure. And what better way to apply pressure than to sit on the back of a horse? he wondered.

His mind clouded by the haze of battle, he decided to ride on, to let the wound close even as he tracked down and slaughtered Asgaroth's scouts.

ಚಿ 11 ಣ

MISTRESS OF THE HUNT

In a good battle, every man is a hunter and every man is hunted.

—*Sir Borenson*

Iome listened for sounds of pursuit, but the burble and rush of the river as it flowed among stones and hanging branches masked everything. She relied upon her several endowments of hearing as she listened for pursuit, but the only sounds that came to her were the wind hissing through trees, the occasional water rat rustling among the reeds at the water's edge, the cries of burrow owls hunting on the wing, and, at last, the soft snoring of the children in their little shelter.

The miles flowed past, and with each mile traveled, Iome rested a little easier.

Overhead, a storm brewed, heavy clouds scudding in from the west, blotting out the stars. The air was heavy, but not with the familiar taste of fog. Instead when Iome breathed, it came in sickly and smothering, so that she found herself gasping for breath like a fish out of water.

A wind suddenly rushed up the canyon, and the boughs of pine trees bobbed and swayed while dried cattail reeds along the bank gave a death rattle.

Myrrima glanced back at Iome, worry on her brow.

There are other Powers at work here, Iome realized. Perhaps Asgaroth is sending the wind to blow the mist off the river. Or perhaps he has other purposes in mind.

For a long while, the storm built, layer after layer adding to the clouds, and the night grew bleaker. Then lightning began to sizzle across the sky, green as an old bruise, and a drear rain simmered over the water and pooled in the hull of the boat.

As Iome poled at the rudder, her robes turning into a sopping weight, she heard the first of the warhorns blow, soft and distant, like the braying of a donkey. They were too deep of timbre to be horns of Mystarria.

Asgaroth.

Upstream behind them.

Someone had found the dead strengi-saats in the shallows, and now they called to other hunters.

For the next long hour, the horns continued to draw nearer. Ten miles back. Six miles. Three.

The steep banks and thick growth along the river seemed not to slow their pursuers. The hunters had to be on foot, but they were men with endowments of brawn and metabolism and stamina, so that they could run faster than a normal man, faster even than the swift current that bore the little boat along at perhaps eight miles per hour here in the hills.

But the longboat would soon be heading into deep valleys where the water grew sluggish and the pursuers' path would grow easy.

Iome looked down to Myrrima and Hadissa. Both of them had endowments of hearing. They too had heard the pursuers and thus held worry on their brows.

"Pull close to shore," Hadissa whispered at last as he reached into a rucksack and drew out his weapons. He held a strange assortment—throwing darts like small daggers, their blades green with poison from the malefactor bush; a garrote woven of golden threads; a curved steel club; a horn bow that would quickly lose its strength in the damp woods. He attached the darts to his belt, looped the garrote around his waist, and otherwise armed himself for stealthy battle.

He hesitated at the horn bow. He dared not remove such a fine weapon from its oilskin case, let it be ruined. The glue that bound the layers of ox-horn in it would turn to mush in a matter of hours.

But he was in great need. At last, he took it, still in its oilskin, along with two quivers of arrows.

Iome steered the boat close to a rock.

"Want help?" she asked.

She feared that Hadissa was on a suicide mission. He might be the most dangerous man alive, but even he could not hope to defeat Asgaroth's army.

He smiled, a show of bravery. "It is time to repay an old debt."

Iome nodded. Years ago, assassins from Indhopal had killed her husband's mother, brother, and two sisters. It was only by luck that Gaborn
had escaped that night, for he'd sneaked down to the garden to play with
the wild ferrins.

Thus, Hadissa had missed killing the child who would grow up to
become the Earth King.

When Gaborn met Hadissa again, years later, he'd looked into Hadissa's
heart and seen what he had done.

It was devastating. Yet in the world of the Runelords, an assassin's trade
was considered necessary. Some even thought it honorable. So Gaborn forgave Hadissa and Chose him under one condition: that from henceforth
Hadissa would guard the family he had once tried to wipe out.

Now, Hadissa would seek to redeem himself.

"The fog will hide you, so long as the wind doesn't pick up too much
more," Myrrima whispered. She knelt and reached into the water, brought
up a handful, and sprinkled it upon him. "Blessed be your blades. May they
strike true against Asgaroth and all enemies of Water."

Hadissa bowed in token of his thanks for the blessing. Then with the
grace of a deer he leapt from the boat and landed upon a rock. He squatted
for a moment, perfectly still, like a dark cat, listening.

Then he leapt under the shadows of a pine bough, and Iome could see or
hear him no more.

He will take a mighty toll, Iome assured herself as the boat flowed inexorably on.

The boat rounded a corner, and spanning above the river ahead was a
land bridge, a huge natural arch of stone, with pine trees growing atop it,
green ferns clinging to its side, and vines hanging toward the water. There
were huge stones in the river beneath it, and the river split. There was a
dark V of water, and the roaring of rapids beyond. This bridge was called
Eiderstoffen, and not far below it, the river came out of the mountains and
dumped into a broad plain. There the river slowed, flowed into the warmer
waters of the River Dwindell, and meandered; once they reached that
junction, though they were but fifty miles from the seacoast and the castle
at the Courts of Tide, it would take many hours for their little boat to reach
safe harbor.

Our enemies will be upon us well before then, Iome knew, and mentally she prepared herself for her death, for she suspected that she would not be able to buy her son safe passage with anything less.

The boat raced toward the archway under the stones, and Iome suspected that Myrrima would turn and ask if they should beach the boat, carry it around the rapids, but Myrrima did not turn. She aimed the prow into the darkest V of water, and the boat rushed through it, then suddenly dropped and lofted again as they hit white water.

Overhead, as they passed under the land bridge, hundreds of swallows' nests could be seen, smears of white mud and twigs against the darker stone.

Then they rode through, and Iome saw a bit of snow in the branches of trees. But as the boat drew near them, the snow suddenly lifted, and white birds flew in a miraculous cloud that took her breath away. Snow doves, they were called. They must have come down from the mountains, where they fed on pine nuts and other seeds at the snow line.

For a long minute, she watched their white wings against the deep gray clouds as the flock veered this way and that. It seemed to Iome to be the most beautiful sight that she had ever seen.

The river twisted ahead, and white water roared and foamed over rocks everywhere. For several long moments the boat rocked, and some of the children cried out as it bucked.

Plumes of water surged over the gunwales.

The boat hit a submerged rock; boards cracked under the impact.

Then it slewed through swift water, around a second bend, and they rushed out of the hills and could see only plains ahead.

The boat hit the slow waters, and Iome spotted a small cottage high up on the banks, its stone walls and heavy thatch roof hidden behind a screen of cattails. A child's rope swing hung beneath an elm that leaned out over the river, and a small fishing boat was perched on the shore.

But the sight of a peasant's cottage offered no comfort. With a cottage near, Iome knew, a road will run beside the river. Our pursuers will make even better time.

The sounds of rapids faded.

For twenty minutes they rode the slow river. Around every bend she feared that Asgaroth's troops would meet them. But she saw nothing, and she realized that Hadissa, brave Hadissa, was indeed holding back an army.

For twenty minutes more they traveled. She heard a horn again, not more than two miles back, high and clear—a horn of Mystarria.

Fierce braying answered from deeper horns.

"The battle is joined," Sir Borenson said, grasping his warhammer and staring back longingly. "Waggit's men have finally arrived."

"One can hope," Iome said.

In the slow water, they rode along, fully exposed.

Iome watched behind. The cottage faded away, but before they rounded a wide corner, Iome saw dark figures running along the riverbank, flashing through trees.

The boat rounded the corner. For a few seconds their pursuers would be hidden.

My turn, Iome thought as she quietly took her long sword and leapt from the boat. The water was shallow, no more than three feet deep, and numbingly cold. Iome landed a dozen yards from shore, then waded in among some cattails and crept up on a bank thick with moss.

Overhead, the skies were cold and gray. Rain fell. The thin mist that had been on the water all morning held. Iome knew that her hunters would be blinded by it.

She quietly crept up to the top of the riverbank and took a post behind a tree, waiting. She did not have to wait long.

Several fat axmen from Internook came huffing along the river at three times a normal man's speed.

Fast, she told herself, but not as fast as me.

Iome glimpsed them through the branches, then hid herself for a moment.

She had ten endowments of metabolism, three times as much as these men. They could not hope to match her speed. And suddenly the endowments that had been sending her racing headlong toward her death for these nine years became an asset, here at the end of her life.

When the axmen drew even with her tree, she leapt in front of them; their eyes went wide with shock when they saw her suddenly rush toward them from the mist.

They tried to halt, tried to raise their weapons. One man cried, "Och!" But with greater speed, Iome dodged their blows and with three quick slices took their heads off.

The bodies were still falling when she whirled and raced along the river-bank, following the boat. She remained in the brush along the riverside, but now the land around them opened up into fields for cattle to forage, and there was little cover at all.

In the morning, she raced through a meadow, where cottontail rabbits held as still as stone, ears pricked up, water sparkling in their fur as she passed. A pair of grouse leapt up from a bush, their wings thundering, and in seeming slow motion they winged over Iome's head.

I am a ghost in the mist, she thought. I am fleet and fierce and untouch-able.

Then she heard shouting on the river, and whirled to glance behind her. Just then, the heavens shook and lightning arced from horizon to horizon, and a fierce wind rumbled through the trees, making proud elms bow before it while drier grasses were knocked flat.

Asgaroth, Iome realized. He is blowing the fog away.

There was a shout from the river, and Iome saw that the wind had shoved the boat against the far bank, and now it was stuck there, lodged between two rocks.

Iome looked back upstream, saw dark figures racing through the trees along the bank. She dropped to her belly and eeled through a patch of tall meadow grass toward the boat, then lay concealed behind a fallen log.

Get Asgaroth, she told herself, and the rest will flee. He's all that matters.

ഌ 12 ര

A BREAK IN THE CLOUDS

I would like to believe that with careful planning, hard work, and adequate resolve, I can create my own destiny. But other men with evil resolve make me doubt it.

—*Fallion Sylvarresta Orden*

Fallion woke as the boat thudded against the shore, the wind screaming all around.

He grabbed his dagger and leapt up, his hand still aching from his wound, and climbed out of the shelter. Borenson and Myrrima were poling the boat away from the rocks, but the wind was so fierce that their efforts did little good. Fallion looked around, realized that Hadissa and his mother were gone.

"What's going on?" Fallion cried, and in a moment Jaz was there at his back.

Borenson turned, his face red from effort, and shouted, "Get back inside!"

"Can I help?" Fallion called.

"No!" Borenson shouted, and he turned and peered upriver, his face stark with alarm.

Fallion followed his gaze. A black wind was driving bullets of rain into his face. On the banks, running between trees, dozens of enemy troops rushed toward them.

"Are we going to die?" Jaz asked.

"Get in the shelter," Borenson shouted, pushing Fallion and Jaz away. The tarp roof of their shelter flapped like a drumhead, thrumming from the wind. Fallion got in the shelter, but scrambled to the back so that he could peer upstream through cracks between the crates.

Something—a strange cloud—was rolling toward them—a ball of night with shadows dancing inside, strengi-saats seemingly carried in a maelstrom.

Lightning flashed overhead and thunder rumbled, troubling the waters. And all around that ball of shadow warriors swarmed toward the boat, moving so swiftly by reason of endowments that Fallion's eyes could not follow them.

Ahead of the maelstrom, one warrior in the dark tunic of an assassin sprinted toward the boat—Hadissa!

Borenson raced to the door of their little fortress, blocking it with his bulk, and stood guard.

"Hide!" he warned the children. "Find the safest corner."

Fallion gripped his own dagger. Though he was only nine, he had trained with weaponry for as long as he could remember, and calluses from blade practice had grown thick on his palm and along the inside of his thumb.

Suddenly from the black storm that came rushing toward them came a howl, deep and almost wolflike, but ululating rapidly—like cries of glee with words in them. At first Fallion thought it might be the hunting cries of strengi-saats.

Then he wondered if it might be the wind, howling like some beast. Fallion listened closely.

The ball of wind rolled toward Hadissa, who shouted a battle cry as he turned in one last desperate attempt to meet the enemy.

The wind screamed, and Fallion saw a dark knot of straw suddenly rise up out of the grass and shoot toward Hadissa, hurtling like bolts from a ballista.

The assassin leapt and tried to dodge as he spun in midair. The pieces of straw lanced toward him, and Fallion thought that they had missed, for when Hadissa landed, he stood on the balls of his feet.

But the wind was buffeting him, propping him up like a marionette. It lifted him in the air slowly, letting him spin, so that Fallion could see the ruin of his face.

The straw had pierced his right eye socket, burrowed through his brain, and left a gaping hole out the back of his head. A small tornado whirled through the hole still, sending more bits of straw through his socket, expanding the hole, so that brain matter and flecks of blood hurtled from the back of the wound.

The wind worked Hadissa's mouth as if he jabbered inanely. Then the wind tossed him high into the air.

Fallion gasped in shock.

Hadissa had always seemed to be a fixture in Fallion's life, a monolith. Now he was dead.

The maelstrom of dark wind boiled toward the boat.

A ball of lightning hurtled from the blackness and shot toward them. Fallion whirled, placing his back to a box for protection, turning away from the attack.

He peered up at Borenson. The ball lightning sizzled just overhead so that Fallion felt his hair stand on end. There was a crackling sound, a grunt and a cry, and for half a second, Borenson's chest lit up so brightly that Fallion could see the red of blood and veins in it, the gray shadows of ribs. The blast hurtled him into the air, knocking him overboard.

Fallion let out a startled cry.

Suddenly he was plunged into utter darkness. Then Fallion's eyes began to readjust.

Myrrima let out a shrill cry and grabbed her bow. Though the wind raged all around, the wizardess seemed calm, collected.

She drew her steel bow to its full and shouted, "Come no farther. You cannot have these children."

The wind howled and raged. Fallion heard it keen over the boat, ripping trees from the bank by their roots.

Suddenly everything went quiet. For half a second, he just crouched, listening. It was as if the wind had disappeared.

He heard a dull thud, and Fallion felt as if he were at the heart of a storm. He could hear wind swirling around in the distance. Darkness had so enveloped the boat that he could hardly make out Myrrima's shadow, though she was no more than a dozen feet away.

The enemy was out there, waiting.

Fallion peered through the crack. Around him the rest of the children huddled, trembling from fear.

From out of the darkness strode a man, all in black. At first, Fallion thought that it was a stranger. But then he saw that it was Hadissa, and he was not striding. Instead, he moved in little hops as the wind picked him up a bit, then let him bounce back down, his feet barely touching the ground.

Behind him, grim warriors strode through the shadows, and dark strengi-saats floated through the air, borne like kites, appearing briefly and then disappearing again. Myrrima let an arrow fly, and one strengi-saat dropped like a wounded dove.

A fierce light shone, ball lightning spewing around Hadissa's head, as if the wind wanted Fallion to see this.

Hadissa drew near, a pale marionette, perhaps a hundred paces across the river; his dead mouth flapped like a scrap of cloth in the wind. His one good eye was fixed and growing cloudy, but it was the ragged hole where the other eye should have been that seemed to focus on Fallion. Wind surged through it, into the dead man's skull, and issued out through his windpipe, causing the ragged flesh to tremble as he spoke.

"Come with me, child," the wind insisted in a strange, rasping voice. "Long have I waited. You are a lord of the living, but I can make you King of the Dead."

Fallion's heart beat so fast that he thought it might break. It took all his courage to keep from running, to keep from leaping into the river, but something inside whispered that fleeing would accomplish nothing. There was something mesmerizing about the voice, haunting.

He could taste the air, a blazing hot streak across the bridge of his cheek—the scent of evil.

"No!" Fallion shouted, his heart hammering with fear.

Myrrima strode to the back of the boat, placing herself between Fallion and Hadissa with another arrow nocked in her bow, and shouted, "Asgaroth, show yourself!"

With a tremendous surge the wind batted her. She went tumbling away to Fallion's right, skidding across the slick hull of the boat. She hit the gunwale with a thud, grunted in pain, and tried to right herself.

Fallion faced the dead man. The wind keened outside, its voice terrifying, and Hadissa's face, growing blue in death, seemed to tower above him.

I should get out of here, Fallion thought. I should run, lead the enemy away from the rest of the children.

"In the name of the One True Master," the wind hissed through Hadissa's teeth, "I claim you. And by the power of the One Rune, I bind you to me."

A gust ripped the roof from their little shelter, leaving them open to the sky. Fallion's shirt ripped, leaving his young chest bare, and he felt wind racing over his flesh—an unpleasant sensation, as if a line of red ants marched upon his skin.

Dimly, a part of his mind became aware that some beast beyond his comprehension drew runes upon him, runes of Air. He could not see them, could not know what they might do. He reached up and tried to brush them off.

But he felt a change taking place, as if cords were wrapping about his chest, making it hard to draw a breath.

"You are mine," the wind hissed. "You will serve me. Though your heart may burn with righteous desires, your noblest hopes will become fuel to fire despair among mankind. That which you seek to build will crumble to ash. War shall follow you all of your days, and though the world may applaud your slaughter, *you* will come to know that each of your victories is mine.

"And thus I seal you, till the end of time. . . ."

Fallion stood for a moment in the darkness, Hadissa's dead face grinning down from the bank, the man's arms flopping lifelessly. Invisible bands held Fallion upright; and he could not breathe. Indeed, each gasp brought only a dark wind filled with dust.

He realized that he was going to faint. His legs felt as frail as willow fronds. It seemed that the only thing propping him up was the wind.

The storm prowled around the boat like a hunting beast. It gave a keening cry, as if the whole of the heavens were shouting in victory.

Fallion stood on the boat, stunned, filled with terror—not a fear of the beast that had assailed him, but a fear of what he might become.

Now Asgaroth's dark minions rushed through the trees toward the boats, warriors and monsters. The clouds overhead kept the whole world in shadow; for the second time that day Fallion wished for light.

Almost as if summoned by his wish, the sky brightened, and through howling wind and driving rain Fallion saw a shadow mounted upon a bloodred horse—Asgaroth himself.

In that instant, a small figure rose up from beneath a fallen log near Hadissa, a woman with silver hair flying in the wind. She moved with blinding speed. She raced to Hadissa, reached into his scabbard with one hand, grasped his sword as she passed, sent it flying end over end into the mist and driving rain—

It struck Asgaroth's chest. For a long moment, Asgaroth sat in seeming astonishment, gazing down at the blade that impaled him.

Fallion's heart pounded as he watched for a reaction. Asgaroth was a Runelord, drawing power through dozens, perhaps even hundreds, of endowments.

There were stories of men who had taken so much stamina that they could hardly be killed. They could fight on in battle with arms hacked off, trailing their own guts, and live to tell the tale.

It seemed improbable that Asgaroth could be defeated with a single blow from a sword, and Fallion half expected him to come shrieking into battle, drawing the blade that transfixed him as if pulling it from a fleshly scabbard, then wreaking havoc upon them all.

But blood gurgled from Asgaroth's mouth. The sword seemed to have pierced his lung, perhaps even cleaving his heart in half.

He leaned his head back and a scream issued from his throat. It became louder and louder, a death cry that shook the heavens; a plume of bloody air spewed out of his throat, went swirling skyward.

Suddenly the wind grew in ferocity. The cry rose from a scream to a rumbling roar. Blood spewed skyward; Asgaroth seemed to explode, his arms and torso ripping away like worn cloth, and a huge wind gusted up, a vortex that rose and rose into a towering tornado that lifted his horse from the ground, sucked up nearby trees, and pulled tufts of grass and dirt into the medley.

An elemental of air, Fallion realized.

Asgaroth had been a servant of Air, a wind-driven wizard, and thus had an elemental within him.

The more powerful the sorcerer, the greater the elemental. The creature rising up now was monumental.

The wind screamed around them, whirling madly, as if the heavens themselves were coming to life, as if the sky would split in half. Asgaroth's troops and the strengi-saats shouted and tried to rush away from the vortex.

The wind tore the voices of men and monsters away, so that their cries came from a seeming distance, like the cries of gulls far out to sea, and

Fallion saw more than one strengi-saat whirl up into the maelstrom, snarling and shrieking as it was torn asunder.

Quickly the tornado grew, its base remaining on the ground while its top whirled up into the slate gray clouds, lost to sight, where suddenly even the clouds whirled and turned green and lightning crackled and shone like a crown.

Many men and creatures ran for their lives, but Iome was the fastest of them, and she raced now, a Runelord in the height of her power, leaping ten yards to a stride. In five bounds she raced down the bank and hit the water, then tried to run across it, her feet a blur. But she didn't have enough endowments of metabolism, and by the time that she was three-quarters of the way across the river, she floundered, bobbed underwater, and an instant later shot up at the side of the boat and pulled herself in.

Meanwhile, Myrrima was shouting to Borenson, "Grab the pole," as she tried fishing him from the river. The boat had beached, but the current was dragging Borenson downstream.

Groggily, Borenson cursed and sputtered, trying to make it to the boat. Fallion gaped in surprise, supposing that Borenson had been killed by the lightning.

Fallion raced to the gunwale and grabbed Borenson's cape, tried pulling him in, but Borenson wore ring mail beneath his tunic, and Fallion could hardly budge him. It wasn't until Iome grasped Borenson that they were able to drag him into the boat.

By then, the tornado had reached its full height, and now it thundered toward them, making the earth rumble, pulling whole trees up by their roots, slinging boulders across the ground.

The wind surged, singing past Fallion's ears, tugging his clothes, slapping his face.

Several of Asgaroth's warriors were racing toward the boat, and now they looked back in horror as the tornado overtook them, plucked them up kicking and screaming, their arms waving in the air, bearing them into the heavens.

This is the end, Fallion thought.

He suddenly became conscious that Rhianna was grasping onto his leg, as if to hold on to him for support. Talon clutched her baby sister and hunched over protectively, while all of the other children screamed in fear.

The only one who showed no fear was Myrrima. She calmly picked up her bow, drew an arrow from the quiver at her back, and fired into the broiling tempest.

The bolt flew true, singing into the funnel cloud.

What is she thinking? Fallion wondered. An arrow won't help.

But the wind suddenly roared like a wounded animal and grew in fury. Dark dirt surged up, blackening the funnel cloud.

To Fallion's utter amazement, the tornado stopped in its course, leapt in the air, and reeled backward over the land, only to touch down a quarter of a mile away, where it plucked up trees and dirt and hurled them in its fury.

It blurred away, at dozens of miles per hour.

In mere seconds it was gone.

He peered at Myrrima in awe, recalled how she had washed her arrows in water at dawn.

She must have cast a powerful spell indeed, Fallion realized.

The world seemed to go still. Fallion could hear the roar of the tornado in the distance, could even feel the rumble through the soles of his shoes, but nearby there wasn't a sound.

And above, the clouds shattered like glass, and to Fallion's delight, the sun burst through clear and strong, its rays slanting in through rain. Suddenly the most brutal gray clouds he had ever seen became nothing but a backdrop for a brilliant rainbow.

Everyone just stood or sat on the boat, breathing heavily, Talon weeping in relief, Borenson looking up at the skies in wonder, Iome laughing and sniffing.

It was in such circumstances that a warhorn blew a moment later, and some of Mystarria's own troops came rushing along the riverbank.

Dozens of Asgaroth's men had escaped, along with no small number of strengi-saats. Many of the enemy troops had crawled into thickets seeking shelter, and all along the riverbank the Mystarrians engaged whatever enemy they could find, dragged them from their hiding holes, and put them to the sword. They sang a battle song as they slew.

"We are born to blood and war,
Like our fathers were, a thousand years before.
Sound the horn. Strike the blow!
Down to grief or glory go!"

Myrrima looked out upon the slaughter, and whispered, "I never knew that such rough old hawks could sing so beautifully."

But Fallion watched it all in dismay, for he could still feel the fiery ants marching across his chest with tiny feet of wind, and he wondered.

Am I cursed?

ಬ 13 ೞ

THE CURSE

No man can fully know the mind of a locus. We are not capable of that much evil.

—*Gaborn Val Orden*

It was Chancellor Waggit who led the troops. Moments later he reached the riverbank, riding a rangy mountain pony bred for hunting more than war. He had fought a bloody battle and managed to rout most of Asgaroth's rear guard, but rather than turn and fight, Asgaroth had elected to forge ahead with the best of his scouts and engage Iome.

As Waggit's men finished the skirmish and hunted among the dead for the spoils of war, Myrrima poled the boat to the far bank, so that the children could get out on the rocks. Fallion smelled the air. The bridge of his nose seemed to burn with the scent of evil.

It's the curse, he thought, and he leapt out of the boat, knelt on some rounded stones, and tried to scrub the scent off from himself, washing his hands in the bone-chilling water first, then his chest, and finally his face.

Waggit strolled down from the fields bringing a helmeted head as a trophy of war, the head of Fallion's enemy. The head was grisly, blood dribbling from the neck, so that Waggit held the thing at arm's length, lest the gore splash upon his boots.

Fallion climbed up the riverbank, finding a path on a muskrat trail, and made his way through cattails to his mother.

Waggit held out the head, turned the face toward Iome, and her mouth went wide with surprise. "Celinor Anders . . . ?"

Fallion looked at the gore-covered face, then back up at his mother. "Who?"

Iome blinked. "I . . . I had thought that it would be old King Anders, that he was the one we fought. But it was Celinor, his son. He was once a friend to your father, one of the Chosen. I thought that he was a good man."

The sense of betrayal was palpable. Fallion could think of nothing to say.

Waggit said, "He's not the first good man to turn to evil."

Iome closed her eyes, wondering what had led Celinor to this. She threw the head down in anger, hurt by his betrayal. "Leave it here, to be gnawed by the foxes."

Waggit reached out a hand, and Fallion heard the tinkle of jewelry as he set something in Iome's palm. She shoved the items in her pocket before Fallion could see.

"Is it over?" Fallion asked. "Is Asgaroth dead for sure?"

Iome looked at her son, perplexed, while a ragged bit of wayward rain spattered across her face. A shadow fell over them, and she realized that the break in the clouds was sealing back up.

"He's dead," Iome said. "Celinor is dead. But the evil that drove him is not. It existed long before he was born and will live long after. There was a creature inside him, a being of pure evil, called a locus. It's gone now, but it will find another host. It can live inside a man like a parasite. The name of the locus is Asgaroth. It will return, in time, when it finds a suitable host, a person of sufficient malice, one with enough power so that it can gather minions to do its bidding. So Asgaroth is not dead. Nor do I think that it can ever die."

Fallion tried to comprehend this, but it was so far outside his experience that his mind rebelled.

Yet as he wondered, he had a strange notion: Asgaroth was my enemy before I was born. Is he bound up in my purpose? Did I come to destroy him? Can he be destroyed?

He looked up to his mother. "How can you tell if a man has a locus in him?"

Iome shook her head. "Your father could tell. He could look into a man's heart and see the darkness there. But common folk like you and me, we can only guess."

Fallion still felt the tiny ants marching across his chest, so he tried to wipe them away. His mother spotted the gesture, reached out, stopped his hand, then gingerly held her fingers near his chest.

"There's movement there," she said softly, "a stirring of the wind, invisible runes . . ." Her voice was thick with worry. She looked over to the river. "Myrrima?"

Myrrima was standing in the water beside the boat. She came out of the river gracefully, as if the water flowed away from her feet, clearing her path. Rhianna and the children stayed behind, sitting on the gunwale.

When Myrrima neared, Iome asked, "What do you make of this?" She placed Myrrima's hand near Fallion's chest.

Myrrima felt the tiny runes, frowning just a bit, but after a moment she covered his chest with her wet palm, smashing the runes, and smiled. "Nothing. There is nothing here that can harm you," she told Fallion. "Asgaroth tried to curse you, but he doesn't have that kind of power."

"But he said I would start wars—" Fallion began to argue.

"Don't let it trouble you," Myrrima said. "He spoke many things that do not make sense. He said that he bound you by the Power of the One Rune, but the One Rune was destroyed ages ago, and when it burst, the One True World shattered into a thousand thousand shadow worlds. The power to bind was lost. And if Asgaroth were ever to regain it, he would bind the worlds into one once again, bind them to himself, and thus hold us all in thrall."

She sounded so certain, so right. And with her touch, the runes of air had broken.

"Are you sure?" Fallion begged.

"Asgaroth only wants to frighten you," Myrrima assured him. "That is how he wields his powers. You saw that."

Iome cut in. "You showed him that you don't fear him, so he wants you to fear *yourself*, fear the evil that you might do."

"She's right," Myrrima said. "Because you are both brave and decent, you do not fear evil in others as much as you fear it in yourself. Asgaroth knows that you will fight him, so he tried to instill within you a fear of battle. There is nothing more to it. Rest easy."

But Fallion couldn't rest easy. He imagined himself leading vast armies to war, armies of men drunk on the blood of slaughter, butchers who reveled in murder, and the vision seemed too alarming to lay aside.

Myrrima reached up. With a wet finger, she drew a rune upon Fallion's forehead, and all of his worries, all of his fears, seemed to lift from him like a heavy mantle. So powerful was the sense of release that he tried to recall what it was that had concerned him, but his mind could not seem to hold the memory for the moment.

Asgaroth. Something about Asgaroth?

Iome reached into her pocket and pulled out a silver cape pin. It was an owl with golden eyes, wings outstretched in flight, as if it were winging toward him. Fallion had never seen anything so marvelous. Inscribed upon the silver wings were tiny feathers so realistic that the owl looked almost alive. To heighten this, its golden eyes had amber pupils that seemed to fix upon Fallion. It was elegant, simple and beautiful, marvelous to behold.

"You should have this," his mother said, "a trophy of your first battle."

Fallion recognized the piece. Asgaroth had worn it when he came against the castle gates. Fallion was hesitant to touch anything that Asgaroth had worn. Yet there was something odd about the pin. The workmanship was finer than anything that Fallion had ever seen. Even the ancient duskins, with their cunning hands and love for silver, had never made anything so fine in detail. Instinctively Fallion suspected that this was some charm crafted in the netherworld. It was too beautiful to have been formed by human hands.

"Take it," Myrrima said. "No harm can come of it. Can't you *feel* that? Even Asgaroth's touch could not sully its power. It was made by Bright Ones. And I'm sure that that is why Asgaroth took it. They would have loathed for him to have it."

Fallion reached out for it. As he clasped it, an image came to his mind, an enormous gray owl with a wingspan much wider than a man is tall, flapping toward him. Fallion stood upon a low hill where the wheat grew nearly over his head, and there was a bright moon shining down, and monolithic oak trees on the distant hills.

The image struck him with such force that Fallion felt as if he had literally been carried away and all of his life had been a dream, for the world that he saw was more substantial, more earthy, than the one that he lived in.

The owl gave a querying call, and Fallion answered, "Ael."

Then the dream ended, and he was standing with his mother and Myrrima.

"What did you say?" Myrrima asked.

"Ael," Fallion answered. "I think that it was the name of the Bright One who owned this cape pin."

His mother said, "You're probably right. The Bright Ones often leave such visions on their items to identify the owner, much as we would write our name upon them."

Fallion smiled sadly. He suspected that Asgaroth had taken this pin as a trophy. He'd killed a Bright One of the netherworld, perhaps one who had come to fight him.

Now the pin had fallen into Fallion's hands. He decided to treasure it, as a thing to be revered.

Yet even as he took it, he was loath to pin it on. Trinkets from the netherworld were not meant as toys; he suspected that this pin might have powers that he didn't understand. Fallion could see runes engraved into the back of it; the rune lore of the Bright Ones was unsurpassed.

It wasn't a thing to be worn casually. It would attract the attention of the greedy and unscrupulous. Unsure what to do, he just stood holding the pin.

Myrrima turned away, strolling toward the boat. Humfrey had hopped off and was marching on the shore, holding his weapon forlornly as he searched for snails or dead fish, or something else appropriately nasty to eat.

Fallion suddenly realized that his pet ferrin had gone conspicuously absent during the battle. Probably hiding among the packs. Apparently, battling wizards and strengi-saats was not to Humfrey's taste.

Rhianna was wading in the shallows, and she suddenly called the ferrin, bent into the water, and tossed something up on shore. A huge red crayfish landed at Humfrey's feet. It immediately raised its claws in the air defensively and began to back away.

Humfrey shrieked in terror and hefted his makeshift spear. After several whistles—calls of "Monster! Monster!" and much leaping about, he managed to impale the crayfish. In moments he was tearing off claws and pulling out white meat with his sharp teeth, grunting from the effort and smacking his lips in delight.

Sir Borenson sat on the boat, wheezing and still in shock, looking at his own hands as if he were amazed to have survived.

Talon and the other children had all gone to the battlefield, and Fallion could see Jaz up there, hunting for treasures among the dead.

Iome followed his gaze, frowned severely, and shouted, "Jaz, get away from there," then added, "I've got a ring for you." She pulled out the black iron signet ring. It was a great treasure. Anyone who wanted to lay claim to South Crowthen would need it.

But Fallion much preferred his cape pin. He held it, squinted as a ray of stray sunshine struck it.

Rhianna came struggling up out of the boat, leaning heavily on a staff. She stared at the pin in dismay, eyes filling with tears. "Mother's pin. Where did you get it?"

"From him," Iome said, nodding toward the head.

"Now I know she's dead for sure," Rhianna whispered. "She would never have parted with it."

"You can have it," Fallion said, holding out the pin.

Rhianna looked at him uncertainly, as if he were offering a gift that was far more valuable than he knew.

"When you touched it, did it tell you its name?" Rhianna asked.

"Ael," Fallion said.

She nodded, as if he had confirmed something. "Then it's yours now."

She stared at him, shaken for a long moment. The pin hadn't really been her mother's for long. And Rhianna felt grateful for Fallion's help, for his strength and courage. She wanted him to have the thing.

Pain and rage had been building up in Rhianna for days.

"I hate you, Da," she whispered fiercely.

Rhianna found herself shaking. She cried out in impotent rage, then hobbled back to the boat.

Rhianna felt her stitches pull with every breath. She wept in terror and relief. Her thoughts felt muddled. After days of fear and sleeplessness and numbing cold, Rhianna was out of words.

She found herself peering at the river. The water was swift and cold and as clear as glass, flowing inexorably past field and stone, making its way to the curling waves and the brine of the sea.

Rhianna stopped at the side of the boat, standing in icy water. She didn't dare climb back in, for fear of injuring herself.

A shadow fell over Rhianna. "Come," Myrrima said, stroking Rhianna's back. The wizardess stepped into the icy cold water. Myrrima seemed not to be affected by its numbing touch at all. She walked out to her waist, wading with unnatural ease, then looked back over her shoulder, inviting.

Rhianna thought that Myrrima was the most beautiful woman that she had ever seen. Her eyes were as dark as mountain pools, and her skin as clear as the stream. She seemed at one with the water, and now she reached out a hand to Rhianna, beckoning. "Come."

Rhianna stepped into the clear, deep flow and caught her breath at its brutal cold.

She waded in, almost blind with tears, and though the rounded stones in the river were slick and she had to search with her numbing feet for toeholds, soon she reached Myrrima, and gazed up in dull pain.

Myrrima cupped a hand, raised it, and let some icy water dribble over Rhianna's forehead. Rhianna arched her neck, and it felt as if the water was not just pouring down upon her, but flowing into her, filling her mind and washing away the weariness and fear that she had borne for days now, for weeks.

"Be at peace," Myrrima said. "Let your thoughts be as restful as forest pools. Let clarity fill you like a mountain stream."

Rhianna stood, neck arched, as Myrrima dipped her hands again and again, letting water dribble on Rhianna's forehead. It seemed not to run down her so much as through her.

Soon Rhianna was weeping again. At first she wept for the loss of her mother, and some dull corner of her mind still hoped that she might still be alive, but Rhianna's heart knew that she was gone. She mourned the young girls who had died in the forest, girls she had known only for a few hours, for they had traded names and told one another the stories of their brief lives in those final hours after the strengi-saats took them.

Then after long minutes it seemed that the waters washed away her mourning. Still, Rhianna found little relief. Her muscles were knotted cords, and as the water rushed over her, she felt as if for years she had borne a heavy burden and now at last she could lay it down. Her fear was the burden. Now the water washing over her brought relief, unknotting the muscles in her shoulders, legs, and stomach, letting Rhianna breathe freely for the first time in days, so that she gasped for air.

And when all of her muscles were unbound, and even the dregs of fear had washed away, still Myrrima washed her, and Rhianna found herself wracked with sobs, not sobs of pain, but sobs of relief, of perfect ease.

Myrrima stopped and smiled down at her. "You're a troubled one, and a strange one. Do me a favor. Cup your hands, as if to drink."

Rhianna held her hands out before her in a tiny cup, and Myrrima reached down and drew a rune on the water, then took it from the river in her own hands and began pouring water into Rhianna's palms.

Rhianna was so weary that at first she did not recognize the import of what was happening. But her uncle had taught her some rune lore as a child, and suddenly she saw the danger. Myrrima had drawn the rune of revealing; now she leaned forward to peer into Rhianna's cupped hands.

A sudden fear took Rhianna, and she hurled the water back into the river. She demanded, "What do you hope to see within the well of my soul?"

What Myrrima had done was an invasion of privacy.

Myrrima smiled, but it wasn't a kind smile, the smile of an elder adoring a child. It was hard and calculating, the grim smile of a warrior who wonders if she has chanced upon a foe. "Where did you learn to scry runes?" Myrrima demanded.

Rhianna did not know what to say. "From . . . a merchant, a traveling merchant. I don't know where he learned it."

Rhianna should have known better than to try to lie to a wizardess. Myrrima gave her a suspicious look. "A rune caster, with no allegiance to the Powers? Some might call you a witch. And where did your mother get the cape pin?"

She waited for Rhianna to cough up the truth.

"I'm not your enemy," Rhianna said with finality.

Myrrima held her eye for a long moment. Rhianna had obviously decided not to answer, and the fierceness in this girl's eyes suggested that she could not be coerced.

At last Myrrima relented. "I would not let you near Fallion if I thought that you were an enemy." She glanced back downstream a few paces where Fallion looked away guiltily and then gazed up at a small break in the clouds, the miracle of sunlight streaming across the heavens. Then Myrrima seemed to come to a decision.

"I heard what you said to Celinor just a moment ago. He was your father. I knew him once. And I knew your mother, too."

She said these words softly. Rhianna looked around. No one else seemed to have heard.

Rhianna blushed with fear and indignation. Her mother had been running for years, hiding from Celinor Anders. Rhianna would never have betrayed her.

"Erin Connell was a friend of mine once," Myrrima said. "She taught me the bow. I had heard that she had fled from South Crowthen, but I never knew why she ran or where she went. She just disappeared. Now, if as you say, she is dead, then I grieve with you.

"You've been through a lot, Rhianna. I saw how much pain washed out of you. I've seen battle-scarred warriors who have shouldered less. No child should have to bear so much. I didn't mean to invade your privacy. I only hoped to find the pain's source, and thus speed your healing."

"I'll beg you to keep your nose out of my business," Rhianna said.

❧ 14 ❧

THE COURTS OF TIDE

A wizard's greatest source of power lies in his ability to retain a child's sense of wonder throughout life, and to maintain a keen interest in dozens of fields of study.

—The Wizard Binnesman

Moments later, Fallion was back in the boat, floating downriver as storm clouds drew back over the heavens and finally grew so heavy that they were forced to relinquish their water. A drenching rain drizzled warm and sweet, and Fallion found himself light of heart.

Chancellor Waggit sent some scouts downstream and dispatched others to hold the path behind, so that the boat traveled in safety. Fallion slept part of the morning, and when he woke it was late afternoon.

The Gyell had met the River Dwindell and now flowed broadly through rich farmlands. The sun shone full.

They passed villages where cottages rested along the shore and tame geese honked at the sight of boaters upon the river. The children broke into the copious supplies and had a fine meal of cheese-bread, ham, and cider.

Talon leapt off the back of the boat and splashed about in the river, grinning broadly, swimming like a seal, and invited the rest of the children to join her. None braved it. Fallion dipped his hand in the water; it was not much warmer than it had been last night.

He lay back in the boat, watched the sun setting golden on the horizon. The sky was mottled with flecks of clouds, blue at the heart with golden edges.

So they had a pleasant trip to the Courts of Tide, where the spires of the castles rose up like spears to the sky, and the great crystalline bridges spanned from island to island, held up by ancient statues.

The Royal Palace stood upon the highest hill of the main island, and by all rights, Fallion and his family should have gone there for the night. Fallion had been born there, but had not been to the palace since he was two or three. His memories of the place were dim and wondrous.

But though Chancellor Waggit reported that the city was safe, free of any sign of assassins or marauders, Iome reminded the children that they were in hiding. "We don't want to attract attention by walking up through the castle gates."

Thus that evening the elders rowed the boat beneath the shadow of Fallion's own palace, its dim lights gleaming through windows. On the east, the stately whitewashed towers seemed to rise straight up out of the water, and Fallion could see the sweeping alcoves built in at the waterline, lighted nooks with broad pools where in the past undines had swum like dolphins right up to the grand portico and held counsel with ancient kings.

Right now, there were no undines resting on the porch—only a few seals lying on the rocks while white gulls with gray backs floated upon the water nearby.

Fallion longed to row his boat into that shelter and head up the steps, but instead the boat rounded the ocean side of the island, into the deeper shadows, to the grungy dockside wharf where hundreds of fishing boats were moored. There the reek of fish guts and boiling crab mingled with salt spray.

In pitch-black, they moored up beneath a pier, and the whole family shambled through the night to an anonymous inn that Borenson assured everyone "is not as bad as it looks."

And he was right. The outside was dingy and dark, but inside the place was more homey. The scent of savory chicken dumplings, buttery rolls, and roast apples soon had the children's mouths watering. Rather than the nasty fishermen and whores and pirates that Fallion imagined might be in such a place, the common room was clean, and most of the patrons seemed to be decent shopkeepers who had brought their wives or friends out for a good meal.

As Borenson rented a room, Fallion looked around. A trio of minstrels played by the hearth. Beside each door and window an image of the Earth King stood—a man in green traveling robes with a deep hood, with leaves for his hair and beard.

Sage, Borenson's three-year-old daughter, saw the decorations and shouted, "Look, it's Hostenfest!"

Hostenfest was a month past, but the little ones had no sense of time and only wanted more presents and games.

"They put up the decorations in honor of the Earth King," Myrrima said, and Fallion knew that she must be right. The decorations were an invitation for his father's spirit to be welcome here.

Borenson secured a room, and just as the children were about to be whisked upstairs, the innkeeper, a fat old man, peered down at Fallion and roared, "Hey, what's that in your pocket?"

Fallion peered up. It seemed that everyone in the room had stopped talking, had turned to stare at him.

"Your pocket, boy? What's that squirming in your pocket?"

Fallion looked down. Humfrey was in the pocket of his tunic, rolling around. "It's just my pet ferrin," Fallion whispered.

"We don't let the likes of them in here," the innkeeper shouted, "the thieving vermin."

"He don't steal," Jaz said, offering up a patent lie. All ferrins stole. It was in their nature.

"We had one that stole bad," the innkeeper said. "Customers were losing gold and jewelry by the dozens. I sacked a couple of my girls, thinking it was them, until we caught the rascal." He nodded to a small crack in the corner where the cobbled floor met the stairs.

They'd killed the ferrin, of course, Fallion realized. Innkeepers were notorious for hating ferrins.

"Humfrey wouldn't steal," Fallion offered; on a sudden inspiration he went to the corner, knelt on the ale-stained stones of the floor, and pulled Humfrey from his pocket.

The ferrin looked about, blinking his huge dark eyes. Fallion thought for a moment. Ferrins didn't have a word for gold or jewels, not that Fallion knew of. Instead, they used a whistle that meant sunlight. So Fallion whistled and snarled, "Sunlight. Hunt sunlight."

The ferrin stood, looking up at the crowded inn, at the angry humans peering down at him. He became more fearful by the moment, his whiskers trembling, nose twitching as he scented for danger.

Borenson must have realized what Fallion was trying to do. "Here. Show him this." He held out a silver eagle in his palm, then let the coin glint in the air.

"Hunt sunlight," Fallion said again, shoving the ferrin toward the crack in the wall.

Humfrey sniffed at the hole, then shrieked in delight as he realized what Fallion wanted.

He lunged into the hole.

Fallion had seen what kind of damage a ferrin could do to a building. They loved to dig their holes under rocks and trees, and thus they were a nuisance to men folk, for they would dig under the foundations of houses and buildings, and at times a ferrin's tunnel would collapse, and a whole wall might come down.

It had happened at the cobbler's shop at Castle Coorm just last spring. A wall had collapsed, and Fallion had gone out to see the cobbler and his neighbors digging up the foundation to expose the ferrins' tunnels. There were a surprising number of small chambers, sometimes lined with stolen cobblestones to bolster them up. And inside them were piles of buttons and scraps of leather, old thimbles, and string and metal tacks. The cobbler was livid to see how much merchandise the ferrins had taken over the years.

"Five hundred shoe tacks!" he'd exclaimed over and over. "What would they do with so many? They don't make boots."

Fallion did not have to wait for more than a minute before Humfrey returned to the mouth of the den. In his mouth he carried a gold eagle, a coin that would easily pay for a week's lodging in the hostel.

Fallion took it from Humfrey and tossed it up to the innkeeper, who bit it to see if it was real, then roared with laughter. He probably wouldn't see a coin like that more than once a month.

He looked thoughtfully at Fallion, as if trying to decide, and said, "See what else he can find down there."

Fallion whistled the command, and Humfrey went rushing back into the hole.

Certainly the innkeeper had to know that a few coins were hidden down there, but like the cobbler, he didn't have any idea what it might amount to. And the cost of tearing out the walls and floors to go looking for them had probably seemed prohibitive. A ferrin might easily tunnel fifty yards in any direction, and an old warren, one that had been built up over years, might have dozens of branches.

It was several long minutes before Humfrey reappeared. This time he held an earring in his mouth, a long thing with several cheap beads dangling from it.

The innkeeper looked disappointed, but said, "Right. He can stay—if you have him do a little more poking around."

"Okay," Fallion agreed.

Then the whole "family" hurried upstairs, Borenson and Myrrima acting as the parents of a large brood, while Iome played the part of "grandmother."

Fallion had never been in such cramped quarters, but soon he found a corner and lay down upon a blanket while his mother lit a fire in the small hearth.

Myrrima put her children down for the night, while Borenson went down to the common room to hear the latest gossip and drink a few mugs of ale.

Humfrey found a hole in the wall, just under the bed, and disappeared. Every few minutes he would bring back a piece of ferrin treasure—a woman's comb, an ivory button, a tin coin. Each time he did, Fallion would give him a bit of food—a crust of bread or a dried date—as a reward.

Fallion watched the flames dance and wondered if the floor was comfortable enough to sleep on. He heard music rising through the floorboards, the steady beat of a drum, like a beating heart, along with shouts of laughter.

To his surprise, Rhianna, who had been lying next to Talon, picked up her blanket and pillow and came and lay down next to him.

"Can I sleep here next to the fire?" she asked. "I'm feeling cold right down to the bone."

"Okay," Fallion said, scooting back, so that she could catch the heat of the flames.

She settled in, leaning against him lightly, and Fallion studied her cheek, her chin. Her fierce blue eyes stared into the flames, lost in memory. Her right hand was under her pillow, and Fallion could see that her fingers clasped her dirk.

Of course, he realized. She'll probably never sleep well again. He couldn't quite imagine what she had been through, getting attacked by strengi-saats, lying half naked in the trees for days while the monsters waited for their babies to hatch and eat their way out.

We each have our own monsters to fight, Fallion thought, his mind going back to Asgaroth. He put his arm around Rhianna and scooted in closer, then whispered in her ear, "It's okay. I've got your back."

He wrapped his larger fist around hers, so that they held the dirk together.

Rhianna stifled a sob, nodded her thanks, and after a long while, when Rhianna was deep in slumber, somehow Fallion fell asleep.

It seemed like hours later when he woke to the creak of floorboards. It was Borenson, back from the common room. Fallion had thought that he had just stayed for the ale, but he now had a whispered conversation with Iome.

"We're in luck," Borenson said. "I found an outbound ship that is leaving in two days: the *Leviathan*. They're taking the southern route. I managed to book us passage."

Fallion was all ears. He had too much common sense to ask Borenson where they were going. It was a secret, and soldiers such as Borenson never revealed a secret. But that didn't mean that Fallion couldn't eavesdrop for clues.

"The southern route?" Iome asked. "Won't that take longer?"

"It will add a month or so to the voyage," Borenson said. "But we can't go by the northern route this time of year—ice storms."

Add a month or two to the voyage? Fallion wondered. They were sailing far away, leaving behind everything that he had ever known.

Iome nodded reluctantly. "You didn't pay too much, did you? We can't arouse suspicion."

"Just about the only people who take this voyage are outlaws," Borenson said. "The price is always high. But I managed to keep it down. I told him that I'd made too many enemies here in Mystarria, aroused too much jealousy. I have too many kids and too much to lose. And I told him that I'd grown tired of the constant fighting. He seemed fine with the story."

"And it's not far from the truth," Iome said. "I've seen it in you. You don't love battle the way that you used to. So, we take the southern route, trading ice storms for pirates. Well, I'll bet he's glad of the bargain. He'll want another sword if we're attacked."

Fallion lay quietly as Borenson grunted agreement, whispered good night, and slipped back out the door.

Rolling over as if in sleep, Fallion peered up at his mother. She sat in a rocking chair, slowly rocking, her silver hair falling loosely over her shoulders, a naked sword across her lap, its blade a brighter silver than her hair.

She's keeping watch, Fallion realized. His mother had so many endowments of stamina that she almost never slept. Instead, she sometimes just paced late at night, letting herself relive a memory or fall into a waking dream, in the way of powerful Runelords.

Iome saw him looking up; she laid the sword aside and smiled, motioning him to her with the wave of a hand.

Fallion picked up his blanket, then climbed into her lap and curled up as she pulled the blanket over him.

"Mother, you said that a locus could be anywhere, in anyone. Right?" Iome hesitated, and then nodded. "That means that it could be in the innkeeper downstairs, the one that doesn't like ferrins. Or it could be in one of the minstrels. Even in you, or me, and no one would know?"

Iome thought a moment before answering. "It isn't good for a child to ask such questions so late at night. Asgaroth's power is too frightening. But it is important that you know the truth. . . ."

She hesitated, and Fallion felt as if he were trying to pry some secret from her. She didn't want to tell him what he needed to know. He decided that he would find out, even if he had to discover the truth himself.

"And you said that it feeds on evil?"

"It seems that they make their homes in evil people," Iome said. "I'm not sure what it feeds on."

"And there is more than just one locus," Fallion asked. "Lots of them?"

Iome began to recognize a pattern. Fallion was asking questions as if he were a captain debriefing a scout. Where is the enemy? That was always the first question to ask. How great are their numbers? What arms do they bear?

"Yes, there is more than one. Some are big and powerful," Iome said, "like Asgaroth. Others are small and weak, little shadows of evil."

"How many are there?" Fallion asked. "If father could see them, he would have told you how many there are."

Iome peered at him, her dark eyes sparkling. "You're so much smarter than the rest of us. It's a good question, and I don't think your father even knew. But I don't think that there are many. Your father told me that not everyone who is cruel or greedy has one."

"So, in a way," Fallion said, "the loci are hunting us. Right?"

"I suppose," Iome said, wondering what he was getting at. It was the next question: what is the enemy target?

"So do they hunt like wolves? Or like hill lions?"

"I'm not even sure what you mean?"

"Wolves hunt in packs," Fallion explained. "They follow herds of elk or deer or sheep."

Fallion had seen some wolves once, from a distance. On an early morning ride with Waggit, he'd topped a ridge one morning to see a pack of hollow wolves chasing a stag. The stag was racing across a field, its head held high so that its magnificent antlers could be seen glinting in the sunlight, all golden and amber, for it was late spring and the stag's antlers were still in velvet.

A trio of wolves ran hot on the stag's trail, and Fallion's heart had hammered, hoping for the stag's escape.

But the stag had bounded down into a draw, through the green grass, past an old fallen log. And suddenly there was a flash of gray as a hollow wolf lurched to its feet, scattering dust as it lunged from the shadows to grab the stag by its haunches.

The huge wolf didn't just nip. It gripped the stag in its teeth and held on, throwing its weight against the noble stag so that its legs twisted out from under, and it fell in the grass, rolling, rolling, while wolves yipped and growled and clung on, one of them holding the stag's throat in its teeth, and then they began to feed even as the stag struggled, peering in a daze for some means of escape.

Fallion suppressed the image and tried to explain his question to his mother. He searched for an unfamiliar word but couldn't find it. "Wolves work together in the hunt, choose an animal and go after it. But a hill lion hunts alone."

Iome licked her lips; in her mind she had a vision of three knights charging toward her on the road south of Carris. She didn't want to frighten her son, but she didn't want to lie to him, either. "They hunt like wolves," she admitted.

So they've chosen me, Fallion realized. They're trying to cut me out from the herd. But why?

"What can I do about it?"

"Prepare," Iome said. "Be courageous, seek to do good. That's how you can fight back, I think," Iome continued. "We can even beat them, your father believed, if we are firm of purpose." This last was only her husband's hope. She had no idea how to beat them.

"You can't kill evil, can you?" Fallion asked.

"I don't think so," Iome said. "You can kill evil men, but I don't think that that kills evil. But you can fight evil. You can fight evil in yourself. You can drive all evil from you."

Fallion squeezed her hand, as if she had told him all that he wanted to know, but then he asked another question.

"Father fought a locus, didn't he? When he went to the Underworld?"

"Who told you that?" Iome asked. Few people had ever heard the full story, and Iome was the only person who had witnessed the battle.

"I thought of it on my own," Fallion said. "People say that reavers are evil. But Hearthmaster Waggit says that they're just animals. So there had to be something more, a crazy reaver or something. That's what I used to think. But then it just came to me: maybe the reaver had a locus."

"You're right. Reavers aren't evil," Iome said with a shudder. She had seen the monsters in their lairs, five times the weight of an elephant, enormous and cruel. She'd seen how they cut men in half for sport. But she'd also seen how they protected and cared for their own young. "But they aren't just animals, either. Don't make the mistake of thinking that they're as dumb as a dog or a bear. They're as intelligent as you or I. Some of them are brilliant. But they're also bloodthirsty, just like some wolves. It's in their nature."

"Was Asgaroth the one that Father fought?" Fallion scratched his chin and looked intently at his mother. Perhaps he thought that this was a vendetta.

"No," Iome said. "It was Asgaroth's master. She was called the One True Master of Evil."

Fallion nodded. "Hearthmaster Waggit says that she tried to take over the netherworld a long time ago. She tried to master the Runes of Creation, and the world shattered into a thousand thousand worlds."

Iome talked to him then for long minutes, telling him of his father's battles against the reavers—how their mages created giant runes that poisoned and polluted the land, and how his father had gone to the Underworld and battled the One True Master, and then afterward defeated Raj Ahten, who also was afflicted by a locus.

Fallion thought for a long moment, then asked, "If loci have to live inside people or animals, why do they want to destroy the world? Wouldn't they die, too?"

"I'm not sure they want to destroy the world," Iome said. "Some think that they just want to change it, make it warmer so that reavers can take our place. Perhaps the reavers make better hosts for the loci."

"Hearthmaster Waggit said that their spells would have destroyed the world, killed all of the plants, and then the animals would have died."

Iome had to admit that that seemed likely.

"And if he's right," Fallion said, "then the loci don't care if they live in us or not. What they really want is to destroy this world. But why?" Fallion asked.

What is the enemy's objective? Iome thought. It was a vital question that any commander would want answered.

Fallion went on, "If there are a thousand thousand shadow worlds in the heavens, why would they want to destroy this one?"

"I don't know," Iome said. "Maybe they want to destroy all of them."

"But the One True Master didn't try to *destroy* the world in the beginning. She just wanted to take over. And Myrrima said that if she could, she would bind the worlds back together under her control. . . ."

Iome had never considered this.

"Why destroy this world?" Fallion said.

"I don't know," Iome admitted.

Fallion wondered, "Maybe destroying this world is a key to getting the rest," he suggested. He peered deep into her eyes. "If we found one, found a locus, do you think we could ask it? Could we torture it and make it talk?"

The notion was so bizarre, Iome was tempted to laugh. But Fallion was in earnest. "Those who are afflicted by a locus," she explained, "aren't likely to tell you anything of worth. Most of the time, the host has no idea what he bears inside himself. Even if you could talk to the locus, would it tell you anything? Gaborn told me that one way to discern a locus is this: a person who hosts a locus can tell you a thousand lies much easier than he can utter a single truth."

Fallion peered up at his mother. "Yet there must be a way to fight them. They're afraid of me. I think they know that I can beat them. All that I have to do is find the right weapons."

Iome fell silent. She didn't want to speak about this anymore. Indeed, she had already said too much. She didn't want to burden her son with more knowledge, not now, not when he had just faced Asgaroth. He needed his rest, and she needed to give him hope.

"There's something that my own father told me when I was a child," Iome said. "It's important for you to understand. It's a secret. I never forgot it. In fact, more than anything else, it has helped shape who I've become."

"What?" Fallion asked.

Iome waited for the expectancy inside him to grow, then repeated from memory, "'The great heroes of the next age are already alive—the Fallions, the Erden Geborens. The child that you see suckling in its mother's arm may someday command an army. The toddler that sits in the street eating dirt may become a counselor to the king. The little girl drawing water from the well may be a powerful sorceress. The only thing that separates what they are from what they shall become is *time*, time and preparation. You must prepare to meet your destiny, whatever that may be. Study the right books. Practice the right weapons. Make the right friends. Become the right person.'"

"So," Fallion said, "I should begin now to build my army?" He looked across the room to where Jaz lay curled by the fire, and Talon cuddled with her baby sister Erin, and then his eyes settled on Rhianna, wrapped in a black blanket by the fire, her dirk in her hand.

"Yes," Iome said. "Now is the time to start. And I think that you'll have need of an army."

Iome was deeply aware that she would not live long enough to see him raise an army, to see Fallion become the hero that Gaborn had said he *could* be. She felt old and stretched, ready to break.

Her tone softened, and she tousled his hair. "I've done the best that I could for you. You've had the best teachers, the best guards to train you. We'll keep giving you all that we can, but others can't live your life for you. You must choose to blossom on your own."

Fallion thought about that. He'd lived in the shadow of the Earth King all of his life, and for as long as he could remember, he'd had dozens of trainers. Borenson had been there to train him in the battle-ax, while Hadissa taught him the arts of stealth and of poison. Waggit had filled his mind with knowledge of strategy and tactics and a dozen other topics. There had been Sir Coomb to teach him horsemanship and the ways of animals, and there were other teachers, a dozen others at least. So many times he had resented these people, but yes, he realized, his mother had given him all that she could, more than any child had a right to ask.

Even his father, who had seemingly gone to far places in the world without reason, had apparently been watching over him from afar.

But is it enough? he wondered.

"You're growing so fast," Iome said. "I think you must be a head taller than all of the other children your age. Sometimes I have to remind myself that you're still just a little boy."

"I'm not little," Fallion whispered. "I'll be ten in a month."

"You are to me," Iome said. "You're still my baby."

"If you want," Fallion said. "Just for a little while more."

Fallion lay against her, his head pillowed by her breast and cradled in her left arm, while his feet dangled over the edge of the rocking chair, too near the fire. He saw Humfrey slinking about the hearth, laying a bright button in the pile of treasures he'd brought up from below.

Fallion smiled.

It was rare that he had his mother all to himself. For as long as he could remember, his father had been out saving the world while Mother seemed busy ruling it. He looked forward to having her nearby, just being with her.

His hand was throbbing in pain, but he put it out of mind and fell asleep, imagining how someday he would drive a spear through Asgaroth's heart—a creature who was somehow a tall thin man with impossibly long white hair, leading an army of minions in black. In his dream Fallion was now the Earth King, and he imagined that he would slay evil once and for all, while the world applauded.

So he lay, his mother stroking his hair as if he were a puppy, content for the moment to be nothing more than a child.

ஐ 15 ௧

A PRIVATE RECEPTION

Military commanders all know the value of training soldiers while they are still young. After all, twist a child enough, and he shall remain twisted as an adult.

—Shadoath

Out on the open ocean, the Pirate Lord Shadoath rode on rough seas, her ship rising and falling beneath mountains of waves. Her crew was panicking, but she feared nothing, for she had laid heavy spells upon the ship. The masts would hold and the hull remain intact. They would find their way through the storm.

So she stood, lashed to the mast, grinning like a skull, enjoying the ride. Her crew was as frightened by her apparent madness as they were of the storm.

It was then that Asgaroth appeared to her in a dream.

"The torch-bearer has faced me," Asgaroth said, "and slain me." He was dispassionate about his death. He had taken countless bodies over the millennia and would take an endless array in the future. "In doing so, he drew upon his powers."

He showed her a brief vision of Fallion thrusting a torch into the face of a strengi-saat, the flames bursting like a flower in bloom; and then he showed her Fallion drawing back storm clouds, so that Asgaroth was limned in light, revealed to his mother's sight.

Shadoath smiled. Fear and rage. Fear and rage were the key to unleashing the child's powers, drawing him into her web.

"Does his every defeat taste like victory?" Shadoath asked.

"Of course," Asgaroth assured her. "And now he is fleeing—right into your hands."

Fear and rage. Fear and rage.

"Excellent," Shadoath said. "I will greet him with open arms."

ೞ 16 ೫

SENDINGS

It is said that the old stonewood trees of Landesfallen reach out with their vast roots, entwining one another, until the whole forest is held fast in one solid mass. Those who watch them say that the old stonewoods actually seem to feel other trees, to seek out younger saplings and hold them safe, so that they are not washed away in the storm. I am convinced that those who are born with old souls are like that, too. They sense the connections between us, and struggle to keep us safe.

—The Wizardess Averan

In his sleep, Fallion had a dream that came startlingly clear, more visceral than any dream he'd dreamed before. It was much like the vision he'd had when he picked up the owl pin, as if all of his life were a dream, and for the first time he tasted reality.

In his dream, he was walking along the side of a hill, in a little port-side market. The houses were strange, little rounded huts made of bamboo with bundles of dried grass forming the roofs. In the distance he heard the bawl of cattle. The road wound along a U-shaped bay, and on the far beach he could see a young girl with a switch, driving a pair of black water buffalo up a hill for the night.

He'd never seen a place like this before, and he marveled at every detail—at the odor of urine by the roadside, the muddy reek of rice paddies, the song that the girl sang in the distance in some tongue that he'd never heard before nor imagined.

As he ambled along the road, he passed between two huts, and in their shadow saw metal cages with black iron bars, thick and unyielding. Two of the cages were empty, their doors thrown open. But in the third squatted a girl a bit older than Fallion, with hair as dark and sleek as the night. She was pretty, all skin and bones, blossoming into someone beautiful. She kept her arms wrapped around her knees.

She peered into Fallion's eyes, and begged. "Help! They've got me in a cage. Please, set me free."

The vision faded, and Fallion woke, his heart pounding. He wasn't sure if it pounded because he was afraid, or because he was angry to see such a thing.

He had heard of Sendings before, and wondered if this was one. Usually Sendings only came between those who shared some deep connection—a family member or a close friend. When one received a Sending from a stranger, it was said that would come from the person who was to be of great import in your life.

But was it real, or just a dream? Fallion wondered. Is there really a girl held captive? Does she need me to free her?

He wasn't sure. Hearthmaster Waggit had told him that most dreams were just odd thoughts bound together by the imagination into what sometimes seemed a coherent story.

The girl could have been Rhianna. She had a similarly pretty face, but the hair and eyes were wrong. Rhianna had dark red hair and deep blue eyes, not black hair.

No, Fallion realized, the girl looks more like the picture of my mother, the one on her promise locket from when she was young and beautiful.

And the cage?

Rhianna is caged, too, he realized, seemingly caught in a maze of fear and pain.

Was I dreaming about her?

And if so, why did it feel like a Sending?

At almost that instant, he heard Rhianna whimper, wrapped there in her blanket by the fire.

Nightmares. She was having a bad dream.

That's all that it was, Fallion told himself. I must have heard her cry out in her sleep, and that's what made me dream like this. . . .

Outside the hostel, a driving wind blew over the sea, thundering over rough waves, lashing them to whitecaps.

The wind rode into the bay, veering this way and that, like a starling that has lost direction in a storm.

It hit the coastline, whistled among the pilings of the pier, and then rose up into the streets, floating over cobblestones, exploring dark shanties.

At one loud inn, where raucous laughter competed with pipes and the joyous shrieks of whores, a pair of sailors opened a swinging door. The wind rode in on their heels.

In a dark corner, at a round table littered with empty ale mugs, sat a man wide of girth, a man with a black beard streaked with gray, and curly hair that fell to his shoulders. His bleary eyes stared at nothing, but suddenly came awake when he felt the questing wind on the nape of his neck.

Captain Stalker came awake. He recognized the two men who had just entered the inn, and as he did so, he kicked back a stool, inviting them to his table.

His table. Stalker didn't own it, except when he was in port twice a year. On those days the inn, with its raucous noise and the reek of fishermen, became his court, while this stool became his throne.

Even lords flocked to his table at those times, dainty men who held perfumed kerchiefs to their noses in disgust. Wheedling little barons would beg to invest in his shipping enterprise, while bright merchants with an eye on profit margins would seek to sell him goods on consignment.

He kept his books on the table, right there by the mugs. He had plenty of ale stains on the parchment.

Though he was none too tidy, Captain Stalker was a careful man. He was used to testing the wind for signs of a storm, watching breakers for hidden reefs. He ran a tight ship, a profitable ship.

He was, in fact, moderately wealthy, though his rumpled clothes and windblown hair suggested otherwise.

Right now, he smelled a storm coming.

It had not been more than a couple of hours since Sir Borenson had booked passage, an aging force soldier straight from the king's court. With the death of the Earth King it was only to be expected that some might flee Mystarria—lords who knew that they would be out of favor under the new administration.

But much that Borenson had said raised warning flags. The man was notorious. Everyone in Mystarria knew him by name, and four men at the inn knew his face. He'd been the Earth King's personal guard, and had taken the task of guarding his sons.

And now he was fleeing the country with his wife and children, only hours after some dark character had come offering a reward for information on folks just like him.

"There may be two boys," the fellow had said. "Both of them with black hair and dark complexions—like half-breeds from Indhopal."

It didn't take the brains of a barnacle to know who he was after. The princes of Mystarria were born to a half-breed from Indhopal—Queen Iome Sylvarresta Orden.

The reward for "information" was substantial.

The two sailors threw themselves down on stools. One whistled for a couple of fresh mugs, and a fat mistress brought a pair.

Both sailors leaned forward, smiles plastered across their faces, and eyed Captain Stalker.

"Well?" he asked. He knew that the word was good. He could see it in the men's bearing, their desire to make him dig the news out of them.

"It's 'em," one of the sailors, Steersman Endo, said with a sly smile. "We 'eard the news over by the palace."

Endo was a wiry little man with the albino skin and cinnabar-colored hair of an Inkarran. Like most Inkarrans, he couldn't bear sunlight, and so headed Stalker's night crew.

"There was a battle last night, just west of 'ere. Soon as the Earth King croaked, someone attacked the Queen's Castle up at Coorm, caught everyone nappin'. So the queen squids off with 'er boys, headin' east to 'er palace at the Courts of Tide. But she never makes it. She just disappears."

Was it possible? Captain Stalker wondered. Was the queen really taking her children into exile?

Possibly. There was some logic to it. The queen had aged prematurely, having taken so much metabolism. She'd be dead in a year or two, and the children weren't ready to lead. She'd want to keep them safe.

And history was against her. There had been an Earth King once before, ages past, a man named Erden Geboren.

Like Gaborn Val Orden, he rose to power precipitously, and folks adored him. He was great at killing reavers, but like Gaborn, he could hardly bear to kill a man.

And when his own sister turned against him, he seemed to have just died, to have passed away from the lack of will to fight.

But Stalker knew something that few others did. There was the matter of Erden Geboren's family, his children.

Many folks wanted to make his eldest son the next king. Whole nations rose up in his support, demanding it.

But the cries were short-lived. In fact, the idea died out within a week—when Erden Geboren's children were found slaughtered in their beds.

Iome would surely be familiar with the tale. And she would have learned from it.

"We're going to make a lot of money," one of the sailors, a deckhand named Blythe, said. "Shall I go find the feller what was lookin' for 'em?"

Captain Stalker whetted his lips, thought for a long moment. "No," he said at last.

"There's fifty gold eagles reward!" Blythe objected.

"Fifty gold eagles?" Stalker asked. "That's only twenty-five for each prince. How many gold eagles do you think that the Court here spends a year, buildin' roads and buyin' armor and repairin' castle walls?"

Blythe shrugged.

"Millions," Stalker said, the word ending as a hiss. "Millions."

Blythe couldn't imagine millions. Fifty gold eagles was more than he would make in twenty years as a deckhand. "But . . . but we could get—"

Stalker needed to make him see the bigger picture. "What do you think will 'appen to them boys?" Captain Stalker asked. "What do you think that feller is gonna do—bugger 'em? Slit their throats? No, he has something else in mind."

Blythe clenched his fists impatiently. He was a strong man, used to climbing the rigging and furling sails, hard work by any measure.

Captain Stalker saw the anger building. "Be patient," Stalker said, reaching to his coin purse. He fumbled through a couple of silver eagles, decided that only gold might win the man's attention for a bit. He threw four gold eagles on the table. "Be patient."

"Patient for what?" Blythe demanded, and the captain realized that it wasn't just money he was after. There was a hunger in the man's face, an intensity common to craven men. He hoped to see the children die.

"Think of it," Stalker said. "We hold the children a bit, and what's this feller that wants 'em goin' to do?"

Blythe shrugged.

"Raise the price, that's what. Not fifty gold eagles. Not five 'undred. Five hundred thousand, that's what I figure they're worth—minimum!"

Captain Stalker had an uncommonly good eye for profit. Everyone knew that. Even Blythe, who knew little but pain and sunburn and the stiff wind on his face, knew that. It's what made the *Leviathan* such a successful ship.

Blythe looked up at him hopefully. "What's my cut goin' to be?"

Captain Stalker eyed him critically. He wasn't a generous man, but he decided that right now he couldn't be stingy. "Five thousand."

Blythe considered. It wasn't equal shares, but it was a fortune. Blood flushed to his cheeks. His pale eyes glowed with undisguised lust. "Coooo . . ." he whispered.

Endo leaned back on his stool and took a swig from his mug, sealing the deal.

"Five thousand," Blythe said giddily. "We're goin' to be rich!" He squirmed on his stool, peered up at his accomplices as if inviting them to celebrate.

"One thing," Captain Stalker said, and he leaned close to Blythe to let the sailor see that he was serious. "You speak a word about this to anyone, and I will personally cut your throat and use your tongue for fish bait."

ಐ 17 ಔ

SMALL ARMIES, SMALL VICTORIES

Children look at the world with an unjaded eye, and so see everything.

—*The Wizard Binnesman*

Iome surprised herself by sleeping. She didn't often sleep. She woke in the morning to the creak of the door coming open.

Sir Borenson entered softly, tiptoeing to the hearth to stir up the embers and get a fire lit.

The children were all asleep, and Fallion still lay in Iome's lap. She drew the blanket back over him and hugged him, regretting that she had not held him more often.

"Lots of folks awake down in the common room," Borenson whispered. "Lots of rumors flying. Everyone in the city has heard how Asgaroth attacked Castle Coorm, and how the queen somehow took his life in single combat."

Iome grinned, even though the news disturbed her. "All of these years we've been hiring spies when we might as well have just resorted to the nearest inn."

"Common folk know an uncommon lot," Borenson quoted an old proverb. He grinned. "Rumor says that the queen is holed up at the Courts of Tide. And to prove it, the queen's flag is flying, to show that she is in residence."

Someone is thinking, Iome realized. Was it Chancellor Westhaven who raised the queen's flag?

"Maybe that's what drew the assassins last night," Borenson continued. "A milkmaid who delivered to the palace this morning swears that she saw thirty-nine bodies laid out on the greens: all of them Inkarrans."

Iome bit her lower lip, imagined the Inkarrans with their bone white skin and silver hair, their strange breastplates and short spears. Inkarran assassins? It would have been a bitter fight, for the white-skinned Inkarrans could see perfectly well in the darkest night.

What worried her more was the sheer number. They'd never made an assault in such force before.

"We'll have to spend the next couple of days inside," Iome said. Though there was little danger from more Inkarrans for the next few days, it seemed likely that other assassins would be watching the court.

"My thoughts exactly. Myrrima can bring the meals in. She can tell our hosts that we've taken sick."

So that was the plan.

They all stayed inside the small room, and Iome spent the day playing child's games—Village Idiot and Three Pegs. Borenson showed the children how to tie some sailor's knots—the thumb knot, the bowline, the rolling hitch and clove hitch—and described in glowing terms what life would be like aboard the *Leviathan*, though he avoided telling anyone of its destination.

Jaz had the good sense to ask if they would see pirates or sea monsters on the voyage, and Borenson assured him that they'd see both, but most likely only from a distance.

Such news disappointed Jaz, who certainly was the kind of boy who would want to catch his own sea monster and keep it in a watering trough.

Fallion remained thoughtful for much of the morning, and held aloof from the children's games.

What his mother had told him last night affected him deeply. He felt that he needed to prepare, and though others had groomed him all of his life, now Fallion considered his own future.

I must get ready, he thought. I must build my army. But why would anyone want to follow me?

He thought of the soldiers he knew, the powerful lords and captains that he liked. They each had qualities that he admired: courage, fortitude, discipline, faith in themselves and in their men.

Am I like that? he wondered. If I work hard, can I be the kind of person that others look up to?

Fallion had known many great lords, men who had taken endowments of brawn so that they had the strength of five men, and endowments of wit so that they had the intelligence of three. He'd seen Anders who had taken endowments of glamour so that his face seemed to shine like the sun. Even Myrrima had taken enough glamour from others so that, despite her age, she remained seductive. He'd heard men with endowments of Voice speak in debates, enthralling audiences.

Fallion was nothing like them.

But I can be, he told himself. I have the forcibles that I need to become that kind of man.

And what of my warriors? He looked at the children playing on the floor: Jaz, Rhianna, Talon, Draken, Sage. Even little Erin still in her diaper.

Iome had told him that greatness could be found in the coming generations.

So it was with some embarrassment that he finally got up the courage to speak to the children. He didn't know how to ask it, so he just broke in on a game and asked, "Do you want to join my army?"

All of the children stared up at him for a moment, giving him blank looks.

"No," Talon answered. "We're playing Rope a Horse."

Sage, who at three never wanted to be left out of anything, blurted, "I'll play dolls with you. Want to play dolls?"

Fallion shook his head. "This is a real army. I'm not talking about playing."

"Who are you going to fight?" Rhianna asked.

"The strengi-saats," Fallion said, "and Asgaroth, and anyone like him."

Nearly all of the children backed away. Talon was maybe the best fighter that Fallion knew, for a seven-year-old. Her father had been training her for years. But she shook her head demurely and looked down at the floor. "I don't want to fight them."

Jaz, Draken, and the other children looked as if they were frightened witless. But Rhianna, the oldest of them, peered up at him, her fierce blue eyes growing impossibly more savage, and said through tight lips, "I'll fight beside you."

"You will?" Fallion asked.

She nodded slowly, surely. There was no doubt in her voice, no hesitation. She understood that this was a serious endeavor. "You saved my life. I'll fight for you anytime, anyplace."

"Good," Fallion said. "As soon as we get on the ship, we start training." He reached out, and the two shook hands at the wrist, sealing the bargain.

For the rest of the afternoon, Fallion felt as if he were floating on air. He had started his army.

Iome watched the exchange, gratified by the seriousness of their tone, but pained by it as well. She didn't want her son to grow up so quickly.

More than that, she worried that she could offer little more in the way of guidance. She had told him to prepare, to begin building his army. But how could a nine-year-old prepare?

She had no answers for him. The truth was, she had never found them for herself.

Once, an hour later, while the rest of the children were playing, Fallion came up and asked his mother, "Do you think you can kill a locus?"

Iome looked to make certain that the others didn't overhear. The children were huddled in a corner, giggling and snorting as they played Village Idiot, a memory game where a child said, "The village idiot went to the fair, but he forgot to take his . . ." and then he would add something bizarre, such as his duck or his pants or his eyes, bringing giggles and snorts of laughter. Each child in the circle then took a turn, adding something new to the list of things that the village idiot forgot—his codpiece, his bowels, his pretty pink pig—until the list became so unwieldy that the children began to forget. When a child messed up, the others would all chime, "You're the village idiot!" and then keep going until only one child remained.

They were deep in play. "I don't think you can kill a locus," Iome said. Then she told him something that she'd never told anyone. "Your father fought one, as you guessed last night. He fought it, and he killed the reaver that housed it, but he could not kill the locus inside."

"So, a locus is like a wight?" Fallion said. "It lives in a body, like a spirit?"

He was grappling with mysteries, and Iome didn't have much in the way of real answers. "I imagine that it's something like a spirit."

"Then . . . cold iron should pierce it."

Myrrima, who had been kneeling on the floor, repacking their clothes, looked up. "I wouldn't recommend that."

Borenson chuckled and said, "She killed a wight once, but it almost killed her back. Froze her arm as stiff as a board."

Fallion glanced at the children to see if they still were playing. The rest of them were giggling. Little Sage was rolling on the floor with laughter, but Rhianna held her back stiffly, listening for all she was worth.

Fallion asked a question now that made him uncomfortable. "So Father couldn't kill the locus. Is that why he was always so sad?"

Borenson glanced away uncomfortably.

"You could see that?" Iome asked.

"Even when he smiled," Fallion said. "It was there behind his eyes."

Iome nodded. Now is the time for truth, she thought. She bit her lip, and said, "Your father traded his life in order to save his people. He traded being a father for being the Earth King. He loved you. I don't think you can understand how much he loved you, not until the day that you become a father yourself. And just looking at you . . . pained him."

"He loved you boys, he did," Borenson agreed. "But he gave too much of himself, until there was nothing left."

"Sometimes," Myrrima said, "I think that he thought he was a failure."

"A failure?" Fallion asked. "But he was the greatest king who ever lived!" Everyone that Fallion had ever met spoke of his father with reverence.

"True," Borenson said, "he saved the world in its hour of need, but he traded everything for that one moment.

"And in the years after, he managed to leave a legacy of peace and prosperity that were unmatched. But I think that he wanted so much more for us. He knew that as soon as he died, everything would collapse. It would all come down around us."

"What more could he want?" Fallion asked.

"He wanted joy," Iome said. "He wanted his people to have joy. He could look into the heart of a good man, a fine child, and see all of the decency inside, and he wanted them to have the happiness that they deserved. But he couldn't give them that. You can't make another person happy, even when they deserve to be."

Iome pierced him with a gaze and said, "Most of all, it pained him that he had taken so many endowments. Hundreds of people gave him their brawn, grace, stamina, wit, and sight. They did it for the love of their families, for the love of their country. But each of them suffered for it, and your father never forgave himself."

"He could have killed himself," Fallion said. "That way, he would have given the endowments back to all of those people." Fallion felt ashamed to even suggest the idea. It made it sound as if his father had been grasping, selfish. Fallion knew that that wasn't the case.

"Would you have wanted that for him?" Iome asked.

Fallion shook his head no.

"Nor would I," his mother said. "I'm sure he thought of it, too. He traded his virtue for power. And once he had that power, he held on to it until the last, used it to try to make the world more livable not for himself, but for you and me and everyone else."

"It must have been a hard choice," Fallion said, feeling somehow disappointed in his father. Surely there must have been a better way.

Borenson peered at Fallion. "The embrace of the forcible comes at a high price. Your father knew that. He took endowments, but he never hungered for them."

"Fallion," Iome said. "There's something that you should know. Your father never chose to take all of those endowments. He was a decent man, and would have faced the reavers with nothing more than his Earth Powers. But I persuaded him otherwise. I talked him into taking a few endowments, and when he went to fight in the Underworld, I had the facilitators at Castle Sylvarresta vector more endowments to him, against his will. I compromised his principles so that he could beat the reavers. And I didn't do it alone. The people of Heredon did it with me. We turned him into the world's champion. We made a sacrifice of him, because he was too honorable to do it himself." Iome choked upon these last words, for in making a sacrifice of him, she'd lost the love of her life.

"If I'm to be a king," Fallion said, "don't I have to take endowments, too?"

Borenson cut in, saying, "Not necessarily. When I was a lad, I thought it would be a grand thing to be a Runelord, to carry a warhammer and have the strength of five men, the speed of three. There was nothing in the world that I wanted more, and in time I won that honor. But it has been as much a curse to me, Fallion, as it was to your father. I killed more than two thousand men in the service of my lord. But if I could turn back time, become a child like you, I'd put my hand to the plow and never hope for the touch of the forcible again."

Fallion didn't know what to say to that. The folks at Castle Coorm had both respected and feared Borenson. Fallion had even suspected that Borenson carried some dark secret. But he was stunned to hear how many men Borenson had killed.

"I don't understand," Fallion said. "How am I to be a king? How can I protect others from Asgaroth?"

"You don't need forcibles to lead," Myrrima said. "A man can lead with wisdom and compassion without them. Kings have done it before. Even in recent history, some lords have chosen to live without them. You may consider that path."

"And remember," Borenson said, "no weapon forged by man can destroy a locus. In time, circumstances may force you to take endowments. But don't be in a hurry to make the same mistakes that I have made."

That evening, as the children sought out their beds, Borenson went down to the common room to learn the latest news. He could feel an electric intensity to the air, the kind that portends a storm. But it was not the weather that caused it. It was the day's news.

Last night there had been an attack on the palace. Now there was talk of cities falling in the far west, a full-fledged war. Queen Lowicker of Beldinook was on a rampage.

So it was that Borenson found himself sitting on a stool, drinking strong ale, while a minstrel shouted out a lively jig and a pair of sailors danced on a table behind him, when all of a sudden he heard a sound that made his blood freeze.

At a stool nearby, just down the bar, he heard a hissing whisper. "Two boys? Both of them have dark hair, like half-breeds."

Borenson peered out of the corner of his eye. The questioner was a scabrous little fellow, as if he suffered from gut worms, with a hunched back and milky eyes. He was leaning up to another patron of the inn, whispering into the fellow's ear.

"Nah," the patron answered in a deeper tone.

"You sure?" the scurvy fellow asked. "They could be in this very inn. Would 'ave stumbled in last night. There's gold for ya, if we find 'em."

The scurvy fellow turned to Borenson with a questioning stare. "'Ave you seen a pair of young lads?"

"About nine years old?" Borenson asked. "Dressed like lordlings?"

The milky eyes peered up at him and the sailor's face split into a grin. "Could be . . ." he said eagerly. "Could be 'em."

Borenson gave a puzzled look. "It's odd that you ask. I saw some boys like that at my sister's house, not two hours ago. They 'ad an old woman with 'em, their granddame."

The excitement in the fellow's eyes turned to a frenzy. "Your sister's 'ouse?"

"She takes in boarders. She doesn't run an inn, really. More of a private house."

The fellow nodded sagely, stroked his scraggly beard.

"Where? Where can I find this 'ouse?"

Borenson licked his lips, drained his mug, and planted it meaningfully on the table. "I'm a poor man, with a poor memory."

The scurvy fellow shifted his gaze to the left, then to the right. "We best continue our negotiations in more private like."

The little fellow turned, stumbled through the crowd as if half drunk, and Borenson fixed his eye on the back of the fellow's long coat and followed him out the door.

The street was dark, with only a crescent moon peering through wisps of clouds, while a low fog was creeping up from the sea. The fellow headed around a back corner, and Borenson followed him down to the pier.

It was lonely and quiet outside, and as the scurvy fellow reached the pier, even that place did not seem secluded enough for him. He retreated to the shadows beneath a fishmonger's hut, and climbed down upon some rocks covered with strands of red kelp. In the pale light, Borenson could see blue-white crabs scrounging for tidbits among the kelp, could hear the clicking sounds of their pincers, the water gurgling from their mouths and joints, the scrapes of tiny feet on rocks.

"There's gold in it for ya, sure," the scurvy fellow whispered when they were alone, "that is, if they're the ones."

"How much gold?" Borenson said. "I mean, I wouldn't want to see anyone get hurt—especially my sister." He feigned being a man of conscience, but a man who could be tempted. "So how much gold?"

The little fellow licked his lips. Borenson felt sure that he had a set price, but he was wondering how much he could shave off of it, pocket for himself. "Twenty gold eagles," the fellow said. It was a small fortune.

"Pshaawww," Borenson said. "You can pay better than that for a pair of fat princelings."

The fellow looked up, and in the moonlight his milky eyes looked strange, like orbs of marble.

"Yes, I figured out who they are," Borenson said. "My sister once served as a maid in King Orden's household. So it's no wonder that they came to her, not after what happened last night."

"Thirty, thirty gold eagles," the scurvy fellow hissed. "All right?"

"All right," Borenson said. Before the fellow could blink, Borenson swung a punch for the little man's ribs, landing the blow with all of his might. Borenson wasn't as powerful as he had once been. His endowments were gone, and he had nothing but his own strength nowadays. Nine years ago, he'd have killed a man with that blow.

Now he just heard a few ribs snap, and the fellow went down with a grunt, holding his gut, trying to suck air. Borenson saw him reach for a dagger, and jumped on his right arm, snapping it like a twig.

The little fellow lay on the kelp, moaning while the crabs clicked and scuttled aside.

"Now," Borenson said as he leaned over the sailor and pinned his arms. "Let's discuss a new bargain. Tell me who sent you, and I'll let you live."

Borenson wrestled the scurvy fellow's arms behind his back, then took the sailor's own dagger from its sheath and laid the naked blade to his neck.

"A big feller," the sailor said, and he began to sob. "White hair, with a black long coat. I 'eard someone say 'e's a captain of his own ship. Maybe, maybe even a pirate lord from the far side."

"His name," Borenson said, digging the knife closer. He twisted the broken arm, eliciting more sobs. "Tell me his name."

"I 'eard tell that his name is Callamon."

Borenson held his breath a moment, taking that in. Fortunately, this Callamon was not on the ship that they'd be taking.

Borenson knew that he couldn't leave the sailor alive. He'd go running to the enemy, telling what he'd found.

Time and time it came down to this. Borenson was a killer, a hired killer.

He was good at it, even though it pained him.

"Thank you," Borenson said reluctantly. "I'm sorry." He bashed the little man's skull with the pommel of his dagger, stunning him, and then slit the fellow's throat from ear to ear, giving him a clean death, which was the most that Borenson could allow.

He hurled the body into the sea as food for the crabs.

The fare at the inn was uncommonly good, and dinner that night for the "sick guests" was spectacular—roast ducklings stuffed with rice and dates, savory pies, honey rolls, and pudding spiced with lemon rind.

When it was done, everyone felt overstuffed, and most of the children fell asleep almost instantly.

Myrrima tidied up, packing for the trip tomorrow. And while Borenson was away, Fallion lay awake beside the fire, watching flames flicker and dance before his eyes. Iome noticed how he hugged Rhianna close, as he had the night before, trying to comfort her. She smiled at his innocence.

Iome felt fulfilled after a day of just playing with her children, eating a fine meal. She had not had a great deal of time to spend with her sons in the past few years, and she had forgotten how refreshing it could be.

Borenson came to the room and found Iome and his wife awake. As he stirred the fire, he gave them the least worrisome of his news: Beldinook had attacked from the north, taking Castle Carris.

It made sense, Iome realized. Paldane had resided in Carris, and she had already seen him impaled on a stick. So the news was stale.

"But there is more important news," Borenson said. "I met a man down in the common room, a bounty hunter. He was searching for news of young boys, princely young men. He was hired by a ship's captain named Callamon."

Iome took this in. "Callamon. I've heard of him. He's a pirate of some repute."

There was no way that a pirate could be looking for them, Iome knew. He wouldn't have had time to gain the intelligence that he needed. Unless, perhaps . . . he was infested by a locus.

This was unsettling news.

Myrrima excused herself to go to the privy out back.

"I'm tired," Iome said to Borenson's back after hearing his report. "Will you keep watch? I haven't slept in so, so long."

"Of course." Borenson glanced back up at her, his head half turned, the fire limning his beard, red streaked with silver. "Are you well?"

Iome smiled. He thinks I'm going to die, she realized. And maybe he is right.

The elderly often feel well just before they die, and Iome realized now that for the entire day she had gone without any of the twinges or aches that come with aging. Indeed, she had not felt so good for many, many months.

Like an apple tree, that blooms best when it blooms its last.

"I just want to go to sleep," Iome said. "I want to hold my boys."

She climbed down from her rocking chair and curled up on the floor with Jaz and Fallion, pulling a single blanket up to cover all three.

Borenson got up from the fire, put a hand on her shoulder, and whispered, "Good night, milady."

"Good-bye," she said. "I think that this is good-bye. But I'm ready for it. Life can be very . . . tiring."

"Rest well," Borenson said.

They did not talk of the boys. Iome wanted to ask him to raise them as his own but she already knew that he would.

She thought, It will be ample repayment for the killing of my father.

She dared not say those words aloud. Borenson had repaid her many times. He was a good servant, a faithful friend.

She lay for a long time, measuring her moments. Does the joy I felt outweigh the pain? she wondered.

She'd given her life in the service of others. She'd lost her husband, and now was going to lose her children.

That didn't seem a fair bargain. But the moments of joy that had come were intense and beautiful: her girlhood friendships with Chemoise and Myrrima, her marriage to Gaborn, and the brightest moments, the births of her sons.

Is my life a tragedy, she wondered, or a triumph?

Her Days had said that she would write that Iome's was a life well lived. But she had given away all that she loved in an effort to win peace and freedom for her people.

So it was neither a tragedy nor a triumph, Iome told herself. It was only a trade.

I'll warn the boys, she told herself in a fit of sudden irrationality. I'll warn them in the morning not to trade away the best parts of their lives.

But she remembered that she had already warned Fallion, over and over again.

He's a smart boy, she told herself. Smarter than I was at his age. He will do well.

Sleep came, deep and restful, until in the night she was wakened by a horn that blew so loud it made her heart clench in her chest.

She clutched at her heart, and opened her eyes to a dawn so bright that she had to squint.

Where am I? she wondered. Am I staring into the sun?

But the light did not hurt her eyes. On the contrary, it was warm and inviting, and grew brighter and brighter. As her eyes became accustomed, she heard the horn a second time, a distant wail, followed by pounding hooves, so much like a beating heart.

Gaborn came out of the light. He was young and smiling, his hair tousled. He wore a riding cloak of green, and tall black boots, and his dark blue eyes sparkled like sapphires.

"Come, my love," he whispered. "The moon is up and the Hunt is under way, and a place is prepared for you."

He beckoned with his hand. Iome saw a horse not far off, a gray mare with a black mane. It was saddled, bridled, and groomed. Its mane and tail were plaited. It was the most beautiful mount, and she longed to ride.

She took a few steps, and a worry made her halt. "What of the boys?"

"Our time is now," Gaborn said. "Theirs will come soon enough."

It was as if his words were a balm, and Iome suddenly cast aside all worries. Our time is now, she thought, and swung up easily into the saddle and nudged her mount forward, until she was at Gaborn's side.

He reached out and she took his hand; her flesh was young and smooth, as it had been when they first met.

He squeezed her hand, leaned toward her, and she into him, and she kissed him, long and slow. His breath smelled earthy and sweet, and her heart hammered at the touch of his lips. For long minutes, he cradled her head in his palm, and she kissed him perhaps for the very first time without a worry in the world.

When he leaned back, she whispered, "I'm sorry."

"Leave it behind," Gaborn whispered. "Leave your sorrows with your flesh."

"I'm sorry that I did not spend more time with you."

"Here," Gaborn said, "an eternity is but a moment, and if you want, we can spend an endless string of them together."

Iome looked around now, and could see the forest. The oak leaves were as ruddy gold as coals in a forge; every blade of grass seemed as white as fire.

The horn blew again, and she heard the hosts of the dead, riding ahead of them, a thundering horde.

Iome leaned her head back and laughed, happy to be at Gaborn's side.

In the night, Borenson sat in the rocking chair, a naked sword across his lap.

Once he heard the floorboards creak outside his door as someone came stealthily to it. The person stood outside for a long time, as if listening, and Borenson thought for sure, We have been found.

But the fellow sniffed loudly, then ambled down the hall to another room, his feet unsteady from too much drink.

And in the pale glow of the coals from the fireplace, Borenson saw Iome's frail body suddenly tremble.

He heard the death rattle out from her throat, and the room suddenly went cold, a feeling that he had long associated with the presence of spirits.

He did not see her shade depart, did not see who had come to escort her into the beyond, but he knew.

"Farewell, my king, my queen," he whispered, "till we are joined in the Hunt."

He waited for several long minutes, just listening to the sounds from the common room. The minstrels had gone silent an hour ago, and he could only hear one pair of boots creaking across the wooden floor down there.

I would like to join whoever is down there, Borenson thought, and raise a mug of ale.

He went to Iome's body. She was smiling, a smile of perfect contentment, but she had no pulse, and she had quit breathing. In a while, she would begin to grow cold.

Borenson unwrapped Iome's arms from around her sons. He tried not to wake them as he lifted her small frame.

Such a small body, he thought, to have held such an enormous life.

He laid it by the fire, and draped it with his own blanket.

There would be time enough in the morning to let the boys know that their mother had died.

They would have their whole lives to mourn.

১ষ 18 ෨

THE LEVIATHAN

Most men live their lives as if they were adrift at sea.

—*Captain Stalker*

When he woke that morning and found the shrouded body of his mother lying before the fire, Fallion felt numb. He sat up and rubbed his eyes, peered at the blanket so innocently draped over her, and waited an eternity for her chest to rise and fall again.

But after a dozen heartbeats, he knew that it was useless. "I'm sorry," he whispered.

Myrrima sat in the rocking chair above him, the sword across her lap, keeping guard, and merely watched Fallion for a moment.

Borenson was gone: the other children still slept.

Myrrima leaned forward, forcing a smile, and whispered, "Sorry for what?"

"It's my fault that she's dead," Fallion whispered.

"How can you think that?"

Fallion wasn't sure. He felt very sad, very lonely and hurt, and somehow he felt that it was his fault. "We wore her out. The flight through the forest, the battle on the river, they were too much for her."

"Life wears us all out," Myrrima said. "Your mother sat on a boat for a day, which is as easy as breathing for a Runelord with her powers. And the battle? She hurled a sword. That's not hard work, not hard at all. No, it's not your fault. We all pass on when our time comes. And it was her time.

"Come here," Myrrima said, and she leaned down over the side of the chair and with one hand raised the blanket so that Fallion could see his mother's face. It was pale, lifeless, with a tint of blue to her upturned lips. "See that smile? She died at peace, beside the two boys that she loved most in this world. She'd want you to be happy, too, be happy for her. She's with your father now."

And the tears came. Fallion tried to hold them back, but the tears came, along with huge wracking sobs.

"Shhhh . . ." Myrrima whispered. "We've got to get ready to go. Would you like something to eat? I can go down and bring you something."

Fallion swiped his eyes. He had thought that Borenson was getting breakfast from the common room. "Won't Borenson bring it?"

Myrrima shook her head. "He's taking a note to the palace, telling them where to find your mother."

"Oh, okay," Fallion said.

Myrrima gave him a hug, and crept out through the door. As she closed it, she bowed her head in wonder.

It had been seven years ago that the Earth King had approached Myrrima and her husband, asking them to take care of his children. He'd known that both he and his wife were destined to die young.

Myrrima had always known that it would come to this. She recalled Gaborn's exact words. He had been standing in the kitchen, holding young Fallion in the crook of his arm. "My son will be greater than me," Gaborn had warned in an ominous tone. "He will have a greater capacity to do good, and a greater capacity to do evil. You must nurture the good in him, lest the whole world suffer."

Greater than the Earth King. Myrrima could not imagine such a thing. Yet she was a servant of Water, and she had to admit, she felt something in Fallion's presence, a force that other children did not have.

Straightening her back, Myrrima hurried downstairs.

Fallion remained alone in the room with the sleeping children, and with his dead mother. He stared at her, feeling numb inside.

Everything seemed so important suddenly, every moment so deliberate, every breath so imbued with life.

To Fallion it seemed that death was a miracle. Last night his mother had been warm and alive, telling stories and dreaming of the future. Now the spirit had fled and her body was as empty and as lifeless as a loaf of bread.

Not death, he told himself. Life is the miracle. The very act of living couldn't be more wondrous if I stretched out my arms and found that I could fly.

He went and lay by his mother, put a hand over her cold flesh, hugging her one last time.

Rhianna woke a moment later. She sat up and rubbed her eyes as she studied the shrouded body.

Fallion was lying there, weeping softly, trying not to be seen or heard. She crawled over to him. She straddled him, placing one hand on the floor on each side of his shoulders, then took his face in her hands, leaned down, and gave him a fierce kiss on the lips. She held it for a long moment, then looked at him appraisingly, to see if he liked it.

Fallion stared up at her, unsure what to do or say.

It didn't matter. At that moment, she imagined that she was in love with him. She'd never kissed a boy before. She wasn't sure whether she had done it right. But it felt good. Her heart had hammered when her lips touched his, and she imagined that someday she would marry him.

She whispered, "Now we're both orphans."

Fallion felt embarrassed by the show of affection. But he heard real pain in her voice, so he hugged her back timidly. Somehow he knew that she needed him to hug her, perhaps even forcefully, as if he could squeeze the pain from her.

Myrrima brought back some breakfast a few moments later, and once Borenson returned, they prepared to leave.

Fallion felt as if this day would be forever emblazoned in his memory. But in truth, as they crept out of the inn that morning, he ambled through a haze. The city was wrapped in a gray mist so thick that he could barely see his own feet stepping one past the other over the grimy cobblestones, and the same mist seemed to cloud his thoughts. In later weeks he would remember almost nothing of that walk.

They reached the docks, where the water was as flat as a vast satin cloth spread upon the ground. A shroud for the sea, Fallion thought.

He heard noises behind them, shouts from far away, the brief sounding of a warhorn. He thought that the soldiers at the palace must be performing some sort of training maneuvers.

He stepped down from the docks into a small coracle, and once all of the little ones were in, he helped row. He looked at Jaz's face, saw that his brother too was lost, weeping, locked within himself. Myrrima put a comforting arm around Jaz as the small boat made its way into the depths of the bay, out where the *Leviathan* was said to be anchored. The mist was so thick that droplets of water beaded upon Fallion's brow and went rolling down his face.

The salt spray in his mouth tasted like blood, and the sea this morning smelled of decay.

Soon they neared a ship, looming above them in the heavy fog, black against the gray.

It was not a huge ship, at only a hundred feet in length, with five masts. A sea serpent's head rose up at the bow, with long jaws full of grim teeth, its eyes as silver as a fish's.

Sailors were rushing to and fro, hoisting up barrels of water, kegs of ale, baskets of turnips and onions, crates filled with live animals—chickens that clucked and pigs that squealed in terror—fresh meat for the larder.

The children reached a rope ladder, and all of them climbed up the sides. At the top they were met by a sailor—a strange little man with a crooked back whose face was as white as death. His hair was mouse-colored, and his eyes a hazel so light, it almost looked as if he had nothing but whites and pupils. His long coat and trousers were both made of black leather, and he wore no shoes. He jabbered at them for a moment and it took several seconds for Fallion to realize that he spoke a mixture of Rhofe-havanish and some other language. Borenson was quick to answer in the same tongue.

"He says that they're loaded and set to sail, but won't be putting to sea until the fog lifts and we get enough wind to fill the sails."

"How long will that be?" Myrrima asked.

"Could be here all day," Borenson said. Myrrima looked worried, and Borenson whispered, "Don't do it. Don't lift the fog. We don't want them knowing too much about us."

Myrrima nodded almost imperceptibly.

For a long while, the children stood on deck while Myrrima and Borenson brought the family's meager possessions up from the boat.

Fallion peered around. He saw other refugees, several families huddled, looking as if they'd lost everything in the world. Most of them disappeared below deck within a few minutes.

The crewmen finished loading the last of the stores, waiting for wind. They were a mixed lot. Most were white of skin, like Inkarrans, as white as albinos with silver or cinnabar-colored hair. But there were tan-colored men from Rofehavan, and even a couple of Blacks from Deyazz.

Their clothes were as varied as the men. The Inkarrans, as Fallion decided to call light-skinned ones, wore what looked to be silk tunics in shades of canary, wine, or crimson, with pants of some fine leather that looked like snakeskin, though Fallion had a hard time imagining where such huge snakes would be found. They wore colorful head rags, too, and most did not wear shoes, only sandals, which they abandoned as they climbed the rigging.

The darker men wore more mundane fare, pants of buckskin or cotton, often without a shirt. More than a dozen could be seen in nothing but loincloths.

Fallion watched a couple of white skins climb up the rigging. They checked the sails on one mast, then grabbed ropes and swung to the next. Both men released a dozen yards from their target, somersaulted in the air, and grabbed the yardarms on the way down—showing a grace that Fallion had rarely seen before, and then only in Runelords with endowments of grace. They looked more like acrobats than sailors.

I could build a strong army with men like these, Fallion thought.

While he was peering up into the sails, a deep voice sounded behind him, and a stout man with long black hair and a black beard said in a strange accent, "Sir Borenson, glad to see you've made it. This your crew?"

Borenson was climbing up the rope ladder with a bag over his shoulder, and the visitor peered down at him.

Borenson grunted and gently heaved his bundle over the railing. Fallion heard the soft clank of blood metal as the bag touched the hull and knew that his forcibles were inside. Nothing else clanked like blood metal. It didn't have the ring of silver or the heavy *thunk* of iron. It was softer, more of a clacking, like sticks of bamboo whacking against each other.

Fallion looked up to see if the captain had noticed.

Captain Stalker peered down at Fallion and smiled. The clank had been soft but perceptible. I'm going to be rich, he thought. And when we sell the boys, I won't even mention the forcibles to the crew.

He saw the briefest hint of worry on the boy's face, and then it was gone.

The princeling wonders if I heard, Stalker thought. There's enough blood metal in that bag to buy a whole ship like this.

Yet the worry disappeared quickly, and Fallion covered it with a question just as Borenson heaved himself over the railing. Fallion asked, "Where are your sailors from?"

Fallion stood straight, showing a poise that Stalker had seldom seen in a child.

This one is trained in arms, Stalker realized. Probably was taught to grip a dagger while other babes were still waving rattles. And he marshals his wits as well as his body.

"Landesfallen," Borenson answered when Stalker didn't. "They're from Landesfallen." Borenson bent over, trying to catch his breath, sweating from the climb. Whatever endowments he'd once had, they were gone now, Stalker realized. A soldier with endowments of brawn and stamina might feign weariness, but they couldn't fake sweat.

That was one less worry on Stalker's mind.

"Landesfallen it is," Stalker agreed. The two men shook hands.

Talon peered up at Borenson in shock. "Is that where we're going?"

Borenson got a veiled look in his eyes, but nodded yes. He gazed down at the children to see their reaction. They'd all heard tales of Landesfallen. It was a place of legendary terrors.

Sage began to cry; Draken hid his face in his hands. Talon just bit her lip and turned away, her face pale with fright. Jaz shrugged and peered around, as if he didn't care. Rhianna glowered, put a hand on her dirk, and seemed prepared to do battle.

Landesfallen was the last place that Fallion wanted to go. It was on the far side of the world, a continent that, according to rumor, had never been fully explored.

In ages past, eight hundred years ago, a race of creatures called the toth had sailed to Mystarria upon strange black ships carved from some sort of stone. They waged a genocidal war that sent the armies of Mystarria reeling in defeat.

A great hero named Fallion the Bold arose and turned the tides of that war, decimating the armies of the toth. But his people feared that more of the creatures would come, so they built huge "worldships" that could hold vast armies, and they sailed across the sea until they found the home of the toth in Landesfallen.

There Fallion's people did their best to hunt the toth to extinction, searching through vast underground warrens for the beasts.

Most folks believed that not all of the toth were dead, that their mates and offspring had retreated farther underground, and would someday issue forth again.

Even Borenson held that opinion.

Landesfallen was so inhospitable that Fallion and his people left within a decade of discovering the continent. The lands in the interior were mostly rock and desert. That's where the toth had lived in their burrows. But only the coasts were hospitable enough for humans, and even those were covered with strange and alien jungles.

Fallion the Bold had left guards of course, men to watch Landesfallen and bring warning should the toth ever rise again. The Gwardeen, they were called, men of mixed Inkarran and Rhofehavanish blood.

It was said that they were valiant men who lived high in the branches of the stonewood jungles, forever vigilant against the return of the toth.

Lesser men had also migrated to Landesfallen over the centuries, too. Some were crazed men who believed that great treasures might be found in the ancient lairs of the toth. Most were outlaws, fleeing from justice. And from such outlaws and madmen sprang the ancient pirate lords, whose folk had been a scourge for generations.

Pirates, Fallion thought, peering up at Captain Stalker. Some of these men could be pirates.

Worse than that, he realized, any one of them could harbor a locus. The captain himself might harbor one.

Stalker laughed at the terror in the children's eyes. "Aye, bound for Landesfallen we are. And a prettier sight you'll never see. When the stonewoods are in blossom, the pollen fills the forest, and the sunlight slantin' through the trees all goes as red as rubies, and the day-bats go flittin' about, 'untin' for nectar. It's a pretty sight, girls, almost as pretty as you."

Stalker grinned and chucked Sage on the chin.

Just then, Myrrima appeared, lugging her own bundle up from the boat.

Stalker said to Borenson, "Stow your gear quickly, man. We're pulling anchor, and we could use your back on the oars."

"In this fog?" Borenson asked.

Stalker looked darkly toward the shore, still shrouded in thick fog. "'Aven't you 'eard? There's trouble at the palace." He hesitated, looked to see the reaction of Borenson and the children. It wasn't that he liked to watch folks squirm, it was that he wanted to see how well they handled pressure. There was a saying where he came from: "You never really know a man until you've spent a week with him in a leaky ship." He continued. "It's a fierce assault, powerful Runelords. Lowicker the Brat is 'untin' for the queen, no doubt. We 'eave off in five minutes, fog or no."

Borenson took the news like a warrior. It seemed hardly to faze him, but Stalker knew that he had to be worried. Even the boys surprised the captain by adapting unreadable expressions.

Myrrima dropped her bundle to the deck, sighed heavily. "I'll be back in a bit." She quickly climbed down the ladder.

Stalker needed to hurry. The boys were worth a fortune, and he needed to make a clean getaway. He had a pair of deckhands that still hadn't reported for duty—probably off drunk or whoring or both. Most likely, they'd come running when the fog lifted. But by then he planned to be far out into the open sea.

Stalker grunted a "Good morning to you," turned, and went trundling off.

Fallion peered out into the fog and petted Humfrey, who was sleeping soundly in his tunic pocket. Fallion had heard a warhorn and shouts, but had only thought that soldiers were parading at the palace, not hunting for him.

Men are dying now, he realized, dying to keep me safe.

The battle would be fierce. Queen Lowicker, whom many called "The Brat," might not need many men to take the palace. A couple of dozen champions rife with endowments formed the heart of any army.

Borenson gave Fallion a reassuring pat on the back, though he felt no assurance himself. Given a choice, he'd not have run off with the boys to the far side of the world. But the Earth King, using his prescient powers, had warned him to do so, and he suspected that though he might face some troubles, he would make it to Landesfallen safely.

So far, everything looked to be going well. Borenson had evaded the pirate captain who was searching for them, and assassins that had struck at the palace.

Soon, he'd be on the open sea, and anyone who might be searching for them would have a hard time following their trail over the open waters.

Draken, Borenson's five-year-old son, dared ask the question, "Are we on a pirate ship?"

Borenson let out a breath, knelt where the children could huddle close, and whispered, "Look, these are merchant marines. It's true some of the Great Houses of Landesfallen have a history of pirate blood, but so does your house, Draken. I was born on Orwynne, an island not far off the coast from here, and your great-grandfather worked as a privateer back during the Hawks War."

Draken looked up at his father and asked, "So *we're* pirates?"

Borenson laughed in defeat. "You could say that."

But what Borenson was really saying went deeper, Fallion knew. Most of these men probably had pirate blood in them. Some may have even worked as pirates.

Borenson was trusting the advice of the Earth King in sailing to some faraway corner of the world, but that didn't mean that they were out of danger.

Fallion peered up through the fog with new eyes at the sailors. Something deep inside him trembled as if in warning. He was riding a pirate ship to the last place in the world that he wanted to go. Borenson wasn't taking him to safety. Borenson was taking them into greater danger.

"Why Landesfallen?" he asked.

Borenson smiled, knelt close. "Your father warned us that the ends of the Earth are not far enough. Right? So we have to go farther."

Fallion didn't understand.

"When we get to Landesfallen," Borenson said, "one of the oldest and safest harbors is at Garion's Port. It's a good deepwater port, in a horseshoe bay. The entrance to the bay is flanked by two huge stones that thrust up from the water. Those two stones are called the Ends of the Earth. That was what your father's message meant, I believe. We have to go beyond the Ends of the Earth, beyond Garion's Port into the wilds of Landesfallen."

"Are you sure?" Fallion asked.

Borenson looked thoughtful, nodded just a bit. "I'm as sure as I can be. There's no better place for a person to get lost. The last we heard, your father was heading that way. He met Daymorra nearly a year ago, and the islands where she lived were not far from Landesfallen."

If that's true, Fallion reasoned, then we're going to where my father died.

Fallion imagined his father in the stronghold of some pirate lair, a port shrouded beneath the vast boughs of the legendary stonewood trees. There he envisioned pirates holding his father in chains and torturing him for their own amusement.

I'll find out how he died, Fallion thought. And I'll avenge him, if I have to.

The children quickly began to explore the ship. The decks had been scrubbed clean by salt and sun and water and wind. Everything looked immaculate. They walked the main deck and could see down through a metal grate to the oarsmen's galley, where crewmen had begun taking seats on stark wooden benches.

Along the way, they passed small wooden catapults with iron baskets. Piles of iron shot were laid out neatly nearby.

At the prow, the children climbed out onto the serpent's long neck, painted golden white on the bottom going to sea green on the sides and black on the back. The long crocodilian jaws were full of oversized teeth, and the serpent's eyes shone like silver shields.

Fallion's heart hammered at the sight, and he climbed out on the neck, his legs straddling both sides, as he peered down into the water. On the hull of the ship, sea stars in orange and purple crawled among anemones like bright flowers of green and gold. Minnows darted in the shadow of the boat, and some leapt to the surface as a sea bass drove up from the depths.

Fallion was in for a grand adventure.

He could smell smoke faintly, and realized that the fog had begun to lift. Then he remembered that Myrrima had been down in the coracle, and most likely, she'd cast a spell while out of sight to lift the fog.

An animal shrieked behind him, and Fallion turned to see a sea ape—a silver-haired gorilla standing eight feet tall, with a spiked club in one hand, yowling at them. It had yellow fangs and a deep red mouth. Its fur was long and wispy, like the fur of a yak. It raised the club as if warning the children to get down from "my spot."

Fallion quickly began to back off his perch, but some sailor shouted,

"Yeep. Yeep!" and the ape leapt up and raced over the forecastle on its knuckles.

"Did you see that!" Jaz cried from the head of the serpent. "A real sea ape!" His face split into a grin so wide that it looked as if he could swallow a plate.

"Yeah," Fallion said in awe. Sea apes were great swimmers and powerful warriors. Sailors from beyond Inkarra sometimes kept them, not as pets, not even as slaves. Instead, the sea apes sometimes became attached to a person, developed a deep reverence for him, something that was said to go beyond love or even worshipfulness.

I shouldn't be smiling at the thought of seeing a sea ape, Fallion thought. Mother is dead.

For a few minutes, he'd managed to forget. But now the memory of the loss hung over him like a pall, and his spirits fell.

Fallion noticed that the ship had begun to move, and he could see the oars splashing the water, raising whitecaps.

None too soon. The fog began to lift rapidly. For long minutes the children just sat on the bow, as if leading the way, while the ship set off for the far side of the world.

Fallion watched for a long hour as they made their way out to sea. The fog lifted altogether, and he could see columns of flame rising from the white towers at the Courts of Tide, a plume of gray smoke like a rising thunderhead.

Behind them, from the harbor, came a smaller ship with black sails, almost as if it were giving chase.

Fallion didn't know if it was really trying to intercept them, but he imagined the ship to be full of enemy troops from Beldinook, powerful Runelords hunting him, led by Asgaroth himself.

Fallion suddenly felt trapped. For the next few months, his whole world would be bounded by the rails of the vessel, and somehow he suspected that he was not alone. Asgaroth had been hunting him since birth.

Would the locus just leave? He could be anywhere. He could be here now, on this ship, inside one of these men. Or he could be on the ship that followed.

He won't leave me alone, Fallion realized.

As if to prove his fears, Captain Stalker took the helm and eyed the black ship suspiciously.

He ordered the sails unfurled, and once they were full of wind he watched for a long time as the black ship began to lose ground. He told the helmsmen, "We can outrun them. Keep this course through the night until second bell, then set course due east."

ᨆ 19 ᨀ

STREBEN

It is in the nature of things that we often get to choose our friends, but rarely get to choose our enemies.

—Iome Sarinnika Orden

That afternoon, Borenson held his long knife at the ready, his right leg forward, his left foot half a pace back, toe pointed out, while his shoulders hunched low and his buckler formed a moving target, protecting his side. It was the classic fencing stance, and like most practiced fencers, Borenson's thighs and calves were overlarge, evidence of his long hours of practice.

But so were Fallion's. The calluses inside his thumb and on his palms fit perfectly against the haft of his blade. Indeed his hand fit the blade so well that it seemed an extension of his body. Only the buckler was unfamiliar. It was an Inkarran device, called a viper, much used on the far side of the world. It was shaped like a teardrop, thick in the middle while the bottom portion tapered into a sharp blade for stabbing. The sides were sharpened so that they could be used as a slashing weapon. The viper was equally handy as defensive armament and as an assault weapon.

Fallion danced back and forth, sometimes feinting an attack in the Deyazz style of fighting with scimitars. It was a form that Fallion liked. It tempted opponents, causing them to strike at imagined openings. But a good fighter in the Deyazz style was always careful to keep his body moving in unexpected directions, so that the opening disappeared even as the opponent committed to his attack.

Borenson smiled. He liked the game.

Borenson lunged, blurring in his speed, aiming his long knife straight at Fallion's eye. Though the knife was blunted, a puncture wound to the eye would still be fatal.

Fallion dodged left, swinging his head mere inches. Fallion was trained to block such a blow with his buckler, bring it up so that the edge clipped the ganglia on the opponent's wrist, numbing his hand and most probably disarming him.

But Fallion dove under the attack, striking Borenson with the blade of his viper, a blow up into the armpit. At the last instant, he pulled his punch, lest he puncture the armpit for real, and the crowd of sailors that looked on, hanging from the rigging and leaning against the railings, shouted "Two!" cheering, even as Fallion leapt back to avoid reprisals.

Two points. Not an instant kill, but a slow one, one that would weaken an enemy, wear him down. The blow would have severed Borenson's artery, causing him to bleed to death in a matter of minutes.

Borenson pushed the attack, lunging while Fallion was off-balance. The boy leapt to the side, putting a mast between him and his opponent. Borenson rushed in, but Fallion leapt to his right again, keeping the larger man at bay.

The sailors cheered as if it were a dogfight.

Captain Stalker peered down from the forecastle and watched with dull interest.

"Pretty good, eh?" Endo asked. "For a kid?"

"Good," Stalker replied. Stalker had an eye for fighters. In his youth, his master had supplied gladiators for the arenas at Zalindar—old warriors from Internook, captured slaves from Innesvale—and so he was no stranger to blood sport.

But Fallion astonished him. In retrospect, he should have known that the boy would be well trained. But many a clod could be trained. No, Fallion had a gift for fighting, Stalker decided.

Even that should not have surprised him. He was bred for it, over hundreds of generations, sired from Mystarria's greatest warriors.

The combination of breeding and training very nearly awed Stalker.

And right now, he was trying to decide if Fallion was merely exceptional for a child, or if he might someday grow to be the best he'd ever seen. "The boy is young yet, but give him six years . . ."

"A Son of the Oak," Endo said. It was a compliment, a reminder of the spooky way that the world was changing, with a new generation growing up stronger and smarter than their elders, better in so many ways.

"Aye," Streben jested, "he may only be nine, but he *fights* like a ten-year-old."

Several men laughed nearby, but somehow the jest angered Stalker. He didn't like someone making sport of another for being good at what he did. That was a pastime for losers.

Streben was his sister's son, and at seventeen he was a tall boy, lanky and strong. He fancied himself a fighter. But he had a cruel streak and a cowardly one.

Oh, he had enough bravado to kill a man, but he'd only done it once, and he'd done it from behind. He had a penchant for picking fights at port. One night, after such a skirmish, he'd ambushed a man in the night, and then bragged about it when they were far out to sea, beyond the reach of any lawmen.

The boy rolled to the side to avoid Borenson's next few blows, keeping the masthead between them, and Streben laughed. "Boy knows 'ow to run!"

But Stalker realized what the boy was doing. He was playing out the fight in his mind, making it real. If Borenson had been a real attacker, he'd know that he was bleeding to death, and he'd press the fight even as Borenson was doing now. At the same time, his quickened heartbeat would pump the blood from his armpit ever faster. By now he'd be down a mugful of his life's blood, and his head would be reeling from the loss. A few more seconds, and the boy would be able to take him with ease.

Borenson feinted left and attacked right, his long knife going slightly wild, as if he were losing focus. He was into the game, too.

The boy struck him a blow to the thigh, one so close to the crotch that many of the sailors actually cried out in sympathetic pain. Another two-point blow.

The crowd cheered wildly, and Fallion smiled. He'd been practicing for three hours, doing all that he could to "prepare" himself, as his mother had warned him to do.

But in his own mind, he was doing more than perfecting his skills. He was playing to the crowd, trying to win their approval. He needed not to win just their applause, but their hearts. Someday, he thought, some of these men may form the core of my army.

His eyes went to the right, where Rhianna watched him, a worried smile on her face.

The small moment cost him dearly. Borenson suddenly lunged like a wild man, slashing with his knife, three blows that Fallion could barely parry. The big man's knife rang against Fallion's small shield, and each blow numbed Fallion's arm.

The fight is everything, Fallion told himself. Focus on the fight.

The cheering faded from Fallion's mind as he watched Borenson's piercing blue eyes. You could always tell when a man would strike by watching his eyes. An accomplished fighter like Borenson wouldn't warn you by focusing on the spot he'd attack, but his pupils dilated a tenth of a second before he struck.

Fallion had to concentrate on his footing. The pitch and yaw of the vessel was still unfamiliar, and his center of gravity rolled with the ship.

Borenson's pupils went large. Fallion dodged left, just as Borenson's shield bashed him in the chest, sent him flying, knocking the wind from him.

Fallion tried to suck air, knew it would be no use. He had to end the fight now.

Borenson rushed and Fallion leapt up and lunged forward, under his reach, bringing his knife point up under the sternum.

"Three!" the sailors shouted. An instant kill.

The sailors in the rigging cheered wildly. Borenson was huffing. He grinned at Fallion, peered over to Rhianna.

Fallion was still trying to suck air. He felt as if he'd lose his breakfast any moment.

"You puke on that deck," Borenson jested, "and you're going to have to clean it up." Then more softly he added, "Hold it in."

Fallion nodded. Borenson poked him in the stomach. "That," he whispered, referring to the blow, "was for showing off. Always keep your mind in the fight."

It was a hard lesson, but Fallion knew that he would rather learn it now than in a real fight.

Fallion got to his knees, tried to hold in his breakfast, struggling for air. Sweat rolled off of him.

The sailors were still cheering, and Captain Stalker smiled in grim satisfaction.

"You saw that!" Streben shouted. "The big fellow pulled his punches. I was that good when I was the kid's age!" He began to jeer.

Stalker turned to his nephew, gave him a dangerous look. "You're not that good. You couldn't beat the kid on the best day of your life."

That caught Streben's attention. There is nothing that a coward hates more than to be reminded of his own weakness.

Several sailors nearby caught the mood and jeered at Streben, "Go ahead, show us what you've got."

Streben looked away in embarrassment, trying to ignore them, but the jests grew crueler.

"Right," he snarled, shouting down at the boy. "You fight me? You want me?"

Fallion looked up at Streben, not quite understanding. Streben shouted another challenge, and Borenson stepped between them and said, "The boy isn't taking challenges. This isn't the arena."

But Streben grinned maliciously, taking the boy's reluctance for cowardice. "Why not?" he demanded. "It's a matter of honor."

Stalker said nothing for a moment. He already knew what Streben was made of: cruelty, cowardice, and stupidity, all wrapped up in a deceptively strong frame. Sometimes he told himself that if Streben wasn't his nephew, he'd have hurled him overboard long ago.

Fallion took a step to the side, so that he could see Streben better. He saw the crazed gleam in the man's eyes, the sneer on his lips.

He is dangerous, the kind of man who would harbor a locus, Fallion thought.

"Is there great honor in beating children where you come from?" Fallion asked. "Or are you just such a sorry ass that you can't fight someone your own size?"

That brought snorts of laughter from the crowd, followed by jeers aimed at Streben, who leapt from the rigging, launching himself toward Fallion, tugging his own dagger from its sheath.

Stalker couldn't allow that. Fallion was too valuable. As Streben raced past, Stalker simultaneously put out a foot, then shoved him.

Streben spilled to the ground like a sack of guts, his knife under him. He grunted a curse, crawled up to his knees, and peered in dismay at his hand. He'd cut it badly, slicing his palm almost to the bone.

But Stalker didn't look at his nephew's hands. He was watching Fallion. The child had drawn his own long knife, and rather than recoil in fear at the sight of Streben, he smiled patiently, as if he would not hesitate to slip a blade between the bigger man's ribs.

I didn't save the boy, Stalker realized. I saved Streben.

Streben peered at his hand and shouted at Fallion, "This isn't over!"

Fallion turned to leave, and Streben made a show of rising up and lunging toward his back. But Endo and Blythe each grabbed an arm, pinning him down.

"Don't spoil the merchandise," Blythe warned his struggling charge. "Them folks is cargo, payin' customers. Anything 'appens to the boy, and you're dead. Understand?"

Streben craned his neck and looked back to Stalker, as if seeking permission to press the attack.

Stalker stepped forward, and as his men held Streben, Stalker struck a heavy blow to his nephew's gut.

Unlike Fallion, Streben didn't manage to hold his breakfast down.

"Listen to me," Stalker said. "I know you. You're a sneak that comes up to men from behind and slits their throats. But I'll not 'ave that from you 'ere. That boy is under my protection. Got it?"

Streben gave a sneer so full of rage that Stalker couldn't resist. He slapped the sneer off his nephew's face.

Streben spent the rest of the day swabbing decks.

ಓ 20 ೮

SMOKER

I serve a higher Power, but I do not always understand its will. I have enough faith in it that I do not need to know its will.

—*The Wizard Binnesman*

Throughout the afternoon, Fallion kept his eye to the horizon behind, catching glimpses of the black ship. It was losing ground, but kept following.

Worrying about it would drive Fallion mad, he knew. He had to keep busy. He could wear himself out for a few hours a day in weapons practice, but he needed something more.

As he and Rhianna wandered the ship, they chanced upon Captain Stalker coming out of his cabin, and Fallion caught a glimpse inside. The place was a pigsty, papers stacked and falling all over his small desk, spilling onto the floor, goods in boxes waiting to be stowed, floors that hadn't been scrubbed in months.

Fallion let the captain close the door, then bowed deeply and said, "Sir, I wanted to offer my thanks for your help this afternoon, for restraining that man."

"My nephew, Streben?" the captain said with a sly smile. "No thanks are needed. 'E's an ass, and asses need to be whipped. I'll see that 'e stays in line."

"Sir," Fallion said, "I was wondering if I could be your cabin boy, fetch things, clean your room." The captain drew back, hesitating, and Fallion offered quickly, "I'd want no pay . . . only, I'd like to learn how to run a ship, to navigate."

"You know your numbers?"

"Some," Fallion said, not wanting to boast. "I can multiply and divide." The truth was that Hearthmaster Waggit had been teaching him geometry, enough so that he could calculate how far a siege engine could hurl its payload. Once you knew how to triangulate, it wouldn't take long to learn to navigate.

Stalker smiled thoughtfully, though Fallion could hardly see the flash of teeth beneath his black moustache. "Is it a life at sea that you're contemplating?" he asked. But secretly he was wondering how to put the boy off. It was a decent offer, and normally he'd have considered it. But he had too many secrets to keep concealed.

"Perhaps," Fallion said. He didn't really want a life at sea, but he was thinking that someday he'd need to know how to run a navy. "It intrigues me."

Children Fallion's age were easily intrigued, Stalker knew. They could be intrigued by pulling the stuffing from a rag doll or peeling carrots.

"A generous offer, lad," the captain said. "Let me think about it for a day or two. . . ."

Stalker had no intention of letting Fallion work in his cabin. Yet he grudgingly found that he admired the boy enough to want to let him down easily.

They said their good nights, and each went their separate ways.

Rhianna took the lead, walking slowly, hesitantly. Fallion kept close by, in case she stumbled. Her wounds were healing quickly, at least on the surface, but she could tell by her pain how deep they went.

I might never be healed, she realized. She'd heard the healers whispering to Borenson after the surgery. They had said that she'd probably never have babies.

At her age, that didn't seem like much of a loss.

But the hurt went deeper. The horror of what had happened would stay with her forever.

So she took her steps gingerly, convalescing.

Humfrey the ferrin had wakened from his daylong nap, and as evening neared, he scrambled ahead of them with his little spear, peering behind barrels, inspecting nooks, seeking for rats or mice to eat, or treasures to collect.

As they moved about the ship, Rhianna noted that Streben watched Fallion constantly, glowering, and they could not avoid him. The young man was on his knees, swabbing decks, and the children had to step past him with each circuit of the ship.

To make matters worse, Humfrey was attracted to the rag that Streben used to wash with, and each time they neared, Humfrey would leap at the

rag and hiss, playfully poking his spear at it, certain that Streben was swabbing the deck for the ferrin's entertainment.

And several times when Fallion drew near, Streben would glance around
to make sure that no adults could see, and then hiss softly through his
teeth, as if warning Fallion to stop walking on "his" deck.

Fallion tried to ignore him. There was nothing else that he could do.
They would be sharing the same ship for months, eating in the same galley.

Still, Rhianna knew by instinct that it was dangerous to antagonize a
man like Streben. She would grab Fallion's hand and hold it whenever he
got too close, trying to urge him away. She warned him once, "Don't go
near him. He'd kill you if he could."

"I don't think so," Fallion said. "He knows what would happen."

But Rhianna wasn't so sure. She'd heard Iome and the others talking
about Asgaroth, the locus, and Rhianna felt sure that he was lurking near.
No matter where they went, Asgaroth could follow, lodging himself in the
mind of the nearest foul person. And what better hovel would a locus find
than in the mind of someone like Streben? And how easy would it be to
drive such a fool to madness?

They were walking past some barrels where an old man was smoking a
reed pipe with a stem as long as his arm, a bald man with skin as white as
tallow and eyes the color of sea foam. Several children, including Borenson's own brood, had gathered round to watch him smoke, for in Mystarria
the habit was all but unknown. Rhianna had never seen anyone smoke
except when they were injured and needed opium for pain. But this fellow
seemed to smoke for enjoyment, and the smoke from his pipe had a sweet,
intoxicating scent.

Right now, he was blowing smoke rings. In the failing light of the evening, the bowl of his pipe burned hot orange as he inhaled, and then the
smoke ring came out between his lips a deep blue-white.

As Rhianna passed, she noticed, not for the first time, that the old man
watched Fallion with keen intensity, and each time that he saw Fallion, he
nodded in greeting, as if to an old friend.

But this time he set aside his pipe and said, "Listen to girl. Beware
Streben. There much of shadow in him."

Fallion stopped and stared at the fellow. "What do you mean?"

"Inside, every man part light, part shadow. In Streben, is great shadow, trying to snuff out light." He tapped Fallion's chest with his pipe and said, "But in you great light, struggle to burn through all darkness. Streben sense this. Hate you. He kill you, if can."

What does he mean? Rhianna wondered. Can he see into the heart of a man?

The smoker peered at Fallion a moment, as if considering a further argument. "Streben has nothing to be proud of. No honor, no courage, no wealth. He hollow. He look inside self, find nothing good. So he imagine to self, rebellion is strength. Rebellion is courage. He not see that rebellion foolish. He kind of man who kill you to make himself feel strong, even if he know must suffer for it." Smoker drew a quick puff of smoke, then leaned close. "Maybe he think punishment worth it. Captain his uncle. Maybe he hope not get punished."

The smoker let some smoke out through his nose, and Fallion peered into the man's eyes, eyes that Rhianna could see were bright, too bright, as they reflected light from a sun that had nearly drifted below the horizon.

Fallion asked, "Are you a flameweaver?"

The smoker laughed. He inhaled from his pipe, blew out a puff of smoke that shaped itself into a wispy gray dove, then flapped up into the air. He turned his pipe and offered Fallion a puff.

"Are you a flameweaver?" Smoker asked, mocking.

Rhianna felt unnerved by the fellow. He was obviously a flameweaver. At first she had thought that he was just bald, but now she saw that he had no eyebrows, no hair of any kind, for the roots had burned away, and that was all the proof that she needed.

She pulled Fallion's arm, urging him to follow. But as if on impulse Fallion took the pipe and drew a deep breath. The other children all peered at him with wide eyes for his audacity. He inhaled deeply, as if the weed tasted sweet in the back of his throat, but he coughed and hacked it out anyway.

The old fellow laughed. "Maybe not flameweaver. Not yet. But great light in you, Torch-bearer. Why you come here, hey? Why old soul hiding in young one's body?"

That seemed to trouble Fallion. "You can see that?" Fallion asked. "You see inside me?"

Smoker answered, "Not see, feel. You walk by, and I feel heat in you, light." He reached out as if to touch Fallion, and Fallion touched the man's fingers, then pulled his hand away quickly.

"Hot," Fallion said.

"You want feel inside of people?" Smoker asked, taking a couple of quick puffs on his pipe. "Take much smoke. Maybe then you will see. . . ."

Fallion didn't want to smoke. "Can you see the shadow creatures that live inside men? Can you see a locus?"

The old man got a secretive look. "Shadoath," he said. "In Landesfallen, we call it a shadoath."

Rhianna hissed in surprise, for it was the name that Asgaroth had used when talking of his master.

Smoker turned to her. "You know this name?"

Rhianna nodded.

Smoker smiled, showed his yellow teeth. "Is pirate lord by that name, yes? Her fame grows. She knows what inside her."

"She?" Rhianna asked. "Shadoath is a woman?"

"Children, get away from there!" Myrrima shouted.

Rhianna whirled. Myrrima had come up behind them, and though Rhianna had never seen her angry, her rage was palpable now.

Water wizards and flameweavers did not get along.

The children stood in shock for a moment, and the little ones were quickest to run to their mother, but the old flameweaver tapped Fallion's chest with the bowl of his pipe. "This one, he not yours. You know that. He know it now, too."

ᛒ 21 ᚲ

A KILLER IN THE DARK

Sometimes I have looked into the heart of a peasant and found something so malign that it fills me with horror. But more often I have found something so beautiful that it causes me to weep for joy.

—*Gaborn Val Orden*

That evening after dinner as the children slept, Myrrima took her husband up on deck for a late-night stroll. The winds were light, the evening cool; stars burned down like living coals.

"I caught Fallion talking to that flameweaver today," she said when they were alone. "I think he suspects what Fallion is."

"Have you caught Fallion trying to shape flames, set fires?"

"No," Myrrima said. "But we will soon enough. You saw how he burned away the clouds when we fought Asgaroth, summoning the light?"

"I saw," Borenson said with an air of resignation. "We knew that this day would come." He said the words, but he did not feel them. It seemed an irony that Fallion's father had fought a bitter war against Raj Ahten and his flameweavers, only to have sired a flameweaver of his own.

"It's a seductive power," Myrrima said. "Those who use it learn to crave destruction. They yearn to consume."

"Fallion is a good boy," Borenson said. "He'll fight those urges."

Myrrima's voice came ragged, "He'll lose that fight. You know it, and his father knew it."

Borenson gritted his teeth in determination. Unbidden, he thought of the curse that Asgaroth had laid on Fallion, predicting a future of war and bloodshed. Is that why Fallion was waking to his powers now?

Or was this part of Asgaroth's plan, to push the boy, force those powers to waken before he was mature enough to handle them?

Borenson had never really known a flameweaver. Oh, he'd fought them in Raj Ahten's army, and he'd seen a couple of folks demonstrate some small skill at bending flames at summer festivals, but he'd never known one intimately. He'd never tried to raise one.

Gaborn had warned him that this would happen, of course. He'd warned him long ago when he begged Borenson to become Fallion's protector.

"Give him something to hold on to," Gaborn had warned. "He won't always need your sword to protect him. But he'll need your love and your friendship to protect him from what he can become. He'll need a father, someone to keep him connected to his humanity, and I won't be there."

Borenson stopped and rubbed his temples. Why did I let Gaborn talk me into this?

But he knew the answer. There were some jobs that were just impossible for common men, jobs that would cause them to falter or break. And some combination of stupidity, audacity, and the need to protect others forced Borenson to accept those jobs.

Wearily, he led Myrrima to their bed.

In her dream, Rhianna lay draped over the limb of an elm, the cold moss and bark pressing into her naked flesh. Her clothes were wet and clung to her like damp rags, and her crotch ached from where the strengi-saat had laid its eggs, the big female pressing her ovipositor between Rhianna's legs, unmindful of the pain or the tearing or the blood or of Rhianna's screams.

The rape was recent, and Rhianna still hoped for escape. She peered about in the predawn, the light just beginning to wash the stars from heaven, and her breath came in ragged bursts.

She could hear cries in the woods. The cries of other children, the snarling and growls of strengi-saats, like distant thunder.

As she listened, the cries rose all around. North, south, east, and west. She dared not move. Even if she tried to creep away, she knew that they would catch her.

Yet she had to try.

Trembling, almost too frightened to move, she swiveled her head and looked down. The ground was twenty feet below, and she could discern no easy path down, no way to go but to jump.

Better a fast death from a fall, she thought, than a slow one freezing.

With the barest of nudges, she leaned to one side, letting her body slide over the limb. As she began to fall, she twisted in the air, grasping the limb. For a moment she clung, her feet swinging in the air, until she let herself drop.

Wet leaves and detritus cushioned her fall, accompanied by the sound of twigs snapping under her weight, like the bones of mice.

Her legs couldn't hold the weight, and she fell on her butt, then on her back. The jarring left her hurt, muscles strained to near the snapping point, and she wasn't sure how fast she would be able to limp away.

Nothing is broken, she told herself hopefully. Nothing is broken.

She climbed to a sitting position, peered through the gloom. There were shadows under the trees. Not the kind of shadows that she was used to, but deeper shadows, ones that moved of their own accord.

The strengi-saats were drawing the light from the air, wrapping themselves in gloom, the way that darkling glories did in the netherworld.

Do they see me? she wondered.

She waited for a brief second, then leapt to her feet and raced to keep up with the rhythm of her skipping heart.

With an endowment of metabolism, she hoped that she could outdistance the monsters.

But had not gone thirty paces when a shadow enveloped her and something hit her from behind, sent her sprawling.

A strengi-saat had her. It held her beneath an immense paw, its claws digging lightly into her back, as it growled deep in its throat.

She heard words in her mind. More than a dream or her imagination. She heard words. "You cannot escape."

Rhianna bolted upright, found herself in the hold of the ship, felt it gently rocking beneath her.

It had been more than a dream. It was a memory from her time with the strengi-saats, a memory that she knew she would never get free of.

The only thing that hadn't been real was the strengi-saat's voice. The creatures had never talked to her, never spoken in her mind.

She had a sudden worry that the creatures still hunted for her. She had escaped, but she worried that it was only for a time.

She wondered even if it was more than a dream. Could it have been a message? Were the strengi-saats capable of Sendings? Could they force messages upon her in her sleep?

She had no idea what the answer might be. Until a week ago, she'd never seen a strengi-saat.

Yet they showed a certain kind of cruel intelligence. They hunted cooperatively, and watched one another's charges. They attacked only when it was safe.

But there was something else that bothered Rhianna: the strengi-saats talked to one another, growling and grunting and snarling throughout the day—not like birds that rise in the morning to sing in their trees, warning others from their realm. No, this was more like human speech, a near constant banter, exchanges of information. They were teaching one another, Rhianna had felt sure, plotting their conquests, considering their options in ways that other animals could not match.

Rhianna got up, peered about by the light of a single candle. Everyone was asleep, even Myrrima, who hardly ever slept. The Borenson family was lucky. They had a cabin in the hold, the only one set aside for travelers. The other refugee families were forced to huddle among crates, camping on blankets.

Humfrey saw that Rhianna was awake, and the ferrin leapt on her feet, gave a soft whistle, and looked toward the door. He wanted out. Ferrins were nocturnal, and the ratlike creature was wide awake.

Rhianna didn't think that she would be able to sleep anyway, so she crept from under her blanket, tiptoed to the door, and pushed. It swung silently on leather hinges. She lifted Humfrey and climbed up to the open hatch, under the starlight.

She set the ferrin down, and he scampered off over the deck, peering behind balls of shot, a tiny shadow that weaved in and out of the deeper shadows thrown by the railing, by barrels, and by lifeboats. Rhianna thought that she heard a rat squeak, and then the ferrin shot ahead, hot on its trail, a killer in the night.

She strolled along casually, letting Humfrey have his fun, just looking up at the stars and breathing. She rounded the corner at the back of the boat and heard the thud of a boot and the crackling of bones, followed by a horrible squeal.

"Got ya," a deep voice snarled, and Rhianna's heart sank as she realized that someone had hurt the ferrin, probably thinking that it was wild.

She raced a couple of steps, rounded the aftercastle, and saw a lanky young man standing on the deck in the starlight. He had the ferrin in his hands, struggling and squeaking, and as she watched, he gripped it hard, twisting it as if to wring water from a rag.

There was a crackling, and Humfrey struggled no more.

In shock, Rhianna looked up, realized that Streben loomed above her.

He grinned at the ferrin, teeth flashing white in the moonlight, and said, "'Ere now. Cap'n says I'm not to hurt your friend, but he didn't say nothin' 'bout you."

He dropped the ferrin to the deck, stood peering down.

Rhianna didn't have time for reason. She knew how devastated Fallion would be at the loss of Humfrey. Fallion's mother and father were both gone within a week, and now this?

And the worst of it was the fear that she felt of Streben. It was cold, unreasoning.

In her mind, he loomed like a great shadow.

Rhianna gave a strangled cry of horror, and Streben turned. He grinned at her, his white teeth suddenly flashing in the starlight.

"Oh, now," he whispered dangerously. "You shouldn't 'ave seen that."

He reached out to grab Rhianna.

A white-hot rage took her. Rhianna did not think about what to do. She didn't even realize that she had her dirk. It was tucked into the belt behind her back. Her hand found it there.

It was like an extension of her body, and the hard calluses inside her thumb and along her palms gave mute testimony that she was well practiced in its use.

As Streben roughly grabbed her shoulder and pulled her toward him, she lunged, the knife flashing up toward his ribs, piercing through a kidney, sinking so far that she heard the blade click against his backbone.

Streben opened his mouth in surprise. "What? What did you?"

He reached down and felt the blade in his side, and suddenly grappled for her shoulders, as if begging for support.

Rhianna stared in shock at what she'd done as his eyes bulged and his mouth worked soundlessly.

He's got a locus in him, she thought. He might have killed me.

Her hand grabbed the dirk, again, and she twisted the blade. Hot blood spilled down the runnel over her fingers and onto the deck.

The tall man was losing his battle to stay alive. Rhianna could feel his weight beginning to sag as his legs gave way. With a fury that she didn't know that she had, Rhianna shoved him. He tried to keep his feet, staggering backward, and hit the railing, then went tumbling over the side and splashed into the water.

Rhianna stood looking down in a daze, watching the V of the backwash behind the ship for signs of movement, but Streben didn't thrash about or cry for help.

He was gone.

Rhianna had a sudden fear that she might be caught and punished, so she raced to the galley, where she spent more than an hour trying to wash the blood from her hand, and from her blade.

In her mind, she replayed the events, tried to understand what had happened.

She'd been afraid. She was used to fear. Her mother had been running for as long as Rhianna could remember, terrified that her husband might catch her. From the time that Rhianna was born, she'd been warned of Celinor Anders.

And then he had come and brought the strengi-saats. "My pets require a sacrifice," her father had said. "And you're it."

She had never imagined that the heart of a man could be so dark, that his conscience could be so dead.

So he'd given her to his pets, left her for dead.

It was Fallion who had given Rhianna her life back, even as her father tried to take it once again.

Her flight from the castle, her days of hiding in the inn—both had left her sick with fear. And when Streben had grabbed her, she'd just wanted it to end. Not just for her sake, but for Fallion's, too.

She was confused by what she was beginning to feel for him. Was it love? They were only children, and weren't supposed to be able to fall in love yet. But she was turning into a woman now, and she felt something that she thought was love. Or was it just gratitude so fierce that it seemed to melt the very marrow of her bones?

Adults don't believe that children can fall in love, Rhianna knew. They disapprove. But Rhianna knew that her own feelings were just as fierce as any that an adult might feel.

It's love, she told herself. That's why I killed Streben. And I'll not be sorry for it, even if they hang me from the yardarms.

And it seemed to Rhianna that they certainly would hang her. Streben was the captain's nephew. He had friends on the ship, and she was a stranger. From what she had seen, strangers tended to get little in the way of justice in an unfamiliar town.

But they'll have to catch me first, Rhianna decided.

There was nowhere to run. If she'd been in a town, it would have been nothing to steal a fast horse and race miles away before dawn.

There in the galley she cleaned herself by candlelight, washed her hands in a bucket of salt water, washed drops of telltale blood from her pants and boots. In the light of a single wavering candle, it was hard to find them all, and she looked again and again. Each time that she thought that she was clean, she found a new dab somewhere.

And she had to hurry, fearful that someone would come in, catch her washing. Daylight was coming. The cooks would be here soon. Twice she heard footfalls as some sailor rushed to the poop deck to relieve himself.

Even getting back down to the hold unnoticed might be impossible. There were chickens down in the hold, and if it got any lighter, when she opened the hatch the roosters would begin to crow. Little Sage had been making a game of it for days, closing the hatch and then opening just to hear the roosters crow. Rhianna needed to leave now.

Worst of all she imagined that Myrrima would be awake when she got back to the cabin. Myrrima, with her endowments of stamina, rarely needed sleep. Not like Borenson, who kept folks awake with his loud snoring.

It was a long, long hour before she finally crept back down to her cabin, stealthily opening the hatch and sneaking to her room, only to find Myrrima sound asleep; it was many hours before Rhianna finally slept herself.

❧ 22 ☙

THE JUDGMENT

Prudence demands that a lord condemn a man only for the crimes that he can prove, not for crimes that he suspects were committed. But the Earth King can see into the heart of a man and condemn him on that basis alone. I would that we were all Earth Kings.

—Wuqaz Faharaqin

It was early morning when Captain Stalker realized that Streben was missing.

A deckhand found the dead ferrin on the poop deck and was about to throw it over when he saw a pool of blood, more than a ferrin could account for. It wasn't uncommon for a sailor to cut himself or get a bloody nose, but this was a lot of blood, and so the deckhand searched the ship, looking to see if anyone was hurt.

It took a long time before he realized that Streben was missing and reported the news to Stalker.

Stalker blew the whistle for an assembly, and all hands reported for the count. Streben was definitely missing; Stalker went to the bloody pool and studied it.

Humfrey's spear lay on the deck still. It had rolled against the railing. A little blood on the point revealed that the ferrin had died trying to defend himself.

The rounded end of the blood spatter was like a comet, pointing the direction that Streben had been traveling at his last, backpedaling toward the railing.

"Think the ferrin got 'im?" the sailor asked. "Maybe 'it 'im in the eye?"

Stalker was an imaginative man, but such a scenario stretched his credulity. Too much blood, he reasoned silently. No, what we have here is murder. Streben's mother would demand vengeance. Of course Stalker could always cover it up. Men fell from the rigging every day, or took too much rum and stumbled overboard.

Yes, he thought, why not? Why not tell his sister that a ferrin had killed her son?

It was ludicrous. It sounded so much like a lie that she'd think that it had to be the truth.

"I don't think a ferrin did this," Stalker admitted.

"The ferrin belongs to that boy," the sailor said, "the one that fought yesterday. Maybe 'e came up in the night to lighten 'is load, and the ferrin came with. So the kid . . ."

Stalker gave the sailor a sidelong look. "He's just a kid. And kids that age don't murder."

"'E's good with a blade," the sailor muttered.

And it was true. But in his heart, Stalker doubted that it was murder. Streben would have terrorized the boy if he'd found him alone at night. Streben might even have tried to cut the kid's throat. It was self-defense, if it was anything.

Maybe one of Streben's victims had finally turned the tables on him.

His mother would still want vengeance, but it would be hard to get.

"Go down to the guest cabin," Stalker said. "Ask Borenson . . . and his son, to come meet me for breakfast."

Stalker went to the galley and took a seat. The rest of the crew had taken breakfast at sunrise, and so the galley was empty. He had Cook fry up some sausages and cut up some oranges to go with their hard bread, then sat at the table trying to compose his thoughts.

When Borenson and young Fallion arrived, they both looked tired, stiff from sleep. Their blood wasn't flowing, and indeed, Fallion was a tad green. Stalker had become accustomed to the pitch and roll of a ship long ago, and he hadn't even noticed that the seas had grown heavier this morning. But Fallion was taking it badly.

"'Ave some breakfast?" the captain asked, letting Borenson and Fallion find their own seats.

Fallion just stared at the platter of sausages, hard rolls, and fruit, going greener by the moment, while Stalker and Borenson loaded their plates.

"Go ahead, lad," the captain ordered. "Nothin' will come up so long as you've got somethin' 'eadin' down."

At that, Fallion grabbed a roll and ripped off a piece with his teeth, swallowing it as if it might save his life.

Borenson and Stalker both chuckled, and took a few perfunctory bites. Borenson ate silently, waiting for Stalker to state his business, but in Landesfallen, men didn't mix food and business, and so they ate through the meal in silence.

When everyone was full, Stalker leaned back in his chair and came straight to the point. "Thing is, see, Streben is dead. Got 'isself killed last night."

Both Borenson and the boy looked surprised.

Neither of them squirmed at those words, but then again, Stalker hadn't expected them to. They could have taken turns hacking the man to death with axes, and he suspected that they still wouldn't have shown any guilt.

"So, gentlemen," Stalker said, "it's your blades I'm wantin' to see."

Borenson raised a brow. "Why, sir, I protest: I haven't killed a man in . . . three days."

From the glittering in Borenson's eyes, Stalker knew that he spoke the truth. He hadn't killed a man in three days. But who would he have killed three days ago?

Not my business, Stalker told himself. Yet he inspected Borenson's blade anyway. Good metal, Sylvarresta spring steel, the kind that would hold an edge for ages and wouldn't rust for a century. It was so clean it might never have been used, and the blade was sharper than a razor. But then Stalker expected that a warrior of Borenson's stature would keep his blade in such condition. First thing after a kill, he'd have wiped it, honed it. Wouldn't have slept or eaten until that blade looked as polished as new.

Stalker returned it.

Fallion presented his own blade, and Stalker whistled in appreciation. Though the haft was a simple thing wrapped in leather, the metal had a dull grayish cast that Stalker had rarely seen. Thurivan metal, maybe six hundred years old, forged by master weapon-smiths who believed that they imbued the blade with Power from the elements. It was a princely weapon, and Stalker, who had done more than his fair share of weapons trade, was duly impressed.

But even more impressive was the blood wedged up in the cracks where the blade met the finger guard.

"Where'd this blood come from?" Stalker asked, peering down at the boy.

Fallion looked up at the captain and struggled to think where it had come from. The strengi-saat, of course! Fallion had stabbed it deeply four days ago, and worrying that others might strike at any moment, he had not cleaned the blade proper.

But he dared not tell the truth. He was, after all, still supposed to be in hiding.

"I cut myself," Fallion said, raising his still-bandaged left hand. The bandage was dirty and gray now.

Stalker shook his head. "Blood only gets in the 'ilt like this when you stab something deep, when it bubbles out all in a frenzy."

Fallion dared not come up with another lie, for that would only hurt his credibility.

Borenson came to his rescue. "He cut himself, like he said. It made a damned mess."

He said it with resolve. That was the lie, and they were both going to stick to it.

Damn, Stalker told himself, Streben's mother is going to be mad.

"Right," Stalker said, rising from his chair with a grunt. "Right. Streben was a rascal. No one will be sheddin' tears for him. Got what he deserved, most like." He forced a smile, peered hard at Fallion. The boy didn't squirm or look away.

Damn, he's a saucy one, Stalker thought. Nine years old, and he draws his own blood when the time comes, like a true warrior.

Stalker's appreciation for the boy ratcheted up a couple of notches.

"Still want that job?" Stalker asked. "I could use a cabin boy of your . . . demeanor."

Fallion nodded, but Borenson shot Fallion a worried look. "A job?"

"I asked if I could be a cabin boy," Fallion said. "I was hoping to learn how to run a ship."

Right now, Stalker imagined, Borenson was trying to understand why he'd be rewarding the lad for killing his nephew. Stalker had to wonder himself.

Because I like cunning and courage, Stalker realized. If I still had kids myself, I'd like 'em feral.

ಋ 23 ಞ

INVISIBLE CHILDREN

It is often said that children are invisible. But I think that it's not so much that they are invisible, as it is that we tend to see children not as they are, but as we expect them to be. And when we expect nothing from them, we learn not to see them.

—Hearthmaster Waggit

Rhianna lay in bed for much of the morning. As the other children rose and climbed up the ladder to eat, she just lay wrapped in her blanket. Myrrima cleaned the room for the day, folding clothes, making beds. She studied Rhianna and asked, "Hey, you, ready for breakfast?"

Rhianna shook her head. "Not hungry. I feel sick."

"Seasick or sick sick?"

"Seasick." It was a handy lie, and wouldn't require her to hold a lamp to her head to produce a fever.

"The whole Ainslee family is down with it," Myrrima said, referring to a refugee family that slept in the hold, near the pens of chickens and ducks and pigs. "Want a bucket, or can you make it topside when the time comes?"

Rhianna's stomach was in a jumble. Murder didn't sit well with her. "A bucket."

Myrrima produced a wooden bucket from under one of the bunks, apparently left for just such an emergency, and Rhianna lay abed.

Borenson and Fallion came back down to the cabin; Borenson told Myrrima, "Streben is dead."

Myrrima held her breath for a moment, and said, "You killed him?"

"Nah," Borenson said. "Someone else did it for me."

"The captain thought I did it!" Fallion chimed in. "They found Humfrey dead."

"Oh, I'm so sorry," Myrrima offered. She leaned over and gave him a long, heartfelt hug.

"And Captain Stalker found the strengi-saat's blood on my knife," Fallion continued. "And he thought it was Streben's blood."

Rhianna felt even worse with that news. She had a sudden vision of Fallion swinging from the yardarm for her crime.

Borenson guffawed with laughter. "Go clean your knife. You know better than to leave it in such shape."

Fallion hurried toward the ladder.

Myrrima hissed. "You can't send him up to clean his knife. The crew will see. They'll see it as a confession."

Fallion faltered in his steps.

"*I'm* not going to clean it," Borenson said.

Rhianna wondered if she should offer to clean it. It would only be fitting that she get the blame.

"No one should clean it," Myrrima said. "Leave it bloody for a couple of days, but leave it sheathed."

She peered at Borenson and said, "So what now? Is the captain going to put Fallion on trial, or what?"

Borenson chuckled. "He asked Fallion to be his cabin boy. I don't think he believes that Fallion is innocent, so he's rewarding him."

"Rewarding him for killing a man?" Myrrima asked, incredulous.

Borenson shrugged. "It's the pirate blood in him, I guess. I'm not worried about the captain. He seems to like Fallion. But we might have to worry about some of the crew."

Myrrima said, "Streben couldn't have had many friends. I don't think we'll have to worry about reprisals too much. Besides, anyone could have killed him."

"Yeah, but it was Fallion's ferrin that's dead."

Myrrima thought for a long moment, then asked, "Fallion, is there something that you're not telling us?"

Borenson guffawed. "A fine family we make, all sitting around the breakfast table accusing each other of murder!"

"I didn't do it," Myrrima said. "And you didn't do it. And Humfrey was in the cabin when we went to bed. He crawled over my feet a dozen times during the night."

"You know how ferrins are," Borenson said. "Most likely he found a rat hole and got out on his own. Or maybe one of the kids went up to the poop deck in the night, and Humfrey bolted out the door."

Borenson held his breath a long moment. Rhianna lay beneath her blanket. She imagined that everyone was peering at her. They'd finally put two and two together. So she peeked up over the edge of the blanket.

No one was looking at her. They all sat with their heads bowed in thought. No one suspected her.

I'm just a child in their eyes, she realized. I'm just a sick little wounded girl.

With that, she knew that no one *would* suspect her, ever.

"I'm sorry about your nephew," Fallion told Captain Stalker later that afternoon when he reported for duty in the captain's cabin. He wasn't sure why he'd said it. He was glad that Streben was dead, and he suspected that Stalker didn't care much either way.

The captain fixed him with an appraising stare and said, "When I was a lad half your age, me father put me on his knee and told me somethin' I want you to remember. He said, 'Many a man, when 'e gets angry, will go about threatenin' to kill a fella. 'E'll scream about it and tell any neighbor who is willin' to listen. That's one kind of fella.

" 'But then there's another kind, the kind who won't tell a soul. But 'e'll come to that man's door one night, and 'e'll have a knife up his sleeve.' " His voice got soft and thoughtful. " 'And 'e'll 'ave a hole dug in the fields nearby. And when 'is enemy comes to the door, 'e'll give no warning. 'E just takes care of business.' "

Stalker went silent for a long moment. " 'That's the kind of man I want you to be.' That's what me da tol' me."

Stalker hadn't taken the advice, of course. For years he'd worked as an honest merchant marine, determined to forget his past, his upbringing. But when you do that, he'd found, you get soft, and the world can come crashing down on you in a hurry. Sometimes he thought that if he could start all over again, he'd have been better off listening to his father.

Stalker thought for a moment. "Streben killed your ferrin, and you killed 'im. Don't cry about it now, and don't pretend to be sorry. When it comes time to gut a man, just take 'im down quietly. That's the dignified way. Got it?"

Fallion nodded, hurt that the captain thought he was guilty.

"Good," the captain said, slapping him on the shoulder. "I'm 'appy to meet a lad of your character."

Fallion peered up at Stalker in surprise. He wanted to proclaim his innocence. He hadn't killed anyone. Yet the admiration in the captain's voice was so sincere, Fallion almost wished that he had.

What's more, he was curious to learn about the captain. It sounded as if Stalker had been raised by wolves in human form. But the truth was even more apparent: Captain Stalker really was from pirate blood.

So as the captain made his rounds, Fallion began to clean his cabin. There was a great deal of booty lying about—wooden crates filled with Mystarria's rarest wines, valuable books, women's finery, valuable herbs and perfumes, jewels, and so on.

The captain had Fallion enter each item into a ledger. The wines went under his bed. The rest went into a secret compartment hidden in the wall above his bunk. Fallion was surprised at some of the items: there were twenty longbows made of Sylvarresta spring steel, for instance. These were in short supply even in Mystarria, and their sale to foreigners—potential enemies—was illegal. The bows were too powerful.

While he was stowing gear, Fallion found a wooden box in the desk. He pulled it out to discover its contents, and found a second ledger, one with ale-stained paper, its list of contents on the last page all duly verified and stamped by the harbormaster from the Courts of Tides.

Fallion compared his own ledger, the real ledger, to the one official one, and found that their contents matched nicely, so long as he only counted what was carried in the hold: hundreds of barrels of liquor, bricks of cheese, bolts of cloth, and so on. But the booty Fallion found stowed in the captain's cabin, items that were small and valuable, were worth almost as much as everything carried below.

Stalker was a smuggler.

The realization jarred Fallion. The captain seemed to be a friendly enough sort.

Fallion dutifully stowed the gear, then got a bucket of hot water and some lye soap, and scrubbed the floors, the desk, everything.

He wanted the captain to appreciate his work. In time that appreciation would lead to trust, and the trust to greater responsibilities. Eventually, Fallion could learn how to run the whole ship.

But it all started here on the floor, he told himself. Getting the grime off.

When he was tired, he lit a candle and checked the cabin to make sure that the room was neat and cozy.

Fallion sagged into the captain's chair behind the desk, weary to the bone. He just peered at the candle for a long moment, mesmerized by the multitude of colors in a single flame—the pale white and blue near the wick, the golds and shades of orange. He studied the way that the flame danced, stirring to unseen winds.

Fallion tried to anticipate the flame, envision which way it would bend, when it would sputter or burn low, or suddenly elongate and grow hot as it found new fuel. But he could not anticipate it. The flame seemed to surprise him, to always be just beyond his understanding.

"Are you a flameweaver?" Smoker had asked, laughing.

Now Fallion began to ask that question of himself.

He remembered how the torch had blazed in his hand when he fought the strengi-saat. He'd imagined at the time that something about the beast had caused it, as if its breath exploded like the gases deep in a mine.

But now Fallion wondered if he had summoned the inferno without thinking, so that in an instant he burned the torch to a stub.

"Torch-bearer." That's what the old man had called him. Fallion liked that name. A torch-bearer was someone who brought light to others.

It's a good name, he thought. A good destiny.

He peered at the flame, willed it to burn brighter, to fill the room with light. But for as long as he watched it, nothing happened.

So he decided to bend the flames. He had heard of a lad in Heredon who could cause cinders to rise up into the sky, to hurtle up like shooting stars, or cause flowers to appear in the flames, or send them up in braids, creating a knot of light.

Fallion studied the light for a long time, tried to work his will with it.

But nothing happened.

"You must make a sacrifice to the light," a voice seemed to whisper. It was a memory, Fallion felt sure, of something that Hearthmaster Waggit had once told him. The greater Powers could not be controlled, only served. Fallion's father had been the Earth King because he served the earth well, suborned his will to the earth's.

But what did the flames desire?

Food.

Fallion recalled an old joke that Hearthmaster Waggit had once told. "What do you call a young flameweaver?"

Fallion knew that there were different names for flameweavers within their order. One who could call flame into existence at will was called an incendiary. One who could burst into flame himself, stand like a fire, was called an immolator. But Fallion had never heard the names for the lowest levels of the order.

Fallion had struggled, guessing words that were unfamiliar: an apprentice? A novice? An acolyte?

Waggit had smiled. "An arsonist."

Because they had to serve fire. They had to feed the flames continually.

Fallion took an old slip of paper from the drawer, a crumpled paper with only a few notes written on it. He wadded it up, held it above the candle.

"Come and get it," he whispered.

The flame bent toward the paper, magically reaching out as if with a long finger, and burning into it greedily.

Fallion held the paper in his hand even as it burned, letting the flames lick his fingers for as long as he could. It surprised him at how little pain there was. He was able to withstand it for quite a while before he threw the paper down.

In that moment, Fallion felt wiser, clearer of vision than ever before.

Are you a flameweaver? the old man had asked.

"Yes," Fallion answered.

Moments later, the captain came in, and Fallion found himself peering up into the man's face. The books were open on the table, though Fallion had all but forgotten them.

The captain sniffed the air. "What you been burning?" he demanded.

Fallion grinned as if at a joke. "Evidence."

Stalker grinned suspiciously, nodded with his chin, and asked, "Understand those books?"

"Your handwriting is all scribbles," Fallion said, "but I understand. You're a smuggler."

The captain looked at him narrowly, as if considering. "Sometimes, a man is forced to cut corners, do somethin' 'e don't care for. Even a man that 'as scruples." And it was true. Stalker had bills to pay, money that went to shadowy types that he didn't even want to think about, and he had been forced to smuggle more and more these past four years. But the truth was, he'd always carried a little load on the side. "So's I work some deals under the table. The fancy lords in their manors don't know. But no one gets 'urt much. Do ya 'ate me for it?"

Fallion thought for a long moment, wondering if Stalker had a locus.

If he does, Fallion wondered, why is he trying to befriend me?

Stalker interrupted his thoughts, "Who owns wealth?"

"Those who create it, I guess," Fallion said.

Stalker considered his own ill fortune, and frowned. "That's who *should* own it, but that's not who *does* own it. Not in the end. Gold flows into your 'ands, and gold flows out. There's many a man who works 'ard for his pay, works his whole life. But in the end you're just food for the worms in the ground. You'll lose it sure, when you die, but probably sooner. Maybe you lose it 'cause you're a fool, so you throw it to the wind on a ship that runs aground. Or you lose it to drink or whores—or worse, you waste it on the damned poor, them what never has figured out 'ow to make it on their own. In the end, we all lose it.

"Now, me father, he would 'ave told you that them what can't keep wealth don't deserve it. It's like givin' a monkey a carriage, or a pig a castle. They may enjoy it for a moment, but they 'aven't the brains or the discipline to hold on to it. And you know why? Because in the end, the ones who *own* wealth, the ones who keep it, are those that are strong enough, cunnin' enough, and cruel enough to take it and 'old on for dear life. That's who the wealth really *belongs* to."

Fallion gave him a questioning look. Hearthmaster Waggit had taught that wealth flowed from the creation of goods. But Waggit's teachings didn't mesh at all well with what Stalker had to say.

Stalker continued. "Look, it's like this. A king collects taxes, right? He takes the wealth from his vassals, sends his lords out every autumn to gather in the 'arvest. But did 'e do any work for that? Is 'e the one who milked the cows and turned the milk into butter? Is 'e the one that broke 'is back with a scythe out in the fields, reaping the wheat and grinding it down to meal? Is 'e the one that dug the clay and burned 'is hands when 'e baked the bricks to build a house? No, the king—'e's just a lord, a man with weapons and an army and the guts to cut down any honest folk what stands up to 'im."

Fallion understood Stalker's reasoning, and he could easily argue against it. He could argue that a lord performed services for the taxes that he collected, that he fought and suffered and bled to protect his people, and in doing so, he was partly responsible for creating wealth.

But Fallion knew better. Even as a child he could see the truth, and the truth was that Fallion was raised in comfort, given the best of everything, and he had done nothing to deserve it.

The only difference between Fallion and the utterly impoverished tow-headed boys who herded hogs in the hills above Castle Coorm was that Fallion's family had a history of taking from their vassals, keeping their families in relative poverty while his own family enjoyed the spoils.

Fallion didn't believe for a minute that he worked harder for his wealth, suffered more, or deserved any better treatment than the peasants who worked the fields. He'd watched the smith's apprentice, breathing coal-fire at the forge all day, hammering out metal. What a wretched, cramped little life the lad lived.

But Fallion had never worked so hard.

Hearthmaster Waggit had tried to explain the truth away, but Fallion saw behind the lie.

"So, 'ow is a king different from any other thief?" Stalker asked.

"He's not," Fallion agreed. "He gives just enough service so that he can tell himself that he's a good man and get some sleep at night."

Stalker gave Fallion a long appraising look, as if he'd expected some grand argument.

"That's a sad truth," Stalker said. "Them what owns wealth is them what's strong enough and cunnin' enough and cruel enough to seize it." He knelt down so that he could peer Fallion in the eye. "So now I ask: why shouldn't that someone be you and me?"

So that was the whole of his philosophy, Fallion realized. We are all destined to end up with nothing, so why not grab all that you can for as long as you can?

The notion sickened Fallion. What's more, he could see that it sickened Captain Stalker, too. He argued, but it was only words coming out of his mouth. His heart wasn't in it.

"Was your da a pirate?"

Stalker grinned. "No. Now, me grandda was a pirate. But Da, he swabbed another man's deck."

Fallion found it intriguing. Stalker was steeped in an evil culture, and Fallion wanted to understand evil, to see the world through the eyes of evil men. He thought that in doing so, he might better understand how to fight a locus. And Stalker was giving him a primer in evil, discussing philosophies that Fallion would never have heard from Hearthmaster Waggit's tame tongue.

Fallion decided that Stalker was a likable fellow underneath it all. And Fallion knew that sometimes even an honorable man got backed into a corner and had to do things that he didn't want to. "No. I don't hate you."

"Good boy," the captain said with a grin. "Now go tell Cook to make you some rum puddin'."

Fallion raced out of the room feeling light of heart, secure in the knowledge that he had made a friend.

❧ 24 ❧

THE PRICE OF A PRINCE

*Every life has value. Some imagine that their life is worth nothing and only
discover too late that its worth cannot be measured in coin. Others value
their own skins far too highly.*

—*Gaborn Val Orden*

A couple of weeks out from the Courts of Tide, Fallion celebrated his
tenth birthday. On that morning, the children spotted a giant tortoise,
nearly fifteen feet long, swimming just beneath the waves, its shell a deep
forest green, and thus Fallion knew that they were in warmer waters.

Captain Stalker was walking the deck and said, "Down in Cyrma, I saw
a 'ouse made out of one of those shells. Big ol' mother tortoise crawled up
on the sand to lay 'er eggs, and some villagers cut 'er throat, cooked up
most of 'er insides, and used the shell to make a nice 'ut. She was bigger
than that one out in the water, of course."

"Do you think the water is warm enough for sea serpents?" Jaz asked
eagerly.

"Close," the captain said. "Serpents all 'ead south this time of year. We
should come up on 'em soon, if the weather 'olds. . . ." He gave a worried
look at the sky. "If the weather 'olds. . . ."

It was late morning, and a thin haze had been building across the heavens all night. Dawn had come red.

The black ship was spotted that afternoon, and the captain came above
decks and nursed every stray breath of air into the sails.

A squall rose that evening, driving the ship inland. They'd been sailing
well out to sea in order to avoid Inkarran warships, but now they were
driven almost to the beach, even when the sails were dropped and the prow
turned into the wind.

The captain was forced to drop anchor in the sand, and the *Leviathan* nearly ran aground.

They hugged the shore all night, and set sail again before dawn, the captain nervously keeping watch for both the Inkarrans and for the ship with the black sails.

For the next few days, Fallion kept busy with his studies—weapons practice by morning, the work of running a smuggler's ship by day, and his magic by night.

The death of Streben was the topic of conversation for much the first week, but soon it faded from memory, just as the death of Fallion's mother and father began to fade.

Fallion took Humfrey's little spear, the polished shaft of a knitting needle with some mallard feathers and horse hair tied to it, and put it in a box under his bed, where he kept the promise locket that showed the image of his mother when she was young and beautiful, and where he kept a gold button like the one on the coat that his father had worn.

That box had become a shrine, a special place for him. Sometimes memories came unbidden to Fallion, like the morning that the cook fixed muffins with dried gooseberries in them, and as Fallion ate, he recalled how much his mother had loved the tart taste of gooseberries, and he'd feel a stab of pain at the memory, deep and bitter.

But he was learning to keep his memories in that box, to take them out only when he wanted.

So the days wore on, blurring into one another the way that the haze blurred with the waterline on warm days, so that one could not see where the haze ended and the sky began.

In three weeks, Rhianna healed enough so that she could join Fallion in weapons practice, and Fallion suddenly found that he had a peer. Until then, he'd always imagined that Talon was the best child-fighter that he'd ever seen. Talon was quick and tenacious. But Rhianna was a little taller than he, and heavier, and she showed a grace, a level of skill, a speed, and a ferocity that Talon didn't possess.

On the morning of their first practice, Borenson watched the two of them spar for an hour, Rhianna weaving back and forth, her movements mesmerizing, the little finger of her left hand always drawing runes in the air.

Fallion had to wonder at that. Were her spells meant to slow his wits or to make him stumble? Or was she just trying to enhance her own abilities?

Then she'd strike with a swiftness and a fierceness that were jolting, demonstrating thrusts and parries in combinations that Fallion had never seen before.

Until at last, Borenson demanded, "Where did you learn to fight like that?"

"From my uncle. He taught me when I was small."

"His name, damn it?" Borenson demanded. "What was his name?"

"Ael," Rhianna said. It was a lie of course, but only half a lie. Instantly Fallion knew that she spoke of Ael from the netherworld, the Bright One who had given her mother the pin. That opened a whole world of new questions for Fallion. Had she been trained by a Bright One? Where had she met him?

But Borenson just searched his own memory, trying to think of a fighter by that name, and came up blank.

Later, Fallion pressed Rhianna, asking her about Ael.

Rhianna's mother had sworn her to secrecy, but Rhianna looked into Fallion's dark eyes and thought, I would do anything for you.

So, haltingly, she broke her silence. "He came here, from the netherworld," she admitted at last. "My mother invited him in a Sending. They can only come if they're invited, you know, and even then, they can't stay forever. There are laws, you know, laws there in the netherworld the same as there are here."

There, I've told him, Rhianna thought. But I haven't given Ael's real name.

"But what was he like?" Fallion said.

Rhianna thought for a long minute, and gave an answer that surprised even herself. "He was . . . like you."

"In what way?"

"He was kind," she said. "And handsome, but not so handsome that you'd think your heart would leap out of your chest when you saw him. He looked like a normal person."

"But he was a Bright One!" Fallion said. In his imagination, men from the netherworld were shining creatures, as if some greater glory sought to escape them.

"No," Rhianna said. "He didn't look special." They were hiding between a pair of barrels on the main deck, crouched with their backs to the captain's cabin. It seemed to Rhianna that you could never really be alone on a ship, and just then, a pair of sandaled feet padded past, some sailor. She waited until he was gone. "You know how everyone says that the world changed before we were born?" Rhianna offered. "They say the grass is greener, and us children are stronger than they were, smarter, more like Bright Ones than children in times past?"

"Yes," Fallion said.

"Well, it's true," Rhianna offered. "At least I think it's true. You look like a Bright One."

"If I look like one, then you do, too. And how do you or I look different from anyone else?"

"Other people, old people, are divided in halves," Rhianna said. "We're not."

Fallion gave her a confused look and she said, "My mother showed me. She held a mirror to her face, and showed me the right half of her face, doubling it. Then she moved it, and showed me the left half of her face. The left half of her face looked like a different person, sad and worn out. But the right half seemed younger, prettier, and still had hope.

"I had never noticed it before, but now I see it all of the time. Most people are torn in half, like they're two different people."

"Hearthmaster Waggit showed me that trick," Fallion said, suddenly remembering a demonstration from when he was very, very young. "Most people aren't the same on both sides."

"But we are," Rhianna said. "You are. When I look at you, both halves of your face are the same, both perfect. It makes you look more . . . handsome than you really are. And both halves of my face are the same, and so are Jaz's and Talon's."

Fallion thought a moment, then said, "But you couldn't have been born before the change. You're too old."

Rhianna smiled and took off her left shoe, then showed him the scar from a forcible on her left foot—a single rune of metabolism. "I got this four years ago. I was born a few months after you."

Fallion thought back to blade practice. No wonder she was so fast!

Hearthmaster Waggit had told Fallion that for both sides of the face to mirror the other was a rare trait. But now he realized that Rhianna was right. The Children of the Oak, the children born in the past nine years, nearly all had that trait, and when he saw someone like Borenson's son Draken, someone whose halves didn't mirror each other, the child somehow looked wrong.

"It isn't just people that have it," Rhianna said. "It's everywhere. In the cows and the sheep in the fields, in the new grass that sprouts. In trees that have sprung up in the past few years."

Has anyone ever noticed this before? Fallion wondered. And what changed the world, made it so common?

His father had slain a reaver in the Underworld, one that hosted a powerful locus.

What does that have to do with me? Fallion wondered. Why are children now different from children born before the war?

There was more going on than just the way that he looked, Fallion knew. It was as if some great wrongness had been mended.

Fallion couldn't see how the pieces of the puzzle connected. He was determined to find an answer.

Each morning, Fallion and the other children made a game of climbing the rigging up the mainmasts and looking out to sea for sign of ships or whales.

Thus one morning they spotted a great serpent finning in the waves, playfully swimming in circles as it chased its tail, its coils undulating as it swam. A sixty-footer—not huge, but respectable.

During the days, Fallion went back to work for Captain Stalker, struggling to gain his trust along with the respect of the crew. Fallion learned how to navigate by the stars, and to trim the masts in a rough wind. He learned the names of every crewman.

By day, he tried to gain their respect, and in the evenings sometimes he even sought to make friends. The men would often go to their quarters at night to drink ale and play dice. Fallion played with them twice, learning games of chance, but learning far more. In their company he began to gain familiarity with the hundred islands and atolls across the Carroll Ocean, learning not just their names, but tales of their peoples. Soon he spoke enough pidgin to speak with any sea hand within a thousand miles.

Myrrima put limits on his visits, telling Fallion, "I'll not have you learning sailors' filthy habits."

Still, Fallion earned some trust. He ran errands for the captain, brought messages, and the men spoke to him with respect. The other refugees were often called "cargo" to their faces, and "ballast" behind their backs. But his shipmates didn't see Fallion as just ballast anymore, like the other refugees. He had become "crew."

Some men would never like him, Fallion felt sure. The steersman, Endo, was one. Fallion often would hang around the forecastle, where Endo steered the ship at night. The sea ape, named Unkannunk, was his. Most of the day, the white ape could be found lying near the forecastle, sunning on the deck, its folds of belly fat hanging over its hips. Often it would leap into the water and hang on to a rope ladder by day, peering into the water in hopes of snagging a fish. Once, the huge ape even caught a small shark by the tail.

Fallion began petting the sea ape, but when Endo caught him one afternoon, the little albino man said, "Hands off. 'E don't like you. Never will."

One night they stopped to take on water and fresh supplies at an island called Prenossa, a place where the fresh stores included mangoes, dragoneyes, breadfruit, and a dozen other things that Fallion had never tasted before.

That night, Stalker took a seat in the local inn, a bawdy place by any standard, where the tables were cleaner and the women were dirtier than most. His seat. His place of business twice a year when he visited the island. He bartered some of his goods with the locals, traded for fresh supplies, then leaned back to get comfortably drunk.

Fallion sat beside him, learning how the trades worked, discovering what fair prices for goods consisted of here. Metal was expensive, food cheap.

Fallion basked in the captain's presence. Stalker treated Fallion well, and he seemed like a fair man despite his tough talk. Fallion liked him. Sometimes, he wondered what it would be like to have Stalker as his father.

Then Blythe and Endo blew in through the doors. Fallion didn't like either of them. Both men were cold, hard. They pulled up chairs. Endo looked at Fallion and said, "Get lost, kid."

Fallion looked to Stalker, to see if he really did need to leave, and Stalker nodded. "Give us a moment?"

Fallion went out under the starlight. A fresh breeze blew through the palm trees, and Fallion walked for a while over tropical beaches where ghost crabs and scorpions fought over scraps that washed up on the beach. After weeks at sea, it felt strange walking on land again. He kept waiting for the world to tilt.

It was just about to do so.

Inside the inn, Blythe gave Stalker some news: "We lost time in that squall. 'Eard a rumor, I did. The black ship was 'ere two days ago. It's one of Shadoath's." Blythe held back the rest of the news, waiting for a reaction.

So, Stalker considered, it was one of the Pirate Lord's ships. That couldn't be good. But Stalker was under Shadoath's protection. He paid thirty percent of his income for the run of the sea. "Any notion what she's after?"

"A pair of princelings," Blythe said, eyes glittering. "Don't know 'ow, but they tracked 'em to us."

Perhaps they only suspect, Stalker hoped. Could they really be sure?

"Shadoath is willing to up the reward. Five 'undred gold eagles for the boys."

Five hundred was a good offer, considering who they were dealing with. But if she offered five hundred, then they were probably worth ten times that much to her. Shadoath was a woman of unsurpassed cruelty. She ruled the sea with an iron fist.

But now that it came down to it, the thought of selling the boys to her rankled Stalker. Maybe he'd have sold to someone else, but not to Shadoath—not after what had happened to his own children, six years past, when Shadoath's hand had first begun to stretch across the seas.

He was away from home at the time, on a trading junket, when his children were taken. At first he thought it was kidnappers, holding them for ransom. It was a common practice among pirates.

Indeed, Stalker himself had spent two years as a hostage on a pirate ship. Looking back now, it had been a grand adventure.

But Stalker's children were placed in greater peril than he had ever been. With the first ransom note he'd received a foot, dried in a bag of salt, to prove it.

Shadoath tortured his children until Stalker agreed to pay for protection for the rest of his life. That's where his thirty percent cut went. But it didn't go to ransom his children and buy their release.

No, the torturers had gone too far. His daughter had lost a foot, and her mind. His youngest son had had his neck broken and could not even crawl. Stalker was forced to pay not for the release of his youngest son and daughter, but for their merciful executions.

Otherwise, Shadoath would have continued to torture them for years without end.

That was the kind of woman he was dealing with.

Stalker was himself the grandson of a pirate, and he'd spent his early years aboard pirate ships. But he'd never seen cruelty that equaled Shadoath's.

Stalker hated the woman.

"So what you think?" Blythe asked. "You ready to sell them boys?"

Stalker forced a smile. "I'm not sellin' to Shadoath. Other lords will pay more. Their own folk would best Shadoath's price ten times over."

Blythe and Endo looked at each other.

"You're not goin' soft on the boy, are you?" Endo demanded. "That's not wise—not wise at all."

The threat behind the words was palpable. If Stalker wouldn't sell, Endo would go behind his back.

I should kill them now, Stalker thought. I should draw my knife and gut them where they sit.

But he'd never killed a man for merely thinking about betraying him, and though his anger was thick in his throat, his hand didn't stray to his dagger.

"Be patient, lads," Stalker assured them. "This isn't a game that plays out in a day or a week. We can tuck the lads away in Landesfallen, nice and safe, and bring them out anytime. The price will only rise as the weeks pass."

"Patience may be fine for you," Blythe said, "but it's the sound of coins in my purse that I like."

It had only been a few weeks since Stalker had paid them both. They hadn't been in port long enough to spend their cash, and so he didn't offer more.

"Hang on," Stalker urged them in his sweetest tone. "We'll be as rich as princes a'fore long."

Blythe left Stalker's table and took a seat in the inn, a thick mug of warm ale in his hands.

He wasn't a patient man.

He wasn't stupid, either. Blythe glanced back over to the captain's table. Fallion had come back, was sittin' there peerin' up at Stalker like he was some damned hero.

Stalker liked to think that he was the smart one, but Blythe knew that you didn't say "no" to Shadoath. And you didn't beg her to wait, or ask for more money.

If she offers you a deal, Blythe thought, you'd best take it before she slits your throat and boils up a pudding from your blood.

Stalker is a fool.

He knew that Stalker paid Shadoath for free passage. But that's what he got, free passage. Nothing more.

The captain was going soft on Fallion, Blythe suspected. Or maybe he just hated Shadoath too much. But he couldn't save the boy.

Maybe there was a chance that Stalker could buy the lad, but it would cost him dear, and he didn't have that kind of money, not anymore.

He'd paid it all to the torturers, to end his own children's pain, paid it all to save his oldest, the one that the torturers had left unmangled. But in the end, Stalker had bought nothing. His oldest son couldn't live with the horror of what had happened, the shrieks of pain. And after Stalker bought his son's freedom, he'd come on his first venture across the sea, and each night he woke in the cabin, screaming. One night, somewhere north of Turtle Island, out in the Mariners, he'd thrown himself overboard.

Now Stalker was too broke to buy a pair of princes.

But Blythe had it figured. He could take the reward himself, keep it all.

That was the smart thing to do. You couldn't stop Shadoath. You couldn't run from her. So you might as well get a little something in your purse from the deal.

He left the inn in the moonlight, stepped in the shadows at the side of the building, and waited for a few minutes to make certain that none of Stalker's men followed him with a dagger for his back, then headed down the street.

There was a shack that the sailors all knew, a place where a man could get a bowl of opium to smoke, sleep with a whore, or purchase just about any other vice that one could dream up.

The proprietor was a tiny woman, an Inkarran dwarf with a crooked back.

"Yes?" she asked when she answered the door, her voice trailing off as she waited for Blythe to name his desire.

"I 'ave a message for Shadoath. Tell 'er that Deever Blythe aboard the *Leviathan* wants his five hundred gold pieces."

The message would take days to deliver, maybe weeks. But Shadoath would get it. It was only a matter of time.

ജ 25 ങ

SMALL BATTLES

No war was ever won by those who stood guard. They were won by those who leapt into a fray, regardless of how slim the chances.

—*Sir Borenson*

Back on the open sea, one evening while Myrrima and the children were all in the galley eating dinner, Fallion sought out Smoker. He found the old fellow sitting at the forecastle, nursing the flames in his pipe.

Fallion bowed to him and said, "Sometimes, when a candle is sputtering, or Cook's fire is guttering, I hear Fire whisper my name."

Smoker nodded. He seemed to understand what Fallion was going through. "Fire will whisper, beg you surrender, give self to it. The big fire talk with loud voice, and strong pull."

"What happens when you give yourself to it?" Fallion asked.

Smoker hesitated. "It share power with you. It fill you. But in time, it consume you. Must be care."

Fallion considered this. It was said that anyone who gave himself to one of the greater powers eventually lost his humanity. Fallion's father had done it, had traded his humanity in order to save mankind.

Fallion stared out to the open sea. Night was falling, but the sea was lit from beneath. Millions of luminous jellyfish stretched across the still water, making it look as if the sea were on fire.

"I understand," Fallion said. "Will you teach me?"

Smoker hesitated, inhaled deeply from his pipe, and Fallion added, "Myrrima will be mad. I know. She'll be mad at both of us. But I'm willing to take the risk."

Smoker smiled. "I not fear her," he said in his thick pidgin. His eyes suddenly blazed as if with an inner light. "But is danger if I teach you. And greater danger if I not teach. . . ."

And so it was understood, Fallion would become his pupil.

Smoker inhaled deeply, blew some smoke, sending it into the air, and said, "Little fire, easier to control. Smoke sometimes easier than fire. You try make shape."

So Fallion began his lessons in stolen moments. Fallion tried turning the puffs of smoke into the forms of fish or seagulls. He tried envisioning shapes while whispering incantations; he tried to force the smoke with his mind. He tried to surrender his will. But hour after hour, Fallion found that he had no knack for it.

"It will come," Smoker assured him. "Must make sacrifice to fire. Must burn something. But not enough wood on ship. We wait. Maybe make huge fire on island. We wait."

So they just talked. Sometimes they talked about how to serve Fire, and Smoker told Fallion some of the secret powers that he had heard about. Some flameweavers became so adept at sensing heat that they learned to see it, as if their eyes suddenly became aware of new colors in the spectrum. "We all flaming creatures," Smoker assured Fallion, "if we had eyes to see."

Fallion learned much in these conversations, but just as often he found that the lessons came as a complete surprise during the course of normal conversations. So it was that he came to what he thought was rather eso-teric. "Why are children born now different from those born before the war?"

Fallion hadn't expected an answer, but Smoker leaned back, pulling a long drag on his pipe. "The world was no balance," he said at last, the smoke issuing from his mouth. "Now, great harmony coming."

"How did it get out of balance?" Fallion wondered aloud.

"One True Master of Evil sought make it her own. That problem. The One World, the Great Tree, even One True Master of Evil—all shattered. All broken and twisted."

Fallion knew the legends. He'd learned them from Waggit and others. But he'd never considered that he was living in a time of legends. "But why is our world changing now?"

Smoker shook his head, as if to say, "Some things even wizards didn't know." But then he drew long on his pipe, and eventually, when the coals were burning hot, it seemed that his eyes glowed with inspiration and he said, "Someone fixing world."

"Right now?" Fallion asked. "Someone is fixing it? How do you know?" Everyone knew that the world had changed when his father defeated the reavers. But few seemed to notice that it was changing still.

"Many powers found in Fire. Not all destroy." Smoker exhaled, and Fallion struggled to make something from the smoke that had formed. Smoker continued. "Light. Is great power in light . . ." Smoker took some puffs on his pipe, until the bowl glowed brightly. "All world is shadow, is illusion. Land, trees, grass, sky. But light pierces shadow, shows us the real."

"So can it teach us new things?"

"Sometimes," Smoker admitted, "like now. Fire whisper, 'There is wizard at heart of world.' That how I know someone changes it. Sometimes, light shows things far away, future. But mostly . . . it make sense of things. It pierce illusion. Watch."

This is what Fallion wanted most right now in his life—understanding. He felt as if everything around him was hidden. There were loci on the ship. Smoker had told him so. But neither of them knew where. Was one in Captain Stalker? Fallion liked the man, but he didn't trust him completely. Maybe that's what a locus would want—for Fallion to like it. But Fallion wanted to pierce through the illusions, to see into men's hearts, and so he eagerly drew near.

Smoker stoked the fire in his pipe, and together they peered into the bowl for a long time, watched the embers grow yellow, then orange, then develop a black crust while worms of fire seemed to eat through them.

"In light is understanding. You, you creature of light, so you drawn to Fire. But why you not touch Fire, use Fire, let it touch you?"

Fallion shook his head, wondering, wishing to know how he could unlock the powers that lay within him.

I'm afraid, he admitted to himself. I'm afraid that I'll get hurt.

Suddenly the bowl of the pipe blazed all on its own.

"You keep light hidden," Smoker said, "deep inside. You not let it out. But when fear is gone, when desire blaze like this bowl, you become one with fire."

"How do you blaze?" Fallion asked.

"Many ways," Smoker said. "Passion. Love, despair, hope. All desires can lead you to power. Rage. Rage is easiest. Let rage build. Must rage like inferno. That release fire in you."

Fallion considered. A seagull cried out on the sea.

He must be lost, Fallion thought.

They were days out from port.

"Is that how immolators do it?" Fallion asked. "They let the rage in them burn?" Fallion imagined himself at the height of power, saw himself drawing light from the heavens, channeling it down into fiery ropes, until he too burst into flame, clothing himself in an inferno and walking unscathed, like the flameweavers of legend.

Smoker gave him a sidelong glance, as if he had asked the wrong question. "Yes," he said. "But you not want be immolator."

"Why?"

"Because, Fallion, is easy throw life away. Living, that hard."

"But immolators don't die."

"Not live, either. When fire take them, when burst to flame, flameweaver's flesh remains, but soul does not. His humanity turn to ashes. His heart goes to other.

"Must take care," Smoker urged. "Fire whisper to you, beg you to give self. But once is done, cannot undo. You be dead, and Fire will walk in your flesh."

"Have you ever immolated?" Fallion asked.

Smoker shook his head. "No."

"Then how do you know that you can?"

"Power is there, always whisper. I know I can do. Fallion, immolation is easy. When rage take you, is *not* become fire that is hard."

For long hours, Fallion had struggled to find any vestige of power. He'd tried shaping the smoke with his mind, imagining fish swimming through the air. He'd even tried pleading with Fire, seeking acceptance.

Now he peered over his shoulder, as if Myrrima might come walking the deck any moment.

And Fallion surrendered to rage. He thought about the past weeks, about how the strengi-saats had attacked Rhianna, about the fresh loss he'd felt over the death of a father that he hardly knew, about his terrifying flight from Asgaroth, his mother lying cold beside the fire, and last of all he imagined Humfrey the ferrin, broken and twisted like a rag.

The rage built as he considered the unfairness of it all. It became a hot coal in his chest, fierce and wild, tightening his jaw.

"Now shine," Smoker said, exhaling, sending tenuous threads of blue smoke issuing from his nostrils. Fallion did not try to shape it, didn't try to imagine anything.

He just let his rage release, like a light that burst from his chest.

A strengi-saat took shape in the smoke and floated up into the air, soaring, its visage cruel as its jaws gaped.

Smoker looked at Fallion with pride and gave a satisfied grunt.

Just then, at the back of the ship, Myrrima called.

Fallion whirled, caught a partial glimpse of her between the ropes and pulleys on deck.

Immediately he ducked, crawled over the forecastle, and went walking down the far side of the ship.

That night as Fallion slept, Myrrima told her husband, "We've got to put a stop to this. Fallion's running with the crew, thick as a pack of wolves. And tonight I saw him with Smoker."

Borenson lay beside her on blankets that had been washed in seawater earlier that day, and so smelled of salt. "Fallion's a good boy," he said with a sigh.

"He's being drawn to evil," Myrrima argued. "The Fire is pulling at him."

"We can't hold him back," Borenson said. "We can't keep him from gaining his powers."

"He's not old enough to choose wisely," Myrrima objected. "Fire draws to its adherents more than any other power. It seeks to consume them. I think we should talk to him."

"If we try to hold him back," Borenson said, "he'll think that what he's doing is shameful."

"Maybe it is," Myrrima said.

From the cabin door came a soft clapping. It was late, and Borenson lay there for a moment wondering who could be calling when everyone else was asleep. Finally, he pulled on his tunic and opened the door.

Smoker stood outside in the shadows, a single candle in his hand, his eyes reflecting the light from it with unnatural intensity.

"Must speak with you and wife," he said.

Myrrima was already throwing a blanket over her, wrapping it around her like a cape. She crept up behind Borenson, put a hand on his shoulder, and peered over.

Smoker said one word, "Asgaroth."

"What?" Myrrima asked.

"Shadow hunts Fallion. Asgaroth is name of shadow. Fire told me. Is near."

"On the ship?" Myrrima asked. She looked out the door. The other refugees in the hold were all abed. The animals slept. No one seemed interested in eavesdropping.

Smoker nodded. "Yes."

"Where? In whom?"

"Not sure. More than one shadow on ship. Two, maybe three. I feel them. Not know where. They hide."

Myrrima peered at the pale old man, the wrinkles of his face, and wondered. More than one locus was on the ship?

Myrrima had worried about this for days. Her water magic was strong in healing power and in protection; each morning she had been washing the children, drawing runes of warding upon them, just in case.

"Your magic help protect boy," Smoker said. "But Fallion need more. He must fight. You know, I know. Day will come when must fight. My magic strong in battle, but is also danger. You know. You feel urge to surrender to your master. Fallion feel, too, thousand times stronger."

Instinctively Myrrima had distrusted this man, but now he was proposing a truce. They had something in common; they both cared about Fallion.

"I don't want him to lose himself," she said. "He needs to understand the dangers."

Smoker closed his eyes and bowed slightly, a sign of agreement. "Power seductive; come with price."

"We both know that it doesn't just come with a price," Myrrima said. "Fire consumes those who serve it—just as it is eating at you. You cannot bear to be away from it. You smoke your pipe and take your dying slow. But you're like a fly caught in a spider's net, and there is no escape for you. You will be consumed."

Smoker nodded, closing his eyes in resignation. "Still, is power he will need. Fallion very strong. You know: he very good, but dangerous. We both must watch him."

ॐ 26 ॐ

ROUGH WATERS

Hope is the father of all virtues. Crush a man's hope, and you will sever him from the source of all decency.

—Shadoath

At eight weeks, the coasts could not be spotted and Fallion was informed by the far-seer in the crow's nest that they were in the realm "Beyond Inkarra."

Inkarra had always been the edge of the world to Fallion. It was a loose conglomeration of kingdoms all inhabited by folks with white skin, who worked and hunted by night. It was a forbidden realm, and no one who ventured beyond its borders came back alive.

Fallion and Jaz were ecstatic. They were sailing into the realms of legend, through the Atolls, following a string of volcanic islands to the Mariners, and then on to the far side of the world.

Stalker bent over his charts one morning, considering his course, when Fallion saw the worry in his face and asked, "What's wrong?"

"This is our course," Stalker said, "right here through the Mariners. We're supposed to stop at Talamok. I've got goods to unload."

"Is there some danger?"

Stalker was slow to answer. He'd been trying to reach a decision. He looked at Fallion evenly. "Pirates," Stalker said. "I think I'll sail around it, strike for open sea. We've got enough food and water to get us 'ere, I think, if the wind 'olds." He pointed at a small island on the charts, a place called Byteen. "It's an unin'abited island. The crew can scurry out and gather fruit, maybe even 'unt pigs. How would you like that, eh? 'Unt some wild pigs?"

Ever since his childhood incident with the boar, Fallion had been terri-fied of pigs. But these island pigs wouldn't be near as large as the ones in Heredon.

Stalker muttered, "Course, we might 'ave to fight some sea apes for the food."

Sea apes often lived among the Mariners, swimming from island to island to gather fish and fruit. Sometimes, whole rafts of them would swim together, hundreds of them with locked arms, forming floating islands.

"Why not go to one of the other islands?" Fallion asked. There were dozens to choose from, maybe even hundreds, including at least one called Syndyllian that was two hundred miles across and showed three ports.

"Shadoath controls them islands."

Fallion stood for a moment, unnerved. He'd heard that name before. "Shadoath is a pirate?" Fallion probed.

"You 'eard of 'er?" Stalker asked.

"I heard her name, once or twice," Fallion admitted. "Who is she?"

Stalker wondered. The boy didn't even seem to know that she had put a price on his head, much less that Stalker had just been worrying about whether he should accept her price. To do anything else was foolish.

"She's a pirate lord," Stalker said. "A bad one, a powerful Runelord. A man that's taken endowments out 'ere is rarer than a two-'eaded goat. Blood metal is 'ard to come by, and we got this saying: ' 'Im what's got a handful of endowments can rule the sea.' She's got more than a 'andful, she 'as.

"She came out of nowhere just a few years back, 'bout the time you were born, and built a fortress down 'ere in Derrabee." He pointed to a large island. "It wasn't long a'fore she got a few ships, took control of the Mariners." He waved, indicating the entire chain of islands.

"Can't anyone stop her?" Fallion asked.

"The only folks that care is them that lives in Landesfallen, and there aren't many of us. Maybe a dozen traders ply the waters these days. Landes-fallen 'asn't got a real navy."

There was a look of such hurt on Stalker's face that Fallion dared not ask about the battles he'd fought. Fallion could see that Shadoath had beaten him.

"I pay protection money to 'er now. She lets the *Leviathan* pass. But sometimes she boards us. That black ship that's been followin' us? That's one of 'ers."

For the first time in weeks Fallion felt truly unnerved. Shadoath was Asgaroth's master. They hunted together. Like wolves, his mother had said. Like wolves.

Shadoath is ahead of us, Fallion realized. And Asgaroth came out of the west, chasing me toward the edge of the world—into Shadoath's path.

Stalker was right to mistrust the course ahead. His plan sounded good—sail around the islands, keep as much distance as he could.

For his part, Stalker looked at Fallion and realized that he could not turn the boy over, no matter what the reward. Stalker had grown too close to Fallion in the past few weeks. He was a good lad—smart, capable. He had become like one of the sons that he should have had.

I'll die before I let her have him, Stalker told himself. Besides, the crew sees him as one of us, now. They'd probably mutiny if I sold him off.

Fallion peered at the map, eyeing it distrustfully. Stalker's plan gave him some comfort. Yet Fallion felt a strange certainty in his gut. It was his destiny to meet Shadoath.

The ends of the Earth are not far enough.

Fallion went to his cabin and spent the morning honing his blade.

The winds didn't hold. Stalker sailed north, trying to bypass the Mariners, but for the next two weeks the sails were slack, and it would take a good storm to drive the ship past the islands.

It was late in the hurricane season, and Stalker had dared hope that he'd not see one this year.

But the sails went slack altogether one morning, and the sea ape Unkannunk began to roar and slam his huge club against the deck, pounding and pounding in a fit of madness. Stalker came out of his cabin and found himself staring at a sunrise that struck fear into his belly.

The sky on the horizon was the blue-green of a bruise, and the air was as heavy as a wet blanket. You could feel the lightning in the air, little pinpricks crawling over the back of your neck.

"Drop the sails," Stalker ordered. "Batten the 'atches, and strap yourselves down."

There was no port to make for. They were fifty miles north of the nearest island, at the very least. Navigating on the open water like this was always part guesswork, and Stalker only had a general idea of where he was.

Myrrima felt it, too. She woke in the morning in solemn terror and didn't take time to eat or clothe her children. She spent the morning on a rope ladder, drawing runes of protection on the ship, runes of strength to hold it together, runes of way-finding to guide the steersman's course.

Then it came. The clouds gathered over the heavens, sealing off the sunlight, and the thunder could be heard in the distance. Then the explosive bursts of light came, high in the clouds.

The seas began to pitch and the storm rolled in lightly, the wind singing through the rigging. When the first patters of rain started, Myrrima brought the children down into the hold, into the dark, where only a single lantern swaying on a hook gave any light.

Captain Stalker stayed above decks and watched the hurricane come in, three men lashed to the wheel, trying to guide the ship.

There are no words that can describe the terror of a storm at sea, winds of ninety miles an hour shrieking through the masts, waves crashing down over the bow so that the boat shudders under your feet as if it will tear apart, that moment when the boat climbs and climbs and climbs up an eighty-foot wave, only to reach the top, and then come crashing down into the wallow with a bone-crushing jar.

Down in the hold, the children wept and moaned. Seasoned crewmen who never got seasick grew ill and lay in their own vomit, wishing for death, wishing with each moment that on the next wave, the ship would tear asunder and yet also fearing to the core of their being that on the next wave the ship would founder.

Lightning took the mainmast. A bolt of it struck the masthead and sent a line of fire running down the beam, almost to the deck.

Stalker didn't worry about the fire. The rain was driving so hard that you couldn't open your mouth without getting a drink, and mountains of water crashed over the railing.

The fire would sputter for a few minutes, then die.

Amid the high winds, the weakened mast gave a tattletale cracking sound, and the ropes in the rigging began to snap.

Before Stalker could shout a warning, it toppled, falling backward into the mizzenmast, snapping spars, so that both masts fell in a tangle of rope.

The ship twisted beneath their feet, listing to starboard.

The heavy masts tangled in the rigging. As the masts fell, the ship lost balance and canted precariously.

If the men didn't cut the masts free, a wave would take them broadside and capsize the ship.

Suddenly a dozen sailors rushed up from below decks, swords and axes in hands, chopping at the tie lines and rigging, trying to cut the fallen masts free. Stalker and the steersmen grabbed the wheel, tried to aim the ship's prow into the waves, but it felt as if the rudder were gripped by a giant hand, and three men together could not budge it. The fallen mast gave too much drag.

Stalker abandoned the wheel and rushed to help cut the damned masts free.

The waves caught the ship broadside, and he lost his footing, went down beneath a wall of water that came cascading over the railing.

Three crewmen went flying overboard, into the white surf, their mouths working uselessly, their cries for help stolen in the roar of the wind, the pounding of the sea.

And then there was a crack, and a line snapped, the rope slapping Stalker's face like a bullwhip, and the mainmast went sliding into the sea.

He himself followed, gravity pulling him downward. He tried to catch himself with his feet, bracing them to take all of his weight as he slid down the slick decks toward the railing.

It didn't work. He hit the rail and his legs gave way beneath him. He found himself toppling overboard. Only years at sea kept his mind steady enough so that he twisted in the air and grabbed onto the railing with both hands, clinging for dear life.

The ship rolled over a smaller wave, and now suddenly the boat lifted and turned. Stalker clung to the railing as the ship seemed to rise beneath him like a mountain. He was suddenly plastered against the outside of the hull, his weight sustained by it, and peering down across the deck to the trough of the next wave.

Inwardly, he prayed that the ship would hold together.

27

SYNDYLLIAN

Children always imagine that evil resides somewhere far away, perhaps in a mysterious land far beyond their borders. But every man knows where it can be found. It is as near as your own heart.

—Gaborn Val Orden

When the storm finally cleared, Captain Stalker found that he'd lost seven members of the crew, including Endo.

The last that he had seen of the man, Endo was treading water in incredibly rough seas, trying to keep his head above the whitecaps. His faithful sea ape, Unkannunk, howled in dismay and leapt into the wash to save him, but a huge breaker crashed over the two, and by the time the water cleared, both of them were lost to view.

The only thing that saved Stalker himself was dumb luck.

The ship was a wreck. The mainmast and mizzenmast were gone completely, and much of the upper deck was broken and in a shambles.

The storm had blown them far off course to the east and north—that much Stalker could tell just by the water: it was deeper green than it should have been, from too much algae, and its surfaces were all hard angles. That only came from cold water funneling down from the arctic currents.

In their current condition, it would take a couple of weeks just to limp to some island among the Mariners. And they wouldn't be able to just dodge onto some uninhabited island. They'd need a proper port, one where they could get the masts replaced, buy enough tarp for some new sails.

Sailing on to Byteen was out of the question. There was only one place to go: Syndyllian.

છ

"We're goin' to get boarded," Stalker told Borenson and Myrrima that night. "There's rumors that Shadoath is searchin' for your boys. I mean to see that she doesn't find 'em."

"Are you sure that we have to go to Syndyllian?" Myrrima asked.

"It's the only island in the chain that's got proper trees on it," Stalker argued. "We might take on food and water elsewhere, even buy some new sails, but we can't repair the masts . . . and without them, we're almost dead in the water. We outran that little black schooner twice, but we won't do it again."

"So what do you propose?" Borenson asked.

Stalker had it all figured. But he needed Borenson and Myrrima to agree to his plan.

"I figure it will take a few days to get the masts fitted," Stalker said. "I've 'ad business dealin's with Shadoath in the past. I pay for free passage through the Mariners. So me and the ship shouldn't be in any trouble. I'm thinkin' we can sail into port at night, under cover of darkness. But before we make port, we'll lower a boat, and you, Mr. Borenson, can row the boys ashore. You'll need to stay 'id. You should be fine for a week. Then just keep watch for the ship at night. When we sail out to sea, we'll drop anchor near the beach, and you can row out to meet us."

Borenson considered the plan. It sounded simple enough. Syndyllian was a big island, from all that Borenson had heard, and had been well settled for hundreds of years. There was plenty of fresh water, plenty of farms and peasant huts.

He looked to Myrrima for approval. She was the wizardess, after all. And she was the one who would have to stay with their children, perhaps even endure the scrutiny of Shadoath. "I can take the boys," he said. "But I'm not sure that I want to leave you and the children. We could all go. We could all hide out together."

Myrrima bent her head, deep in thought. Her heart was full of misgivings. She didn't know what kind of shelter they might find in the wild, what foods they would be forced to eat. Myrrima could handle it, but it would be harder on the little ones. Worse, Myrrima was still nursing Erin, and at three, Sage would never be able to remember that they were in hiding.

"I'll stay with the children, and keep Rhianna," Myrrima finally decided. "You take the boys into hiding."

Her misgivings were fierce, though, and she rocked back and forth on her stool, wondering.

In her fortress on Syndyllian that night, Shadoath walked upon the veranda of her palace, under the stars.

Outside in the valley below, the barracks of her armies stretched for miles, dark tents covering the land. And as the stars twinkled in the heavens above, the campfires and forge fires glittered below her.

Shadoath had taken hundreds of endowments of stamina, brawn, grace, and will. She no longer needed to sleep.

But she rested, walking alone under the starlight, her eyes unfocused, in a waking dream.

That's when the Sending came.

Asgaroth appeared to her not in any human form, but with a hideous face, as if to reveal the monster that he was. He spoke only two words: "We come."

The vision faded, and Shadoath smiled. For nine years she had been on this miserable little world, preparing.

Now, the torch-bearer was on his way.

Nine days later, the *Leviathan* reached Syndyllian. Captain Stalker had apprised the crew of his plan and sworn the men to secrecy.

It was only at the last instant, as the boat lay under the stars on the north shore of the island, that Rhianna informed them all that she would be going with the boys.

Myrrima was prepared for it. The girl was growing more and more dependent upon Fallion. At night, evil dreams kept her awake, and it wasn't until she was lying by Fallion's side that she could sleep.

Reluctantly, Myrrima gave her consent. Borenson and the children climbed down the ladder to the ship's boat. Borenson rowed away, the big boat riding lightly on the sea as it made for the gentle white sands of Syndyllian.

The captain marked the spot with the navigator, choosing a pair of mountains in the distance as a point of reference for their return.

An hour later, the *Leviathan* sailed into the port city of Mannesfree under a gentle breeze as the moon rose so huge out above the sea that the last of the roosters down in the hold thought the sun was rising and began to crow.

They eased into port and found the waters still and glassy, with four other ships already lying in harbor. It was not a huge port. A steep hill rose to the south, and they were at the mouth of a deep river. A few inns and shacks crouched along the pier. Myrrima could see the fishermen's nets hanging by the docks, where they were dried and mended.

To the north, a small city sprawled across a fertile plain.

It felt cozy and idyllic.

There was singing coming from a little shanty by the waterside, and the sounds of woodwinds and drums. So late in the night, few other folks in the city seemed to be awake. A single lantern gleamed over the water.

The city seemed almost abandoned.

No smoke rose from the chimneys. No lights shined from the windows.

Stalker studied the scene with evident concern. " 'Aven't been in port 'ere for five years. Used to be a jumpin' place. Busier than this."

Myrrima stood on deck, peering anxiously. One of the ships lying in port had black masts.

Sitting upon a barrel behind her, Smoker inhaled deeply on his pipe, a red glow forming in his hands around the bowl, and peered out over the water, his face wrinkling in concern. He said to Myrrima, "Something wrong."

Myrrima could not fathom why everything was so dead.

28

THE BEACH

In Carris, when the reavers charged, I saw men grow weak at the knees and faint, while others leapt into battle and performed superhuman feats of strength. Thus I propose that the fear that weakens one man only serves to make another man strong.

—Duke Paldane

They all helped drag the away boat up onto the beach, Borenson lifting the prow while Fallion, Rhianna, and Jaz tried to get the back and sides. None of the children were slackers. Borenson drove them too hard in weapons practice for that. But they were still young, and Jaz especially had a hard time of it.

They wrestled the boat up over the sand dunes, through tough grasses that rasped beneath their feet, and it was a quarter of a mile before they neared the tree line.

As they struggled toward it, in the hills above them Rhianna heard a familiar growl, like distant thunder: the hunting cry of a strengi-saat.

Her muscles melted at the sound of it, and she dropped her corner of the boat.

Borenson whirled and drew his saber. Rhianna already had her weapon in hand. Fallion hadn't heard the sound, but recognized that something was up, while Jaz just grumbled, "Come on. Let's go."

The surf splashing over the beach was a constant hiss, and Rhianna stood, straining to hear more, another cry in the darkness, or the thud of footfalls as one of the creatures dropped to the ground.

She heard a swoosh, the movement of branches as something heavy leapt from a tree, and moments later another hunting cry rose to her left, and oh so faintly, almost as if she imagined it, a third cry farther up in the hills.

The moon was rising, huge and full out over the ocean behind them. Rhianna searched across the beaches for sight of any shadows in the coarse grass, any dark patches where a strengi-saat might hide, but she could see nothing.

The creatures did not like open spaces.

Palm trees rose up ahead. There, giant ferns shadowed the ground, and vines corkscrewed up among the foliage. It was a jungle. The strengi-saats could be anywhere in there.

Borenson crept toward the children, had them huddle together, and put a big hand on Rhianna's shoulder comfortingly as he whispered, "All right. This is as far as we go tonight."

"What's wrong?" Jaz asked. "What's going on?"

"We'll turn the boat over," Borenson whispered. "Rhianna, I want you and Fallion to crawl under it, use it for a shelter, and get some sleep. I'll keep guard out here."

"What's going on?" Jaz demanded again.

Borenson gave him a look, warning him to be silent, and whispered, "Now, I've a question for you. I'm thinking that it might be good to have a fire. It keeps most animals away. But it will also light up this beach for miles, and show us up to anyone or anything that's out there."

So he wanted a vote. He looked mainly at Rhianna though, as if the choice were hers. He knew that she was terrified of the dark.

Each time that a strengi-saat approached, it brought the night with it, and she had learned to be afraid.

She had to balance the hope that a fire would give her with other very real dangers, though. Shadoath's people were supposed to live on this island. Were any of them left? How long could they survive if strengi-saats were about?

Could it be that Shadoath somehow controlled the monsters?

Rhianna wasn't sure.

"A fire," Fallion suggested. He was nervous, shifting from foot to foot. "A small one. I can build a tiny one, and keep it small, until the moment we need it."

Borenson peered at Fallion, measuring him. "Are you sure you can handle it?"

Rhianna wasn't sure what he meant. Could Fallion keep a small fire going, or was he asking something more?

Fallion was a flameweaver, Rhianna knew. And Myrrima had fought against Fallion's training. She thought that he was too young for it, and fire was too seductive. Would Fallion be tempted to trade his humanity for Fire?

That's the question that Borenson is really asking, Rhianna decided. He doesn't want to bring Fallion to this beach as a child, only to watch him become an immolator.

"I can control it," Fallion said. But Rhianna could see that he was worried.

He needs the fire as much as I do, she decided.

And so they flipped the boat over, and Rhianna and Fallion scooted beneath it. Borenson told Jaz, "Look around here, bring over some driftwood and put it in piles, along with some dry grass, so we can set it afire at need."

So Borenson and Jaz remained outside, and Fallion put his arm around Rhianna and they lay together.

They had not been lying for more than a few seconds before the fire started.

Fallion didn't wait for his brother to bring some dry grasses or driftwood. The fire just seemed to sprout from the empty air, as if the heat were so great that it could not be contained.

It was a small fire, as promised. A tiny flame no bigger than a candle; Rhianna saw that it had formed on a twig of driftwood that Fallion had found in the dark.

But it was enough. It gave them some hope.

The curve of the gunwales on the boat let them see out a bit, to where Borenson's feet marched past nervously.

Rhianna trembled in fear, her heart fluttering madly.

Fallion whispered, "How did strengi-saats get here? Asgaroth opened the gate between worlds months ago, thousands of miles from here. Did they come by ship?"

"They couldn't have been brought by ship," Rhianna decided. "We're too far from there. Besides, the strengi-saats that caught me were running wild."

So Shadoath must have summoned her own monsters. But why? Why would she loose them upon an island, one where she kept her warriors?

"They're part of her army," Fallion whispered as if she had asked the question aloud. She realized that he was drawing upon his powers; he'd seen into her mind. "They're her night sentries. Darker things stir in the hills."

She turned, just enough to see his face. His eyes were wild, his face pale and drawn. Sweat was rolling from his brow, and he peered intently at his little flame, as if the fire were showing him things.

What has Smoker been teaching him? Rhianna wondered. He hasn't been training for long. Is he really that gifted as a flameweaver, or is it desperation that makes him strong?

It could have just been the tiny fire, but it seemed to Rhianna as if there were too much light in Fallion's pupils, as if distant stars were captured in his eyes.

❧ 29 ☙

THE MERRY JIG

Knowing when to strike and when to hold still, that is half a battle.

—*a saying of Rhofehavan*

Stalker took the captain's chair at the inn. It was a sloppy dive called the Merry Jig, one that he remembered well. It was famous for featuring sour ale to go with its overcooked fowl, all served by wenches so ugly that they threatened to give womanhood in general a bad name. But the inn did have one redeeming feature: it had kept musicians playing nightly now for over a hundred years.

Once a lively place, it had apparently fallen on hard times. The serving wenches were gone, replaced by a couple of lads with greasy hair and bad teeth. The other ships lying in the harbor apparently didn't have crew ashore, for the establishment was empty of all but the most hardened of customers—a pair of the drunkards.

"Let's have some ale, and some of your lousy bird for dinner!" Stalker shouted as soon as he took his seat, waving his hand in general so that the lads would know that he was buying for the whole crew. He waited sullenly.

His men were coming ashore in waves, a dozen at a time rowing across in the ship's boats. It would take the better part of an hour to unload.

Just after the fourth shore boat had unloaded, bringing some of the guests from the ship—which included Myrrima, the babe in her arms and her brood of children clinging to her robe, Shadoath arrived.

Shadoath strode into the inn wearing no armor, for she needed none. She was a Runelord at the height of her power. Her speed and her grace served as her armor.

Shadoath was a petite woman of tremendous beauty. It was as if sunlight had entered the room, all somehow captured and subdued beneath a surface that glowed like a black pearl. She held her back straight, eyes high, a study in poise.

Her beauty contrasted greatly with the creatures that followed on her heals. They were not apes, at least not of any variety that Stalker had ever seen. They were hairless, with warty gray skin as thick as a warthog's, and arms so long that they walked on their knuckles. They had no ears that he could see, just dark circles, tympanums behind their jaws. Their huge eyes had no whites to them at all, and they squinted as if the room was too bright for their liking. They wore no clothes, only belts that carried strange weapons—clubs with animal teeth for spikes, curved knives that fit around the hand like brass knuckles, and other things that were stranger still.

And there was no joy in their eyes, no emotion that he could discern. The deadness of them, that's what made Stalker shiver.

Shadoath's eyes were dark and sparkling, as if her pupils were black diamonds. Her ebon hair fell over one naked shoulder, curling in toward her cleavage.

Every curve of her—shoulders, breast, stomach, thighs—seemed to drive him mindless with reptilian desires, and Stalker had to struggle to restrain himself.

Stalker had often admired Myrrima when she walked the decks, but Shadoath—Myrrima was a pale shadow beside her. Shadoath had to have forty or fifty endowments of glamour at the least. No man could linger in her presence and not desire her. The smell of her alone ensured that.

She killed your children, Stalker reminded himself, hands shaking while his whole body quivered with desire.

Among the men, only Smoker seemed immune to her charms. The wizard stiffened as she passed, and his eyes glowed brighter, as if he struggled to keep from unleashing some hidden fire.

"Captain Stalker," she said, her voice as sweet as any birdcall, "I've missed you."

He forced a smile. Her voice was high, and though she tried to move casually, she did so with great speed. Four endowments of metabolism, at least, he imagined.

She stepped to his table, took a seat. Her body was all air and poise.

This woman is battle-ready, he realized. Brawn and grace to the hilt.

A hundred endowments brawn and grace and stamina she has at least, perhaps even hundreds.

He could see the scars left by forcibles there deep between her breasts. Her body, beneath the silks, was a mass of scars.

Where are the townsfolk? he'd wondered when he first peered out from the ship. Now he suspected that he knew. She'd put the forcibles to them, and now held them prisoner in her Dedicates' Keep.

She sat beside him, leaned forward. Stalker's eyes fastened on her cleavage, the mesmerizing sway of her breasts, the skin so rough down there, like rippling waves above a clear pool.

"So," she said, "tell me, where are the boys?"

"What boys?" Stalker asked.

"The princes of Mystarria. The Sons of the Oak." Shadoath said loudly enough so that all could hear. She smiled, but there was a predator's hunger deep in her eyes.

"Not on my ship," Stalker said evenly.

She looked at him as if she'd caught him in a lie. "Two boys, dark of skin, with raven hair, both of them nine or ten years of age."

"No one like that on my ship," Stalker said. "See for yourself."

She peered as if her eyes alone could pierce him, shatter his wall of lies, tumble down a fortress of deceit. All around them, sailors muttered, "That's right," "That's the truth, ma'am."

Without turning, still peering into his eyes, she said softly, "Is that the truth, Deever Blythe?"

Blythe stepped away from the bar and stammered, "In a manner of speakin'. We dropped 'em off, up the north shore, 'bout an hour ago."

There were gasps from the crowd and soft little cries. Stalker tried not to let Shadoath see the rage boiling up in him. Smoker gave Blythe a fierce look.

You're a dead man, Blythe, Stalker told himself.

Blythe smiled broadly at Stalker, downed his beer, and hurried out the door. Smoker made as if to follow, but one of the crew grabbed his arms, restrained him.

"Go and get the boys," Shadoath ordered the ugly creatures at her back.

The pair whirled and headed toward the door, walking on their knuckles.

There was a ring of metal, a swirl of robes. Myrrima plunged a dagger into the neck of one of the imps.

The blade should have driven between the monster's top vertebrae and its skull, but the steel was no match for that ugly gray skin. The blade snapped and the creature fell forward, flailing to the floor, knocking over stools.

Before Stalker had a chance to rise to his feet, Shadoath was up from the table.

What happened next was a blur. Myrrima whirled toward Shadoath to do battle, and there was a hiss as fog came pouring in under the door, rushing through cracks in the window. The whole inn suddenly filled with mist so thick that Stalker could hardly see from one wall to the next.

But Shadoath was faster still, too expert for Myrrima. She became a blur. She leapt in the air, kicked Myrrima in the face, somersaulted, and landed lightly on her feet. Somewhere in that time, there may have been a roundhouse kick to the legs. Myrrima went flailing backward with a groan, her flesh smacking to the floor.

The other imp caught Myrrima and held her firmly.

Blood flowed freely from Myrrima's face, running from her nose, from a split lip, from a scrape above her eye. Stalker wondered what had stopped the fight, and then stared in horror as he saw that Shadoath had grabbed baby Erin from the counter.

Myrrima struggled lamely, the little imp gripping her, grunting with delight, his face pressed against hers.

The babe shrieked in terror as Shadoath held it by the feet, a dagger laid to its throat.

Shadoath whispered, "You have a choice: you can die while your children watch, or I shall kill your children as *you* watch—starting with this babe. . . ."

At the end of the bar, Smoker exhaled a breath of smoke while fire blazed in his eyes. He was ready to go incendiary.

"No!" Stalker shouted, throwing the table aside. But he didn't dare attack. Shadoath, with her endowments, couldn't be beaten by the likes of him.

And he knew that she would gut the baby quicker than another man would gut a rabbit.

"They're under my protection," Stalker shouted. " 'Safe passage.' That's what I pay for. Safe passage for me and mine. These folks is cargo, bought and paid for."

Shadoath smiled for an instant. Stalker knew that she was thinking about killing them all. There was nothing that any of them could do to stop her.

All he could do was to appeal to whatever vestiges of humanity remained in her.

At last she tossed the babe to Myrrima.

"These you can have," Shadoath said, "but not the princes. The princes are mine."

Myrrima caught the babe, fumbled to get her upright. Little Sage was screaming, fighting to get to her mother, but one of the crew had grabbed the child to keep her safe. Draken and Talon both were weeping bitterly, but had the good sense to keep their distance.

One little imp surged out the door, eager to do his master's bidding.

Outside the inn, there was a strange snarling, a roar like thunder, and Myrrima's eyes went wide with terror.

Shadoath peered at Myrrima and whispered, "Relax. By now, I'm sure that the boys will be eager to be captured."

Shadoath smiled at her secretively and strode from the inn. It was as if the sunlight went with her, the glory departing, leaving the room to look dull and dingy. Without her, the room was a cave full of cobwebs and shadows. It almost surprised Captain Stalker when Smoker moved, went to the door to watch her depart. Compared to Shadoath, they were all dead things.

❧ 30 ☙

ON THE BEACH

To rob a man of his money is a foul thing, but to rob a child of his childhood is far more grievous.

—Jaz Laren Sylvarresta

Fallion lay beneath the boat with Rhianna, sweat pouring from him, and struggled to keep the flames at bay.

There was a fire in him indeed, he discovered. It glowed, and it was strong enough to light other fires.

He was feeling helpless and outraged at the fates that had tossed him here on the beach.

Why can't the world just leave me alone? he wanted to shout.

But the fates would not leave him alone. Fate seemed to hunt him, shadowing him like wolves, and now he lay upon the beach with Rhianna beside him while Borenson bravely held off the strengi-saats.

Jaz had not hunted for firewood for more than three minutes before he raced back, his teeth chattering from fear, and proclaimed softly, "There are shadows out there."

The strengi-saats had found them.

"Stay close to the boat," Borenson whispered. "Watch my back, and when I tell you, dive under the boat with the other children."

Jaz was silent for a long, long moment, and then whispered, "What good would that do?"

What good indeed? Fallion wondered. The strengi-saats were huge. If Borenson lost against them—and he surely would lose, Fallion believed, for he was but a common man now—then the strengi-saats would take them all, play with them, batting the children around, nipping at them with massive teeth, the way that a cat takes pleasure in tormenting a mouse.

And so the fear grew in Fallion, fear and a bone-crushing sense of help-lessness. He peered at his little flame, one that had sprung to life not from any match or any piece of flint, but from his own heart, and he struggled to keep it from growing, to keep it from raging across the island.

For he was filled with wrath.

Rage is born from desperation, he thought. It came like a memory, and Fallion wasn't sure if he was just repeating something that Waggit had once said, or if he had just heard it from fire.

But then he seemed to remember. "Whenever we grow angry," his father had once said, "it is in response to a sense of helplessness. We all yearn to control our lives, our destinies. Sometimes we wish to control those around us, even need to control them. So whenever you grow angry, look at your-self, and figure out what it is that you want to control."

Fallion remembered now. It was back when he was a child of four. His father had come home from his wanderings, from the far corners of Ind-hopal. He had brought Fallion a present of bright parrot feathers—yellow, red, green, and blue—to wear in his hats.

His father's voice came clear now, almost as if he were still speaking. "Once you know what it is that you want to control, focus your efforts upon that thing."

His father had always seemed so reasonable. He always took specific instances and tried to draw larger lessons from them. He was like Smoker that way, always trying to see beyond the illusion, to learn the lessons that he insisted "life" was trying to teach.

What had it been that Fallion was angry about? A puppy. A little hunting hound that he had brought up to his room to play with. The puppy had peed on the floor, and Fallion had grown angry, for even as he told the pup to stop, it stared at him with sad eyes and finished its business.

Fallion smiled at the memory, and his anger diminished somewhat. His rage shrank, along with his desire to make a furnace of this island, burn it and everything on it.

"Sir," Jaz whispered to Borenson. "There's three of them on the beach behind us, I think. Maybe four."

Fallion heard the rustle of clothing as Borenson craned his neck to see. Fallion wished that he'd heard the clink of chain mail, but Borenson had been on ship too long, where mail was bound to get rusty or bear a man down into a watery grave. He wore no mail tonight.

"Just two," Borenson said. "Those others are driftwood. Tell me if they come closer."

So Jaz was imagining things.

Fallion's heart was pounding. Rhianna squirmed a bit, and Fallion clung to her. He could feel her heart, too, pounding in her chest, like a bird fluttering against the bars of its cage.

The moon continued to rise; a silver light spilled out over the white sands. A ghost crab came scuttling under the boat as if seeking to hide under a rock, and Fallion watched it dully, then flicked it back out with his fingers.

At long last, Borenson breathed softly in resignation. "Fallion, light the fires."

Fallion did not have to think about it. Light poured from him. He did not see it, but he could feel it. It raged from his chest, slammed into the pile of grass and driftwood, and suddenly there was a beacon of fire, blazing with light, sending oily smoke into the sky.

The light was far brighter than any normal fire, brighter even than a forge. Fallion wanted it what way. He wanted to flood the sands with light.

There was a snarl of surprise from a strengi-saat, and faintly Fallion could feel a pounding through the sand as one of the monsters leapt away.

"All right," Borenson said with a chuckle. "You can stop now. They're gone. For the moment."

What Fallion didn't know was that Borenson breathed a huge sigh of relief. He'd seen a shadow growing before them, knew that a strengi-saat was sneaking in. But he'd never imagined how close it had come. The monster had almost been breathing on him.

Fallion crept out from under the boat, and Rhianna followed. Both of them held naked blades, and it felt good to see the firelight reflect from them.

The little bonfire was still blazing, pulsing like a star. Fallion felt inside himself. His rage was gone. He felt spent, empty, like a fire in a hearth that is remembered only as ashes.

Rhianna took his free hand in hers, looked up at him with admiration and a hint of fear. "Your hands are very warm. You're an incendiary now."

Borenson grunted, peered down at Fallion with sadness in his eyes, as if

Fallion had lost something dear. He hadn't wanted to leave the boy here on the beach, trade him for a flameweaver. But that is what he had done.

And Fallion knew that next time that he needed fire, it would be easier. His master would heed his call.

Even now, he knew what he had to do. "Help me get more wood for the fire," Fallion said. "We have to keep it burning."

It wasn't to keep the strengi-saats at bay, Fallion knew. It was more than that. He needed to show his gratitude, his reverence. He needed to feed the flames.

It was while Fallion was dragging driftwood to the fire that the soldiers came.

There were seven of them, seven men in dark chain mail that jangled as they rode.

Rhianna was the one who spotted them first, lances glinting in the moonlight.

At first, Fallion thought that he imagined them. They moved at a strange gait, leaping high and then floating back to earth.

They're riding rangits, he realized. A rangit was like a hare or a jumping mouse in shape, but much, much larger. They lived upon the plains of Landesfallen among the sand dunes at the edge of the desert.

Like all mammals from Landesfallen, they were strange beasts. They laid eggs in late winter, as soon as the sun began to warm the sand, and guarded their nests through the spring until their young hatched. Then they nursed their young, though the mothers had no nipples. Instead, the rangits squirted milk from glands in their mouths, feeding their young like mother birds.

And so the men rode rangits, creatures broad of feet, that hopped like hares over the sand, racing along the beach much faster than any horse could have managed.

As they neared, Fallion saw that these were no common troops. They were handsome men and women, unduly so, as if they had stepped out of a dream.

"Force soldiers?" Fallion wondered aloud. But he'd never heard of anyone nowadays that granted endowments of glamour to force warriors. There was a time when forcibles were plentiful, in ages past, when vain lords would endow their honor guards with glamour. But blood metal was now too rare, and forcibles were put to better use.

Borenson seemed to accept that these men were force soldiers, but

Rhianna disagreed. "Bright Ones," she said with a tone of certainty. "From the netherworld."

At that, Borenson just opened his mouth in surprise, unsure what to say. The fighting skills of the Bright Ones were the stuff of legend.

They were like men in form, but more perfect in every way—stronger, faster, wiser, kinder.

"We're saved!" Jaz said, jumping up and down in glee.

By the time that the soldiers approached the bonfire, their helms and mail gleaming dull in its light, Borenson and the children were ready to fall at their knees in gratitude. Indeed, Borenson planted his scimitar in the sand and knelt, as if to royalty.

The Bright Ones merely smiled. Fallion noticed a twinge along his cheek, across the bridge of his nose, something that he had associated once with the smell of evil, and he knew by that, more than by the lack of humanity in the men's eyes or the bemused expressions on their cruel faces, that these were not the Bright Ones of legend.

Loci, Fallion thought. In all of them.

The men rode up, ranged around the campfire. The rangits leaned forward, their lungs pumping like bellows, snorting from the effort of carrying their inhuman charges.

"Are you folks well?" one of the Bright Ones asked, playing the part of the rescuer.

Fallion felt inside himself, tried to summon flames that would consume this man whole, but he felt empty, tired. The fire behind him suddenly blazed brighter, as if fed by a strong wind, but nothing more.

"We're well," Borenson said, "thanks to you."

In all of the legends the Bright Ones were full of virtue. "May the Glories guide you and Bright Ones guard your back," was a common prayer.

But where would these evil ones have come from?

The same place the strengi-saats did, Fallion realized: the netherworld.

"Come," their leader said, eyeing Fallion. "We'll take you to safety." He urged his rangit forward a small hop, and Fallion smelled its breath—heavy and sweet, like some exotic grass, with undertones of hair and urine, much like a very large goat.

Borenson suddenly backed up a step, placing himself between Fallion and the stranger. He smelled the trap.

"Who sent you?" Borenson demanded. "What are you after?"

"We came to save the princes," their leader said. "That is all."

Borenson reached for his sword. His skills were legendary, but these men were Bright Ones, and quicker than Fallion could see, one of them lunged forward, his long red lance plunging into Borenson's gut.

Borenson dropped his sword, stood there holding the lance.

It was not a deep wound. Fallion suspected that only the tip of the lance, the first six inches, had penetrated Borenson's girth. But it was a serious wound, one that could well be fatal.

The Bright One shoved the lance a little, and Borenson clung on for dear life, letting himself fall back rather than have the lance driven deeper into him.

Two rangits bounded forward, one of them heading straight for Fallion. He turned to run, and a lance drove through the shoulder of his heavy woolen cloak.

Suddenly he was lifted into the air, kicking and squirming, his feet well above the sand.

The knight lifted his lance point, and Fallion found himself sliding inexorably down the shaft, into his captor's arms. He peered to his right, heard Jaz screaming and kicking as one of the Bright Ones seized him.

Suddenly the rangits turned, and they were bounding away, racing along the dark beach the way that the soldiers had come while the surf pounded in their ears, the smell of salt water heavy in the wind.

Fallion was devastated.

He peered back, over the Bright One's shoulder, and saw Rhianna there by the fire, frantic, torn between her desire to follow, her desire to help the wounded Borenson, and her terror of the strengi-saats.

Fallion reached for his own blade, trying to wrench it from the sheath. His captor shook him so hard that the blade slipped from Fallion's hand and fell to the sand.

"What about Rhianna?" Fallion pleaded with his captor. "What about Borenson?"

The man chuckled mirthlessly. "We must leave the strengi-saats *something* to eat."

❧ 31 ☙

LEFT IN THE DARK

A man's fears are like grains of sand on a beach. Ofttimes the tide strips them away, but then sends them sweeping back.

—Asgaroth

Rhianna stared at the retreating backs of the soldiers as the rangits hopped gracefully away, like hares on the run.

Not knowing what else to do, she went to Borenson and studied his wound. He was looking faint, sweating badly, and just holding his guts in.

Fortunately, there were supplies in the boat: a little food and water, some spare clothing, Fallion's forcibles.

Taking a rag, Rhianna washed off his wound first with water, then disinfected it with wine. She found one of Talon's dresses, altered to be big enough for Rhianna, ripped off the lower part of the skirt, and gave it to Borenson for a bandage.

The whole time, he just stared at her forlornly, panting.

"Crawl under the boat," she told him. "I'll keep watch."

But he shook his head. "I'll stay here with you."

Not that you can do anything, she thought.

She picked up his saber and sat atop the boat, keeping watch.

I'll last through the night, she told herself. *And if I live till morning, I'll walk south, to town, and find help.*

She didn't know how far town might be. Three miles or thirty.

I'll run, she told herself. *As soon as the sun comes up.*

Rhianna heard growls and snarls in the jungle. A stray gust of wind brought the acrid scent of a strengi-saat. Borenson just lay in the sand, fading in and out of consciousness, getting ready to die.

After an hour, the fire began to burn low. Rhianna rushed away from the boat, out into the shadows, and got some firewood. A shadow followed her.

She turned to face it, sword gleaming in her hand, and then walked backward to the fire.

Thus she scavenged the area, forced on each trip to walk just a little farther than she had gone before. And each time that she left the fire, the strengi-saats became more daring and drew closer.

As the night waxed and the temperature dropped, she huddled near the fire for warmth as much as safety, saving her wood, nursing each tender coal. The smell of smoke was thick in the air and permeated her skin.

The most dangerous time came at moonset, when the great silver orb dipped below the mountains. Blackness seemed to stretch across her then, the shadows of the night, and strengi-saats hidden from sight snarled in anticipation.

She dared not go hunting for more wood.

Dawn was still an hour or more away. The stars had not yet begun to fade in the sky.

Rhianna heard growling and looked to Sir Borenson, who lay stretched on the ground, unconscious, his left knee in the air, his back twisted as if he were lying on a rock, seeking to get comfortable. His breath came shallow.

He'll probably die in that position, Rhianna thought.

One of the monsters hissed, and Rhianna spotted a shadow on her left. She whirled to face it. There was no more wood. She dared venture no farther.

But she was ready for them. She took a log from the fire and set it under the gunwale of the boat, then threw her spare clothing atop it.

Soon the boat was ablaze, creating a bonfire.

Now we can't use it to get off the island, a small voice seemed to whisper to her in despair.

It doesn't matter, she told herself. If I don't live through the night, nothing matters.

So she planted her saber in the sand and squatted beside it, her back to the fire, both hands gripping the hilt of her sword.

Her eyes grew heavy as she fought sleep.

Finally, she decided to rest her eyes for a moment, relieving them from the stinging smoke.

Only a moment, she told herself.

She closed them.

When they flew open, the sun was a pink ball out on the horizon, and the boat lay like the smoking corpse of some beast, its blackened ribs all turned to cinders.

Rhianna heard a cough, peered down at Sir Borenson. It was his coughing that had wakened her.

He was still breathing shallowly, but he peered at her through slitted eyes. "You made it," he whispered. "Now get out of here. Bring help if you can."

"I will," she promised.

She dropped the saber at his side, in case he needed it. She didn't want to lug the thing down the beach. So she took only her dirk, jogged to the beach where the sand was wet and firm, threw off her shoes, and ran.

Three miles or thirty? she wondered.

She ran, feet pounding the sand, heart hammering, ignoring the stitch in her side and the burning that came to her legs. She gripped her dirk firmly, just in case.

Run, she told herself. Nothing else matters.

Hours later, in the heat of the day, Myrrima, Captain Stalker, Smoker, and a dozen other crewmen marched up the beach. It was hours past noon when they found Rhianna's blade lying in the surf, half buried in sand.

Myrrima picked it up, wiped it dry, and called out nervously, "Rhianna? Borenson? Is anyone here?"

There was no reply, only the soughing of the wind over the sands.

Smoker inhaled deeply from his long-handled pipe and peered toward the shore. "I cannot feel their heart fires," he whispered. "They are either dead or far away from here."

Stalker and the others searched for tracks, but found none. What the tide had not washed away, the morning wind had.

"Rhianna would not have left her weapon like this," Myrrima said. She grieved, fearing the worst.

So they marched on for an hour, calling for Rhianna and Borenson, the despair gnawing at Myrrima's gut, until at last they saw the black ribs of the boat lying in the sand, and found Borenson beside it.

He was pale and sweating, looking as if he would die. But he wept when he saw Rhianna's blade and heard the news.

"Rhianna left just after dawn," he told them. "She waited for daylight, so the strengi-saats wouldn't attack, and then ran for help."

With a heavy heart, Captain Stalker whispered, "My guess is that she did not wait long enough."

ஐ 32 ය

THE CELL

Why should I weep for a man in prison, when I am held captive by my own desires?

                 —Mad King Harrill (upon the imprisonment of his son)

Fallion clung to his rangit as it raced along an open road. The dusty road itself shone a steady silver-gray in the starlight, but the foliage beside the road ranged in hues. Open fields that basked in the moonlight were a darker gray, while in the shadowed woods the boles of trees were black slats beneath the foliage.

Strengi-saats, attracted by the sight of running beasts, raced beside them, but dared not attack the well-armed troops.

The land seemed dead. No dogs barked or raced out from the shadowed cottages at the sound of approaching strangers. No cattle bawled in the barns as if wanting to be milked. No smoke coiled lazily from chimneys.

The land had been swept clear of life. Even the sheep were gone.

Where? Fallion wondered. But he knew.

The strengi-saats had eaten everything that moved.

The ride was jarring. Within an hour, every bone in Fallion's body seemed to ache, and he could hear Jaz whimpering on the rangit behind him.

They climbed hills and rode through shadowed vales. And in the cool hours of morning, when a chill wind had begun to numb his hands, they topped a mountain pass and looked down into a valley beyond.

At last, there was a city with smoke coming from chimneys. The valley below was black with fires, choked with them, and in the silver moonlight, he could see masses of men—or something that looked like men—toiling in the darkness.

It's an army, he realized. An army hidden here at the edge of the world. And what an army!

As the rangits bounded down the slopes with renewed energy, eager to be home, they passed fortified bulwarks and deep trenches, until at last they reached the encampments. Fallion soon saw that what he'd thought to be cottages were in fact tents. What he'd taken to be hearth fires were forges, burning in the open air.

Hammers rang in the night, and manlike creatures called out with strange groaning cries.

As he neared, he saw creatures with warty gray skin scampering about on their knuckles, bringing fuel for the forges. Others were dragging logs down from the hills, denuding the mountainsides.

They stared up at him as he passed, and their gazes chilled Fallion to the bone. The creatures were not human, he was sure. There was no joy in their eyes, no sadness or any other emotion that he could name.

Just deadness, yawning emptiness.

At the forges he saw workmen, some Bright Ones, some gray men, hammering blades, fashioning helms and axes.

They're preparing for war, Fallion realized, but with whom?

And quickly he figured it out. Once, long ago, in days so far past they seemed to be legend, black ships had sailed from the west, surprising the folk of Mystarria.

The ships carried the toth, and their assault had nearly decimated the world.

The creatures hammering out weapons in this dark vale would be far more dangerous than toth, Fallion suspected. They formed the heart of an army from the netherworld.

There would be men who would join their cause, Fallion knew, men like those that had ridden with King Anders—mercenary warlords from the north, embittered nobles from minor houses, cruel and cunning men eager for a profit.

Fallion tried to guess how large the army might be. Two hundred thousand? Five hundred? He could not guess. The unending city sprawled across the valley, rose into nearby hills, and spread beyond them for unguessed distances.

How will anyone save me? he wondered.

He thought of Borenson lying on the ground, his belly pierced by a lance.

They won't save me. He realized. They can't. Even if whole armies sailed from Mystarria, they wouldn't be able to bring enough men to penetrate the enemy defenses.

It was with a rising sense of despair that they passed through the vale, rode up a winding mountainside, and entered a bleak fortress, its walls crude but thick and functional.

Once inside the city walls, the Bright Ones dragged Fallion and Jaz to a heavily guarded building, and into a dungeon where the tortured cries of men and women could be heard.

They passed a cell where a young woman sobbed noisily, cradling her right arm, trying to stop the bleeding from a stump where her hand should have been.

They were taken to a small cell and chained to a wall, their hands stretched overhead, the weight of their whole bodies resting on their wrists.

The prison cell consisted of three walls made of heavy black basalt blocks piled one atop another. The fourth wall was formed of iron, bars with a small door in it.

The bottom of the door had a clearing of perhaps three inches, just tall enough so that a plate could be slid under, for those who were lucky enough to eat.

Fallion and Jaz were not afforded the luxury of food. They were left hanging against a cold stone wall, slick with greasy water and mold.

There was no light.

Fallion could sometimes hear the snarls of strengi-saats deeper in the prison, and he feared that they prowled the hallways. He hoped that the bars would keep the monsters out.

And he heard Jaz crying, his young frame shuddering.

Fallion wanted to hold his little brother, offer him comfort, but he couldn't even see Jaz's face.

Jaz asked after a long while, "Do you . . . . think that they'll kill us?"

"We're worth . . . more alive." Fallion could not get his air. "They'll probably hold us—for ransom."

"What kind of ransom?"

"Forcibles, gold. Maybe . . . land," Fallion said.

He wished that he believed it. They were the Sons of the Oak, the children of the Earth King. Borenson believed that with a word, whole nations would rise up to follow at their command.

And so, Fallion realized, to someone like Shadoath, they might represent a danger. They might just be worth more dead than alive.

The manacles were cutting into Fallion's wrist; he wriggled painfully, trying to ease the pressure.

"How long?" Jaz asked. "How long will they . . . keep us?"

"A few weeks," Fallion calculated. "Someone will have to sail back to Mystarria, raise a ransom, come back."

"Oh," Jaz said forlornly.

Fallion offered some more words of comfort, and after a bit he asked, "Would you like me to sing to you?"

That had always worked when Jaz was small and troubled by bad dreams.

"Yes," Jaz said.

Fallion remembered a song about rabbits, one that had been Jaz's favorite a few years ago, and he began to sing, struggling for breath.

> "North of the moon, south of the sun,
> rabbits run, rabbits run.
> Through winter snow, summer gardens,
> having fun, having fun.
> Faster than wolves, fast as birdsong,
> Rabbits run, rabbits run.
> North of the moon, south of the sun."

Someone came marching toward them. Fallion saw a flicker of light and heard the jangle of keys. His stomach had begun to tighten, and he hoped that it was someone bringing food.

But it was only a brutish man who stubbed past their cell, bearing a smoking torch. He wore a loincloth, a blood-spattered vest, and a black hood that hid his face. In his right hand he carried an implement of torture—a bone saw.

Fallion peered at Jaz, saw his brother's face pale with fear.

The torturer went past their cell, and Jaz asked, "Do you think he'll come for us?"

"No," Fallion lied. "We're too valuable."

Down the hall, the torturer went to work, and the screaming began—a man whimpering and pleading for mercy.

He must have been round a corner, for Fallion could see little light.

"Are you sure?" Jaz asked.

"Don't worry," Fallion told him. "They . . . just want to scare us."

So Fallion hung against the wall, his weight born by the manacles around his wrists, and sang to his little brother, offering comfort whenever he could.

His were small manacles, made especially for women and children, he realized.

They cut into his wrists, made them swell and pucker. He had to wiggle his hands from time to time, try to find a more comfortable position, in order to keep the blood flowing to his fingers. He'd seen a man once, Lord Thangarten, who had been kept hanging in a dungeon in Indhopal so long that his fingers had died, and he was left a cripple.

Yet if I wiggle too much, he knew, in a few days my wrists will chafe and begin to bleed.

So Fallion hung on the wall and tried to minimize his pain. With his wrists bearing all of his weight, his lungs couldn't get air. After the first few hours, he learned that it would be a constant struggle.

In the darkness, Fallion was left to focus on sounds, Jaz's breathing as he hung in his cell, deep and even in sleep, ragged when he woke. His brother's weeping and sniffing, the clank of chains against the wall, the sobs of the tortured as they lay in their cells, the squeaking of rats, the snarling of strengi-saats.

He would not have minded the rats, normally. But after he had hung against the wall for a few hours, he heard one squeaking below. It rose and bit his big toe.

He kicked at it. The rat squeaked angrily as it retreated.

It will be back, Fallion knew. It will be back, when I'm too tired to fight.

He found that he had to pee. He held it for as long as he could, then let it go.

In the darkness, deprived of light, accompanied only by the smell of mold and urine and cold stone and iron, as days began to pass, Fallion despaired.

Several times the torturer passed by their cell, never looking toward them, his torch guttering, his keys jangling.

He came at dawn, Fallion surmised, and left at night.

"How long has it been?" Jaz asked time and again.

Only three days, Fallion suspected, but he told Jaz that it was a week.

One cannot despair forever, even in the worst of times. The body is not capable of sustaining it. And so the despair came in great waves, crashing around his ears sometimes, threatening to drown him, and then ebbing away.

Sometimes he dared hope. Straining for every breath, he'd babble to his brother.

"Maybe they've sent . . . messages to Mystarria, demanding payment for our release," he'd offer. "We've been, at sea for eight weeks. It will take a ship that long to reach Mystarria, another eight weeks back.

"Four months. In four months we'll be free."

"When will they feed us?" Jaz begged.

"Soon," Fallion promised time and again.

But they had been hanging on the wall for days. Fallion's mouth grew dry and his tongue swelled in his throat. Greasy sweat became his only blanket. He woke and slept, and hung on the wall, sometimes unsure if he was awake or asleep any longer.

Now when the torturer passed, Fallion and Jaz would both cry out, their dry throats issuing only croaks. "Food." "Water." "Help." "Please."

Down the hallway, lost in time, Fallion heard a woman's scream echo, followed by the snarl of a strengi-saat, the sound of it grunting, and more screams. The strengi-saat was filling the woman with its eggs, he realized.

Who are all of these people? Fallion wondered. What have they done to deserve such pain?

He had no answer. Like him, he suspected, they had done nothing.

Waggit had taught Fallion about the lives of evil people. He knew that there had been lords in the past who tortured others for their own amusement.

What had Waggit told him? Oh, yes. Such people eventually went mad. "They ride into power on a steed of fear and violence, doling out favors to those who support them. But as their inhumanity grows, their supporters fade away. Fearful of losing support, they begin to kill the very lords who brought them to power, and the foundations of their empire crumbles. In time, in fear and madness they dwindle away, and at last they tend to die by their own hands, or the hands of their people."

Waggit had cited examples of men and women so cruel that even to tell of it was harrowing.

Is that how Shadoath will end? Fallion wondered.

At the time, the lesson had seemed . . . boring, a mere recitation from the pages of dusty old books.

Now, Fallion was learning of such things firsthand.

Hunger gnawed at his belly. Thirst became a nagging companion.

It was under these circumstances that the boys received their first visitor. Fallion had expected Shadoath herself to show up, but instead he woke in his cell, his vision blurred, and peered up to see Deever Blythe peering through the bars, a torch in his hand, grinning inanely.

" 'Ow they treatin' you boys?" Blythe asked.

Jaz was unconscious. Fallion peered at him, saw him pale and vulnerable. For the first time, Fallion began to worry that his little brother would die.

"Last couple o' days been nice, 'ave they?" Blythe asked.

Fallion did not want to let Deever see him beaten. Choking, he said, "I'm well, and you?" But his voice betrayed his outrage.

He's the one that told on us, Fallion realized. He's the one that betrayed me.

"Not like back 'ome, I'd imagine?" Deever asked. "Not like those hoity-toity dinner parties, what with the lords in their silk tights, struttin' about and dancin' with their plump ladies. Not a bit like that, is it?"

Fallion had never been to a ball. He'd seen one or two, and it sounded to him as if Blythe had only some garish approximation of what it was like at a ball.

Outside the cell, down a hallway, an echoing groan came loudly.

Fallion said, as if he were a lord at a dinner party, "The music does leave something to be desired."

Blythe peered at him, his eyes glowing with delight. Fallion wondered what message Blythe had come to bear, and realized at last that he had brought none. He'd come only to gloat.

"Mr. Blythe," Fallion begged. "Can you get . . . food and water? At least for my brother?"

"What?" Deever Blythe asked. "You tired of chewin' on your tongue already?"

His teeth were flashing broadly in a smile, half hidden by his scraggly beard. There would be no food or water.

Blythe held his torch loosely.

Fire. So close, so easy to tame. Fallion could feel it calling to him, could feel the rage rising in his chest, the flames ready to leap out.

"Oh, look at that," Blythe said. "There's a nice 'ungry rat down in the corner, come to visit ya. Better watch out!"

Fallion hung his head. It wasn't hard to do. He barely had the energy to lift it anymore.

He saw the rat trundling toward him as it edged along the wall. There were rat bites on his ankle and feet, little red patches already swollen. The wall was slimy and dark between his legs, wet with urine.

The rat nosed around Fallion's feet, peering up at him, black eyes reflecting the torchlight.

"Go ahead, little feller," Blythe said, "'ave another bite."

Fallion kicked at the rat, and it backed away an inch. It knew that Fallion couldn't reach him.

Blythe laughed and lurched down the hall.

᪥ 33 ᪣

THE SEA APE

Man learns in his youth that he must submit to indignities, for nature itself heaps them upon us.

—*Asgaroth*

Rhianna rode through the green hills by daylight, passing cottages and fields all left fallow, drifting in and out of consciousness. She did not know whether the men who had found her running on the beach were her saviors or captors. She felt tired beyond caring.

She discovered the truth when they reached the palace, and the men took her in and dumped her at the feet of Shadoath.

"Your Highness," one of the Bright Ones said. "We found her on beach patrol, just north of Port Syndyllian."

Shadoath studied the young woman, a pretty thing. Not many like her could be found on the island anymore.

Rhianna peered up. Shadoath was easily the most beautiful woman that she'd ever seen. The palace was astonishing, its high windows all draped in white silks, with heart-oak panels upon the walls, and beams all gilt with silver. The room was resplendent, and Shadoath was its crown jewel.

Only one thing marred this picture of perfect beauty. On each side of Shadoath's tall throne, a strengi-saat was chained like a lion. The beasts slept at the moment, or at least rested lazily, but Rhianna felt certain that they were aware of her.

Rhianna gaped, unsure what to say. Finally she asked, "Where's Fallion and Jaz? What did you do with them?"

Shadoath walked around to Rhianna, studied her as she circled. "You should be worried about yourself."

"Please, let me see them," Rhianna asked. "I'll do anything."

"You're in no position to barter," Shadoath said. "Do you know what we do with little ones like you?"

Rhianna was afraid to ask.

Shadoath frowned down at her. "We give you to the strengi-saats."

Rhianna swayed on her feet, nearly fainting, the terror written plainly on her face.

"Are the boys all right?" she begged.

Shadoath made no answer.

Tears filled Rhianna's eyes. She was trembling. She dropped to one knee, bowed her head, and said, "Please, spare them. I'll do anything for you. Anything. People don't think that I can do much, because I'm still just a girl. But I killed a man once, and I could do it again."

Such a bold declaration was not to be taken lightly.

Shadoath had few servants that she could trust. If this girl feared her enough, she might become a proper tool.

"Give me your hands," Shadoath asked.

Fearfully, Rhianna held out her hands. Shadoath grasped her wrists and studied Rhianna's palms.

Yes, I can feel the bloodstains there, Shadoath realized.

"You love these boys?" Shadoath asked.

Rhianna bit her lip and nodded.

"Do you love them enough to die in their place?"

Rhianna nodded again, but more slowly. Too slowly.

From the back of the throne room came the sound of a throat clearing, and Shadoath's son Abravael said loudly, "Mother, may I have her?"

Shadoath hesitated, turned to her son. He had crept into the room quietly. Sneaking—that was his way.

He was sixteen, still in that awkward period when he was still half a boy but had the lusts of three grown men. Shadoath had no doubts as to what services his son might desire from a pretty young girl.

Rhianna peered up to see Abravael, not nearly as handsome as his mother, come striding into the room. He stared at her, bemused.

In her heart, Rhianna dared to hope that Shadoath would give her to him, let her become his slave. She'd give anything rather than die.

Shadoath got a sly grin on her face, and still holding Rhianna's hands, said, "I think that you would make a fine servant. I'm not sure that I can trust you completely yet, but there is a fierceness in you that I admire."

Rhianna tried to force a smile, but failed.

"And so I will give you this one chance: I will teach you the true meaning of devotion. Do you understand?"

Rhianna nodded, for she understood that Shadoath wanted her complete devotion.

"No, you don't," Shadoath said. "Not really. Not yet. But soon you will. I want an endowment from you. Do you think you could give up an endowment?"

Rhianna nodded.

Shadoath smiled.

Taking Rhianna by the hand, Shadoath led her deeper into the palace and out the back. There, beside a pool, squatted a young sea ape, a female with long yellow fangs, and hair that was almost as white as snow. She stood perhaps only seven feet at the shoulder, and when she saw Abravael, she rushed to his side and squatted next to him, gently inspecting his skin as if seeking lice.

Total adoration shone in the sea ape's dark eyes.

"Love without wisdom is useless," Shadoath said. "I want you to give your endowment of wit to her. She will teach you devotion, and with your help she can learn many things."

Rhianna nodded slowly. To give an endowment of wit was dangerous. It was supposed to allow the recipient to use a portion of your brain, to give him an expanded memory. The recipient would thus become a genius, while the Dedicate was left an idiot.

There was a danger, Rhianna knew, that the Dedicate would give too much, that she would grant so much of her intelligence that her heart would forget how to beat, her lungs forget how to breathe.

I won't do that, Rhianna promised herself as a servant brought a facilitator, the wizard who would transfer the endowments.

The facilitator was surprisingly young, dressed in rich robes of deepest crimson. His face had a solemn, drugged look.

"You promise?" Rhianna begged Shadoath. "You'll spare the boys?"

Rhianna was in no position to make demands. Shadoath could kill her before she blinked her eyes.

"You keep your end of the bargain," Shadoath said, "and I'll keep mine."

Rhianna nodded, and dropped to her knees in submission, for she could do nothing more.

The facilitator had her sit beside the sea ape, peering into its enormous eyes, as he began to sing the incantations, his voice sometimes dropping low and liquid, like the solemn tones of a bell, then piping high and frenzied, like the distraught calls of a mother bird.

Sometime as he chanted, he reached into the sleeve of his robe and brought out a forcible, a tiny branding iron no thicker than a nail, about the length of his hand. The forcible was cast from blood metal, and so was the color of dried blood, rough and granular. At its tip was forged a single rune.

The facilitator held the forcible out, spread over one palm, as if to display it to Rhianna.

He wants me to get used to it, Rhianna thought. He doesn't want me to be afraid of it, and indeed, a moment later, still singing the incantation, he brushed it against the back of her arm for a long moment.

Shadoath was sitting behind Rhianna, and she whispered, "Now, child, look into the ape's eyes, and give yourself to her. Will yourself to her."

Rhianna tried to obey, but it was hard. She was frightened. She had heard that giving endowments was painful, and now the facilitator placed the forcible to her forehead.

"Will it hurt?" Rhianna asked, panic shooting through her. She suddenly clenched her knees together, afraid that she might pee.

"Only a little," Shadoath assured her, "only for a moment."

The facilitator held the forcible against her skin for a long minute, singing faster and more frantically. His voice was like a distant drum, pounding and pounding on the edge of her consciousness.

The forcible began to grow warm, and Rhianna could see the metal heating up, glowing red like tongs in a forge. She smelled a strange metallic smoke, and then it began to burn.

She heard her skin sizzling, and there was a light as the forcible glowed white-hot. But she felt surprisingly little pain. It was as if the forcible flared so quickly that it merely fried the nerves off of her head, and mercifully, the facilitator chose that moment to remove it.

He waved the white-hot forcible in the air, and an afterglow followed it, but mystically seemed to hang in the air between them.

It's like a snake, Rhianna thought, a snake made out of light.

Its head was at the tip of the forcible, but its tail extended back to some point inside Rhianna's forehead.

There was a dull ache between Rhianna's eyes, a pulling sensation, as if the contents of her skull were being drawn out.

The facilitator sang and waved the forcible in the air, peering at the snake of light, seeming to judge its heft and thickness.

He turned to the sea ape, and the ape just peered curiously at the glowing forcible. He plunged the tip of it into the hair between her breasts, and the sea ape peered down, her mouth open in dull wonder.

The facilitator sang louder and louder, more frantically. There was a yanking sensation between Rhianna's eyes, and then she saw it: a bright actinic flash traveling through the pale pipeline of light.

The facilitator cried out in triumph. The air stank of burning hair and scorched flesh as the forcible went white-hot.

Rhianna felt a pain blossom, one that started between her eyes but that shot to the back of her skull. It was as if her skull were suddenly shrinking to the size of a walnut, and everything inside would gush out.

Just when Rhianna realized that the pain was greater than anything she had ever hoped to bear, it suddenly intensified a hundredfold, and an endless cry was torn from her throat.

Rhianna collapsed, and as she did, she found herself staring down at her own body, watching herself collapse. She flared her broad nostrils, sniffing, and got up and paced about on her knuckles, too energized and too alarmed to sit any longer.

Rhianna *was* the sea ape.

❧ 34 ☙

A CHILD OF EVIL

One of the sweetest victories in life comes when we discover who and what we are.

—Fallion Val Orden

Twice more the torturer came and went. But the hulking, hooded brute never turned to look Fallion's way.

But the time will come when he will look my way, Fallion thought.

No food or water appeared.

Jaz had grown weary of asking for it, and both times that the torturer passed by, Fallion saw that his brother only hung limp now, barely alive.

Fallion knew that torturers liked to soften their victims, to withhold nourishment before putting them to pain. It weakened their wills, weakened their resistance. A man who could withstand the burning tongs often could not withstand the eroding weakness brought on by hunger.

Or maybe the torturer won't come at all, Fallion wondered. Maybe they've forgotten about us, and they'll just leave us here hanging on the wall until the rats gnaw the flesh from our bones.

Jaz woke later that day. He did not speak. Only hung on the wall, sobbing.

Fallion mustered enough energy to sing him a lullaby that their mother had taught him.

"Hush, little child, don't you weep.
The shadows grow long and it's time for sleep.
Tomorrow we'll run in the fields,
And wade in the streams,
But now it's time for dreams.

Hush, little child, don't you weep.
The shadows grow long and it's time for sleep."

Fallion wondered at the words. His father had warned him to run, that the ends of the Earth were not far enough. Borenson had promised the children meadows to play in, and hills to climb. In Landesfallen they were to enjoy their childhood, put their fears behind them.

It's all a lie, he realized. They've got nothing to give.

Or maybe we did something wrong? Fallion thought. Maybe I didn't understand the message?

Fallion tried to remember the message, but his mind wouldn't work.

"Jaz," Fallion croaked after a long time. Jaz held silent, and Fallion wondered if he had fallen back to sleep when finally an answer came.

"What?"

"What were the last words that Father said when he was dying?"

Jaz stayed silent for a long time, then grunted, "He said, something about . . . 'Return a blessing for every blow. . . .'"

The words seemed to strike Fallion like a mallet. He'd forgotten. He'd forgotten those last words. They'd seemed like only the rants of a dying man, the idle chatter of one who was fading from consciousness.

"Learn to love the greedy as well as the generous, the poor as much as the rich, the evil as well as the kind." The words seemed to resound, rising up from his memory. His father had said something like that when Fallion was small, a babe of two or three, cuddling in his father's arms. He'd been talking about his own personal credo, the guidelines that he'd chosen to live his life by. But Fallion didn't remember that last, "A blessing for every blow."

Could his father possibly mean that literally? Was he supposed to show kindness to those who now kept him in chains?

Fallion had nothing else to do but ponder this.

And fortunately, it was only a few hours later that a visitor came to the cell again.

Fallion had drifted into a half sleep, and woke to keys rattling in a lock, and a squeaking door.

A girl was opening their cell, a young girl perhaps a couple of years older than he, pretty, with raven hair.

She held a candle in one hand, and had set a silver jug on the ground while she carefully tried the keys.

Fallion thought that he recognized her, though he'd never seen her before. He managed a groan, and the girl looked up, startled, almost guiltily.

Yes, he recognized her dark eyes, the hair falling down around her pale face.

"You!" she said in surprise. "I know you! You're from that dream!"

Fallion peered at her, and the world seemed to somehow tilt askew.

"Yes," Fallion said. "You were in the cage."

And she'd begged him to set her free.

She peered at him, trembling lightly, and Fallion realized why she had come.

Here is my tormentor, he thought.

Not the man in the dark hood with the tongs, but this girl.

Jaz had wakened. His breathing came raspy, and he peered at the silver ewer as if to drink with his eyes. "Wa," he whispered. "Wa."

The girl said no more. She looked away guiltily, then picked up the pitcher and stepped forward carefully, as if to keep from spilling a drop.

Near Fallion's feet, she set the pitcher down.

Is there water in it? he wondered. Or maybe even cider? He was so thirsty, that being this close to drink made his head reel.

The girl stared up at him, her dark eyes boring into his. "We got it wrong, didn't we, in that dream? You're the one in the cage. Not me."

Then Fallion's mind seemed to leap, and he said, "We're both in the cage. We're both in chains, but just of different kinds." She stared at him, confused, and so he added, "I hang in chains on the wall, but you are caught in the chain of command. There's nothing for us in that pitcher, is there? You brought it only to torment us. You're waiting for me to beg. What are you supposed to do if I beg?"

She peered up at him, but did not answer. She was forbidden to answer their questions, to tell them anything but lies, to give them any hope.

I'm supposed to spit in it, she thought, and then leave it at your feet, to torment you for two more days.

She looked over to Jaz, saw that the younger boy was unconscious. He'd be dead in two days. She'd seen enough of the beggars die to know that.

She turned and began to hurry away, candle in her hand.

"Thank you," Fallion said.

She whirled on him, unaccountably angry. "For what? I didn't give you anything!" She was to give them nothing. She'd be punished if she broke the rule. And if he ever claimed that she'd given him a drink, she could lose a finger.

"Your eyes gave me drink," Fallion said.

She glared.

She rushed from the cell, and turned the key in the lock.

"What is your name?" Fallion called, just as she finished.

She was not supposed to answer questions.

She looked this way and that, up and down the hallway. "Valya," she whispered, then ran.

35

THE RANSOM

You cannot make a fair trade with an evil man. Either he will not make a fair trade in the beginning, or else at the end he will rue the choice, and change the deal.

—a saying of Indhopal

Aboard the *Leviathan*, Borenson lay abed while the crew secured a pair of properly cured logs to use as masts, then shaped them with hatchets and set them—a difficult task under the best of circumstances. The work would take them three more days.

Borenson wasn't sure what had saved him—his own toughness, luck, or magic.

Stalker and the crew had found him early in the morning and carried him back to the ship, a difficult march of nearly twenty miles along the sand. They arrived just as the light was fading and the strengi-saats began their nightly prowl.

On the ship Borenson hovered near death, a vile infection brewing in his gut.

Smoker thought that he was lucky. A horseman's lance is made to breach armor. The point is steel, sharp enough to puncture plate mail, but it is only as the lance is driven home and the shaft wedges into an opening that the weapon does its damage, ripping a man apart.

Borenson had taken only a shallow hit, the lance puncturing his gut and driving six inches, nicking his backbone. Had the blow hit his liver or pancreas, he'd have died within moments. The acrid stench of the wound and the quickness with which it became infected showed that the lance had punctured his bowels, nothing more.

Luck. He stayed alive partly out of luck, and maybe just a bit of stubbornness. He'd decided that even though his time had come, he was not going to die in the night. He'd felt determined to save Rhianna, to stay with her till the morning, and then die.

After she'd left, he'd clung to life a little longer, hoping for rescue.

Under normal circumstances the wound would have killed him. In the end, it took more than stubbornness and luck to save him—it took magic.

Smoker laid his left hand on the wound, where the swelling and pus were the worst, and peered at a candle as he "burned" the infection away.

Borenson felt no pain, only a warmth not much hotter than a fever.

When Smoker finished, Myrrima ministered in his place, washing the wounds away and drawing runes upon his wet flesh, bidding him to heal.

They managed to save his life.

But the wound didn't leave him with enough vigor to do much of anything. He lay abed, fretting, while Myrrima scouted the island, hunting for Rhianna and the boys.

She was beside herself with worry, and stayed up much of the night pacing. She'd lost three charges in a single day, and though she searched the beach for Rhianna for two days before turning her hopes to finding the boys, she found no peace. She was wearing herself out.

"You're a mother," Borenson told her. "You've got a babe that wants your breast, and other children that need a mother. Let someone else go. Smoker can hunt for them, and some of the crew."

"I can't leave it to others," she said. "They were my charges. Besides, I'm Water's warrior still, and a Runelord. No one aboard the ship is even close to being my equal in battle."

"Captain Stalker will send men out," Borenson assured her. "Stay with your children."

Myrrima searched inside herself, and could feel no peace. "It's not just that I lost three children," she said. "It's *who* I lost. Gaborn told us that Fallion could be a greater king than he, that he could do greater good, but also greater evil. Asgaroth knew what Fallion was before he was even born. He wanted Fallion even then. And now, Fallion is in their hands. . . ."

Borenson was too weak to care for his own children. Erin needed her mother's breast, and when her mother left for the day, Erin whined and cried. Talon would bounce her on her knee, try to keep her satisfied until nightfall. Draken, at five, would wander around the little room making messes, bored out of his skull, while Sage would beg to know, "When is Mommy coming home?"

The time that Borenson spent without Myrrima was pure torture, but it was a torture he would have to endure.

"Go find him then," Borenson said, "and be quick about it."

He sighed, and considered for the thousandth time how hard it was to raise a king.

On her fourth day of scouting, Myrrima found the fortress where Fallion was held, and she despaired.

She peered out over a valley filled with dark tents where at least a quarter of a million soldiers camped, while a vast fortress crouched on a hill above them like a bloated spider, its various outbuildings spilling down the hillside like appendages.

"What can we do?" she wondered.

Smoker stood at her back, a small pipe in his mouth. He looked down, but his eyes did not focus.

"We get boys."

She looked up at him in disbelief, studied his pale, expressionless face.

"We'll be discovered," she objected.

He closed his eyes, in agreement. "I be discovered. You, though, have endowment—look like Bright One."

He was right. The army was made up mainly of the gray creatures, which the locals called golaths. But the Bright Ones seemed to serve as their masters.

A commoner would never make it past the guards.

But with her endowments of glamour, Myrrima might well be able to pass for a Bright One.

Do I dare risk it? she wondered. If I'm caught, I'll leave my own children motherless.

There was no right choice. She didn't dare risk it. But she would never be able to live with herself if she left the boys alone.

Better to die swiftly, she told herself, than to live as a shell, a mere hollow thing.

"Let's do it then," Myrrima said.

They couldn't try to rescue the boys now, she knew. The ship wasn't ready to sail yet. Rescuing the boys wouldn't help, if they couldn't make a clean getaway.

But there was one chance.

Myrrima needed to scout ahead, get a closer look.

"Stay here," Myrrima told Smoker.

She strode down the hill, onto the muddy road, and made her way through the vast encampment, studying the terrain.

To her surprise, no one stopped her. Shadoath's people had not needed to worry about security for a very long time.

It wasn't until she reached the palace gate that she was challenged. Several Bright Ones watched the gate, handsome men, perfect men by their looks, all in elegant burnished black mail with black capes.

"Halt," one of the men demanded. "State your name and business."

"Myrrima Borenson," Myrrima said. "I've come for an audience with Shadoath."

"On what business?" one of the Bright Ones asked.

"I've come to offer a ransom for the princes."

The Bright Ones looked at one another, and presently one of them raced up the road, into the confines of the palace itself, a tall black building made of basalt.

Meanwhile, Myrrima had to step aside as locals pressed through the gates—golaths carrying food and other gear about as if they were an army of ants.

Myrrima studied the Bright Ones, taking special notice of their mail. It was splint mail—a suit of light and sturdy chain mail hooked to metal plates to cover the vital areas. The plates were enameled, and so shone brightly.

The epaulets curved elegantly at the shoulder, and at the cuff thickened into lip, a design that Myrrima had never seen before. It would have severely reduced any damage from a downward stroke with a blade or an ax, and would deflect a blow away from the vulnerable spots on the arm. She decided then and there that she must have some, even if it meant ripping it from these dead men's bodies.

The breastplates that they wore showed a similarly innovative design and high level of craftsmanship, and were engraved with runes of protection. Myrrima recognized some of those runes, but others were strange to her.

The man that she was studying smiled at her, perhaps imagining that she fancied him. Myrrima smiled. "Nice armor."

But she wasn't studying it to admire it. She was studying it to discover its weaknesses.

It will take a blow to the armpit to defeat that design, she realized. There is a good space there under the arm that is still unprotected. Likewise, the throat is open, along with the base of the neck, and behind the knee. Many of the usual places.

Arrows wouldn't do for such a fight. Even a saber would be tricky. A dirk might be best, something short and sharp.

The messenger returned, and bade Myrrima to surrender her weapons and follow him. She handed her bow and knife to one guard, then was escorted up a short hill, to the steps of the keep.

The basalt exterior was ugly, but the thick stones looked almost impenetrable.

Inside, the palace was grand. The tall roof soared three stories, stone arches offering support. Many high windows made it feel as if the room were open to the sky, and indeed finches and other songbirds could be seen flitting about in the rafters. There was no antechamber or offices for minor functionaries. The palace was open, a vast hall. The walls covered in polished white oak and burnished silver, with tapestries of white silk, made the palace seem full of light.

Shadoath reclined upon a couch covered in white silk. Today she wore enameled black armor, with a cape of crimson. Near her feet was a smaller couch, and resting upon it were two youngsters, a boy of perhaps seventeen, and a young girl, perhaps eleven. Her children.

Myrrima approached the queen. Shadoath watched with the glittering eyes of a serpent.

Myrrima knelt at the bottom of the dais.

"Your Highness," Myrrima said. "I've come to offer ransom for the princes." It was the only believable story that she could think of.

Shadoath smiled, and Myrrima had never seen such a beautiful face marred by such a cruel expression.

"What do you offer?" Shadoath asked.

The only thing that she had that was of worth was Fallion's forcibles.

They might just be enough to buy his freedom. But would he regret the price? Myrrima wondered.

Those forcibles were his legacy. He might never see their like again.

Is this what his father would have wanted?

"Three hundred forcibles," Myrrima said. It was all that the boys had. "For the pair of them."

"Do you have three hundred forcibles?" Shadoath asked. Myrrima was intensely aware of Shadoath's predatory gaze. If the woman knew that she had so many forcibles, she'd steal them. The weight of her stare was overwhelming, and Myrrima had a sudden suspicion that she would never make it from the palace alive.

Myrrima sought to be her most convincing. "I don't have them here. I would have to return to Mystarria."

"Then why not offer three thousand forcibles?" Shadoath suggested, "and a thousand pounds of gold for good measure?"

Myrrima licked her lips, told the first lie that came to mind. "Forgive me, Your Highness. I am but the daughter of a poor merchant. I was taught that one should never make one's best offer first."

Shadoath seemed offended. "You expect to haggle as if I were some peasant dickering over the price of parsnips?"

"Forgive me. It seemed wise."

Shadoath smiled. She peered at Myrrima as if she had penetrated her secret.

"If I were to give you time to bring the ransom, would you really bring it? Or would you return with a flotilla of warships and try to seize the boys?"

"That would be unwise," Myrrima said. "You would still have the children at your mercy."

"But if Chancellor Westhaven tried to rescue the boys, and they died in the skirmish, who would blame him? It would leave him free to assume the throne. . . ."

"Westhaven is not that kind of man," Myrrima said, surprised that Shadoath would think so ill of him.

Shadoath only smiled. "All men are that kind of man."

Was that really true?

In a few years, Fallion would reach his majority and be ready to assume the throne. Would Westhaven refuse to turn it over?

Myrrima believed that he was better than that.

"So," Myrrima pressed. "Three thousand forcibles and a thousand pounds of gold. . . . Do we have a deal?"

Shadoath shook her head.

"I don't know if I could go any higher," Myrrima said. "Blood metal is growing rare, and I doubt that Mystarria has more than three thousand forcibles to its name. The Brat of Beldinook recently invaded, and on that account, many of the forcibles may have already been put to use. A higher price could bankrupt the nation."

"Sadly," Shadoath said. "None of that matters. I can't give you the boys. They're already dead."

Myrrima stared in shock.

"It was not their fate to be rescued," Shadoath continued. "Had I left them alive, I'm sure that they would have come after me in time."

Myrrima felt her eyes misting over, her heart wrenching with grief. She succumbed to it, knelt there sobbing.

"May I take their bodies?" she asked, her mind in a fog. "They should be entombed in the halls of their fathers."

Shadoath shook her head. "There is nothing left. I fed them to my pets." She waved to the right and left, to her strengi-saats chained at the base of the throne.

She has beaten me, Myrrima thought. She knows it and takes delight in my pain.

Myrrima felt herself sliding into an emotional abyss. But then she caught her footing, just the tiniest bit.

No bodies? Myrrima wondered. Even in her shock, this seemed odd.

Myrrima studied the children on the couch for a response, wondering if Shadoath had told the truth, but both of them just stared at her, their faces calm and unperturbed, perfect masks.

"Very well," Myrrima said, still in something of a fog. "I thank you for the audience." Heavily, she turned away and went slinking from the palace.

But once outside, with each stride she grew stronger and more encouraged.

She had never believed for a moment that she might ransom the princes. It was too much to hope for. Shadoath was building an army here at the edge of the world. Not a vast army by the standards of Rofehavan or Indhopal, but it was an enormous army for such a small kingdom. Obviously she had ambitions. And if the princes of Mystarria were released, they might thwart those ambitions.

No, Shadoath wasn't likely to sell, not unless she had some overwhelming need for gold or blood metal.

Nor was she likely to kill the boys. In some future year, she might need them as hostages.

The boys are alive, Myrrima realized. Were they dead, Shadoath would have taken delight in casting their broken bodies at my feet!

The boys are alive, and I will steal them back.

❧ 36 ☙

DYING BY DEGREES

A wise man dies by degrees. He dies to greed. He dies to fear. He dies to all worldly desires. And when he is ready, he dies to all else.

—Aya'ten, a lord of ancient Indhopal

In his cell, Fallion passed in and out of consciousness, learning to ignore the snarls of strengi-saats, learning to be a prisoner.

Each time that the torturer stomped past, Fallion would be alerted by the sound of jangling keys, followed by the thump, thump, thump of booted feet. Then the light would come, blessed light, and for long minutes after the brute was gone, Fallion would savor the afterimage of the torch, its flames twisting gently, sputtering, the delicious aroma of oily smoke lingering in its wake.

Sometimes, Fallion would look to see if his brother was still alive. Jaz rarely roused himself anymore. His chains did not rattle; his breathing came slow. Only every few hours did he struggle for a breath, suddenly gasping.

They're going to kill him, Fallion realized.

Jaz was second in line for the throne. Those who wanted Mystarria badly enough to kill children would place a great value on him.

But Fallion was the prize. He held the birthright. He was the one that the killers would want most.

And maybe even the people of Mystarria, he hoped. They might want me, too, enough to pay my ransom.

He couldn't imagine that. He was a child, more trouble than he was worth. He was not some great king, skilled in diplomacy and wise beyond the understanding of the common folk.

I'm nothing, Fallion knew. They would not want me.

But they would pay nonetheless, he suspected, if only to soothe the national conscience.

"See," Chancellor Westhaven would tell himself, "I did not let my princes die. I am a good man."

Mystarria was wealthy, one of the wealthiest nations in the world. Surely Westhaven would pay.

If he could.

Fallion recalled the smoke rising from the palace at the Courts of Tide. There had been a fierce battle, the kind where nations fall.

Lowicker the Brat might have prevailed, or the Warlords of Internook might have invaded by now. Mystarria might be nothing more than a fading dream of glory.

No one can rescue me, Fallion realized. And so I must rescue myself. But how?

The manacles were too tight for him to wriggle loose. In the days since his imprisonment, they had only grown tighter. His flesh had swollen, and now his wrists were as large as a man's. No matter how he moved, he could not get comfortable. Sometimes wounds opened if he squirmed too much, and blood flowed down his arms into his armpits, smelling of iron.

He had only one asset. Fire.

But there was nothing to burn in his cell. No cots or mattresses, no wooden chairs or beams. Perhaps his captors knew of his powers, so they gave him no fuel.

Even if I had fire, what would I do with it? Could I make it hot enough to melt my chains?

Perhaps.

But in order to survive such heat, Fallion would have to accept Fire as his master, become like the flameweavers of legend who were so powerful that they clothed themselves in nothing but living flame.

And thus wrapped in flames, they gave in to their passions, their hunger, and went from place to place, seeking to make the world an inferno.

Fallion's father had battled such creatures. They were no longer human.

Why would I want to? Fallion wondered. Why would I want to serve something that doesn't serve me?

"To live," Fire whispered. "To grow. It is only Fire that can set you free."

ဆ

Fallion was hovering near death when Shadoath finally entered his cell. He did not hear the keys rattle or the grating of the door as it swung on hinges that were almost never used. He became aware of her only gradually, first when he heard the sound of Jaz gulping, greedily drinking, the water splashing on the floor, as the child whimpered in relief.

He thought it was only a dream at first, some nightmare that featured sustenance that would never come. It was not until he heard Shadoath's voice, gentle and seductive, that he realized that she had come, "There, Child. Drink. Drink your fill. I'll save you. I'll be your mother now."

Fallion's eyes flew open. The room was lit by a narrow candle, tall and thin, lying upon a silver plate, beside a silver bowl. Jaz was down from his manacles, and now he lay in the arms of the most beautiful woman that Fallion had ever seen. Jaz's dull eyes stared up at Shadoath, and Fallion had never seen such adoration in the eyes of any being. Shadoath had saved him. She was beautiful beyond dreams. She had no ewer from which to drink. Instead, Jaz drank from her cupped palm.

His eyes said it all: his soul was hers, now, if she wanted it.

Shadoath took a crust of bread from the pocket of her black robe, fed it to Jaz. He wept at the taste of it, and she stroked the tears from his cheek, then bent her head and kissed his forehead.

"So hot," she whispered. "Your head is so warm." She lifted him, peered up at Fallion, and smiled. Then strode away, leaving the light.

Fallion's own tongue was leathery, and felt as if it had swollen in his throat. His stomach cramped so hard that it felt as if it were wrapped around a stone.

Yet his body seemed almost weightless now, and he could no longer feel the pain of the manacles slicing into his wrists, or the muscles stretching in his arms.

He was hot, too. Feverish. And as his brother was carried away, Fallion burned for release, yearned to be carried with him, and wept for want of water.

But there was only fire in the room.

Fire!

Fallion closed his eyes, felt the heat of the candle. He was more sensitive to the flame now than he had ever been. It was a bright and steady presence in the room, like the impotent rage that was building in him.

There is fire all around, Fallion realized. There are flames inside me, burning for release. There are fires inside the other prisoners.

I don't need torches to build an inferno. I could draw the fire from them.

It had been done. Fallion had heard of flameweavers so sensitive that they could draw light from the sky, or suck the heat from a human body.

It could be done again.

Fallion reached out with his consciousness, let it surround the candle, bask in its warmth. The candle sputtered, seemed to come alive.

A rage built inside Fallion. His brother had been carried away, refreshed, weeping in gratitude.

Had Jaz died, Fallion would have mourned. But Jaz had been claimed by Shadoath, and there was no word for the grief that Fallion felt now.

Jaz will be kept as a slave, Fallion realized. Perhaps he'll be pampered and treated well, like the Bright Ones who brought us here. But he'll be hers, and he'll learn to serve her without thought, without compassion.

From the shadows of the room, Valya strode, and knelt to pick up the light. He had not seen her there.

She had heard him crying.

"You can have food," Valya said. "You can have water, too. All you have to do is beg."

Fallion shook his head. He didn't want to live as a servant of Shadoath.

"Mother can give good things, too," Valya said. "It's not all punishment."

The words were just one more blow. "Mother?" Fallion asked. "She's your mother?"

"Yes," Valya said too loudly, as if it were nothing to be ashamed of, as if she'd fight him if he uttered a single syllable of condemnation.

There is light in her still, Fallion thought. She sees the truth about her mother, and hates her.

"I can set you free," Fallion promised.

Valya stormed from the room.

Shortly afterward, perhaps only hours though it might have been days, Fallion woke again.

He'd been dreaming a dream unlike any that he'd ever had before. All of his dreams now were of the prison, of the torturer stumping past his cell, keys rattling. Sometimes in the dream, the torturer turned and leered at Fallion. Sometimes he opened the door, hot tongs in hand, and smiled grimly. Sometimes he brought water, and just as Fallion was taking a drink, he would plunge a blade into Fallion's chest and begin to twist it, twisting, twisting, so that Fallion's innards wound around the blade and eventually began to pull free.

But this dream was different. In this dream, Fallion was filled with a dull rage, and he had sent his consciousness throughout the prison, drawing heat from torches and the tormented bodies of the prisoners.

Not all of the heat, just enough to sustain him.

And then the torturer came stumping through the darkness. The jangle of keys, the thud of boots.

Even though Fallion's head hung and his eyelids were so heavy that he knew that they would never open again, he saw the guard, saw him as he'd never seen anyone before.

The guard stumped past, his torch sputtering grandly. Fallion reached out to draw heat from it, but the guard did not look human in form. His body was there, but Fallion saw it now as if it were the body of a jellyfish floating among the waves. The flesh was clear and insubstantial, barely a hint of form. And there at the heart of the being, hidden beneath the flesh, was a dull gray-blue light, with tendrils shooting in every direction.

Like the jellyfish that I saw at sea, Fallion thought, radiating light.

The torturer stumped past, boots thudding, keys clanking on his chain, and was lost as he passed the stone walls of Fallion's cell.

Fallion was left alone in the darkness.

Except now, there was no darkness.

There was a light inside of him. A light that hardly brightened the room, but which burned fiercely nonetheless. It was not a dim gray light, a shadow yearning to be seen. It was an inferno, a sliver of the sun.

I am a Bright One, Fallion realized. I am a Bright One.

His father had said that Fallion was an old soul. In the legends of Mystarria, there were stories of mystics and wizards who were said to be "old souls." It was said that some folks chose to be born time and time again, accruing wisdom over lifetimes, wisdom that somehow came with them to each new life. Some of these old souls even claimed to recall bits of their past lives. "The body is a shadow," they taught, "and the soul is a light that can pierce it."

Fallion did not necessarily believe the legends. It seemed as good an explanation as any as to why some children were born with wisdom beyond their years.

But Hearthmaster Waggit had warned him against such notions.

"Those who claim to have old souls are mostly fakirs," Waggit had said, "poor folk who pretend to be great, starving for applause.

"Some invent the tales because they can't stand to be seen as the wretches they are. They tell themselves that only wise men suffer, and since they are in pain, they imagine that it must be because they are wise.

"Others use their supposed wisdom to gain money. Out in Indhopal, they prophesy to the poor about impending doom, and offer to use their 'vast spiritual powers' to deflect imaginary ills."

"So all of them are frauds?" Fallion had asked.

Waggit had given him a deep, penetrating stare, one filled with respect.

"Some are genuine," Waggit said softly.

At the time, Fallion had imagined that Waggit was thinking of some wistful encounter. Fallion had not been aware that his father had declared that Fallion was an "old soul." Now he realized that Waggit had been referring to him.

Fallion observed the light within himself, radiating from a central point just beneath his heart.

This is a flameweaver skill, he realized. I'm drawing on powers that I didn't know I had. But what good does it do me to see this?

Not much.

There was some comfort in it. Fallion expected his life to end soon, and he knew that if it did, he would come back again.

He peered inside himself, examining the light. He could see tendrils, thin filaments that stuck out from a burning center, like the spines on a sea urchin.

The spines did not flicker and sputter the way that the flame in a candle does, nor did they seem as if they could die. They were just there, like antlers on a stag.

Fallion twisted this way and that in his chains, and the spikes of light moved with him.

How brightly can they shine? Fallion wondered. I'm a flameweaver. I can nurse a twig into flame from nothing. What can I do with the fire within me?

He willed the light to come forth, and suddenly it blazed, astonishingly bright, so that it seemed to him that the whole room was alight.

He hung there, knowing that he was enveloped in total darkness, yet seeing the room in stark detail—the manacles that had held his brother hanging empty, the locks open, while a stain of sweat and urine darkened the stone wall.

Bits of dust and rubble threw shadows on the floor.

A rat gamely rounded a corner from another cell, the shadowy light within it bouncing as it moved, completely unaware of Fallion's penetrating gaze.

Fallion was marveling at the sight when Shadoath came. He did not hear her, did not see a candle or torch. She came in utter darkness, as if she preferred it that way. Only her voice announced her presence as she rounded the edge of the cell.

"So," she said cheerfully, "the sleeper awakes."

Fallion peered through the darkness at the edge of his cell, and saw her behind the iron bars. Her flesh was as clear as jelly, a mere hint of form. There was a light in her still, a struggling little gray spirit no brighter than the rat's. But there was something more, a blackness that seemed to be attached to the back of it, some creature of indistinct form, like a worm, and it clung to her spirit via a small mouthlike orifice, the way that a lamprey uses its mouth to hold on to a shark.

Fallion opened his eyes. There was no light to reveal her form, and so he let the light within him shine, and studied her by the light of his spirit.

She watched him with keen interest.

"I'm awake," he said. "What do you want from me?"

Shadoath did not answer, not because she did not have one. Fallion could see that much in her eyes.

She opened the lock to his cell, stepped inside, then kept a steady pace as she came close. She did not stop until she touched him, stood leaning against him, her chest to his, peering up into his eyes.

She was beautiful, and Fallion stirred uncomfortably. He was a child still, and his fantasies about women consisted solely of holding hands or tasting a kiss, but he felt in small part what it must be to be a man, to want her more than life or breath.

"You should see yourself," she said. "There is light bleeding from every pore of you, just as in days of old."

Fallion had no idea what she was talking about. "The days of old?" Was she talking about the Bright Ones of old, or did she mean him, in some previous life?

"Why are you here?" she whispered.

"You brought me," he said.

She shook her head. "Not here in this cage. Why are you here on this *world*, now?"

Fallion shook his head, bewildered. He only wanted a drink. For a drink, he would tell her everything he knew and make up lies the whole day long.

"You *do* know the answer," Shadoath said. "It's there in the flames, inside of you. Peer hard enough and you will remember. . . ."

But Fallion felt too tired, too weak, to peer inside of himself for the answer. He surrendered to his weakness, just let himself hang loosely. It did not matter if the chains cut his wrists. The fresh flow of blood that came streaming down his elbows didn't matter.

He hung his head and fainted.

Hours later, he came awake again and tried to recall the conversation.

He was fully aware of the light inside him, and just as aware of the dark creature that dwelt in Shadoath.

Did it really feed on her spirit? Fallion wasn't sure, but he recalled now that his mother called the locus a "parasite." If that is what it was, then it clung to Shadoath like a bloated tick.

Yet if the locus had been feeding, Fallion had not seen it. He'd not seen a gut or some muscle that sucked sustenance from the spirit.

Perhaps, he thought, the locus only clings to a spirit the way that an anemone clings to the hull of a ship, mindlessly catching a free ride across the sea.

No, Fallion decided, the locus is not a mere rider. It is something more than that. It's manipulative. It controls things. It has a purpose.

But what?

Fallion sifted through Shadoath's words for clues. She had not asked about a ransom, as a pirate should. Nor had she sought the location and disposition of his kingdom's Dedicates, the way that a sworn enemy to the realm would.

She had really asked only one question. "Why are you here on this world?"

The answer seemed paramount to her.

She knows me better than I know myself, Fallion thought. She's known me for millennia. But she doesn't know why I'm here.

"The sleeper awakens." She could have just been referring to the fact that he was awake. But Fallion had been gazing at the tendrils of light within himself when she came. He'd let it flood the room.

Had she sensed that? Had it drawn her?

I am the torch-bearer, he thought, recalling Smoker's name for him. I am the light-bringer.

And then it hit him: She wanted to waken him to his powers.

But why? he wondered.

She was his enemy. He could feel that in the marrow of his bones. They had been enemies for endless eons.

What could she hope to gain from him?

Fallion had no answer.

≈ 37 ≈

BECOMING ONE

So many men seek only a union of the flesh, never guessing the joy that comes from a union of the minds.

—Jaz Laren Sylvarresta

Where the sea ape ended and Rhianna began, Rhianna wasn't sure.

She had no volition. She was not Rhianna anymore. Now she was a sea ape, a girl named Oohtooroo.

Oohtooroo walked where she wanted, ate what she wanted. She squatted and peed on the grass while others watched and thought nothing of it.

Rhianna could observe the world at times, her consciousness weak, as if she were half asleep. But even in her most lucid moments she could not do one thing on her own. She could not move one of Oohtooroo's thick fingers or blink an eye.

She was merely an observer, peering out through the eyes of an ape, an ape who loved Abravael more faithfully than any human ever could.

She craved his presence. He was the one who fed her sweet plantains and succulent pork. He was the one who groomed her skin, as her mother once had.

If Abravael had wanted it, she'd have given herself as his mate.

He could not move without Oohtooroo watching. Her eyes followed him everywhere. Her nose tasted the air for his scent as she slept. Her hands longed to touch him.

Oohtooroo wanted to keep him safe, fed, protected.

Until she got her endowment, she had not realized how that might be done. He had made noises and she had done her best to understand.

But with a single endowment of wit, Oohtooroo's eyes seemed to open and her mind to quicken.

"Oohtooroo, come here," her love said softly, and she understood. "Come" was one of only seven words that she had understood, but until now, she had always been unsure of its meaning. Abravael might say, "Come here one moment," and she would go to him. But when he said, "How come you're so stupid?" a moment later, she would go to him, and he would slap her as if she had offended him.

Now, there were so many layers of meaning exposed. "Come quickly" meant to hurry. "Come outside" meant that she should follow him out onto the palace green.

Many times, Oohtooroo wept tears of wonder as she suddenly discerned the meanings of the tiniest of phrases.

Rhianna in her lucid moments had to remain content to watch.

She watched Abravael at his studies, watched him practice with the blade and ax, and even when he slept at night, Rhianna, in Oohtooroo's body, would lie down beside him, tenderly watching him, her heart so full of love and devotion that she thought it might break.

No beagle ever loved its master as perfectly as Oohtooroo did.

And one day, Abravael sat stroking Oohtooroo's neck, whispering sweet words. "Good ape," he said. "You're a sweet thing."

Oohtooroo sniffed in gratitude, her eyes welling with tears, and Rhianna realized that after only three days with endowments, the ape understood everything that was being said. She'd learned quickly, perhaps because Rhianna had already known how to speak, and Oohtooroo was now just learning to use the pathways of Rhianna's mind. It was a marvel in itself.

"Love," the ape said, her lips stretching out into nearly impossible shapes as she sought to duplicate the human words. "Love you."

Abravael smiled and quipped, "You're becoming quite the orator, aren't you?"

"Love you," Oohtooroo repeated, then reached out and took his hand, hugging it.

"How sweet," Abravael said. "Do you love me enough to kill for me, when the time comes?"

"Yes," Oohtooroo said.

"Sweet girl." Abravael hugged her, reaching up to put an arm around her, his face pressed against Oohtooroo's small breasts.

Waves of gratitude and adoration swept through Oohtooroo, and in some measure, the ape's feelings for him mingled with Rhianna's, becoming one.

৪৩ 38 ೮೩

THE RESCUE

All men are free to wander in the realm of thought. I only hope for the day when we are also free to act out all our most wholesome desires.

—Fallion Sylvarresta Orden

Aboard the *Leviathan* the mainmast and mizzenmast were now firmly ensconced, and all of the rigging had been repaired. New sails replaced those that had been lost.

The *Leviathan* was ready to sail. Only one thing remained. . . .

A man named Felandar stood guard at the gates to the outer wall of Castle Shadoath. Thick fog had gathered for the night, and even the brightest torches did not let him see a dozen feet.

It didn't matter. The island was dead on nights like these. Even the golaths went into hiding. The strengi-saats were supposed to confine themselves to the jungles, but when a fog came thick, the monsters often prowled the edge of camp. Indeed, on such nights, a score of golaths might well be dragged from their beds, kicking and screaming.

So in the dead of night Felandar relaxed, a pair of torches at his back to keep the monsters at bay.

He almost didn't see the woman. He had glanced to his left, along the castle wall, and caught a movement from the corner of his eye.

Suddenly she came striding toward him as if she'd coalesced from the mist, a beautiful woman with silky black hair, eyes like dark pools, a stunning figure, and a gait that made her seem to flow rather than walk.

Instinctively he smiled, eager to make her acquaintance. She smiled apologetically, and with blinding speed struck him under the chin.

At first, he thought that she had slapped him, until he realized that cold metal had lodged in his throat.

She twisted the blade, and he heard gristle crackling along his vertebrae.

As Felandar gasped for breath, he grabbed the wrist of her knife hand, trying to stop her.

Myrrima twisted the blade again, and Felandar was no more.

Amid a cloud of thickening fog, Myrrima stalked onto the grounds of Castle Shadoath. Smoker came pacing behind, the coals in his pipe burning brightly.

The locals would not be able to see through her fog, yet Myrrima's eyes pierced it easily enough. She was surprised at what she saw. It was well past midnight, and the grounds were dead. No guards patrolled. A single strengi-saat crouched atop the west tower, seemingly lost in the fog.

Apparently, Shadoath felt that her monsters were guard enough. Certainly Myrrima would not have felt safe walking along those walls at night all alone.

There were three main buildings in the compound. Ahead, Myrrima knew from her previous visit, was the palace itself. She doubted that the dungeons would be there. To the left there appeared to be barracks for the palace retainers, though Myrrima could not be certain. To the right was another building, monolithic and low to the ground, lacking windows. It would be dank inside, and dark. Several guards huddled outside the front door, beside a small fire.

She raced to the guards and found as she neared that two of them were dead asleep. The others were playing dice.

These were Bright Ones that Myrrima was attacking, men whose skills and strength were the stuff of legend.

But they'd never done battle with a Runelord that had four endowments of metabolism. She had the advantage of superhuman speed.

She nailed the first one before he was even aware of her, her blade plunging into the back of his neck.

The other guard grunted and tried rising to his feet. He grabbed for his blade. His speed surprised her, and she recognized that he had endowments to match her own. A bright blade sprung from the scabbard at his back. It glowed like living fire and struck fear in the pit of Myrrima's stomach.

Nice sword, she thought.

He took a wicked swing, and Myrrima dodged beneath it, felt the blade swish perilously close to her scalp.

Her dagger drove into his groin.

He leapt back, blood gushing from his leg, and tried to shout for help, but Myrrima lunged and plunged her blade up under his ribs, into his heart.

I really like your armor, too, she thought. But it didn't do you much good, did it?

One sleeping guard startled awake as the dying man fell on him. Myrrima ended his life without a cry.

The last guard died in his sleep, blissfully unaware of the attack.

Myrrima sheathed the glowing sword, hiding its light. She tried the heavy door, found it locked. She stooped over the dead guards, searching for a key. Smoker came up and found it, turned the outside lock.

Myrrima went in, carefully, watching for more guards. But inside she found none.

Myrrima felt a thrill of surprise. She had expected more resistance. But then, they were on a small island in the middle of nowhere, and with an army outside. The dungeon was as secure as it needed to be.

She hurried down the hall, into the dark. The dungeon smelled of carrion and human filth. The coals in Smoker's pipe suddenly blazed, giving Myrrima the only light that she needed. Myrrima still had endowments of sight, and her eyes were as keen as a cat's.

She passed two cells, found that they were empty, but discovered an old man in the third. She studied him for a long moment before she realized that he was not old at all; he was a young man, mummified and rotting.

She almost dared not look into any other cell until she reached Fallion's. What she found there horrified her.

Fallion hung from the wall, blood running from his wrists, unconscious, possibly dead.

They unlocked the door to his cell, and Myrrima lifted Fallion in order to take the weight off of his swollen wrists. As Smoker fumbled with the keys, Myrrima studied the boy to see if he was still breathing.

He was alive, barely. He smelled of stale urine, feces, blood, and sour sweat. His cheek, resting on her shoulder, burned with fever.

Smoker got the manacles unlocked, and Myrrima was about to carry Fallion outside when he moaned.

"Can't go," he said. "Not yet. Must free Jaz. In the palace."

Myrrima had expected to find Jaz in a cell.

"He's in the palace?" Myrrima asked.

Fallion nodded. "Shadoath took him."

Myrrima trembled. She wasn't strong enough to face Shadoath. But if Jaz was inside the palace, she'd have to go for him.

"Okay," she whispered. "I'll get him. I want you and Smoker to leave. We have rangits tied up outside the gates. You'll need to get as far away as you can, as fast as you can."

Fallion opened his eyes, peered at her through dark slits. His lips were swollen and crusted with blood. "What about the others?"

"What others?" Myrrima asked. Fallion nodded down the hallway.

He wanted her to free the other prisoners.

To what end? she wondered. The night was dark; they'd have to sneak past an army. Once they managed that, the woods were full of strengi-saats. What would she be giving these people?

Hope, she realized. A slim chance. But it was better than none.

Smoker rushed out and began checking cells. Myrrima heard the rattle of keys, the snick of locks, the sound of people groaning and weeping in relief.

Myrrima lay Fallion down; he sprawled on the floor, too weak even to crawl.

Her heart was racing. Shadoath was a powerful Runelord, with endowments of hearing and sight and smell. It would be almost impossible to enter her home in the middle of the night without being detected.

And she would most certainly be awake. Her endowments of brawn and stamina would make it so that she needed no sleep.

Dare I risk this, Myrrima wondered, even for Jaz? He was not the heir apparent, and as far as children went, he didn't show the maturity, insight, or even the strength of Fallion. In short, she expected little from him in this life. And if she had to choose to sacrifice one of the boys, she'd certainly have chosen to sacrifice Jaz.

But she couldn't just leave him.

Myrrima still had endowments of her own. She'd taken endowments of hearing and sight years ago, and she had those. And she had four endowments of metabolism, and still had the brawn of two strong men. Compared to a commoner, she was a ferocious warrior.

But Shadoath would be far more powerful.

Gathering her resolve, she wiped her blade, went out into the night, and headed for the palace.

She found the main gate barred from the inside.

She walked around the eastern wall to the back and found some stairs that led toward some upper apartments. Large apartments, she decided, too large for servants. One apartment was grand, and stood on columns that formed a portico. This would be Shadoath's apartment. But there were smaller rooms on the other side—children's apartments.

Myrrima had seen Shadoath's son and daughter. They'd be sleeping up there. Would Jaz be sleeping with them?

Myrrima crept up the steps, knowing that a Runelord of Shadoath's powers would hear the tiniest scuff of a shoe or rustle of cloth.

She gingerly pulled at the door. It too was barred from the inside.

Softly, she made her way back downstairs.

The servant's quarters. That would be the only way that she might get in.

Sneaking along the outer wall, she came to a tiny room outside the kitchens, and found a window open, where some cook or maid sought to get a little fresh air. The window was in an apartment above the bakery, a room that would be hot here in this clime. Shadoath would have been outraged to see such a breach in security.

It was fourteen feet up to the window. Too far to jump.

Myrrima took off her boots and began to climb, her fingers and toes seeking purchase in the tiny cracks between the stone blocks of the building.

She controlled her breathing so that she did not pant, held her mouth so that she did not grunt. Even when she slid back a bit, breaking nails, she did not cry out.

In a few moments, she reached up over the windowsill and pulled herself inside.

A smelly baker lay on a dirty mattress with his wife and three kids. He snored so loudly that he wouldn't have heard Myrrima if she'd started to dance.

She made her way across the room, carefully stepping over the little ones as if they were her own.

She thought about the guards that she had killed.

They may have wives and families, like my own, she told herself. I'll have to be careful with them.

But she knew her duty.

When she opened the apartment door and found a corridor outside, with another guard—a powerful man, strong and handsome—she didn't hesitate to rush in and stab him hard in the throat.

The man struggled fiercely as he died, reaching for his own blade, kicking at her. She wrestled him—until she stuck her blade in his throat once again, breaking his neck, and then laid him gently on the floor.

She waited for long moments, afraid that the sound of the struggle would have alerted Shadoath.

When she was certain that no one had heard, she followed the corridor upstairs to the royal apartments.

She moved as silently through the hallways as an apparition.

Just outside the queen's quarters, she heard another guard pacing the floor. She ducked into an alcove as he walked downstairs, peering this way and that.

If he turned to his right, he'd stumble over the body of his dead comrade.

Myrrima's heart hammered, and she silently prayed that he would turn to the left.

She studied the layout. There were only three doors—the queen's apartment to her left, and the children's rooms.

Myrrima went to the nearest of the children's doors, tried the lock. It came open, the door creaking slightly. She stood for a long moment, fearing that Shadoath would have heard, that she'd come rushing out from her own room.

She stepped inside.

The apartment was large, with more than one room. A privy took up one small room, and down a short hallway, Myrrima found a bed.

The canopy above the bed was covered in golden samite, which glittered like gems in the wan light of the moon, which shone through a tiny window.

Lying in the bed was Shadoath's daughter, the dark-haired girl that Myrrima had seen two days earlier, when she'd come to ransom the princes.

A third room beckoned around a corner. Myrrima quietly walked toward it, a loose board creaking under her weight, and peered in. It was only a wardrobe, filled with clothing and mirrors.

Myrrima heard a startled gasp, the rustling of clothing, and turned to see the girl peering at her, face pale from terror.

Myrrima flung herself across the room, dagger drawn, prepared to kill the girl. She threw one hand over the girl's mouth, grabbed at her throat with the other, thinking to snap her neck.

But the girl didn't squirm, didn't fight. She just held her finger up, as if warning Myrrima to be quiet.

Taking the girl's cue, Myrrima cautiously pulled her hand away. She could see the track of tears on the girl's cheeks.

"Are you here for Fallion and Jaz?" she whispered so softly that she could almost not be heard.

Myrrima nodded.

"Take me with you?" she asked, even softer.

Myrrima was puzzled.

The girl hesitated. "Fallion said that he could save me. Will you save me?"

Save her from what? Myrrima wondered. But instinctively she knew: Shadoath. Even a dull child knows when her mother is evil.

Again, Myrrima nodded.

"Follow me," the girl whispered.

Quietly, she crawled out of bed, wearing only her night clothes. She did not stop to grab a cloak or shoes. She went straight to the door and opened it, peered into the hallway, and led Myrrima back down two flights of stairs toward the kitchens.

At the bottom of the stairs, a single candle gave light.

Valya hesitated a moment, peering about as if searching for the guard, then headed down a hallway.

They neared the buttery, and Myrrima heard a big man sniffing and moving about, apparently raiding the leftovers from dinner. It was the missing guard. They crept past the buttery, went down two doors, and the girl stepped into a poorly lit room.

It was the kitchen. There, lying before the hearth where the only light came from dying coals, Jaz lay curled up in a large basket.

He's sleeping on the kitchen floor like a dog, Myrrima realized to her dismay.

She rushed to him, peered down. He had not been taken from the prison long ago, she decided by the smell. He hadn't even been bathed. He smelled of his own sweat and urine and feces.

But it seemed that he'd been fed. He was fast asleep, and a salve had been put on the wounds at his wrists, where the manacles had cut him.

"This way," the girl whispered, and headed out a back door, quietly lifting the iron bar that locked it.

Myrrima gently picked up Jaz and carried him out in the back, where the moonlight shone down into a small herb garden.

The girl led Myrrima down a cobblestone path, under an archway, and Myrrima found herself on the west side of the palace.

She'd made it out alive!

Across the green, Myrrima saw Smoker leading two dozen souls out of the prison, many of them maimed. There was a woman with no hands, only bloody bandages. An old man scarred by hot tongs. A golath that limped about on one foot.

All of the women had bloated wombs, as if they were pregnant, and many of them looked pale and wounded; with mounting horror Myrrima realized that they carried strengi-saat young in them.

Smoker had Fallion in his arms, and he was leading his band of refugees out toward the front gate.

"This way," the girl whispered at Myrrima's back, and went racing for the front gates.

Myrrima followed in the dark, bearing Jaz.

Smoker and the others came after. As the prisoners exited, some could not stifle their sobs of relief or tears of joy.

Myrrima had to turn and beg them, "Quiet!"

But fifty feet scuffling over cobblestones were not quiet. One prisoner, wounded and weak, fell with a splat; someone gave a tiny shriek.

Myrrima peered about, growing more worried by the moment. No alarm had sounded.

It couldn't last.

They raced down to the city gates. The city wall was set atop an earthen mound; a tunnel ran beneath the mound, through the wall. There stood the iron gates.

Jaz stirred in Myrrima's arms, moaning just a bit, and he nuzzled against her shoulder, lovingly.

"Quiet, sweet one," Myrrima whispered. "We're almost free."

In the fog and wan moonlight, he suddenly came awake. He peered up at Myrrima, as if he'd expected someone else, and his whole body went taut as he woke from a sweet dream into a nightmare. He peered over Myrrima's back at the cripples and maimed prisoners.

"It's all right," Myrrima whispered as she saw his agitation. "We're almost free."

But Jaz peered at her as if she had slapped him, and screamed in his loudest voice, "Help! Shadoath, help me!"

Myrrima drew a hand over his mouth, but it was too late. The cry was out.

In shock, she realized that Jaz *wanted* to stay with Shadoath.

From somewhere on the palace grounds, Myrrima heard an echoing report, "Murder! Murder in the palace!"

She heard the clank of steel boots, the ringing sounds of chain mail, the palace doors being thrown open.

Cries and screams rose from the prisoners, and they began to stampede. One front-runner was the golath with the amputated foot. It hopped about painfully. Someone pushed it from behind, and half a dozen people fell.

Myrrima urged Shadoath's daughter to hurry. "We've got to get out of here. We've got rangits tied to a tree just down the road. Only a little ways."

But a warhorn sounded up by the palace, deep and brutish, like the grunt of some great beast. In a moment the whole camp would rise up, hundreds of thousands of soldiers.

And now they had a fifth rider to slow them, Shadoath's daughter. Myrrima hadn't planned on that. She hadn't stolen enough rangits.

"Hurry!" Myrrima said, even as Jaz began to fight, trying to get out of her arms, get back to the palace.

The palace doors flew open, and Shadoath stood there on the porch, peering out into the fog, limned by the light. She held a wicked sword with a wavy blade.

A pair of guards rushed out behind her.

The old flameweaver peered at Myrrima, eyes glowing ominously, as if embers had lodged in them, and said softly, "You go. I guard your back."

Smoker saw the danger. He knew that the prisoners would never get free unless he bought them some time.

"Are you sure?" Myrrima said, backing away. She'd seen flameweavers in battle, and she did not want to get too close.

Smoker nodded.

He had been carrying Fallion, but now he carefully handed the boy to one of the prisoners, leaving his charge with another, and stood at the mouth of the tunnel with his pipe glowing in his hand. He raised it overhead and the contents of the bowl burst into flame. He whirled the pipe in a circle, creating a glowing afterimage, a circle of light, and as he did, the prisoners raced past him, pushing, bumping.

Shadoath heard the sounds of scuffing feet and came rushing toward them, running at perhaps six times the speed of a normal mortal, guards sprinting at her back.

Myrrima carried Jaz in her arms, still struggling, and raced down through the tunnel. At the far end, she turned and glanced back.

Smoker stood in the tunnel, waving his pipe in the air, as Shadoath charged toward him.

He raised a dagger and lunged forward a step to do battle.

Shadoath raced toward the tunnel. An old man with skin as white as a sheet barred her way. He had a long-stemmed pipe in his hand, and he swung it slowly in a great arc as he peered into the fog and darkness. He held a long knife in his off-hand. From his stance, she could see that he was no warrior.

She lunged out of the darkness with six times the speed of a normal human, swinging her sword so fast that it blurred. She felt the blade catch slightly as it slid through his guts and met his backbone, but with her great strength, Shadoath merely forced the blade on past.

For half an instant she slowed, wanting to savor the terror in his expression as he realized that he was going to die.

But instead, he merely grabbed for her with one hand, clutching her cloak for all that he was worth, and instead of fear or horror or surprise, she looked in his face and saw . . . a victorious smile.

She expected to be washed in his blood. Instead, a shower of flames roiled out of the wound, scorching her, boiling her flesh instantly, sending a scent of charred flesh and cooking meat into the air, searing her eyes and face.

Shadoath wailed and threw up her hands for protection as burning flames washed over her. She whirled, trying to run, but the old man grabbed at her, as if to hold her in death's embrace.

She pulled away, hot pain embroiling her, as a powerful elemental of flame began to rise from the old man's corpse. It sent fingers of fire rippling through the air; one slammed into her back.

Her robes were aflame!

The guards that had been racing toward her stopped, recognizing the danger. They turned to run, even as fiery arms seared them, boiling their guts instantly.

Groaning in agony, Shadoath lunged away, weaving this way and that in an attempt to elude the elemental's attacks. Lances of fire whipped past her shoulder.

She made the palace doors and raced inside, screaming in pain, and hurried out the back door, placing the palace between her and her attacker.

Her right eye was blind. Her left eye seemed cloudy. She could barely see. She ran to her private garden where a reflecting pool lay, and threw herself in.

Myrrima had seen fiery elementals escape from flameweavers like Smoker before. She knew enough to run.

The inferno came. A rush of hot air roared through the tunnel. Some of the slower prisoners were caught in the wash, screaming in pain and terror as they died.

The heat was so great that it smote the tunnel walls, melting the stone, fusing it into molten glass.

The heat of it blasted Myrrima, singed her hair, scalded the back of her legs.

Myrrima could hear Shadoath wailing in pain, her powerful voice, amplified by the reason of many endowments, keening through the night.

Shadoath's daughter led Jaz, and now she turned and peered toward the inferno, her eyes wide with terror.

Myrrima saw the elemental reflected in her eyes. It rose up on the far side of the wall, forty feet tall. For half a second it still held the form of Smoker, but then it morphed into something more hideous, more brutal, and went stalking toward Shadoath's palace, slaughtering guards and palace workers with every stride.

No one would be safe, Myrrima knew. The elemental was almost mindless now. It would no longer be guided by Smoker's intellect. It existed only to consume.

Reeling from pain, Shadoath threw herself into the reflecting pool and rolled, extinguishing the flames.

She had never imagined such torment.

She raised her searing right hand to survey the damage. Her two smallest fingers had burned off completely. Much of her palm was blackened. She hoped that it would heal, but even as she watched, a ragged scab of flesh dropped away, exposing bones.

Her whole torso ached where the fire had ripped into it. She reached down to her right breast, touching it experimentally, and felt nothing at all.

Burned. The flesh was destroyed.

The elemental on the far side of the palace was doing its damage. It lit up the night sky, and by that light, Shadoath knelt on all fours in the reflecting pool and peered at her ruined face.

Her right eye was a milky white orb, nestled in a swollen socket of bloody meat. Her left eye was cloudy at the center. Her right ear was burned away, along with most of her hair.

The flesh of both of her hands was cooked.

But none of that mattered.

For at the moment she was mindless with agony. Gone were all thoughts of revenge or escape or of rescuing her daughter.

Shadoath wished for the release offered by death, but with hundreds of endowments of stamina, death would not come.

Myrrima rushed toward the rangits. One escaped prisoner, a man whose back was lashed and shredded, had found their rangits tied to a tree, and now he struggled to untie one.

"Sir," Myrrima said, "those are for the children."

The fellow leapt up at the sound of her voice, terrified, and for a moment Myrrima feared that she would have to fight him for a mount, but he looked at her, at the children, and nodded his head stupidly, then ran toward the woods.

Myrrima found that Fallion was too weak to hold on, so she set him in the saddle with Shadoath's daughter. And since Jaz still fought her and cried for Shadoath, Myrrima did not trust him to ride alone. She put him on a mount in front of her, and clung to him, hoping that in time he would regain his senses.

Now she saw that there were two spare rangits. A pregnant girl of perhaps fifteen came and mounted one. Myrrima took the other to use as a palfrey, so that the mounts could take turns getting a rest, and off they went, the rangits bouncing down the dirt road, then floating up again.

Behind them, Shadoath could be heard shrieking in mortal agony, and the sky was ablaze. Smoker's elemental seemed intent on igniting the world.

❧ 39 ☙

THE FURY

Our rage may give us power, even as it diminishes us.

—Erden Geboren

Fallion rode in a hot fury. Thick fog hid everything, the road ahead and the inferno behind, but Fallion could feel the flames licking the night sky behind him, and it took little to reach out with his powers and summon the heat, use the energy to renew his own depleted strength.

Numb with pain and fatigue, Fallion wasn't even sure how he'd gotten here, riding a rangit with Valya's arms holding him tightly, but for a moment he resented the pain. Each time the rangit hit the ground, the jarring threatened to dislocate his bones.

His eyes itched and his head ached, and at that moment, he wanted nothing more but to fall back into unconsciousness.

On the road ahead, he saw men rushing up out of the fog, or something like men. Golaths, their warty gray skin sagging around their breasts and bellies.

"Clear the way!" Myrrima shouted to them. "Clear the way! The prisoners have escaped."

The golaths leapt out of her way, fearing that some dire soldier would ride them down. And after the prisoners passed, the golaths stood beside the road peering at their backs in wonder.

Let them try to stop us, Fallion thought, summoning heat from Smoker's inferno. Let them try.

"Stop that," Myrrima said from the rangit that raced beside them.

"What?"

"Don't give in," Myrrima whispered. "Don't give in to your rage."

Fallion tried clinging to the saddle as the rangit bounced ahead, and his mind seemed to spin.

He'd asked Shadoath what she wanted, and she had not answered. Only now was he really certain.

She'd wanted the sleeper to awaken. She'd wanted him to summon the fire, to lose himself.

But why? What would the loci hope to gain from him?

Did they want him to join them? Or did they need something else from him?

Behind them, Smoker's inferno was raging, roaring in intensity. The fire crackled the bones of his enemies and sent clouds of smoke spewing into the heavens.

Smoker had given himself to the flames so that Fallion would not have to.

I'm a fool, Fallion thought in dismay, and he tried to let go of his rage. He sagged against the rangit, struggling for the moment to remain a child.

When the riders reached the mountain pass, they came up out of the fog and the rangits found themselves on a clear road, hopping by starlight.

In the valley behind them, the palace was aflame and Smoker's elemental was dutifully attacking the barracks, blasting row upon row of tents, sending out fingers of flames that seemed to have an intelligence all their own, pure malevolence bent on destruction.

The whole valley seethed like a hornet's nest.

Myrrima could hardly believe that a single wizard could cause so much annihilation.

At the edge of the woods, she got off her mount and drew a rune in the dirt, one that would lock the valley below in fog for a week.

Then she lit a torch and they were off again. She worried about patrols in the woods, even though she and Smoker had done their best to take care of that.

So they raced for hours under the starlight. They picked up some strengi-saats as they rode. The great beasts snarled in the woods, and floated behind them like shadows, leaping from tree to tree.

Myrrima shivered and kept the children close. Jaz quit fighting her after a while, and seemed to realize who she was, and that she was taking him to safety. He clung to her and wept.

"I'm sorry," Jaz said over and over again.

"You've no need to be sorry," Myrrima said.

"I got Smoker killed. Shadoath was so beautiful. I wanted to be with her."

"Don't feel bad," Valya told Jaz in a soothing tone. "I've seen grown men give themselves to her that way, thanking her even as she twisted a blade into their hearts. Beauty was just another of her weapons."

Myrrima worried at that, wondering what kinds of things Valya might have seen.

After two hours, a half-moon rose, adding a wan tone of silver to the night.

With a clear road, the rangits picked up speed, and the faster they hopped, the less jarring the ride became.

They neared town just an hour before dawn.

Fallion seemed to sleep most of the way, until they reached the docks, where Captain Stalker and some of his men were waiting with a ship's boat.

They transferred the children into the boat, and Stalker peered up the road.

"Smoker comin'?" he asked, his voice tinged with worry.

"I'm afraid not," Myrrima said. "His elemental burnt down the palace and set flames to at least half the camp."

"Ah, he always was one of the good ones," Stalker said. "Don't know how I'll ever replace him."

A good flameweaver, Myrrima thought. She'd never met one that she would have called *good* before, but now, sadly, she realized that Stalker's assessment was right.

I'll never meet his equal again, she told herself.

They rowed out to the *Leviathan*, and carried the children aboard. Myrrima held Fallion on the deck, while one of Stalker's men ran to fetch some water. Fallion's forehead was burning up.

Some of the crew began pulling anchor, while others rushed about unfurling masts, ready to make way.

Stalker peered at the other ships in the harbor darkly. Four ships. Shadoath's ships. He dared not leave them, lest they give chase.

"Fire when ready," Stalker said, and his men went to the catapults, put torches to iron shot wrapped in pitch, and sent the balls arcing out into the night. The nearest two ships each took a ball, and soon Myrrima could see crewmen racing to put out small fires.

The ships were only manned by a skeleton crew, two or three men aboard each.

"That ought to keep 'em busy," Stalker said, grinning.

The crewman brought Fallion a ladle filled with fresh water, and he raised his head to drink. For a moment he peered at the ships out on the wine-dark water, with their little flames.

Myrrima felt the heat in him, a fever that suddenly felt explosive. Then it raced out in an invisible ball that could be felt but not seen, and struck out over the water.

The fires surged, went twisting up the mastheads and washing over the decks. A ball of flame leapt from ship to ship; in seconds all four pirate ships had become an inferno. Their crewmen shouted in fear and leapt into the sea.

Stalker peered at the conflagration in astonishment.

Fallion smiled. He could hear the flames sputtering, the voice of his master, gleefully hissing in appreciation.

He had used his powers, and given glory to Fire.

Not until Fallion was sure that his fires would do their job did he take a drink.

❧ 40 ❧

A MOTHER'S VENGEANCE

Even a wolf bitch loves her pups.

—*a saying from Internook*

In the dim hours of morning, Shadoath strode through the tunnel under the palace gate. The stone walls were charred and darkened. The bodies of those who had been too close when the flameweaver had immolated himself were stretched out on the ground, their clothing incinerated, flesh charred and burned beyond recognition. Twenty-seven people had died there at the heart of the flames.

Some had been soldiers, others prisoners. But judging from the skeletal remains, none were children.

Fallion and Jaz had escaped and taken Valya with them.

Shadoath seethed.

She had hundreds of endowments of stamina to her credit, but even those had barely kept her alive. Gone were fingers and an ear, her right eye and most of her vision. Gone was the better part of her nose.

Her face was a mass of scars. Every inch of her was a searing pain. She would live, but never again would she be beautiful.

Her son Abravael came up behind her, the sea ape knuckling along at his back.

"Captain Stalker will go to Landesfallen," Shadoath said. "We'll find him there."

"How do you know?" Abravael asked.

"He has a wife there, and a son. He knows that I know where they live. He has no choice but to rescue them."

"He'll have a good lead on us."

"Ships will come soon enough. Stalker will be wallowing his way to

Landesfallen with a hold full of cargo. He's at least six weeks out. We'll lighten our load. With any luck, we'll meet him at the docks."

Rhianna listened through Oohtooroo's ears, and her heart ached. She longed to warn her friends. But the sea ape's body would not respond to even her most urgent needs. Rhianna was a prisoner.

Shadoath turned to Oohtooroo and smiled. She must have realized Rhianna's distress. She reached up and scratched the sea ape's head. "Good girl, Oohtooroo. Good sea ape. You'll help us catch those nasty people, won't you? And when you do, we'll have fresh meat for you—the tasty flesh of a young boy."

At the words "fresh meat," Oohtooroo grew excited and began grunting. She leapt in the air repeatedly and banged the earth with her mighty fist.

Shadoath smiled cruelly, peering not into the ape's eyes, but through them, as if into Rhianna's mind, and through Shadoath's scarred visage, Rhianna saw the torture that she had in mind.

She would feed Fallion to the sea ape, and Rhianna would be able to do nothing as the ape ripped the flesh from his body, tearing away strips of muscle in her teeth, while Fallion screamed in pain.

That night, as Myrrima and Borenson lay abed with the children sleeping all about, Borenson took stock of the situation.

Fallion had taken the news of Rhianna's death hard.

"I was sworn to protect her," Fallion said.

Borenson had been a guard. He knew how much it hurt to lose a charge.

"We can't always protect the ones that we love," Borenson said. "Sometimes, even after all that we can do, we lose them."

"I was able to save her from the strengi-saats once before," Fallion objected. "Maybe she's still out there. Maybe she needs our help."

"Myrrima searched everywhere," Berenson said. "She's just . . . gone." Fallion had insisted on blade practice before bed, despite his worn and weakened condition.

With muscles wasted from fatigue, with mouth swollen from thirst, Fallion reeled across the ship's deck in the lantern light, his eyes glowing unnaturally, fighting like a crazed animal.

Afterward, he had cried himself to sleep.

Borenson worried about him. One by one, it seemed that Fallion was losing everyone he loved. What would happen when he lost them all?

Would there be room left in his heart for anything but hate?

"We got Fallion and Jaz back," he told Myrrima as he lay spooned against her, whispering into her ear. "But if Shadoath is still alive . . . ? You're sure that she's alive?"

"I saw her and heard her cries," Myrrima said.

"Then what have we won?"

Myrrima wasn't sure. "We have Valya. We could pretend to hold her hostage if Shadoath comes for us."

"Do you have the heart for such games? Neither one of us would ever put the girl's feet to the flames or cut off an ear."

"Shadoath doesn't know that," Myrrima said.

"At least we have a head start," Borenson said.

Some of Shadoath's ships had burned, but others still patrolled the ocean. Captain Stalker had assured them that Shadoath would hunt them with a vengeance in short order.

He'd had his men go down to the hold and begin dumping his cargo, throwing overboard anything that they couldn't eat. It would ruin him financially, but he was worried only for his life. Captain Stalker intended to get to Landesfallen as soon as possible. There, he'd get his wife, the last surviving member of his family, and take the northern route to some unnamed port.

As Myrrima lay in bed, she whispered to herself as much as her husband, "I wish I could have beaten her. She has too many endowments."

"If Shadoath has endowments, then she has Dedicates," Borenson said in a dangerous tone. "Did you see any sign of them?"

"No," Myrrima said. She glanced pointedly toward Valya, who lay asleep on the floor. The child didn't know where to find her mother's Dedicates. Borenson had already asked her. But she had been able to provide a clue. Her mother's Dedicates had always been taken east, perhaps to some hidden port in Landesfallen or to another island, in a ship called the *Mercy*.

In time, Myrrima hoped that the girl might provide more clues to the whereabouts of Shadoath's Dedicates.

Borenson held Myrrima tightly. She could tell that he was worried. He had played the assassin once in his life, and now it seemed that fate was casting him in that role again. Myrrima knew that he could not bear it.

She couldn't ask Borenson to hunt down Shadoath's Dedicates. Nor did she believe that she could do it herself. Besides, Gaborn had not told them to fight. He must have known the dangers that they would face better than they did.

There was only one other hope.

"Do you really think that we'll be safe once we reach Landesfallen?" Myrrima asked.

Borenson hesitated. " 'The ends of the Earth are not far enough,' Gaborn said. Once we reach Landesfallen, we'll have to go past them, far past. Deep into the inlands."

Only the coasts of Landesfallen were well inhabited. Here and there, where the roots of the stonewood forests touched the sea, cities had been built in the trees.

Shadoath would have a hard time searching even the coast. But the inland desert? That was huge, big enough for a man to get lost in and never be found.

"We'll be safe," Borenson said hopefully. "We'll be safe."

ೞ 41 ೞ

THE BROKEN CHILD

Children have legendary healing abilities. I have seen a newborn babe lose a finger to a dog, and grow it back again. No matter what wound is inflicted, one can always hope for healing with a child.

—*The Wizard Binnesman*

In the mornings Fallion got up and walked the decks. He climbed the rigging for exercise, and enjoined the other children to follow him. His muscles grew strong, but not large. Instead they felt thin and ropy, as if in the prison he had starved enough so that even now his body fed upon his own flesh, and he wondered if he would ever regain his bulk again.

By day he'd practice harder with his weapons now, his mind returning again and again to Rhianna, to thoughts of how it had been when she died upon the beach. Perhaps she'd been killed and eaten by a strengi-saat, but Fallion feared that she'd been taken instead—carried into the trees and filled with strengi-saat babies, the way that she had been when he first found her.

He tried to act normal, to force smiles when he saw his friends or to laugh when he heard a joke. But the laughter always came too late, sounding hollow; and though his lips might turn upward, there was no smile in his eyes.

Borenson and Myrrima worried about him, as did Captain Stalker. But the one who could perhaps have offered the best comfort was Smoker, and he was gone.

"He'll get over it in time," Borenson said. "He was starved. One doesn't heal from that easily."

And it was true. The welts around Fallion's wrists tried to heal, but they scabbed over and became infected. Myrrima washed the festering wounds, but they just seemed to swell the more. Often they would bleed, and four weeks later, when it seemed that the infection had finally subsided, Myrrima had to satisfy herself with the knowledge that the wounds would leave deep and everlasting scars.

But though the scars on Fallion's wrists had begun to heal, the darkness still called to him, and he found himself longing for oblivion.

It was a few weeks after they left that Myrrima was awakened one night in the hold of the ship.

"Nooooo!" Borenson cried, his voice keening like some animal. He began to thrash about, as if enemies attacked and he was holding them at bay. "Noooo!"

Sage woke at the sound, whimpering, and Myrrima shook Borenson awake, carefully.

He'd been troubled by bad dreams for years, and she'd learned long ago that it was best to leave him asleep, let him thrash and weep until the dreams abated. But with Sage crying and other guests on the ship, she dared not let him sleep.

She shook him and called to him, dragging him from his slumber, and when he woke, he sat at the edge of the bed, trembling. His heart pounded so hard that she could hear its every beat.

"Was it the dream again?" she asked. She leaned up and kissed him on the forehead, then secretly drew a rune with her spittle.

"Yes," he said, still sobbing, but suddenly seeming to regain control. "Only this time, I dreamed that Valya and Fallion were there."

He had dreamed of Castle Sylvarresta, long ago. It seemed like a lifetime ago, though the dream was as vivid as ever.

Raj Ahten had taken the castle, and then abandoned it on a ruse, leaving his Dedicates behind. Upon the orders of King Mendellas Orden, Borenson was sent inside to butcher Raj Ahten's Dedicates. All of them, any of them, including the king's own son Gaborn, if need be.

Borenson had known that he would have to kill some folk that he had counted as friends, and it was with a heavy heart that he did his duty.

But after slaying the guards and walking into the inner courtyard, he had gone first to the kitchens and bolted the door.

There, staring up at his naked blade in terror were two deaf girls, Dedicates who had given their hearing to Raj Ahten.

It was considered a crime against nature for a lord to take endowments from a child. An adult with enough glamour and voice could beguile a child so easily. For Raj Ahten to have done it was monstrous.

But from Raj Ahten's point of view it had to have been a seductive choice. What true man would slay a child, any child? An assassin who somehow broke into the deepest sanctuaries of a castle with the intent of slaying Dedicates would find it hard indeed to kill children.

No, a decent man would let the children live, and thus give Raj Ahten a better chance to fight back.

Thus, beyond the walls of stone and the heavy guard, Borenson found one last barrier to his assassin's blade: his own decency.

He had managed to fight it to a standstill, but he had never conquered it. Indeed, he hoped that he never would.

"The dream was different this time," Borenson said, his voice ragged. "The girls were there, as in life, but I saw Fallion there, and Rhianna, and Talon and Jaz. . . ." He fell apart, sobbing helplessly. She'd seen the way he had been slashing in his dream, murdering his own children.

"I killed them," Borenson said. "I killed them all. Just like I did in life— thousands of Dedicates, some that I called friends, some that had feasted with me at their tables. King Sylvarresta was there, grinning like an idiot, as innocent as a child, the scar from his endowments ceremony fresh upon him, and I killed him again. How many times must I kill him before he leaves me in peace?"

He broke down then and sobbed, his voice loud and troubled. He turned and buried his face in a blanket so that other guests of the inn would not hear.

Sage had already gone back to sleep.

A single candle was sputtering beside the bed, giving light to the whole room, and by it, Myrrima looked over the children, to see if they were all asleep.

She saw a pair of bright eyes peering at her, reflecting the light of the candle. It was Fallion, his eyes seeming to glow of their own accord.

Well, Myrrima realized, now he knows the truth: the man who is raising him, who has been all but a father to him, is the man who executed his grandfather.

The man whom all call a hero sobs himself to sleep at night.

I wonder what Fallion thinks of us?

She whispered to Fallion, "Don't make the mistakes that we have made."

Then she turned over and held Borenson. But as she did, she worried for Fallion. This was but another scar for the boy to bear.

Fallion sat on the balcony at the back of the ship, between the barrels where he and Rhianna used to hide, just hoping for a bit of peace. Valya sat beside him.

They were peering out the back of the ship, watching the sun descend toward the sea in a molten ball of pink, the clouds overhead looking like blue ashes falling from the skies.

They had not spoken for a long hour, and finally Valya put an arm around Fallion's shoulders and just hugged him, holding him for long minutes.

"Don't give in to it," she begged. "Don't give in. That's what my mother wants you to do."

"What?" Fallion asked.

"She told me not to give you anything—" Valya answered. "No food. No water. No comfort. She said, 'All that I want is his despair.'"

Fallion had felt despair in the prison, wave upon wave of it. But he'd always held on to some thin hope that he would be released.

Yet suddenly, here on the ship under the bright light of day, it was as if the despair thickened, and he could not escape it.

His mind flashed back to Asgaroth's prophecy. What had he said? "All of your noblest hopes shall become fuel to fire despair among mankind."

It was almost as if Asgaroth wanted Fallion to become one of them.

But why despair? he wondered. Do loci feed on despair?

Fallion recalled something that Borenson had once told him. The purpose of every war was to cause despair. "We don't fight wars for the love of battle," he'd said. "We fight to cause despair, to force surrender, so that we can enforce our will."

He'd gone on to explain that most conflicts seldom reached the point where one side took up arms. The costs of marshaling troops, feeding them, sending them off to foreign lands—or worse, defending your own borders and lands—was too prohibitive.

And so other means had been devised. First, diplomacy took place. Grievances were made, petitions filed.

If the problems were not rectified, then the complainant might wage economic warfare, raiding supply trains going into and out of the country, seizing merchant ships, or convincing other nations to suspend trade.

Only as a last resort, after many warnings, did one invade.

Fallion sat in the sunlight, his mind dulled from abuse, and realized that for reasons that he did not understand, Shadoath was waging war upon him.

That alone seemed to spark his rage.

I will not surrender, he told himself. She will surrender to me.

"What will I have to do to cause your mother despair?" Fallion wondered.

Valya laughed. "Just keep on doing what you're doing?"

"What's that?"

"Smiling."

Fallion suddenly realized that he *was* smiling. Not a happy smile, but a cruel smile, the kind of smile that Borenson carried with him when he went into battle.

He'd found a reason to live: revenge.

ಬಿ 42 ಅ

GARION'S PORT

Home is whatever place you feel safest.

—*a saying of Rhofehavan*

The *Leviathan* sailed near Garion's Port on a cool spring evening almost four months to the day from when it had left the Courts of Tide. The night was cool, marbled with gauzy clouds that shaded the moon, and the brisk wind snapped the sails and lashed the water to whitecaps.

Fallion was stunned at his first sight of stonewood trees. The ship had neared Landesfallen three days ago, but remained well out to sea as it inched north, and so though he saw the gray trees from the distance, rising like menacing cliffs, he had not been able to see them closely.

They grew thick at the base of two cliffs of stark sandstone: the Ends of the Earth, and as the ship eased near the port, Fallion peered up in wonder.

The stonewoods were aptly named. Their massive roots stretched out from gray trunks into the sea, gripping the sand and stone beneath. The roots were large enough so that a fair-sized cottage could rest comfortably in a crook between them. Then they joined in a massive trunk that rose from the water, soaring perhaps two hundred feet in the air.

"There are taller trees in the world," Borenson told the children much in the same tone that Waggit used to lecture in, "but there are none so impressively wide."

The roots of the trees soaked up seawater, he explained, which was rich in minerals. Eventually, the minerals clogged the waterways within the trunk of the tree, and over the years, the heart of the tree became petrified, even as it continued to grow. The starving tree then broadened at the base, in an attempt to get nutrients to the upper branches. The tree could even put down new taproots when the old ones became clogged, thus becoming ever wider, and becoming ever stronger, its heart turning to stone.

The result was a tree that went beyond being *hoary*. Each stonewood was tormented, like something from a child's fearful dream of trees, magnificent, its limbs twisted as if in torture, draped with gray-green beards of lichen that hung in tattered glory.

Within the bay, the water was calm. Fish teemed at the base of the huge trees, leaping in the darkness, and Fallion could see some young sea serpents out on the satin water, perhaps only eight feet long, finning on the surface, seemingly bent on endlessly chasing their tails.

High above, in the branches of the trees, lights could be seen from a forest city.

"Are we going to live up there?" Talon asked her father, fear evident in her voice.

"No," Borenson said. "We're going inland, to the deserts."

In the distance, near the city, Fallion saw a pair of graaks flying along the edge of the woods, enormous white ones large enough to carry even a man, sea graaks that were so rare they were almost never seen back in his homeland. Their ugly heads, full of teeth, contrasted sharply with the beauty of their sleek bodies and leathery wings.

The graaks were both males, and so had a ridge of leather, called a plume, that rose up on their foreheads. The plumes had been painted with blue eyes, staring wide, the ancient symbol of the Gwardeen. A pair of young men, perhaps thirteen or fourteen years of age, rode upon their backs.

They're on patrol, Fallion realized. He longed to be up there, riding a graak himself. It was something that his mother had never allowed him to do.

Even if I fell, he thought, the worst that would happen is that I'd land in the water.

And end up a meal for the serpents, a niggling voice inside him whispered, though in truth he knew that a young sea serpent, like the ones he saw finning now, were no more dangerous than a reef shark.

The ship didn't even bother to drop anchor. The captain just let it drift for a bit.

"I'll let you folks row in from here," Captain Stalker said. "No sense attracting any notice, if you can help it."

That was the plan. They would row in during the night and follow the river inland for miles, hoping not to be seen for days perhaps, until they were far from the coast.

Meantime, Captain Stalker would rush home and get his wife, then sail north and scuttle the ship near some unnamed port.

Fallion was suddenly aware that he'd never see Captain Stalker again, and his heart seemed to catch at his throat.

"Thank you," Myrrima said, and the family grabbed their meager possessions as the crew lowered the boat.

There were some heartfelt good-byes as Fallion and the children hugged the captain and some of their favorite crew members.

Stalker hugged Fallion long and hard, and whispered in his ear, "If you ever get a hankerin' for life on the sea, and if I ever get another ship, you'll always be welcome with me."

Fallion peered into his eyes and saw nothing but kindness there.

I used to worry that he had a locus, Fallion thought, and now I love him as if he were my own father.

Fallion hugged him hard. "I'll hold you to it."

Then he climbed down a rope ladder to the away boat. Borenson, Myrrima, and the children were already there, each child clutching a tiny bundle that held all that he or she owned.

Myrrima was deeply aware of just how little they had brought with them: a few clothes that were quickly wearing down to rags, some small mementos, Fallion's forcibles.

We must look like peasants, she thought. She took the oars and rowed out toward the city.

"Make north of the city, about two miles," Stalker warned her, and she changed course just a little. The sound of waves surrounded them, and the boat splashed through the waters with each small tug of the oars. Droplets from the oars and spray from whitecaps spattered the passengers.

Fallion watched the *Leviathan* sail away, disappearing into the distance.

All too soon they neared shore, where small waves lapped among the roots of the stonewoods. The scent of the trees was strange, foreign. It was a metallic odor, tinged with something vaguely like cinnamon.

Two hundred feet up, peeking through the limbs, lanterns hung. Among the twisted limbs, huts had been built, small abodes made of sticks, with roofs of bearded lichens. Catwalks ran from house to house.

Fallion longed to climb up there, take a look around.

But he had to go farther inland, and sadly he realized that he might never set foot in Garion's Port again.

"The Ends of the Earth are not far enough," he recalled, feeling ill at ease. He scanned the horizon for black sails. There were none.

So the boat crept among the roots until it reached a wide river. The family rowed through the night until dawn, listening to the night calls of strange birds, the rasping sounds of frogs or insects—all calls so alien that Fallion might just as well been in a new world.

As dawn began to brighten the sky, they drew the boat into the shelter beneath the great trees, and found that it was a place of eternal shadows.

The murk of overhanging trees made it as dark as night in some places, and the ground was musty and covered with strange insects—enormous tarantulas, and various animals the likes of which Fallion had never seen— flying tree lizards and strange beetles with horns.

They found a barren patch of ground and met up with Landesfallen's version of a shrew: a tenacious little creature that looked like a large mouse but which defended its territory as if it were a rabid she-bear. The bite of the shrew was mildly poisonous, Borenson was later warned, but not until after he discovered it through personal experience.

The shrew, disturbed by his approach, leapt up on his leg and sank its teeth into Borenson's thigh. The shrew then squatted in the clearing, squeaking and leaping threateningly each time that he neared. Sir Borenson, who had battled reavers, Runelords, and flameweavers, was obliged to give way for the damned shrew.

As Fallion nursed a fire into being, using nothing but wet detritus, the others set up camp.

He marveled at the raucous cries of birds unlike any that he'd heard before, the weird twittering calls of frogs, and the croaks of lizards.

The earth smelled rich, the humus and dirt overpowering. He had been at sea for so long, he'd forgotten how healthy the earth could smell.

But they were safe. There was no sign of Shadoath's pirates. They were alive, and tomorrow they could push farther inland.

For at least today, he thought, we are home.

❧ 43 ☙

THE NIGHTMARE RETURNS

We cannot always run away from our problems, for too often they follow.

—*Hearthmaster Vanyard, from the Room of Dreams*

Five years passed before Shadoath heard the words "We have found him."

The spring that Fallion had gone missing, she'd sent her agents through every port in Landesfallen, searching for the boy. Bribes were offered, threats were made. After a few months without any progress, innkeepers went missing and wound up in her torture chambers.

The Borenson family had disappeared, and apparently never made it to any port.

Yet Captain Stalker had found his way home, Shadoath knew. His wife, in the village of Seven Trees Standing, disappeared, and six months later Shadoath got word that the remains of the *Leviathan* were crashed upon some rocks on the shores of Toom. The captain and all hands were reported dead.

Shadoath had changed the focus of her search then, sending men to the north countries of Rofehavan. She imagined that the Borensons had decided to flee back home to safety.

He might be in Mystarria, she reasoned, or even off in his mother's old haunts in Heredon.

Thus, the trail grew cold, and in time Shadoath turned her thoughts to other things. Her armies began making raids into the southlands of Inkarra, slaughtering villages and bringing back gold and blood metal. Her assassins struck down powerful leaders in far places.

She took endowments of stamina, sight, and glamour. In time, she smoothed the scars from her body. Though her right eye remained forever blind, with enough endowments of stamina and sight, she regained vision in her left.

She sent out an army of minstrels to sing new songs, powerful songs that called for change, songs that reviled decent lords, accusing them of tyranny, while true tyrants were praised within their own borders as men of great strength and vision.

And the peasants responded.

Chaos washed across the world, and in a dozen countries revolutions arose. In Orwynne, good men refused to serve as Dedicates to their young king, suspecting that he was a tyrant. He responded by outlawing all minstrels—a group that by ancient law could not be silenced—and thus in the minds of many proved that he was a tyrant indeed. When the Knights Equitable slaughtered his Dedicates, and then put him to the gallows, only his wife and children protested.

In the northlands of Internook, folk who had always been too poor to afford forcibles heard songs that decried the "tyranny of the Runelords," and were taught to long for a day when none existed. It was no surprise when the peasants revolted, slaughtering the few Dedicates that lived within Internook's borders.

The folk of Alnick soon tried to follow in their footsteps, marching upon the castle. There Queen Rand threw herself from the battlements, ending her life so that she might free her Dedicates, sparing them from murder.

The call for revolution spread, even as the blood-metal mines in Kartish gave out.

The world grew ripe for destruction, and as it did, Shadoath prepared. Her army of strengi-saats had multiplied and grown fat on the carrion left in the wake of her small wars in Inkarra.

Shadoath had almost forgotten Fallion. But last fall she had been visiting a small port in the north of Mystarria, and as she walked down the busy streets, studying the work of local weapon-smiths, she spotted a sailor that she recognized.

She'd only seen him once, for a few seconds, yet with a dozen endowments of wit, Shadoath remembered his face vividly. He had been just another sailor in the crowd on the night when Shadoath had fought Myrrima. He was supposed to have been dead, washed up on the rocks of Toom.

She took him then, and a few days under the hot tongs loosened his tongue.

Fallion had gone ashore near Garion's Port.

She sent her agents out again, had them search up the Hacker River with its many tributaries, and told them what to look for.

She knew Fallion better than he knew himself. She'd fought him time and again, over many lifetimes.

"Look for a lad well versed with a blade, one who has made a reputation for himself. He will be quiet and unassuming, driven and as sharp as a knife, but well liked by others."

And so now one of her scouts had returned, a minstrel in green-and-yellow-striped pants with a shirt of purple and a red vest. He looked like a fool but sang like a sweet lark, plucking his lute as he danced around.

"I found him. I found him. And for a fortune I'll tell you whe-ere," the minstrel sang, doing a jig around the throne, glee shining in his eyes.

Shadoath grinned. "Fallion?"

The minstrel nodded secretively.

She reached down to her belt, threw her whole purse full of gold onto the floor. "Where?"

"He's a captain among the Gwardeen, and goes by the last name of Humble. For three years he has led graak riders at the Citadel of the Infernal Wastes, and only recently has he been transferred to the Gwardeen Wood, just north of Garion's Port."

"A captain—so young?" she wondered. Instinctively she knew that it was true. Young, ambitious, well liked.

The name "Fallion" was common in Landesfallen, and the boy had apparently kept it, changing only his last name.

The Gwardeen were notoriously closed and secretive, and their graak outposts were often difficult to reach. The Citadel of the Infernal Wastes was a fortress only eighty miles east of Garion's Port. But it was high in the mountains, some said "impossible" to reach by foot.

Shadoath tried to imagine the life that he had been living. Fallion would have spent years flying missions over the inland deserts on his graak, making certain that the toth had not returned. He might even have spent the midsummer and winter months down in their ancient tunnels.

No wonder she had not found him.

The minstrel plucked his lute, as if begging attention, and then continued. "He has a brother serving under him: a boy named Draken. And there is an older woman that he visits in Garion's Port—petite and beautiful, with raven hair." The minstrel strummed a few notes to an ancient love ballad.

Valya.

Shadoath smiled.

The minstrel strummed and sang, "How will we catch this bird? How will we clip its wings? For with only a word, other larks will warning bring."

Obviously he had been thinking. The Gwardeen kept watch at all times, and Fallion would be ready to fly away at a moment's notice.

"I don't have to find him," Shadoath said with a smile. "He is a Gwardeen, sworn to protect Landesfallen. I shall make him come to me."

❧ 44 ❧

HEIR OF THE OAK

In times of trouble, the world always looks for a hero to save it. Be careful that you don't heed their call.

—Sir Borenson, advice given to Fallion

On a lazy summer afternoon at a tiny inn called the Sea Perch, built high among the branches of the stonewoods, Fallion sat listening to a minstrel sing.

> "Where, oh, where is the Heir to the Oak,
> Strong of heart and fair of face?
> His people mourn, and their hearts are broke,
> They say he dwells in some far-off place.
>
> In Heredon's wood, on Mystarria's seas,
> one can hear the ravens cry.
> Their calls disrupt the dreams of peace
> That in tender hearts of children lie.
>
> Where, oh, where is the Heir to the Oak?
> Exiled to some fairer realm?
> Does he follow his father's roads?
> Calling a field his fort, the forest home?
>
> Where, oh, where is the Heir to the Oak?
> 'Lost,' some say, to light and life.
> But faithful hearts still hold this hope:
> His return will herald an end to strife."

The song struck Fallion to the marrow. It wasn't just the quality of the singer's voice. Borenson had warned Fallion that the people would cry for his return.

Not yet, Fallion thought. I'm not ready yet. Do they really want me to come so soon?

Fallion had hoped to wait until he was sixteen. On his sixteenth birthday, it was customary to crown a prince as king.

But Fallion doubted that there would be anyone to crown him by the time he returned home. By all accounts, Chancellor Westhaven had tried his best to hold Mystarria together. But the Brat of Beldinook had torn it from his hands, and then had begun a reign of horror over its people, "punishing" them for the death of her father at Gaborn's hands, persecuting any who dared admit that the Earth King may have been right in executing him.

There were tales of starvation in Mystarria, of forlorn crowds rioting at the Courts of Tide.

In Fallion's mind, such "nobles" were waging wars that only weakened themselves and destroyed the very people they hoped to govern.

The song brought a little applause. Few people were in the inn at this time of the day. Fallion tossed a small coin to the minstrel.

"Thank you, sirrah," the minstrel said.

The man was fresh off a ship from Rofehavan, and Fallion hoped for more news from him.

"Are all the songs that you sing so forlorn?" Fallion asked.

"It has been a rough winter," the minstrel said. "The folks in Heredon liked it well enough."

"How fares Heredon?" Fallion asked, for it was a place close to his heart.

"Not well," the minstrel said. He was a small man, well proportioned, with a gruff voice. "The Warlords of Internook seized it two years back, you know, and the peasants there all remember a time when they were ruled by a less-cruel hand. Many a tongue was singing that song last summer at the fair, and so in retribution, the lords at Castle Sylvarresta set fire to wheat fields. They say that the sky was so full of smoke, that in Crowthen it became as dark as night."

"It seems to me that any lord who made war against his own peasants would only weaken himself."

"Aye," the minstrel said. "Still the people croon for the return of their king. It's that Earth Warden Binnesman that put them up to it. He told them that 'the stones' woke him at night, troubling him, calling for the new king. Lord Hagarth would have sent the old wizard swinging from the gallows, but the Earth Warden ran off into the Dunnwood, where it is said that he lives among the great boars, gnawing wild acorns."

Fallion wondered at that. Binnesman had anointed his father to be the Earth King. Fallion had never met the man, at least not since he was very small, but he knew that Binnesman was a wizard of great power.

"Do those beyond the borders of Heredon share the hope for a new king?" Fallion asked.

The minstrel smiled. "About half and half, I'd say. Some hope that the Earth King will return from the dead, or that his son will reign in his stead. But there's a good many that never want to see a Runelord sit a throne again. 'Death to all Dedicates' is the call of the day."

"What would we do without Runelords?" Fallion asked. "What if the reavers were to attack again, or the toth?"

"Our people have more to fear from evil leaders than they ever have from outside forces," the minstrel said. "There's some that whisper that it should not be so. It's said that long ago, the Wizard Sendavian and Daylan of the Black Hammer stole the knowledge of rune-making from the Bright Ones of the netherworld. They took it, but such knowledge was not meant for man. Only the truest, the noblest among the Bright Ones, were permitted to bear such runes, and no man is *that* good."

Fallion had heard this rumor before, too, not six months back. Yet Shadoath had come from the netherworld, and she bore such runes.

The door to the inn opened, and outside stood a young girl, nine years of age, with skin as pale as milk. Her silver hair fell to her shoulders. She wore the gray robe of a graak rider, and held under her arms a pair of baskets of fruit and bread that she had bought at the local vendors. She was one of Fallion's troops. It was time to head home.

Fallion nodded at a young maiden with raven hair who was scrubbing tables, getting ready for the nightly crowd. Valya had been living in town now for nearly three months.

She smiled back, went to the hearth, and began to set the fire. Fallion felt uncomfortable. He had seldom practiced his skills as a flameweaver through the years, yet month by month, the call of the flames grew stronger.

Valya was a sister to him now, but a sister that he hardly knew. Soon after they landed, Borenson and Myrrima moved to some hovel up on Jackal Creek, an area so sparsely inhabited that it was easy for the family to get lost, but hard to make a living. The farm was too poor to support much of a family, so Fallion had volunteered to join the Gwardeen. Draken joined a few months later.

Shortly afterward, Jaz had gone to work for Beastmaster Thorin, an elderly gentleman who raised exotic animals.

Now Valya had moved here, coming to the coast, waiting for a ship that would carry her far, far away.

Fallion had seen his family rarely in the past few years, only on winter holidays.

So Fallion went outside where three other children had gathered with today's purchases, and stretched his arms, enjoying the sweet cinnamon scent of stonewood trees. The evening light was turning golden as the sun plunged into the sea.

The boles of the stonewood were gray, streaked with brown, like petrified rock. Only the upper branches really seemed to be alive. The elegant limbs were more of a dark cherry in color, hung with mosses and lichens and flowering vines. Epiphytes grew on their bark and put out brilliant crimson blossoms that smelled faintly like ripe peaches. As the evening sea wind stirred the leaves, the air filled with pollen, and then in the slanted sunlight that broke through the boughs the vibrant-colored day-bats flitted from flower to flower.

It was a scene that was as eerie to Fallion as it was beautiful.

"Come," he said. So they trundled across a catwalk that spanned through old stonewood trees. The bridge was made of gold-colored planks that seemed to be hundreds of years old. In places it was rickety and worn, and the handrails looked as if they'd fall off. But always the bridge was in at least a usable state of repair.

Fallion walked slowly, bearing the children's stores of food from time to time so that they could rest.

He was the oldest and largest of the graak riders, and bore the title of Captain. But he was more than a captain to these children, he knew. Many of them were orphans, and they looked up to him as something of a father.

Below them they could hear choruses of peeping frogs and the squeals of wild boars.

Fallion was deep in thought, wondering about the plight of his people—not just the children of the Gwardeen, but the people that he should rightfully be leading, the people of Heredon and Mystarria.

They walked for half a mile before they could glimpse the Gwardeen Wood, which could be seen ahead as a knot of stonewood trees on a peninsula that jutted out into the sea.

There, among the trees, stood an ancient fortress, a high tower used as a graakerie.

These were all sea graaks, white in color, the kind with the widest wingspan. They could fly from island to island out here in the Mariners, and if a storm came, they would sometimes ride its front for hundreds of miles inland.

The group was rounding the bay, still a mile from the Gwardeen Wood, when trouble struck.

Fallion heard a buzzing noise just overhead, almost a loud clacking, and a giant dragonfly, as long as a child's arm, flew past. In the shadows it had been invisible, but then it lunged into a slant of sunlight, and Fallion saw it—a vibrant green with mottled yellow on the carapace, the color of forest leaves in the sun.

It buzzed into the air and grabbed a cinnamon-colored day-bat that was no larger than a sparrow; the day-bat screeched in terror.

As Fallion's eyes followed the creature, he became aware of the dim clanging of bells. A deep-pitched warhorn sounded, as if the very earth groaned in pain.

The call was almost too distant for him to discern. He barely picked it up, buffered as it was by the trees and the sounds of the sea.

But instantly he knew: Garion's Port was under attack.

When he held his breath, he could discern distant cries. Not all of the cries were human. Some were the deep tones of golaths.

Fallion had passed the last house trees nearly half a mile back. From here forward, there was nothing but the catwalk.

"Run," Fallion told the children. "Run to the outpost and don't look back."

The children all peered up at him with wide eyes. "What's wrong?" the youngest girl asked.

318 DAVID FARLAND

"Shadoath is coming," Fallion hazarded.

So the children ran.

Fallion followed at the rear, where a young boy named Hador tried in vain to keep up with the older children.

For several minutes, no one pursued.

Fallion heard footsteps slapping behind and turned to see Valya racing toward them for all that she was worth.

Fallion sent the little ones ahead. They were only half a mile from the fort when he caught sight of the first of the golaths. The gray-skinned creatures came rushing from the city on their knuckles, thumping along the catwalk, curved reaping hooks and strange clubs in their hands.

The children heard their grunts, so they screamed and redoubled their pace. A pair of young Gwardeen skyriders came flying along on graaks, their course bringing them near the catwalk. Fallion could see fear on their faces.

"Pirates!" one of them shouted needlessly. "Pirates are coming. There's a worldship just off the coast!"

A worldship? Fallion wondered. Eight hundred years past, Fallion the Bold had created huge rafts to bear his army across the oceans to fight the toth. Those strange rafts had been dubbed worldships. But none of their kind had been seen in centuries.

Now he recalled the denuded forests on Syndyllian, and he realized what Shadoath had been up to. She had been building vessels to carry armies to Mystarria.

Valya reached him, and with her longer legs could well have raced ahead. Instead she pulled even with him.

He could hear the golaths coming, glanced back to see a dozen of them only a couple hundred yards back.

The Ends of the Earth are not far enough.

"Go," Fallion told her. "Get on a graak and head inland to safety. The Gwardeen can protect you."

"What about you?" Valya asked.

"I'll hold them back."

Valya stood there a moment, obviously fighting her desire. She didn't want him to stand alone.

"You go," Valya said. "You're the one Shadoath is after. If she gets you now, all of our efforts will have been wasted!"

Fallion knew that she was right, but he wasn't prepared to let Valya die in his place.

Fallion peered up the catwalk the last quarter of a mile. Ahead he could see the graakerie, huge white graaks nesting in trees devoid of leaves. Here, even the trees were white, stained by guano.

A high stone wall surrounded the Gwardeen Wood itself. The only easy way into the fort was over the catwalk.

As the children raced ahead, Fallion saw a young man run out from a small wooden gate, Denorra. He was watching them, waiting. He had a hatchet in hand and looked as if he'd cut the rope that held the last little span of bridge.

"Hurry!" Denorra shouted.

Fallion heard an animal cry, excited grunts and shouts. He glanced back. A golath with tremendous endowments of speed and brawn was rushing toward them, taking fifteen feet to a stride. He made as if to pass a pair of his slower kin, and merely leapt ten feet in the air.

Valya drew a boot dagger, but Fallion knew that it would be useless.

"Cut the ropes!" he shouted to Denorra even as he suddenly hit a span of bridge held only by rope.

He raced for all that he was worth, stretching each stride to its fullest, his lungs pumping. Valya matched him stride for stride. They were in the shadow of the fortress now. He heard the thump of heavy feet rushing behind him, became aware of two large graaks rising up from the tower. A few arrows and stones came flying over his head, thudding onto the deck.

The children were fighting back!

The golath warrior grunted and wheezed, its iron boots pounding the walkway only paces behind.

An arrow whipped over Fallion's head, and *thwacked* its iron tip into golath hide. But a golath with endowments wasn't likely to be stopped by a single arrow.

"Jump!" Fallion shouted to Valya just as Denorra swung the ax down on a rope.

They hit the ground together, and the left half of the bridge dropped from under them. Fallion grabbed on to the rope that held the right half of the bridge up. Valya got only a single hand on it.

The golath cursed, just feet behind, and grasped onto the rope.

Fallion held there for a second, swung up so that his feet hit the landing near Denorra, even as the young boy swung wildly, trying to cut the second rope.

The golath cursed, and a pair of children rushed out of the fortress with long spears. The oldest, a girl of eleven, blurred past Fallion and stabbed at the golath, hindering its progress.

Fallion grabbed Valya and pulled her to safety just as Denorra swung one last time, severing the rope.

The golath cried out in rage as it fell into the sea.

Valya turned and caught her breath, stared in shock for half a second. On the far side of the causeway, golaths growled and cursed. Some threw double-sided blades that spun in the air like whirligigs falling from a maple tree. One blade spun just overhead, then Fallion, Valya, and the rest of the children raced into the fortress.

It wasn't much of a fortress. The stone walls would keep a determined force warrior out for only a few minutes; inside there were only a couple of small rooms to give shelter from the weather.

A dozen young Gwardeen boys and girls cared for the graaks. The oldest of them, besides Fallion, was only twelve. These were children of mixed Inkarran blood, with skin as white as bone and hair of pale silver or cinnabar. Fallion was the closest thing to an adult.

The Gwardeen were hastily throwing bridles onto the graaks. Most of the children were already mounted. Indeed, Draken had saddled a beast, and a young recruit was clinging to it tightly. Her name was Nix, and she was only five years old.

"But how do I steer?" Nix was crying.

"Just lean the direction that you want to go," Draken said, "and gouge with your heels. The mounts will head that way."

"But what if I fall?"

"You won't fall if you don't lean too far," Draken replied.

Fallion wondered why the children hadn't left yet, but then realized that they had been waiting for him.

"Draken," Fallion shouted. "Go inland. Take a message to Marshal Bellantine at Stillwater. Warn him what we're up against. Tell him that we'll await his command at the Toth Queen's Hideout. Afterward . . . go home."

Draken peered hard at him. Fallion was sending him to safety, he knew, and Draken resented that. But Fallion was also sending him on a vital mission. He nodded his acceptance.

With that, Draken leapt onto his own reptile and gouged its sides. In a thunder of wings it jumped into the air, and several other riders followed.

Fallion rushed forward to the landing platform as some boys led two more graaks forward, the huge reptiles waddling clumsily, tipping their wings in the air.

Fallion peered about. Eight hundred years ago, Fallion's forefathers had left the Gwardeen on vigil, commanding them to watch for the return of the toth.

Since that time, it seemed to Fallion, the famed Gwardeen had dwindled to little more than a club for youngsters who liked to ride graaks.

Most of the older Gwardeen were out making a living, marrying and having babies, planting gardens, growing old and dying together—the way that people should.

Few of them took their ancestors' promise of eternal vigilance seriously.

The Ends of the Earth are not far enough, Fallion thought.

A young man of eleven brought a bridled graak forward, a large male, a powerful thing that smelled as strong as he looked. It glared down at Fallion, as if daring him to ride. His name was Banther.

Valya stood at the edge of the platform. She looked at Fallion, as if begging him to ride this monster, leave her to a tamer beast.

"You'll need a large one," Fallion told her, "and Banther is not as dangerous as he looks."

The large sea graaks could carry an adult, and a small woman like Valya would not be hard in most cases, but they would be flying high into the mountains where the air was thin and the flight steep. She needed a sturdy mount.

"He's yours," the boy told her, "if you dare."

Valya raced forward, as she'd seen other skyriders do, and planted her foot in a crook at the back of the graak's knee, then leapt and pushed off.

Her second step took her to the graak's thigh, and she leapt from there onto its long neck.

Valya settled onto the beast's neck and grabbed the reins.

"Go inland," Fallion said, "to the Toth Queen's Hideout. Know where that is?" Valya shook her head no. "Just follow Carralee and the others through the flyway."

Valya nodded, gouged her mount lightly in the pectoral muscles at the joint of its wing. With an angry grunt, the graak lunged forward, took a pair of clumsy steps, leapt, and flapped its wings.

They say that if you're going to die, it will most likely be on the landing, Valya assured herself.

The beast's wings caught air, and it was suddenly flapping over the water and into the woods.

Fallion helped the last of the children onto their mounts, assigning some to fly to various forts and warn the Gwardeen, sending others into hiding, and then got upon his own huge graak.

Its name was Windkris, and he was the one of the largest and strongest graaks within a thousand miles.

It was only upon such a mount that a boy Fallion's size could fly. Fallion ate little and kept his body fat down to nothing so that he could remain a Gwardeen. Even so, he was growing, putting on muscle, and by the year's end he would be too heavy for a graak to carry far.

Fallion spurred the beast into the sky. Ahead he could see other graaks flitting through the trees, and his mount gave chase.

He looked back over his shoulder, hoping to see if the fight for Garion's Port went well. Distantly, he heard the sounds of crashing blades, cries of pain. The battle was raging down there, but he could see little through the trees, only the smoke of raging fires.

Dozens of Shadoath's warriors raced along the burning gangplank, helpless to catch him.

He peered back one last time, and then looked ahead as his graak soared into the trees.

That's when he entered the flyway.

From the ground it was invisible, hidden by the limbs and leaves of ancient stonewood trees, concealed behind curtains of lichens and flowering vines.

But the Gwardeen children had cleared a path. It had been done over generations, at great cost and effort. The children had cut away limbs high up in the trees, a path sixty feet wide and forty feet high.

It led through the deep forest, inland.

Now that he was airborne, Fallion's heart raced. He was in a precarious position, perched aback the enormous beast. He had no saddle, nothing holding him to safety.

Beneath him, he could feel the enormous lungs of the graak working for every breath, feel its iron muscles ripple and surge as it sought purchase in the air.

For long minutes the creature flew, and only once did Fallion hear any sound of pursuit. He was winging through the flyway, with the day-bats ahead flitting among shafts of sunlight, the air mellow crimson and sweetly scented by pollens, when he heard a whoop below, the gruff voice of a golath.

They're trying to follow us, Fallion realized.

ও 45 ৩

THE HUNT

The flight of a graak oft heralds the coming of gore.

—a saying of Inkarra

Borenson trudged along a muddy track beside Jackal Creek, a name that was something of a misnomer. There were no jackals in Landesfallen. The early inhabitants had probably named it after something else—the bushtiger. And there was no creek for most of the year. It was early afternoon, and he had been out hunting for wild burrow-bears for dinner. The creatures were gentle and easy enough to take, if you found one in the open. No luck there.

He had just vowed to himself to climb up into the far hills, where there was better hunting, when he saw a fish: a muddy brown fish eeling along the road, half submerged in a rut from wagons that had traveled this way during the winter.

It was a walking catfish, about four feet in length, as muddy brown as the water, and had four tiny vestigial feet. Its broad mouth was full of teeth, and beneath its mouth were whiskers.

He circled the thing, and it peered at him with dull brown eyes, hissing and baring its teeth.

He didn't like the taste of walking catfish. It was about like eating mud, and he was wondering if he should kill it and take it home for dinner when a shadow fell over him.

He looked up to see a huge white graak winging just overhead.

"Father," Draken shouted, leaning precariously to his right. The graak grunted angrily, but finally veered right. In moments, the graak landed gracelessly not a dozen yards away, smack in the middle of the road.

The walking catfish hissed and scurried off into some thick ferns.

"Father," Draken shouted. "Shadoath has found us!"

Quickly he described the attack on Garion's Port.

It took several moments for Borenson to gauge the situation. Shadoath had brought reinforcements—a worldship full of them. How many men that might be, Borenson couldn't guess. It was said that Fallion the Bold had built strange rafts large enough to hold five thousand men each.

For now, the children seemed to have headed to safety at some place called the Toth Queen's Hideout. But how long would they remain safe?

Borenson swallowed hard. It was a long way to Garion's Port—eighty miles by air. But he was getting to be an old fat man, and he would have to travel a lot farther than eighty miles. There were no passes through the mountains for a hundred miles to the north.

And he couldn't just charge toward the city blindly. There were ten thousand Gwardeen in Landesfallen, but they were spread all across the wastes. It would take weeks to warn them of the danger, form an army, and march on Garion's Port.

"I'll head to the fort at Stillwater. If I'm lucky, I'll reach it in a couple of days. But first I have to go home and tell your mother where I'm going.

"As for you, I want you to fly to Beastmaster Thorin's ranch and warn Jaz that Fallion is in trouble. He'll be needing your graak. Give it to him. He'll need it to fly back to the hideout. Understand?"

Draken nodded, then leapt onto the back of the graak. With a cry it rose into the air.

Shadoath followed a pair of golaths along a wooden bridge, until they reached a point near the fortress where it just fell away.

"This is where you lost them?" Shadoath asked.

"Yes," a golath answered, its voice emotionless. "Fast they were, and cunning fighters. They shot arrows, and pricked at us with spears. Gone they are, I think."

Shadoath peered over the bridge. One of her most valuable warriors lay broken below, on rocks stained black from blood.

Ahead of her, Shadoath could see the little island fortress. There were still a dozen graaks nesting among the white trees. In the full sunlight, it was a dazzling sight.

"So you saw children flying away from here, heading inland?"

"Yes, yes," the golath answered. "All of us spotted them, we did."

"Which way?"

The golath pointed almost due east, into the trees.

It had to be Fallion. She and her men had searched the city, and come up empty.

"Search the forest," Shadoath said. "Look for any trace of them—footprints, smoke from a fire."

The golath lowered its eyes in acknowledgment.

Shadoath backed up, then raced along the bridge toward the fortress. Ahead, a portion of it had been cut away. Sixty feet of rope bridge now dangled uselessly to the stones below. But with her endowments of speed and brawn, Shadoath sprinted up to a speed of ninety miles per hour, then leapt high in the air, seeming almost to glide across the span as she hit the bridge on the far side.

Ahead, a wooden door was locked, a bar wedged across the inside.

Shadoath slammed a mailed fist into it, shattering the bar. The door fell open, and Shadoath entered the fortress.

She found harnesses and bridles inside a crude tack room, then came out.

The graaks were nesting, each of them sitting in a bowl formed from sticks and soft seaweed. They rested atop leathery sand-colored eggs with flecks of brown and white.

The mother graaks could not be coaxed from their nests, Shadoath knew. They were good mothers. But the males could be tempted. They were used to hunting for food for their mates at this time of the year, and quickly grew restless.

She found a nest that still had a pair of graaks, and then bridled the male.

She peeled off her mail, left it lying in the nest.

Shadoath was a petite woman, not much heavier than a child. She'd be able to ride a graak for a few miles at a hop.

She leapt upon its back, and urged it into the sky. It leapt forward clumsily, the branches in its nest crunching and snapping under their combined weight. At last it launched forward over the edge of the nest.

It seemed to fall a dozen feet before its wings caught the air and it lumbered upward.

The graak was small for a male, and Shadoath could feel it strain as its leather wings flapped heavily, gaining purchase in the sky.

Then it was airborne.

She aimed it to the east, let it fly above the ocean for a moment, and above the trees, giving it its head.

My mount may have seen which way the children went, Shadoath thought. It knows the paths in the sky. Let's see if he will lead me to their hideout.

To her delight, the graak thundered toward the trees for a few minutes, then dove toward a broad expanse, a place where limbs and branches had been cleared, creating a hidden flyway.

She was hot on Fallion's trail.

ೞ 46 ೕ

THE RISE OF A KING

You men here in Landesfallen, though you were once enemies, have shown yourselves to be true friends. I offer you your lives and your freedom, asking in return for only your eternal vigilance.

—Fallion the Bold, upon forming the Gwardeen

Fallion winged away from Garion's Port, flying slowly, stopping every few miles to let his graak rest, letting his huge mount take its time.

He had come up out of the flyway just moments ago, exiting the stonewood. His troops were flying low above the trees, following the curves of the valley.

A graak is so large that it can be seen hundreds of miles away by a vigilant far-seer. But it can only be seen if it is flying in plain view. Fallion's troops were expert at flying unseen. Their mounts now were winging over a river valley, the graaks skimming just above the treetops. Flying thus did more than keep the graaks hidden. The warm thermals rising up from the woods coupled with the dense air at lower elevations let the graaks' wings get a stronger purchase in the air, fly more easily.

Fallion looked all around. Hillsides rose up in every direction. His troops would remain unseen.

The sun was a golden ball in a hazy sky. Far ahead of him, perhaps eight miles, the young Gwardeen flew toward the hideout in a staggered line, each upon the back of a graak.

At the edge of the stonewood, Fallion let his mount perch in a tree and rest. He waited for a long while, listening for sounds of pursuit. He heard none.

It was twelve miles back to the city. Following the children on foot so far would have been all but impossible. The stonewood was almost impenetrable. The huge roots of trees lay in a tangle on the forest floor.

Perhaps a powerful force warrior might manage to follow us, Fallion thought.

But the flyway was meant to baffle such pursuers. It led through dense foliage, over bogs filled with quicksand, up steep cliffs, and wound this way and that so that even if a pursuer spied them from below, he would not know their true direction.

Still the danger was very real. If Shadoath's scouts spotted them, they could follow the children like bees to their hive.

The only way that Fallion would be able to keep the kids safe would be to have them stay hidden.

Back toward the city rose billowing clouds of smoke. Shadoath, it seemed, had set fire to the ships in the bay, perhaps even to the city itself.

Below him, tangles of stonewood gave way to smaller white gums with stands of leatherwood.

Ahead of him the wind had sculpted the deep red sandstone mountains into bizarre and beautiful configurations, and at the base of the mountains he could see blue-green king's pine on the ridges.

Here, the landscape opened up into stony fields. There were no farms, no tame herds grazing on the hills, but he spotted various animals found only on Landesfallen—gentle burrow-bears that looked much like young bears from back home, but they had gray hair and ate only grass. The burrow-bears watched him fly overhead as they grazed, unperturbed by the sight of humans or graaks.

There were scores of rangits, lying in the shade of fallen gum trees, that would jump up and leap away, the whole ground trembling as they did, for they tended to jump and land in unison.

There were smaller poo-hares, creatures related to rangits that were the size of large hares, but which hopped much more quickly than any hare.

He saw spiny anteaters that swung their heavy tails like clubs; and once he even spotted a rare arrowyck, an enormous flightless bird nearly twice as tall as a man, a cruel carnivore that could crush a burrow-bear in its heavy beak.

Ahead was a stony mountain of red rock, sculpted by the wind. It thrust up from the trees, and its sides—formed from petrified sand dunes—looked almost as if they had stairs carved into them. Natural ridges in the stone created a stairway that rose up and up.

The Gwardeen had come up into a relatively narrow canyon, and the mountain lay straight ahead. They had already circled it, so that their climb could not be seen from the west.

The graaks flew upward, skimming the treetops, while the mountain-sides around them grew steep.

Soon, the rims of a canyon flanked him, the rock walls carved by wind and water into tall columns. The path beneath him was safe. A roaring brook surged through the canyon, its surface white with foam. The steep sides of the canyon gave purchase to only a few king's pines. There was no way that anyone could climb those rocky banks without being spotted.

Ahead, a stone bridge spanned the canyon. The graaks flew toward it steadily.

They know the way, Fallion thought with pride, giving his mount its head. In moments they passed beneath the monumental arch, and from this point on, he knew that any scouts on his trail would lose sight of him, for there were steep ridges of rock on either side. The canyon split, and his graak winged to its left.

The trail below them looked impassable. The swollen creek rampaged over the rocks; stone columns seemed almost to sprout up out of the river.

A few minutes later, they neared the top of the canyon when the graaks began landing in a shadowed crevasse.

The refuge was almost completely hidden, even from the air. Stone columns rose up all around, sculpted by wind and rain into ugly shapes reminiscent of half-men or gargoyles; the landing site was secreted in their shadows.

Fallion rode up and his graak dropped neatly onto the bluff, just before a dark tunnel.

He leapt down from the beast as a pair of young Gwardeen came to handle his graak. To his right and left, iron rings were set into the stone walls, and each riding graak had a single leg tethered to a ring.

Overhead, a stone arch led to a tunnel. Beneath the arch, the red rock had grown black, stained by mineral salts as water dripped over the ages, and there on the stone was an ancient tothan mural painted in vibrant

colors—purples and blacks, titanium white and coral. It showed a scene of
a tothan queen—a four-legged creature with two heavy arms—riding upon
the shoulders of a huge crowd of lesser toth, as if being borne to victory.

The lesser toth carried long metal clubs as weapons, while sorcerers
among them wielded staves made of purple toth bones, as clear as crystal.

Where the queen had been or what battles she had won, Fallion could not
guess. Nor did he understand why she had a fortress hidden here in the mountains. But for the thousandth time he hoped that her people were no more.

At the mouth of the tunnel was a huge alcove filled with graaks. Farther
back, sitting around an old campfire, a dozen Gwardeen had assembled,
along with Valya.

None of the children under Fallion's command was older than twelve.
That was not surprising. The only way to reach this place was by graak, and
graaks couldn't carry the weight of an adult for any distance.

That night, the children huddled in a circle around a small campfire, arguing.

"I say we stay in 'iding," one young woman said. "We don't leave the
cave till Shadoath's army is gone."

"You mean sit and starve?" a boy asked.

"There's food in the valleys," an older boy, Denorra, said—the boy who
had cut the ropes to the bridge. "The farmers still have some stores."

The children were having a moot, a counsel where all voices were to be
heard.

"The stores won't last for long," Fallion said. "It's just past spring planting season, and the winter's stores are all but gone. They'll become scarcer
still once Shadoath's troops finish burning and looting. And what will we
do then, rob our own people for food?"

The children all looked up to him. He was their captain, and their
friend, and though he tried to refrain from usurping authority in a moot,
his voice counted for more than did the voices of some of the smaller ones.

Fallion wandered over to the fire but didn't sit. Hearthmaster Waggit
had impressed upon him the importance of making sure that when he
spoke to a crowd, he assume a position of authority.

"He's right," Valya offered. "Shadoath is building worldships, and she'll
need slaves for that. She'll take folks here captive, like she did on Syndyllian."

Those who go into hiding won't be able to hunt or farm. In time, they'll be forced to forage for food, and that's when her men will catch them. Shadoath is patient that way."

She spoke as one who knew, but Fallion noticed how guarded her tongue remained. She hadn't told these children that Shadoath was her mother.

I wonder, Fallion thought, if Shadoath is just hunting me. Maybe it's Valya that she's after. Perhaps Shadoath would even offer a ransom?

He would never think of selling her, of course, but the thought made him curious.

There was a stir at the mouth of the cave as a late rider landed.

One young Gwardeen, a girl of seven, said, "Aren't we supposed to warn someone if the toth come back? Shadoath is like a toth, ain't she?"

"The king of Mystarria," another added. "That's 'oo we're supposed to tell. But 'ow do we get 'old of 'im?"

"The king's already here," someone said from the darkness. Jaz marched in from the mouth of the cave and nodded meaningfully toward Fallion.

Fallion had not seen his brother in months, and he was amazed at how fast his little brother was growing. Jaz had become tall and lean. He threw a bag at Fallion's feet. Forcibles inside clanked in their peculiar fashion, echoing loudly in the small cavern, and a pair rolled onto the ground. "You'll be needing these, Your Highness."

The Gwardeen children stared at Fallion in disbelief, mouths open in surprise. Could their captain truly be the king in exile?

"Show them your ring," Jaz urged.

Fallion fished into the pocket of his tunic and pulled out his signet ring—an ancient golden ring with the image of the green man upon it. Fallion had not shown it to anyone in years, not since he'd left Mystarria.

Most of the children fell silent, awed, unsure how to conduct themselves before a king. A couple of the older ones crept up from their sitting position, and managed to kneel.

One child, the girl named Nix, said, "But I thought the *Earth King* was the king of Mystarria?"

"He was," Fallion said. "The Earth King was my father. But he died.

That's part of why I came here: to see if I could discover what happened in his final days."

Now even the youngest of the children began to kneel, and Fallion saw to his dismay that even Jaz chose this moment to bow.

"What shall we do, milord?" Jaz asked.

A wisely chosen question, Fallion realized. By asking it, Jaz was subtly urging all of the others to submit to Fallion's will.

They were all looking to him for answers, each of them with eyes shining, full of hope.

I wanted an army, Fallion realized, and now I've found one: but only an army of children.

What could *they* do to battle Shadoath?

Fallion said, "The closest Gwardeen fortress is at the City of the Dead. That's a four-day march from here, and it holds only four hundred good fighting men. That's not enough to face Shadoath, not nearly enough."

He looked to one of the scouts for help, the boy who had first warned him of the enemy approach. "How many men do you think we are fighting?"

"I saw twenty ships, big ones, and lots of away boats. I'd think that each could hold a thousand men."

Fallion knew that the locals would not be able to repulse so many. Not everyone on the island was Gwardeen. There were plenty of local farmers, the descendants of outlaws. Tough men, many of them. But such folk weren't necessarily fighters.

Fallion suggested, "Even if anyone can come to our rescue, it will take a good week for them to get here."

A girl of eight said, "My father told me that there are ten thousand Gwardeen." She said it as if it were a phenomenal number, an unimaginable host, and the number alone might scare away the enemy. Obviously, she hadn't been listening when they spoke of the enemy's numbers.

"Yes," Fallion said, "but they're spread out all over the land. It would take a year to gather them all. So we can't rely on them to save us," Fallion said. "We have no food, and we can't forage. We won't last a year."

"There's something else," Jaz said. "Bright Ones fired arrows at me on my way to the hideout. One of their arrows took my graak in the wing. They're hiding in the trees along the river, watching for graak riders. Every time one of us tries to fly out of here to forage for food, it gives them one more chance to spot us."

As if to emphasize his point, there was a flapping of wings at the mouth of the tunnel, and a graak croaked as it announced its presence. A new rider had just arrived.

Fallion made a mental note to check the wing on Jaz's graak. The membrane could be easily torn and become infected. They'd have to sew the wound closed and let the beast rest for a few days.

"What do we do?" the oldest of the Gwardeen girls asked. "Everyone knows to come 'ere. We could 'ave riders stragglin' in all night."

And if everyone knows to come here, Fallion thought, then this is no hiding place at all.

He wondered if he should run, just tell the children to fly away. They could go to the Fortress of the Infernal Wastes, and from there head inland.

But there were problems with even that simple plan. Even by flying out of the fortress, they might reveal its location, and Fallion needed to keep it as secret as he could. It had tremendous strategic value.

Besides, he thought, even if we fly away, what kind of life would that be? Would I really be solving anything?

Waggit had always told him not to run from problems, but toward solutions.

"Tonight, I want a sentry at the door," Fallion said. "And I want another about two miles down the canyon. If any of Shadoath's scouts try to make their way up here, I want ample notice. Depending on their number, we can either choose to fight or to run."

"And what then?" someone asked. "Do we stay up here forever without any food."

"Maybe we could fight them," one boy said. "We could drop shot on them from high up, from our graaks."

Fallion doubted that such an attack would do much harm, but it was Denorra who objected first. "We might kill a couple o' golaths that way, but for what? It's not likely that we'd 'it Shadoath 'erself. And they'd be on our tails sure then, and we'd be next to die."

"There are other ways to fight," Jaz suggested. He nodded toward the leather bag on the floor, the forcibles in plain sight. To the children the forcibles were more an emblem of Fallion's kingship than his signet ring, for what was a king without endowments? "Perhaps it's time," Jaz said, peering into Fallion's face.

Valya offered, "Milord, I will give you an endowment."

"As will I," Jaz said.

Fallion looked at his friends, and his heart felt so full that he thought it would break.

"I'll not take endowments from the people that I love best," Fallion said. "Besides, we don't have a facilitator. We must find another way."

Valya mused, "This may be our chance to strike Shadoath's Dedicates. She has just sacked a city. She'll be taking endowments tonight and sending the new Dedicates to her keep. We know that she sailed east from Syndyllian with her Dedicates in the past. It's likely that she's got them hidden here on Landesfallen, or somewhere nearby. We only have to follow her ship. We could go out in force, hunt for it in the night."

Fallion wondered if it would work.

The other children looked at Fallion hopefully, and Denorra said, "It's better than sitting on our asses, just waitin' to starve—or for one of 'em to come kill us."

Could it really be so easy: just fly old Windkris out to where Shadoath hid her Dedicates and dispatch them along with their guards?

But Fallion had no army to attack with, or at least no army that he was willing to risk. He wasn't about to send the children into battle.

He had only his own strong arms, and he doubted that they were enough.

But I've been training for this fight from childhood, he thought. His small size belied his prowess in battle.

What's more, there was a hidden fire within him, yearning to blaze.

He had no endowments, and he knew that if he were to proceed, he would be placing himself in tremendous peril.

I could find her Dedicates, he told himself. I could strike them down.

Afterward, killing Shadoath herself would not be hard. Fallion knew a dozen good warriors who might manage it.

Fallion needed only to seize the opportunity.

He'd never taken a human life with his own hands, and he was not eager to do so now.

But he thought of Captain Stalker's advice: when it comes time to gut a man, you don't cry out or make threats or apologize. Just be the kind of man who quietly goes and takes care of business.

"That's the kind of man I want you to be," Stalker had said.

Fallion wasn't sure that he trusted the advice, but with nothing but uglier choices before him, it was the only decision that he could make.

ॐ 47 ॐ

FLYING AMONG THE STARS

I rode my first graak at the age of five, and never have I forgot the wonder.
Now I am old and fat, and can fly only in my dreams.

—Mendellas Orden

As evening fell, Fallion built a fire up, a bonfire that belched smoke and filled the cavern with light.

As he did, he felt a familiar tug. A voice whispered in his mind: *Sacrifice to me.*

The time for battle was at hand, and after many years, Fallion gave in.

Yea, Master, he said in his mind. *My work shall bring you glory.*

The children took ashes from the fire and mixed them with water, then daubed them upon Windkris, Fallion's great white graak, painting it black.

In the darkness, he'd be almost impossible to spot. Then Fallion painted his own face and hands black, and wiped the sweet-smelling ashes upon his clothes.

Last of all, he honed his blade to razor sharpness.

Fallion peered through the gloom, taking one last long look at his friends, and then bade them all good-bye.

He felt as if he were looking upon his own children, and it broke his heart to be forced to leave them now, alone and helpless.

He went out to the ledge, untied Windkris's leg, and leapt onto the back of his mount. The graak lumbered forward to the edge of the cliff and leapt, then soared out over the valley.

A wind was rising from the land, and it bore the graak aloft, sent the great painted reptile soaring through the night beneath stars as bright as diamonds.

ॐ

He circled east and then south, hiding the direction of his approach from any unfriendly eyes, and soared through hidden flyways among the stonewood trees until he reached the hills above Garion's Port.

There, east of the city, his graak perched in a tree, and he watched a small black schooner.

Is it the *Mercy?* he wondered.

He watched for hours as away boats rowed up to it, loading their cargo. Fallion saw humans being carted up by the score, most of them unconscious or incapacitated to the point that they had to be carried.

Sometime well before dawn, still hidden by the darkness and a rising mist, the ship stole out to sea.

He studied the ship's bearings, and knew where it was headed. Valya had said that it sailed due east from Syndyllian. Now it was taking a course southwest. By triangulating the courses in his mind, he was able to fix an approximate location, one that he recalled from Captain Stalker's old charts—the island of Wolfram, or one of the other atolls close by.

Fallion waited until the ship was far out to sea before he gave chase.

He flew south through a hidden flyway among the trees until he reached the beach, and then let his mount drop into the mist, so that its wingtips brushed the water and he felt the salt spray in his face.

For long hours he soared above the sea, watching it undulate beneath him, its waves dimpling like the skin of a serpent as it coils.

As he rode, time seemed to pass slowly.

I am growing old, Fallion thought. My childhood is vanishing behind me, failing.

And in the solitude as he rode under the stars, he had a long time to think, to firm his resolve. He imagined the Dedicates' Keep, filled with cruel people who'd given themselves into Shadoath's service—twisted Bright Ones from the netherworld that had grown perfect in evil. Perhaps she used animals, too—golaths and strengi-saats and darkling glories.

Monsters. Shadoath's keep could well be filled with monsters.

But there would be others, too. Some of the folk from Garion's Port might be there—the innkeeper or his wife, or perhaps the tanner's pretty daughter.

How would he feel about taking her life?

৪৩

Nix was crying. Jaz held her in the night and tried to get some sleep. The watch fire had burned down to coals and gave almost no heat.

And here so high on the mountain, the air felt thin and frigid, almost brittle. Jaz tried to warm Nix with his body, but could not even keep himself warm.

Fallion had been gone for hours. Jaz could not sleep. The graaks had been restless. Most of them were males, and at this time of the year, they were overwhelmed by the urge to hunt for food for their mates and to search for branches and kelp to use as nesting materials.

All through the night they let loose with *graaak* cries, then rustled their wings, eager to be off.

What would happen if I let the mounts go? he wondered.

He imagined that most of them would head straight for the sea, back to their nests, and try to rear their young. But not all of the graaks looked to be adults. The adolescents, those under nine years of age, wouldn't have bonded with a mate yet, and would be more likely to remain close to their masters, soaring along the mountain ledges to hunt for wild goats or heading to the valleys to hunt for rangits and burrow-bears.

They'd return after they fed, and that was the problem. They might attract unwanted attention.

The only thing that he could do was to leave the graaks tied to their iron rings. Let them sit quietly and feed off of their fat. In a few days, without food or water, the reptiles might die—or worse, they might gnaw off their own feet in an effort to escape.

He imagined the graaks coming after the children, so crazed by hunger that they were willing to eat their masters. It had happened before, many times.

Jaz pitied the creatures. He knew what it felt like to be chained to a wall, with no food or water.

At long last, Jaz slept.

It seemed that he had only been down for a minute when he heard a guttural cry, and woke, his heart pounding in his throat.

Several of the graaks grunted, and he heard the rush of wings. Someone was riding away!

Jaz leapt to his feet. Nix was gone.

He raced outside and saw that the sun was rising, a great ball of pink at the edge of the world.

Down below him, he saw a graak flying just above the trees. Nix was riding it.

Gone to get food, he realized, and water. The children would need it.

Jaz was filled with wrath and foreboding. But there was no stopping her now. He could only hope that she did well.

Now was the time for her to get supplies, if she was to have any hope at all—now, before Shadoath's troops looted all of the nearby towns.

Fallion had warned them all not to go scrounging for food. But you cannot command a child to starve, Jaz realized.

For all of their sakes, he wished Nix luck.

Shadoath waited on a pinnacle of a mountain, studying the night sky. She had three dozen endowments of sight, but even then she was blind in the right eye, and everything in her left eye looked as if it were shrouded in the thinnest of mists.

To the west, her golath armies were marching through the night, fanning out. The golaths were tireless, and by dawn they would have prodded beneath every rock and mossy log within twenty miles of Garion's Port, looking for Fallion and Valya.

Shadoath had tried to follow the flyway, had taken it through several long detours and dead ends. Without someone to lead, her graak had lost its way.

At last she'd come to the end of it, rode out above some trees. She'd wondered if perhaps the children's hideout was somewhere just at the end of the flyway, there in the jungle, and so she'd landed her graak and searched on foot for a time, sniffing in the shadows for the scent of children, listening for human cries, all without luck.

But late in the afternoon she spotted a pair of graaks far to the east and suspected that the hideout had to be elsewhere.

She'd lost sight of them as they flew into the mountains.

Now for the first time she spotted something in the distance, miles away: a sliver of white, almost like a cloud, appearing and then disappearing, appearing and disappearing.

A graak, she realized, flapping its wings in the dawn. She could even make out a shadowy rider.

Perhaps one of the children was on patrol or carrying a message. In either case, it meant that the child would return.

And when that happened, Shadoath would follow the child to the hideout.

ℬ 48 ℭ

THE ATOLL

Each man thinks himself an island of virtue, surrounded by a sea of louts.

—Jaz Laren Sylvarresta

In the long night, Fallion's graak grew tired. It was a far journey, and even with light winds Windkris could not go on forever. The poor reptile began to cough as it flew, and the flesh at its throat jiggled, as if it grew faint from thirst.

Fallion considered abandoning the beast. He did not want to cause its death. But he was too far out to sea now to turn back.

By some good fortune, he spotted a small atoll, a rock that thrust up from the ocean. He stopped for a long while and let Windkris rest. The rock was hardly big enough for him to get down from his mount, perhaps fifteen feet across. So he sat upon Windkris as the black water surged all around them and watched the sunrise.

It was not until late in the early morning, when a pink sun had climbed into the sky, that Fallion reached Wolfram.

He recognized the island from the charts, its white sand beaches and the play of waves around it.

He let Windkris drop, and it flapped along its length.

The island seemed empty, uninhabited. There was no sign of the *Mercy*.

He flew up and down the coastline at such a slow speed that it seemed to him that he spent hours observing its every detail.

There were no fires to warm Dedicates, no hidden towers or compounds to house them.

They're not here, he realized. But there are two other islands nearby. I'll let my mount rest for the morning, and then leave.

He let Windkris drop to the beach and take a young sea lion as a meal.

Fallion found a pile of driftwood and curled up in the sand beneath it, gaining a little shelter from the wind as his mount rested.

As Fallion slept, Sir Borenson made his way toward Stillwater on the family rangit, bouncing and jostling all along the road until his head pounded in pain.

At each little village, he shouted warnings to whomever he could, telling them of the invasion, thus raising the countryside.

It was hard work, long work, made all the harder because he was traveling over rough roads in the heat of the day.

The journey to Stillwater normally took two days by rangit. He intended to make it in one.

Time and again, his thoughts turned back to the children, and to Myrrima. He'd left her with the family. A couple of years back, she had lost her endowments—all but her glamour. She was no longer the warrior that she had once been. She was a healer, a water wizardess living at the edge of the desert. Most of all, she was a mother, and she liked it.

She longed for another home, one with a stream or a lake nearby, but had forgone that. "Anyone who is looking for us will know to look near water," she'd said, and so Myrrima insisted that they move to the hottest, most inhospitable patch of rocky land that they could find.

"Someday," Borenson had promised her time and again, "I'll find us a proper home."

Borenson worried that his wife and children would be captured, or worse, and it was only with great difficulty that he turned his mind away from such thoughts.

It does no good to worry, he told himself. I can't change what might happen. My course is set, and to turn back is worse than to press on.

And as he raced over the hillsides, into lush country where wild rangits grazed on the green spring grass, he stopped at the top of a hill and looked down upon a silver river. The grass was of a kind that he'd never seen back in Rofehavan. Rangit grass, the farmers called it, and it had a scent and texture like no other. It was exotic and spicy sweet in its smell, like oat grass with just a hint of sandalwood, and when he sat down upon it, it felt almost silky to the touch.

As his mount sat huffing and coughing from the labor of climbing—
Borenson was a big man, after all, and growing fatter by the year—Borenson
marveled at the beauty of the hills and vales that spread before him.

There was nothing like this that he could remember back in Rofehavan.
Nothing half so lovely. And if the journey to Landesfallen had not been so
far and the tales of it so frightening, Borenson imagined that folk would
stampede to reach this place to lay claim to a few acres of its lush grounds.

The beauty of it threatened to overwhelm him.

"I'll come back here when the war is over," he told himself. "I'll buy a
place as beautiful as this valley, and I'll never leave."

An hour before dusk, Fallion flew above a nameless atoll and knew by the
smell that he had found Shadoath's hidden Dedicates.

The island was small, a single volcanic cone rising from the sea. Its surface was almost solid basalt, a hint of smoke rising from the cone of the
volcano. In ages past, seals and seabirds had harbored here; fertilized by
guano, plants and trees had sprung up in profusion. Thus the lower edges of
the volcano were a riot of green.

There was no harbor, no sign of easy access to the island. The *Mercy* had
come and gone. He'd seen it sailing north back toward Garion's Port, and had
given it a wide berth. But this was the place, Fallion knew as he approached.

The smoke hung in the still evening air for miles around, and to Fallion's nose, the attuned senses of a flameweaver, it was the taste of the
smoke that told him that humans were about.

If the smoke were coming from the cone of a volcano, it should have
smelled of sulfur and ash, the heart of the world.

Instead, it tasted of wood and meat—of cooking fires.

Fallion urged Windkris higher. The old reptile was flagging, fading fast.
But it took him above the rim of the volcano, and Fallion peered down
into its crater. Even then, Fallion did not see the encampment at first. The
crater was filled with stones and a shallow lake, and it was only near one
rim that smoke issued.

Fallion spotted shadows in the sheer cliffs, even in the dim light, suspicious shadows that whispered of hidden caverns.

He let Windkris make a single pass, gliding above, and the scent of smoke and bread became stronger. A beaten path in the grass led to a single open-ing, a shadowed tunnel.

The encampment appeared to be asleep. At least no warhorn sounded at his approach; Fallion saw no guards.

But a single guard did see him. Lying deep under the shadowed arch, her sea green eyes peering warily out a door, the giant ape Oohtooroo spotted the black shadow of a graak glide across the evening sky.

She growled in outrage.

Grabbing a heavy spiked club in one hand, she went to a cot in a corner and shook her beloved master awake.

Abravael rubbed at his eyes, peered up warily. He hated this assignment, hated this place. The rock seemed to freeze each night by dawn and then bake in the afternoon heat. He hated his mother for sending him here. But she had insisted. She was going to war and needed someone that she could trust to guard her Dedicates; Abravael was the person in the world that she trusted most.

It took him long seconds to realize that Oohtooroo was frightened. She peered outside, nostrils flaring, growled, then rumbled, "Bird. Big bird."

"It's all right," Abravael said. "You don't have to worry about birds."

"Evil bird. Stranger rides it."

Abravael shot up. A stranger riding a graak?

Abravael hastened to pull on his pants, unsure whether to grab them first or his warhammer. His mind dulled by his afternoon nap, he peered around for his boots.

Oohtooroo growled, and Abravael heard footsteps crunching in the gravel outside.

"Kill the stranger," Abravael hissed.

With a grunt like a wild boar, Oohtooroo charged out from the Dedi-cates' Keep.

In the early evening, Jaz stood guard at the Toth Queen's Hideout.

The mountain blocked his view to the west, but he could smell fires ris-ing from the jungle out toward Garion's Port, and smoke had turned the sky a hazy yellow.

Far below, he saw something rise up out of the woods, a graak winging toward him. It had been soaring above the forest, and with the slant of the evening sun, it had been hidden in shadow. But now it climbed high enough so that the afternoon sun touched its wings, and suddenly it appeared, blazing white.

The small rider had some heavy bags slung over the graak's back.

It had to be Nix, bringing back supplies. Jaz felt his stomach grumble in anticipation of food.

For a long minute Nix winged toward him.

Then he spotted a second graak, flying low above the trees, miles behind. The rider was too large to be a Gwardeen; instantly Jaz felt a sinking in the pit of his stomach.

He knew that rider. It was Shadoath. He felt certain—not because he could see her face or recognize her outline. It was just an instinct, one that sent a shiver down his back and drew a strangled cry from his throat.

"Shadoath is coming!" he shouted, warning the others.

Fallion was stalking toward the cave quietly when a pair of shadows unfolded from the cliff walls above, came gliding down toward his mount.

Strengi-saats! he realized, pulling his long knife.

They floated toward him, thinking him to be just a child. Perhaps in the past they had killed others, taking them easily as they stood rooted to the ground in fear, or stumbled off into the brush.

But Fallion was ready. He stood, mouth open, feigning terror, letting his hatred for the beasts lend him strength.

He felt rage welling inside him, mindless and consuming, and the fire inside him begged for release.

Yea, my master, he whispered, *I consecrate their blood to thee. Let these be the first of my kills this day.*

As the largest one neared, Fallion lurched forward and rolled, blurring in his speed.

He struck the throat of one great monster, raking it, and blood gushed as it roared. Fallion rolled beneath it, and the strengi-saat swiped vainly at him with its claws, then winged away, snarling in pain.

The other strengi-saat saw what had happened, tried to veer away, and Fallion rushed toward it.

He felt like a force of nature as he leapt into the air, twisted away from its gnashing teeth, and slammed his blade into the strengi-saat's tympanum.

The monster roared, but the cry cut short as Fallion's blade pierced its brain.

Fallion and the beast both dropped to the ground heavily, and as Fallion hit, he twisted his ankle.

For a moment he stood above the monster as it heaved and grunted, some part of its brain still struggling for breath, while its claws raked the air.

Fallion tested his ankle, stepping on it gingerly. He felt like a fool. Taking a fall like that could leave him with broken bones that would take weeks to heal.

The first strengi-saat had raced off into the woods, and now was roaring. I left it wounded, he thought. And now it is more dangerous.

But the roars of pain became keening cries, and Fallion knew that the monster would bleed out in time.

I need to be more careful, he thought as he limped toward the hidden keep ahead.

Fallion's head was down, watching the path, when the sea ape lunged from the shadows of a tree.

Instinctively, Fallion leapt aside, clearing the trail. The ape bolted past, teeth bared, knuckles digging into the dirt.

Only years of training had saved Fallion.

The ape whirled and peered at him in surprise.

She rose up on her hind feet and waved an enormous club overhead, white spikes bristling from it.

Shark's teeth, Fallion realized, gazing up at the triangular teeth in the club.

The sea ape swung it down in a great arc, seeking to smash Fallion.

He rolled aside.

The impact shattered the club; the sea ape peered at it in astonishment.

Fallion had no desire to hurt the beast. He knew little about them, and knew that this ape was not acting on its own. It stupidly served its master.

"Leave," Fallion said slowly, "and I will let you and your master go in peace."

To his surprise, the ape's eyes widened in understanding, and it stared hard at him.

In a vague dream, Rhianna peered at Fallion. The ape's heart pounded with bloodlust. He was not food, she knew. He was not flesh to eat. But he posed a threat. He had come to slay Abravael. She could not allow that.

Rhianna felt torn and powerless, even as the ape watched for openings in Fallion's defenses.

The sea ape Oohtooroo growled and thumped her chest with her left fist—once, twice, a third time.

"You go!" the ape cried. "Go now or die."

Fallion's mouth fell open; he stood, unsure what to do or say.

Oohtooroo watched intently as Abravael stepped out from the shadows and crept up behind Fallion.

For his part, Fallion merely studied Oohtooroo, blade in hand, and spoke softly. "There is no need for this. I wish you no harm."

Fallion heard the scuff of a footfall and whirled.

A man lunged toward him, scimitar in hand. He was fast, and even as Fallion stepped aside, the man twisted his blade, nearly slipping beneath Fallion's guard.

He has endowments of metabolism, Fallion realized.

Years of training took control of Fallion's blade. He struck with his long knife, pulling the blade up quickly and reversing its edge, in order to strike the young man's wrist.

Fallion slashed a deep wound, drawing blood. The wound jarred the man's wrist, striking ganglia, causing the attacker to drop his sword.

Fallion pushed the attack, slamming his fist into the man's face, then laying his blade to the man's throat. Fallion called, "Surrender!"

The huge ape roared and charged, bounding toward Fallion, and he had no choice.

He shoved his captive forward and the ape clumsily tried to step aside, hoping to avoid hitting her master.

As she did, Fallion stepped forward and slashed her across the belly. Red blood flowed over white fur, and the ape roared in pain. She whirled toward him, now standing between Fallion and the wounded man.

Fallion stared. The young man was handsome by any standard, with dark hair and a face like his mother's. He pressed his badly bleeding wrist against his chest, peering at Fallion maliciously.

"Truce!" the young man called. "I surrender!"

The huge ape began wheezing, and Fallion cringed to see the damage that he'd done. Her rib cage had opened up, and he could see the pale purple of intestines and the pink tip of one lung. The ape panted, stood in shock, still keeping itself between Fallion and its beloved master.

The young man was holding his wrist as if Fallion had chopped off his arm. He was worried about a minor wound while his faithful servant died.

"Go," Fallion whispered. "Get out of here." He stepped aside, giving the huge ape leeway. It just peered at him, breathing heavily, unsure what to do.

"Come, my pet," Abravael whispered. "We're outmatched. Mother will be so unhappy."

The way that he said it, Fallion almost imagined that the young man wanted his mother's Dedicates to die.

No, Fallion realized, he *does* want them to die. It's not my imagination. How he must hate her.

Taking the sea ape by one hand, Abravael led the beast along the path. It glared back at Fallion, hurt and bewildered, dying, but it did not attack.

Fallion had an uncanny sense that the battle was not over, that Abravael still had some trap for him.

But the young man merely retreated to the shadow of a rock, then sat down, his huge sea ape beside him. Abravael smiled and nodded at Fallion, as if daring him to enter the Dedicates' Keep.

There are more guards inside, Fallion realized, suddenly worried. Perhaps these guards are even powerful Runelords.

He licked his lips. His legs suddenly felt too weak to carry him farther into battle.

My body is a tool, Fallion told himself, repeating an old mantra of the Gwardeen. It must obey.

He stalked into the Dedicates' Keep.

"Run!" Jaz shouted, warning the children in the cave. "Shadoath is coming."

The children clamored to escape. Some grabbed weapons or sought to pick up coats, but most just rushed toward the graakerie, some of the bigger ones knocking the little ones aside.

Jaz had no time to help.

Grabbing Fallion's forcibles, he raced to the rookery and freed a graak, a big male. It was tied with a rope, and Jaz fumbled as he tried to undo the knots. Finally, in a fit of panic, he drew his knife and slit the rope.

Then, realizing that he had time to help some of the younger children out, he raced to a second reptile and cut it free, and another and another.

The older children were quickly preparing their mounts, heaving huge saddles upon their backs, tying them down, fitting bridles.

Jaz raced to a corner where his own tack had been laid, then bridled and saddled the nearest great reptile. After he did, he helped a young girl onto the graak, then slapped its rump. The huge reptile lunged toward the ledge and soared into the air.

Jaz felt sick with fear and hunger, as if he would topple at any moment.

He stood on the ledge, gasping for breath.

Jaz looked down into the valley. Shadoath's mount came up behind Nix's. The girl wasn't even aware of the danger.

Suddenly Shadoath hurled a dagger. Bright steel flashed as it blurred toward its mark. Nix got struck full in the back and went hurtling headlong from her graak.

The mount veered away and roared in fear, heading down into the forest.

Shadoath kept flying toward the hideout.

Two minutes, Jaz told himself. She can't be more than two minutes away.

For half a second he wondered. Could Fallion have found Shadoath's Dedicates by now? If so, had he killed them yet? And if he had, what did that mean?

Shadoath could be as weak as any commoner. Jaz wasn't half the warrior that Fallion had become, but Jaz had been practicing with the blade for years.

Dare I fight her? he wondered. If she is a commoner, she might underestimate me. I might be able to strike a killing blow.

But Jaz was no warrior. He never had been.

A young boy was struggling to throw a heavy saddle over a huge graak, using all of his strength.

It gave out and the boy collapsed.

He'll never make it, Jaz realized with horror. He'll never be strong enough to saddle it.

He peered at the young children at work, their faces all whiter than ash, as was common among the Gwardeen, and the full horror of what was about to happen struck him.

They were all struggling to escape, but the process of bridling and saddling a graak took too long.

The forcibles, he told himself. I have to save them. They're more important than the children.

Valya had just helped a child with a saddle, and now she helped the child mount a graak, and slapped the beast's rump, sending it over the cliff.

She whirled and went to help another, a broad smile on her handsome face.

Jaz wasn't sure if he'd even be able to save himself. Riding a graak wasn't easy. How would he carry both the forcibles and himself?

He didn't have time to answer as he raced outside.

Another child had managed to pick up a bridle for a graak, and was trying to throw it over the head of her mount, but she was too small. Jaz finished the job as she carefully climbed onto the reptile's neck, without a saddle, and perched there, clinging with fright.

Jaz peered up at her. "Get out of here. Fly inland and find the fortress at Stillwater."

The girl nodded, and Jaz slapped the graak's rump, yelling, "Up! Up!"

His heart skipped a beat as the reptile hopped forward. In that moment, when the beast lunged, if the child was going to fall, this would be the time.

The graak dropped from the sky a dozen yards, its wings unfolding gracefully, and then it caught the wind and was gone, flying away. The girl cried out in fright, but managed to hold on.

Jaz peered down below. Shadoath was close now. No more than a minute away. Jaz didn't have time to harness more graaks.

Expert riders could command a graak even if it wasn't harnessed, Jaz knew, but he wasn't an expert rider. Such riders usually had years of experience to help them.

Jaz had none of that.

Weary to the core of his soul, he scrabbled up the side of the nearest graak, somehow climbing from knee, to hip, to back, and to neck by sheer will.

Shadoath was drawing near, less than a quarter of a mile away.

Maybe she won't hurt me, Jaz thought. She'd treated him gently when she took him from the prison. He'd seen her then as a vision of mercy, a savior, someone to be adored.

But she was the one who put me in irons in the first place, he told himself, and he knew that it was true. She could show kindness, but it didn't come from the heart.

He had only one chance. He was taking a rested mount. Shadoath's would be tired. He could hope to outfly her.

He looked to the side. Valya was throwing the bridle on another graak, sending off another child. She wouldn't have time to get away herself.

"Valya," Jaz shouted, "come with me." It would be dangerous for his graak to try to carry them both, he knew, but it was their only chance.

Valya raced toward him as if she would climb on, but then she slapped his graak on the rump and shouted, "Up!"

The graak surged, stretched its neck out, and with a little warning cry took flight. The warm evening air smote Jaz in the face and whistled through his hair, and he felt the great reptile take flight beneath him.

Valya is staying behind, he realized. She's giving her life for mine.

Shadoath was racing toward him, her graak twenty yards above his. Her face shone with an ethereal beauty, despite the scars from her burns, and she sat astride her graak with the easy grace of one who had hundreds of endowments.

I was fool to think I might be able to fight her, Jaz realized. She's a powerful Runelord still, and there is no way that I could win.

Jaz worried that she'd dive, have her mount claw his, knocking Jaz from his seat.

But Valya shouted, "Mother, I'm here."

Shadoath turned her face up to the cave and urged her mount toward it, willing to let Jaz go.

Jaz felt miserable inside as his graak dove toward freedom.

There were still several children up in the cave. They were screaming now, abandoning their mounts, racing into the depths of the cave in the hopes of escaping.

Jaz was buying his own life with theirs.

THE TORCH-BEARER

In a reign of darkness, the fallen saw a great light.

—from "An Ode to Fallion"

Warily, Fallion made his way into the Dedicates' Keep, convinced that at any moment a dozen guards would ambush him.

But as he passed the small guardroom where Abravael and the ape had slept, he found it empty of all but a cot.

Fallion marched forward, past the bakery with its open hearth, beyond a hallway that led to some more guards' quarters, then to the buttery and the kitchens. A pair of matronly women worked inside. They huddled away in a corner, terrified, as he passed.

At the end of the hall, he opened a door to a darkened chamber. There he found the Dedicates.

The room was lit by a few candles, enough so that Fallion could see everything well enough.

The room was full of children, dozens and dozens of them. Some were toddlers, not more than a year or two. Others were Fallion's age or older.

Many laid upon cots, invalids. Some cried out or moaned in pain. They'd given brawn and grace, given their sight or their beauty, and could only wonder why they hurt so badly.

Of course, Fallion realized. When Shadoath captured a city, she used the elderly, the infirm, as food for her strengi-saats. The strong ones she'd keep as workers. And their children served as Dedicates.

It looked more like a nursery than a Dedicates' Keep. Fallion had never seen an instance where a Runelord took endowments from children. Such a deed was horrific.

But he understood the cunning of it.

Fallion stood there numb, as if wounded. He dared not advance.

He remembered Borenson sobbing in the night, and Myrrima warning Fallion, "Do not repeat our mistakes."

He'd heard Borenson cry out in his sleep many times over the years. Now Fallion began to understand why.

He looked at the faces of the children, some lying fast asleep, others peering at him in terror, and searched in vain for an adult target, someone evil, someone cruel, someone worthy of death.

He'd imagined that Shadoath's servants would be vile, like her. He'd dreamed that their cruelty would be written plain upon their faces, and that in slaying them, he would feel secure that he'd done the world a favor.

But there was no evil in this room. Only innocence.

And then he saw her, there across the room, not forty feet away. A young woman with pale skin and dark red hair, slumbering, perhaps lost in a dream. She had aged in the past five years. She now looked to be more than twenty. It was Rhianna.

Without thought he moved across the room and found himself peering down, trying to make sure that it really was her.

Over the years, a thousand times he'd dreamed of going back to Syndyl-lian to rescue her. Or he dreamed that she found her way to him somehow.

A rune of wit was branded on her forehead, the scar a cold white and puckering.

She's given Shadoath her wit, Fallion thought. I could kill her now, and she'd never even know what happened. I could slice her throat, and strike a blow against evil. If I am going to do this, if I am to defend my people, then I should take her first.

Fallion peered down at Rhianna, and a seemingly ancient oath suddenly rose from his throat, escaped his lips. "Sworn to serve."

He let his blade clatter to the floor.

He sank to his knees and hugged her while fierce tears welled up in his eyes.

Shadoath's graak struggled for purchase in the air, its leather wings ripping the sky as it made its way up to the little bluff.

Half a dozen white graaks still waited in the shadows. They were hungry,

and their reptilian brains seemed to not be quite awake. They were going to
sleep for the night. And so they stood, almost like statues, while Shadoath's
own mount landed on the bluff, panting from exertion.

Shadoath leapt off of her graak onto the sandstone, her powerful muscles catching her weight as if she were as light as a windblown leaf.

She drew a long knife and stalked into the little cave.

The room was small and bare. It held the embers of a fire, but no water
or other supplies. There was nowhere that anyone could hide.

Most of the children had raced down into the tunnel ahead. Only Valya
stood her ground.

She had grown. She was lithe and beautiful. Her breasts had filled out.

"Mother, leave here," Valya begged. Her lips trembled, and her hands
were shaking.

"I've searched for you for years," Shadoath said.

"I . . . didn't want to be found."

Shadoath stepped up to her daughter and lovingly stroked the girl's
cheek. Valya tried to recoil in fear, but then stood her ground, head bowed.

Shadoath kissed her forehead.

She betrayed me, Shadoath realized. She chose to go with Fallion.

"Come," Shadoath said, using all the persuasive power of her Voice. The
command slipped beneath the girl's defenses like a knife, and she lurched
forward a pace.

"Come," Shadoath said again.

Shadoath took Valya's hand and strode out of the cave, toward the ledge
where her graak waited.

She stood by her mount for a moment, peering up into its eyes, and the
reptile watched her.

Valya stood, trembling. She was no match for her mother. She didn't
have the strength or speed to fight her. Any attempt to flee would have
been futile.

Without a word, Shadoath took Valya's arm and hurled her over the ledge.

The young woman screamed once, then made soft thumping sounds as
she dropped, bouncing off of rocks, a hundred yards, two hundred, then
landed with a rip like a melon splitting as it hits the ground.

Shadoath stood for a second, then turned and stalked back into the recesses of the cave to hunt for the rest of the children, hoping that Fallion would be among them.

Fallion felt a strange sensation, an emptiness inside.

The world seemed a darker place, as if someone had blown out a candle in the corner of a room.

For years now, Fallion had been growing more sensitive to heat and light. He was aware of it on a hundred levels. He could feel the soul-fires of his friends.

Now he stretched out with his senses, questing, to discover what had changed.

And like the great flameweavers of legend, he recognized when one of his friend's soul-fires went out.

"Valya?" he cried, fearing the worst.

He climbed to his feet, sure that Shadoath had found his friends.

Shadoath's own Dedicates lay before him, easy prey, and he knew that if he did not act quickly, the guards could come. He might never have another chance.

Do I kill them? he wondered. Dare I?

Killing the children is evil, he knew. But so was letting them live.

He knew the arguments, had heard them all of his life.

He reached down to the floor, retrieved his blade, and peered around the room. He couldn't kill Rhianna, not first, so he moved to the bed next to her. A boy no more than three lay there so still that he might have been dead.

Fallion leaned close, smelled his breath, a baby's sweet breath. Metabolism, he decided. The little boy had given Shadoath metabolism.

He had a vision of Shadoath sitting with the child, her arm wrapped around the boy, whispering softly into his ear. "Do you have a present for me? Do you want to give me something nice?"

And the boy would have loved her. He'd have been mesmerized by Shadoath's beauty, beguiled by her liquid voice. He'd have ached to give Shadoath something, anything.

Kill him, Fallion thought. Do it now, before you have time to regret it.

More guards could come rushing back at any moment. Maybe Abravael has gone for reinforcements.

The world hangs on your decision.

That thought stopped him. It was true. Shadoath was raising an army from the netherworld. Fallion didn't know her plans, but it was obvious that she intended to invade.

And Fallion was the only person in the world who knew where her Dedicates lay hidden. With them intact, there was a very real possibility that she could take control. The world's supplies of blood metal were dwindling. No great Runelord would arise to fight her.

Fallion needed to play the part of a hero now.

I wish that Sir Borenson were here, Fallion told himself. Borenson the assassin. Borenson the Kingslayer.

But even Borenson would shirk from this task, Fallion knew. He had killed innocents once before, and it had wounded his conscience, crippled him.

Now it's my turn, he told himself.

Oohtooroo knew that she was dying. She clung to Abravael with one hand, and with the other tried to hold in her innards.

"Love you . . ." she told him. "Love oooo."

She was gasping, trying to hold on, wanting to protect him with the very last of her strength.

But Abravael fought her, tried to shove her away.

"Let go!" he shouted desperately. "You're bleeding all over me."

He struggled to escape, his strength boosted by endowments, but it was not enough. He swatted at her face, and Oohtooroo grasped him harder, as if by doing so, she were clinging to her own life.

"Love ooooo," she said desperately, her heart pounding as fast as a hummingbird's wings. She needed him to understand. She had loved him fiercely for years, and always would.

She took him by the neck, her enormous hand encompassing it, and tried to cling to him for one last moment, one last loving moment.

Abravael frantically kicked and struggled as Oohtooroo's heart suddenly gave out, and her vision went gray.

Rhianna woke, her heart pounding in terror. "Abravael!" she shouted, her love for him seeming to swell as big as the universe.

She found herself peering up at Fallion, who stood nearby, both hands wrapped around the hilt of his blade, ready to strike down a sleeping boy. She did not know where she was.

Her last memory was of holding Abravael, trying to explain to him the depth of her love, trying to bore the knowledge into him with her eyes.

She had heard a snapping sound, the crunching of bones in his neck.

And now she was staring up at Fallion, and with the same ferocity, wanted to bore the knowledge of her love into him.

He turned at the sound of her startled voice.

She stared into his eyes, and memories came flooding back—her bargain with Shadoath, the torturous touch of the forcible, her time spent as Oohtooroo, loving her master with a fierceness beyond man's ability to understand.

She knew that she was in some Dedicates' Keep. Fallion stood nearby in the darkness, only the candlelight revealing his shape.

Sweat poured down his forehead and broke out upon his arm. He trembled, his whole body shaking, as if he had been standing for hours, or might stand thus forever.

"Do it, if you must," Rhianna whispered.

Fallion gasped, as if to cry out, but managed to hold his pain inside.

Carefully, Rhianna climbed to her elbows and peered at the children still sleeping nearby, innocent children by the dozens, and she understood his predicament.

"And if you can't do it," Rhianna whispered, "then I'll do it for you."

Reaching up, she gently unclasped his fingers from the hilt of his knife, and took the blade into her own hand. There was a little girl nearby, a child with blond hair and a pinched face. Her skin was leathery and wrinkled, for she had granted an endowment of glamour.

Silently, Rhianna whispered to herself: By the Glories, let her feel no pain.

Rhianna raised the knife overhead.

This is how I will serve Fallion, she thought. This is how I will prove my love. She let the knife plunge.

"No!" Fallion screamed and pulled on her wrist, spoiling her aim. The blade buried itself in a straw mattress.

For what seemed an eternity, Fallion had stood above Rhianna, unable to strike either her or the boy beside her. Part of his mind knew that this was a trap.

Shadoath had taken endowments from babes, knowing that he could not cut them down.

Sweat had broken out on his forehead; his hand trembled and would not strike; his mind raced down a thousand paths, seeking an alternative. Time stopped, and the earth ceased its course through the heavens. Rhianna awoke and bade him to give her his knife.

And in despair, Fallion reached out and felt the heat of a dozen candles, and the life-warmth of hundreds of bodies. As his rage grew, he wanted nothing more than to cease to exist.

Serve me, the fire whispered. *Take them all.*

Let the fire come, he told himself. Let it take me, eat away my soul, and take these others with me.

It would all be so easy to burst into flame, to feed his own rage, let it blossom into an inferno.

He exhaled, and smoke issued from his throat, even as Rhianna raised the knife, preparing to strike.

Sacrifice to me, Fire whispered.

He had grabbed her hand as it fell, wrested the blade, and just stood for a moment as it sat buried in the straw.

"Let go," Rhianna said, "you're burning me!"

She peered at him, and Fallion could see himself reflected in her pupils. There was a brightness in his eyes, a hidden fire about to be unleashed.

He peered around the room.

There's something I'm missing, he thought. There has to be a way out of this. All that I need to do is *see!*

Instantly, the candles around the room blazed, as if responding to his need. Fallion keenly felt the heat of the room, conscious of how hidden flames played through the bodies of the children, how their own life heat was exhaled in every precious breath.

He peered closely at the children before him, and as in the prison, it suddenly seemed that their flesh fell away, exposing the faint undulating lights of their tiny souls. Blue lights were everywhere, like rafts of luminous jellyfish in the summer seas.

All that he had to do was look.

There was a brightness in them, a brightness in each and every child.

They are all Bright Ones, he realized.

Shadoath took for her Dedicates only the best.

Rhianna was trying to pull away from him and at the same time grabbing for the knife. He saw her flesh and bones in a vague outline, saw warm tears streaming from her eyes.

"If you won't kill them, I have to do it myself!" she shouted. Grabbing the knife, she went after the nearest girl.

Then he spotted it: there beneath her flesh, a shadow attached to the back of her spirit, a dark parasite that fed upon her.

A locus! he realized.

He had never seen one so close.

She raised the knife, and Fallion shouted, "Rhianna, you have a locus."

She turned to him, her face a mask of terror and disbelief.

"We must kill them," she said, shaking. "Help me."

"Is that what *you* think?" Fallion said. "Or is it the locus speaking?"

Rhianna trembled, and with great difficulty threw down the blade.

Fallion peered at the locus, saw it there. It was obviously alive. It had a form, vaguely shaped like a worm or leech, and where the leech's abdomen should have been, it latched on to Rhianna's spirit.

Fallion saw movement at that point, as if some attachment on the locus were tearing into her, doing mortal damage to Rhianna's soul. But the whole creature was wrapped in shadow, and he could not see it clearly.

More light. I need more light to see by.

There were torches in sconces on the wall. Fallion reached above Rhianna's bed, grabbing the nearest torch, and at his touch it burst into flame.

He raised it high and held it above Rhianna, willing it to brighten, but as if in response, the locus wrapped itself in deeper shadows, as if seeking to hide.

More light, he told himself. Let the earth blaze.

The torch blazed in his hand, and all around the room, other torches burst into flame.

Feed the flames, a voice whispered in the back of Fallion's mind.

He drew heat from the torches, thin coils that raced through the atmosphere, until his own flesh felt hot to the touch. He let the heat escape from every pore in the form of light, so that at first he glowed warmly, and then began to blaze.

He was in a rage and felt as if at any moment his skin would take fire like parchment, and when it happened, he would destroy this place, let it all burn.

Yes, a voice whispered, *that's what I need.*

Rhianna staggered back, tripped, and fell to the floor.

"Stay back. You're getting hot!" Rhianna said.

Fallion struggled to maintain control. He fought the urge to burst into flame. But he knew that he had to do something. *There are many powers among flameweavers*, Smoker had said. *Not all of them are evil.*

Rhianna's voice softened, and she pleaded, "Fallion, help me kill the Dedicates."

Then Fallion understood! Suddenly he let the heat out of him in a gush of radiance. Brilliance washed through the room, light bleeding from his every pore.

Rhianna gasped, and her face seemed to go white, all colors washed away. She held up her hand as if to keep from going blind, and the whole room blazed.

"Now let me see you!" Fallion commanded the locus, and the light shining from him smote the creature, revealing it in every sickly detail.

It trembled and shook, seeking to escape, and as the light flowed through Fallion, it seemed as if pure knowledge came with it.

He peered at the locus in all of its filth and ugliness, and he knew its name.

"Asgaroth!" Fallion shouted. "I see you!"

But how had it come here?

"Asgaroth?" Rhianna cried, her voice high and frightened; she cringed and tried to scurry backward.

Fallion would have none of that. He raced near, loomed above her. Rhianna glanced at him briefly, and when she did, the locus shuddered, until she glanced away.

"Look at me!" Fallion commanded Rhianna. "Look into my eyes!"

Rhianna peered up at him, and her pupils constricted down to pinpoints. Fallion saw himself reflected in her eyes, a luminous creature as bright as the sun, and for a moment he worried that he really would blind her.

He could see beyond her eyes, through them, into her soul. His father had used Earth Powers to see into the hearts of men. Now Fallion used Fire to do the same.

And he saw how Rhianna had succumbed to despair and given herself to Shadoath, surrendering not only her wit, but her soul. That was when Asgaroth had taken her.

Fallion felt as if he were blazing with righteous indignation. The locus shuddered and trembled, seeking to escape his burning gaze.

"Why?" Fallion demanded. "Why are you here? Why now? Why do you trouble me?"

Rhianna fought Fallion then, fought him savagely, twisted onto the floor and tried to crawl away, but Fallion threw her onto her back, pinned her with a knee, and forced her to look into his face.

Asgaroth trembled and shuddered, and in a fit of rage, Fallion blazed. It was as if the sun suddenly flared, and Fallion heard children screaming and realized that many of them had come awake. Rhianna was screaming as Asgaroth shuddered and bulged and tried to break free.

"Answer me!" Fallion demanded, and the flaring light seared the locus, burned off an outer layer of skin.

"Nooooo!" Rhianna wailed, but Fallion did not even register her complaint, so intent was he upon the locus.

As it burned, layers of skin and flesh peeling under his scorching gaze, Fallion stripped away its secrets.

This world. For ages the loci had searched for this world, for it was like a large shard of a broken mirror, or a key piece to a vast puzzle. There was information written upon this world, a memory of the Great Rune.

The loci needed this information, this piece of the rune, to bind all of the shadow worlds back into One True World, flawless and brilliant, and under their control.

Asgaroth had taken Rhianna in the hopes that through her, Asgaroth could lead Fallion astray, make a tool of him, until a locus infected him, as it did the Bright Ones that were under Shadoath's sway.

Fallion saw it all so clearly, he was amazed that he had never understood. In that moment his attention flickered, and Asgaroth fled.

One moment the locus gripped Rhianna and the next it released, surging off quicker than thought, so that Fallion saw it only briefly, escaping from the corner of his eye.

"Kill it!" Rhianna was shouting, and her voice suddenly rose above the pounding of blood in his ears. "Kill me if you must. Just get rid of it!"

Fallion suddenly found himself growing cold, shaking. The light in him had died, and the torch in his hand and the torches all around the room had all but burned out.

Dozens of children had come awake, and they huddled around him, peering with huge eyes, some of them screaming in terror, many of them coughing from smoke.

Fallion heard guards rushing toward the keep, iron shoes clanking down the hall. With a thought, he sent the smoke hurtling from the room, billowing down the corridor toward the guards, filling the narrow passage.

Fallion had Rhianna pinned to the floor, his knee in her chest, and now he crawled off.

I've burned her, he thought. I've blinded her.

But Rhianna was crying, shouting, "Kill it. Do it now!" and Fallion realized that whatever harm he had done to her, she would bear it gladly.

"It's gone," Fallion told her. "The locus has gone from you."

Rhianna choked on a sob, reached up and hugged him, weeping bitterly. "Can you see?" he asked.

"I can see," she said. "I'm fine. I'm good. I'm good. I'm good. I'm good." She repeated the words over and over, as if to comfort herself or to comfort him.

Fallion held her, hugged her tightly. "I know," he said. "I know you're good."

Far away, Shadoath rode upon the back of a white graak, soaring above the tops of the stonewood trees, when suddenly a shadow whispered to her soul.

"The torch-bearer has awakened. He comes to destroy us all."

She closed her eyes, and in her mind saw what had happened to Asgaroth. Fallion had burned him with light, pierced him, devastating the locus.

Indeed, even as Asgaroth whispered to her, Shadoath could sense that he was dying.

For long moments, the shadow wailed in pain, until at last it fell silent.

Shadoath was stunned.

No locus had ever died.

We are eternal, she thought. We are spread across a million million shadow worlds, and not one of us has ever died. Asgaroth was one of the great and powerful ones.

But Fallion had awakened, had summoned a light that even the Bright Ones of old could not match.

If Asgaroth can die, so can I.

In rising fear, Shadoath raced her graak to Garion's Port. Fallion would be coming for her, that much was certain. There was a new terror in the universe.

Shadoath was not ready to face him.

ಬ 50 ೞ

FIRE IN THE HEAVENS

His power smote the wicked, and his rage burned the sky.

—from an "Ode to Fallion of the Flames"

Fallion led Rhianna from the Dedicates' Keep, into the outer corridors and to the guards' chamber.

There, Fallion shoved on the door, found that it was unlocked.

The golath guards in the darkened chamber cringed and hacked, trying to clear the smoke from their lungs.

Some of them moaned in pain, their voices sounding strangely musical.

They had retreated here, fleeing. Fallion held his torch aloft, and he could see the flames dancing in their eyes.

"Take good care of the children," Fallion warned them. "Or when I return, your cries of pain will become a symphony to me."

He shut the door, walked out into the evening light. It limned the bowl of the volcano, all along the ridges.

A hundred yards away, near a rock, the sea ape lay on the ground, her huge paw still wrapped around Abravael's throat.

Both of them were dead. Fallion could tell even at a distance by the whiteness of Abravael's face, by the frantic way that his fingers clawed at the sky even though he lay perfectly still.

Rhianna stumbled to the pair, reached down, and petted the sea ape's shoulder. "I'm sorry," she whispered. "He could never have loved you half as well as you deserved."

Then Fallion led Rhianna past the dead strengi-saat, where she cringed in terror, and to the sea graak.

The great beast lifted off, lugged them both the three miles to the island of Wolfram. But the weary graak could not carry the weight of two for any great distance, and at Wolfram the children landed near the deserted docks, where they found a leaky sailboat.

They scrounged up some food—strange bread from the netherworld that tasted sweet and filling, along with some old dried figs.

A strong wind and a single sail was enough to let them reach Garion's Port by late morning.

Fallion had no endowments with which to do battle. Instead, as the boat sailed toward port, he raised his left hand to the sky and drew down sunlight, ropes of light that came twisting out of the heavens in cords of white fire, running down his arm, filling him with light.

The sky darkened as he did this, and the ropes of fire blazed in the false night like lightning.

By the time he reached port and sailed between the Ends of the Earth, he was prepared for battle.

He saw the remains of ships in the harbor, but Shadoath's armies had gone.

One great worldship lay beached a mile north of the city. Even from a distance, Fallion could see that it was empty.

Fallion and Rhianna climbed up a rope ladder into the stonewood trees at the port, and everywhere they found refugees returning to their homes.

"The armies ran off," the innkeeper at the Sea Perch said. "They all took off last night, heading inland. They were blowin' retreat on their warhorns, runnin' like mad. And all of us folks that they'd captured, they just left us to ourselves."

Fallion nodded thoughtfully, and told the innkeeper, "There's an island to the south of Wolfram, a small island with a volcano. At its top you'll find a couple hundred children, Shadoath's Dedicates."

The innkeeper looked outraged. "We'll 'ave to kill 'em," he said. "There's no other choice!"

Fallion shook his head and promised, "Shadoath will be dead by the time you reach the children."

Fallion looked inland, wondering how far away the armies would be, and because he was filled with fire and light, he suspected that he knew the answer: he might never reach them.

Shadoath and her followers were fleeing far beyond the bounds of this world.

Shadoath had known that he was coming, and had grown afraid.

Fallion went to the Gwardeen Wood, and there found some male graaks. He and Rhianna rode them inland for several miles, following the river, until at the edge of the woods they spotted a large rune upon the ground, a green tracing of fire in a circle of ash. Within the circle, the flames formed something that looked vaguely like a serpent.

Golaths were charging from the woods by the hundreds, racing into the circle and then leaping but never landing, simply disappearing.

It was a gateway to the One True World.

Fallion saw no sign of Shadoath or even a single Bright One that served as her guard. The leaders had been the first to flee.

It would have taken little for Fallion to close the gate, to suck the last of the flames away and make the exit disappear. But then the folks of Landesfallen would only have had to face a cruel enemy, the stranded golaths.

Besides, he had one more task.

Nodding to Rhianna, he jutted his chin, pointing upstream. "Up in the hills about thirty miles from here, the river will fork. Take the right fork up. There, about fifteen more miles up, you'll find a Gwardeen fortress."

"What about you?" Rhianna asked.

But Fallion was already diving. His graak swooped out of the sky, and Fallion reached up one last time, drawing cords of light from heavens that suddenly went black, and then his graak was almost on the ground, skirting the flames.

Its wings thundered, and the world blurred and changed, and suddenly the graak was rising up from the ashes, into a sky where a million stars blazed profoundly.

He was in a stony valley, and all around were dark pines, towering, mountainous, almost blocking out the light.

Below, a vast army had congregated—tens of thousands of golaths and Bright Ones, all camped beneath the shadows of the giant trees.

Fallion soared above them, and he heard frightened shouts, saw golaths pointing upward.

There in the midst of her army, Shadoath sat beside a campfire. Fallion's sharp eyes were quick to spot her, sitting so regally, a diaphanous jewel in the night.

Fallion let the graak dive, winging only three dozen feet above the heads of the golaths, and he saw Shadoath rise from her chair as she spotted him, her mouth falling open in rage.

Make an offering of her, Fire whispered. *Burn her.*

Fallion did not give her time to cry out.

He released the heat stored in him, blazing brighter than the sun. It felt as if his skin caught fire, and everywhere cries of pain and dismay rose up from those that were infested by loci.

Bright Ones cringed and cowered, unable to mount a defense. The golaths saw their masters' fear and then turned to run.

Fallion peered down at their souls, saw wounded loci by the hundreds breaking free from their hosts, then streaking away to safety.

He bent his will most of all upon Shadoath.

She cried out in horror, the locus ripping free from her, a shadow hurtling away like a comet.

When it was gone, Shadoath stood, raging at him in defiance. She grabbed a great bow from a cringing golath, drew it to the full, and fired an arrow.

It blurred in its speed.

Fallion unleashed a fireball, sent hurtling toward it. The fireball raced down far faster than a horse could run, caught the arrow in midair, and turned it into cinders. The fireball roared along its course.

Shadoath took another arrow, fired again. But it met the same fate.

Shadoath barely had time to curse before the fireball took her full in the face.

An inferno washed over her, and she raised a fist and shook it, screaming in pain. The fireball turned those around her into flaming torches, yet with her endowments, Shadoath refused to die.

Shadoath cursed and raised her hands, shaking her fists, even as flames lashed out all around her, charring her flesh, bubbling her skin, melting her fat.

Her cries, by reason of many endowments, were amplified a hundredfold, so that her voice seemed to shake the heavens.

She roared and reached down to pick up a huge stone, and suddenly the cooked meat of her joints gave way, so that the bones of her hands ripped free, borne away by the weight of the stone.

The fire roared all around her, and she stood in the midst of the inferno, as if she would keep screaming endlessly.

Slowly, she began to collapse. First one cooked knee gave way, and she stumbled to the ground, as if compelled to kneel to her young master.

Still she shouted obscenities, even as her tongue boiled. By now her hair was gone, and her face a bubbling ruin.

Then she lowered her head as if in pain, and at last collapsed among the flames, falling forever silent.

Now the children are free, Fallion thought.

He fought back tears and pulled his mount up, soared back toward the world gate, and in moments he was gone.

And in Shadoath's Dedicates' Keep, babes that had not seen in years suddenly opened their eyes to the light.

The deaf heard other children shrieking in delight and laughing.

Those who had been too weak to walk suddenly leapt in the air and cavorted like frogs.

The sick became hale, and fools suddenly recalled their names, while many a child who had given away beauty discovered a new luster to their skin.

There was not enough room in the Dedicates' Keep to contain all of the joy that was unleashed, and so the children ran out of the shadowy retreat into the sun and rolled about on the green grass.

It was a short journey to the Toth Queen's Hideout. Fallion did not want to make it, but he had to. He needed to see if any of the children had survived.

When he returned from the netherworld, rising up from the world gate, he was surprised to find that Rhianna had waited for him. Her graak was high above, circling the field.

There was a fire in him now, a constant companion, endlessly burning.

He flew by the bright light of the sun, with Rhianna beside him, and at the fortress he found a twig and summoned a flame, and held it as if it were a candle.

As he held it, he peered at his hands and saw that they looked smoother than before, as if they had been shaved. The hairs on the back of his arms had turned to ash. He reached up, found that the hair of his head had met the same fate. He'd come perilously close to bursting into flame.

He hesitated outside the entrance to the tunnel and steeled himself. Nix could be there, dead, or Denorra or Carralee or any of a dozen other children that he had been training. He loved them as if they were brothers and sisters. He did not know if he could look upon their corpses and remain sane.

Rhianna landed her own graak and stood at his back.

"Stay out here," he told her.

He took a deep breath and dove under the stone arch, into the blackness.

Inside, he found the corpses. It had been a bloodbath, and the sight of it left him ill, but he was relieved not to find Jaz or Nix or several others.

There was no sign of Valya.

He searched everywhere in the little tunnel, following it back into the mountain for nearly a mile.

One of the most dangerous times to ride a graak is on the takeoff, he thought. And a certainty filled him. He knew where to find Valya.

He raced to the mouth of the cave and peered down, two hundred yards below.

In the full sunlight, his eyes made out her form.

Valya lay on the rocks at the edge of the stream, her arms and legs splayed wide, as if she were reaching out to embrace the heavens. Her skin looked as white as parchment.

He let out a strangled cry, and Rhianna came up behind him, put a hand upon his shoulder, and tried to offer some comfort.

He left Rhianna on the bluff, and had his graak land beside Valya, and then waded through the shallows and pulled her to shore.

He'd never touched a human body that felt so cold. It wasn't just the cold of death. The water had leached the heat from her, too.

He brought her up on the shore and peered into her face. Her eyes were closed, her face expressionless. It did not look as if she had died in pain.

Fallion combed her dark hair with his fingers, and just held her against his chest for a long time, until the body warmed a bit.

He did not know what to feel for her. Pity. Sadness. Regret.

I promised to set her free, he told himself. But what did I give her? If she could talk now, would she thank me for what I've done, or curse me?

Late that night long after the sun had set, Fallion and Rhianna flew high into the mountains up onto an arid plateau where an eerie fortress stood, a compound formed of white adobe bricks that gleamed like the bones of a giant in the starlight.

They landed at the gates, only seconds before a weary Sir Borenson arrived, hopping along on a tired rangit.

The travelers dismounted at the same time, and Borenson gave Fallion a long hug. He stared at Rhianna for a long moment, as if trying to place her, and then cried out in recognition.

"Rhianna?"

"Yes?"

"You look older," he said. "You have an endowment of metabolism?"

She nodded.

"I never knew," he said, astonished.

He looked to Fallion, his eyes locking on to Fallion's bald head. "And Shadoath?"

"She's dead," Fallion told him. "Shadoath's dead. In body, at least. I killed her, and her locus has fled."

Sir Borenson had already seen Jaz earlier in the day. He'd flown ahead, had beaten Fallion here. He knew what Fallion had done, how he'd gone to slay Shadoath's Dedicates. He'd known the price that Fallion would have to pay.

And now he imagined that by some miracle, Fallion had slaughtered the Dedicates and then slain Shadoath in single combat.

It was not an unreasonable leap of the imagination. The boy was well trained for battle; he was growing tall and strong. And he was a flameweaver.

He saw pain in Fallion's eyes, and the weariness that can only be known by those who have witnessed terrible evil. He saw light in Fallion's eyes, like a fire, endlessly burning.

He's done it, Borenson thought. His hands are every bit as bloody as mine.

Borenson found himself weeping, crying in relief to know that both Rhianna and Fallion lived, but crying more for the innocence that they had lost.

ॐ 51 ॐ

FALLION'S END

Happy endings come with a price, a price that must be borne from the beginning.

—Fallion

Weeks later, long after the uproar at Garion's Port died down, Borenson and Myrrima found the house that they had once promised to Rhianna and the children.

The new home lay on the edge of a town called Sweetgrass, fifty-seven miles upriver from the Ends of the Earth. So far inland, the stonewood trees were all but a memory. To each side of the valley, the land rose precipitously into red-rock canyons with their fantastic bluffs sculpted by wind, their hills of petrified sand dunes, and their majestic sandstone arches.

But there in Sweetgrass the hot hill country was still far away, as was the dense forest at the ocean's edge. Instead a clear river ran down out of the canyons, through rolling hills, to form a rich alluvial plain, and there in the deep soil, grasses grew thick and tall.

Land like this wasn't to be found anymore on Landesfallen, Borenson was told by a local farmer. There were places that you could homestead, desert hillsides so barren that goats could starve even with fifty acres to forage.

"I already own a piece of land like that," Borenson had said with a laugh.

But this was rich country, grabbed up by settlers eight hundred years in the past. An old widow owned the homestead, the last in her line, and she could no longer maintain it. The farm had fallen into disrepair, all but her little square garden of flowers and vegetables out by the back porch.

So Borenson took his family to have a look. He had heard many a farmer curse the poor soil on their land back in Mystarria, and so he disregarded the shabby state of the cottage and barns, the fallen stones from the fences.

Instead, he gauged the farm by its soil alone. He took a shovel and went out into the fields and began to dig. The topsoil was rich and black, even to a depth of three feet. No hint of sand or clay or gravel or rock—just rich loam.

Land like this is a treasure greater than gold, he knew. Land like this will feed my children for generations to come.

As he dug, the kids raced along the river and chased up a pair of fat grouse and a herd of wild rangits. Little Erin thrilled to see turtles in the millpond and fat trout in the river.

It was paradise.

So Borenson bought the land with its thatch-roofed cottage; its stone fences and a pair of sway-backed old milk cows; its pond full of perch and pike and singing frogs with a quaint mill there at the river's edge; its rope swings and rolling green meadows filled with daisies; its orchard with cherry trees and apples, pears and peaches, apricots and almonds, black walnuts and hazelnuts; its vineyard full of fat grapes and the wine press that hadn't been used in twenty years; its dovecotes and doves; its horse corral where a tabby cat lived; and its old cattle barn where the owls nested.

It was, quite frankly, the kind of place that Borenson had only dreamed about, and though he knew little of farming, the land was fertile enough to be forgiving.

Even a fool like me couldn't botch it, he thought as he opened the barn door and found a plow.

He looked at the rusty old thing and wondered how to sharpen it.

Much as I would a battle-ax, I guess.

There so far from the coast, the days were free of fog and rain. The sunlight filled the valley each morning like a bowl, so that it seemed to spill out everywhere.

And life grew easy. The children found their smiles and learned to be children once again. It didn't happen in a day.

There were wars in Heredon and Mystarria, and in various far places. Borenson heard about it that fall at Hostenfest.

Fallion's kingdom is slipping away, he thought.

Heredon seemed so far away, it could have been on the moon. And Fallion had been a prince so long ago, it could have been never.

Fallion came home that Hostenfest, as did Draken. Both of them had quit the Gwardeen, giving up their graaks. Fallion's hair had begun to grow back. It looked only as if it had been cropped short.

"I'm too heavy to ride anymore," Fallion said, and he went out on the farm and helped bring in the harvest, picking buckets full of apples and laying up a store of winter wheat as if he had never been a Gwardeen.

Unknown to his foster parents, Fallion still kept watch, as he had while serving in the Gwardeen. Sometimes he would climb the hill out behind the house and peer down over the valley. From its height he could see all of the cottages in Sweetgrass, and many of them up and down the river. He'd light a small fire, and by its power he would peer about, into the souls of men.

He could see them, even down in their cottages, their soul-fires burning brightly, guttering like torches; if any of them had borne a shadow, he would have known.

But as the weeks and months dragged on, he realized that there would be nothing to see. The loci feared him. They would stay away.

He did not wonder at his destiny any longer. His father had been the Earth King, the greatest king that the world had known, and Fallion had no desire to try to walk in his father's footsteps. He did not long to build armies or fight wars or squabble with barons over the price of their taxes or lie awake at night with his mind racing, trying to decide the fairest punishment for some criminal.

I am something different from my father. I am the torch-bearer.

Shadoath was still alive, he knew. He had been too far away from her to burn the locus when he released his light. But he had scarred her.

What his destiny might be, he did not yet know, but he did not fret about it. He left that to Borenson.

He does a good job of it, Fallion thought. The old guardsman was still protective of Fallion, and probably always would be.

Fallion practiced with his weapons for no fewer than three hours per day. He grew more and more skilled, showing blinding speed and more natural talent than any young man should have.

After all, he was still a Son of the Oak.

But he lost some of his drive, his consuming need to be better than his opponents.

I will not win this war with a sword, he knew.

And in time, even he seemed to find his smile. One autumn morning as Myrrima and Talon were busy in the warm kitchen baking apple tarts, he came from hunting for mallards alongside the river, and Myrrima saw him smiling broadly.

"What are you so happy about?" she asked.

"Oh, nothing," he said.

She looked for a reason, and realized that it was true. He was just happy.

He deserves to be, she thought, wiping a tear from her eye with the corner of her apron.

Rhianna was another story. She didn't smile for many long months, and often at night she would wake in terror, sweating furiously, so frightened that she could not cry out, or even move, but only lay abed, her teeth chattering.

On such nights, Myrrima would lie down beside her, a comforting arm wrapped around the young woman.

Over the course of the summer the dreams faded, but came back sharply in the fall and through much of the following winter. But by spring they were gone, and by early summer, she seemed to have forgotten the strengi-saats completely.

Myrrima would never have known, but little Erin, who was now seven, came into the house eating some particularly fine-looking cherries, deep crimson and plump. Sage claimed that they were hers, that she had hidden them in the barn in order to save them from the predations of her siblings, but Erin had found them hidden in the hayloft.

In a rage, Sage shouted, "I hope the strengi-saats take you!"

Myrrima had whirled to peer at Rhianna, to see her reaction to such a foul curse. But Rhianna, who was washing dishes, seemed not to have noticed.

As Borenson marshaled Sage out to the shed for punishment, Myrrima told her, "You apologize to your sister, and to Rhianna, too."

She apologized, but Rhianna seemed baffled by the apology.

Myrrima added her own words of regret, saying, "I'm sorry for what Sage said. I've told her never to mention *them* here in the house again."

Rhianna seemed distracted and only vaguely alarmed. She didn't even look up from her work as she replied, "Oh, okay. What's a strengi-saat?"

Myrrima peered hard at her, astonished. Rhianna still bore scars over her womb, and always would. But she seemed to have totally forgotten what had caused them.

"Maybe it's better that she forget," Borenson told Myrrima later that night as they lay in bed. "No one should have to remember that."

And so Myrrima let it go as completely as Rhianna did. She watched the young woman revel in her beauty. She was the kind that the boys would flock to at festivals. Rhianna's skin remained clear, and her red hair grew long and flaxen. The fierceness was gone from her eyes now, and only rarely did Myrrima ever see a flash of it. Instead, she seemed to have learned to love, had developed an astonishing ability to feel for others, to be considerate and watchful. And it was Fallion she loved the best.

Of all her features, it was Rhianna's smile that was the most beautiful. It was broad, and infectious, as was her laugh, and when she smiled, the hearts of young men would skip a beat.

One chilly spring night eight months after they'd moved to Sweetgrass, Borenson had a dream.

He dreamed that he was shoving down the door to the old kitchens, inside the Dedicates' Keep at Castle Sylvarresta.

He used his warhammer to bash through the locking mechanism.

Inside, two little girls stood with brooms in their hands, as if they had been sweeping the floor. They peered up at him, screaming in terror, but no sound came from their mouths.

Mutes, he realized. They'd given their voices to Raj Ahten.

In the dream, time seemed to slow, and he advanced on the children as if a great weight had descended upon him, horrified to the core of his soul, knowing what he had to do.

And there, at last, he dropped his weapon to the floor, and refused the deed.

He took the girls into his arms and hugged them, as he wished that he had done so long ago.

He woke with a sob, his heart pounding wildly.

In a panic, he threw himself out of bed, fearing that he would retch. It was no dream, after all. It was a memory, a false memory. The girls had been just the first of thousands. The blood of thousands was on his hands.

But in the dream he had refused to kill them.

He felt as if he had made some kind of breakthrough.

He groped through the darkness, moaning in horror at the memory, crawling on the floor, blinded by grief, yet hoping that somehow he had made a transition, hoping that he would not have to relive that slaughter for an eternity.

It had been the first time in days that he'd dreamed of them. Oh, how he wished that he could never dream again.

He reached the front door to the cottage, went out into the yard, and found himself gasping for air beside the well, sick to his stomach and fighting the urge to vomit.

Jaz's dog, a mutt that had no name, came and peered up at him, perplexed and eager to give comfort.

"It's okay, dog," Borenson said.

And so he stood there, leaning against the well, peering out under the cold moonlight, listening to the river as it flowed beneath the hills, and waited for his heart to still.

All was safe on his little farm. All seemed well with the world. There were no assassins from Mystarria. No one knew where the Sons of the Oak might be, or if they did, they did not care.

But the loci still knew that Fallion was their enemy.

So where are they? Borenson worried. Why aren't they fighting now? Are they really so afraid of him? Or are they plotting something worse?

And then a nagging worry hit him, one that he would chew on for years.

Or maybe they think that they've already won?

Borenson admired Fallion, admired and loved him like no other. But always in his memory he heard Asgaroth's resounding curse: "War shall follow you all of your days, and though the world may applaud your slaughter, *you* will come to know that each of your victories is mine."

Those who knew Fallion best considered him to be a quiet and unassuming hero.

But Borenson had seen the destruction after Fallion's battle at the port of Syndyllian. He'd seen the fire-gutted ships. He knew what kind of damage the boy could wreak.

The loci were said to be cunning and subtle. *Are they plotting something more?* Borenson wondered. *Or do they just leave him alone because they know that they have already won?*

Borenson came into the house a few mornings later to see Fallion sitting in front of the hearth, peering into the fire, smiling as if at some secret, a faraway look in his eyes.

"What's going on?" Borenson asked.

"Trouble," he said. "There's trouble ahead."

"What kind of trouble?" Borenson looked about the house. Myrrima had gone outside to feed the sheep. Most of the little ones were still asleep.

"I remember why I came here," Fallion said.

"To Landesfallen?"

"To this world."

Borenson peered into Fallion's eyes.

Fallion continued. "Once the world was perfect. Once it was whole and complete. But when the One True Master sought to take control, she tried to bind the world under her dominion, and it shattered into a million million worlds, all of them hurtling through space, all of them broken and incomplete, each of them a reflection to some degree of the One True World, shadows, each of them like shards of a broken mirror."

Borenson knew the legends. He merely nodded.

"Now," Fallion said, "the shadow worlds have turned. Now they're coming together, a million million worlds all set to collide at a single point. Here."

Borenson could not imagine any number so vast, and so he imagined a dozen balls of dirt, like little islands in the sky, all crashing together with explosive force, knocking down mountains, sending seas to hurl beyond their shore. "Everyone will be killed," he said, unsure if he believed that it were even happening, unsure if it *could* happen.

"No," Fallion said. "Not if it happens as it should. Not if the pieces fit together. The world won't be destroyed. It will be healed. It can be perfect once again."

"You really think this will happen?" Borenson asked.

Fallion turned his face upward. "I'm going to *make* it happen."

Borenson drew back in astonishment, unsure whether to believe the boy. But something inside him knew that Fallion was serious. "When?" he asked.

"Soon. A year or two," Fallion said. "I must return to Mystarria." He turned and peered into the hearth, and his eyes seemed to fill with fire. "There's a wizard at the heart of the world, one who seeks to heal it, a woman. I must find her, warn her of the dangers of what she is doing."

"Averan?" Borenson asked. He'd never told Fallion about the girl, or anyone else for that matter. Gaborn had warned him not to. The work that she was doing was too dangerous, too important.

"So that's her name," Fallion said. "She's the one that made me what I am. . . ."

The Heir of the Oak, Borenson realized. More perfect than children born in ages past. More like the Bright Ones of the netherworld.

At midwinter, Borenson learned the truth of what had happened at Shadoath's Keep. A traveler came upriver, bearing news. The children in Shadoath's Keep had been rescued, and were being given over to loving homes.

Did Borenson want one?

"No, thank you," Borenson said. "I've got more than I can handle as it is."

But Borenson dug the details from the stranger, and learned the truth of Fallion's battle: Fallion had faced Shadoath at the height of her power, and had put her down.

Borenson had once wept for the boy's lost innocence. Now he found himself weeping in gratitude to learn that the boy had retained it.

"He did not repeat my mistakes," he told himself over and over.

That was something grand.

It was only three weeks later, in early spring, that Fallion solved the mystery of the death of his father.

From the time that they arrived in Sweetgrass, he'd heard rumors that the Earth King was seen in the area mere days before he died.

Back home in Mystarria, Fallion had dared imagine that his father had been murdered by Asgaroth, and that someday he would avenge him.

So Fallion collected rumors of his father's whereabouts.

He was delivering eggs to the innkeeper in Sweetgrass, a lean man named Tobias Hobbs, when one of the guests at the inn said, "There's an oak tree growing up on Bald Mountain, not two days' walk from here."

"An oak tree?" some stranger asked. "How would you know?"

And Fallion wondered how he would know indeed. There were stonewood trees down by the sea, and white gums along the river, and king's pine in the mountains, and leatherwood and other types of trees that Fallion couldn't even name. But there were no oaks in all of Landesfallen, and Fallion himself could barely remember what they looked like. His only real clue was a button that he kept in an old box, a gold button with the face of a man, his hair and beard made up of oak leaves.

"I'm sure. It's the only one in all of Landesfallen," the stranger was saying.

And so, on a hunch, two days later Fallion took a pack and followed the river upstream, past the towns of Mill Creek and Fossil, and then turned inland and climbed Bald Mountain.

He reached the top near sundown, and there discovered the oak tree, a young tree with golden bark, new leaves unfolding in green while only a few tattered brown remained from the previous fall, and boughs that spread wide over the ground, as if to shelter the world beneath.

Fallion circled the tree.

They called him a son of the oak, but he had not seen one in so long that he had almost forgotten how beautiful a tree could be.

My father planted this, he thought. He stood here once, just as I am now.

For Fallion, the tree was a thread that bound him to a father he had never really known.

He looked for a place to sit, so that he could just admire it. Nearby was a tall outcropping of red rock, and he thought that he could lean against it, soak in its sun-drenched warmth like a lizard. He walked toward it, saw a vertical slit of blackness that revealed the presence of a tiny cave.

Fallion peered inside and found a weathered pack on the ground, its leather surface blending into the dust. Mice had nibbled at it, tearing a hole.

Upon the back of it, a leather cord acted as a latch, and a single gold button held it closed. Fallion peered at the button. The image of the green man stared back.

My father's pack.

He opened it, looked inside. There had been food inside once, grain and herbs, but the mice and bugs had gotten to it.

A leather pouch held a portrait with a silver backing and a glass cover. The picture was painted on ivory, and showed Fallion and Jaz as children with their mother and father, all of them painted side by side. The boys could not have been more than four. They all smiled, grinning so innocently at the future.

Fallion marveled at it, for he did not recall having sat for the painting. Hours of his life, wasted, forgotten.

Beneath the painting was a change of clothes, a razor and mirror, a few coins, and an old leather book.

Fallion opened the book, and saw that it was a journal, containing notes about his father's travels, the people he had met, the things that he had learned, his hopes and dreams and fears. It was a window into the soul of the world's greatest king.

There in the shadows, Fallion could not read it. He thought to take it outside, and reached out for support as he rose to his knees. By chance he touched a staff, an oaken walking stick with a brass base, nicely carved. Gems were set in the handle, and runes had been carved along its lengths.

The Wizard Binnesman's work, Fallion realized.

He took the staff and the book out into the bright sunlight and squinted as he peered around.

Father wouldn't have left these, Fallion told himself. His body will be nearby.

Behind him was all rock, a sheer rise of petrified sand dunes, the stone cascading down as if to make a stairway into the heavens.

Below was the hillside, covered with sparse grasses.

The only place that a body could be hidden was there beneath the tree.

Fallion took the staff and prodded the old leaves beneath the tree. They formed a mat, brown leaves splotched by dark lichens and mold. Many had gone skeletal, showing only the bones of leaves.

There Fallion struck something round and heavy, and a skull rolled out from the leaves, grayed by age, its walls thinning as it decalcified.

"There you are, Father," Fallion whispered, picking up the skull.

He prodded some more and found a collection of bones, a few thin ribs, finger bones, and a hip. There was no sign of foul play, no dagger protruding from the back, no arrow in the heart. Just bones.

Finally Fallion understood.

Father had been a wizard, an aging wizard. Just as a flameweaver carried an elemental of flame within him, or one of the wind-driven would unleash a cyclone, something of the earth had to make its way out of his father upon his demise.

Fallion peered out over the valley, the land that he called home. From up here, he could see the river snaking through green and peaceful fields, cottages down below with red-and-white cattle or black sheep dotting the fields. There were orchards and hay fields stretching as far as Fallion could see.

Fallion's father had not been murdered. He had been old and decrepit, dying.

So he sought out a fertile place, and had planted himself there.

He wanted me to be here, Fallion realized. He wanted me to be where he could watch over me.

Fallion had never really known his own father. At times he had wanted Waggit to be his father, or Borenson, or Stalker. And as such children do, he had learned from each of those men, had taken something of them into himself.

Squatting there in the shade of the oak, Fallion pulled open the book and began to read, determined to become intimate with a father he had never really known.